COASTAL PATH

A Soldier's Quest for Peace

COASTAL PATH

A Soldier's Quest for Peace

by

Steve Bracken

DIADEM BOOKS

Published by Diadem Books

For information, please contact:

Diadem Books
8 South Green Drive
Airth , Falkirk.
FK2 8JP
Scotland UK

www.diadembooks.com

Front cover painting by Luci Manfredi

ISBN: 978-0-244-67170-9

To Eleftheria

Chapter 1

Cape Wrath, Scotland

THE SEA AND SKY had teamed up to knock seven bells out of the granite cliffs as giant combers tore chunks from the shoreline. The shipping forecast threatened an enormous low pressure system stretching from Newfoundland to Norway: 'Wind north-west, storm 10, increasing to violent storm 11, visibility poor, snow showers.'

"That's us Steve."

The slamming gusts made the van lurch uneasily. Caroline cleared a porthole in the windscreen's condensation. A long malevolent swell, driven by anvil-headed nimbus thumped the coast, forcing vast tons of spume into the saturated sky.

"This is getting scary Steve. My dad will kill you if I get washed away."

"No he won't. Last time he was sober he said he'd be glad to get rid of you."

"You pig. Hold me tight; make up for that."

I gave her a smiling kiss, the storm focusing our warmth. She wanted to hunker down; I wanted to get out into nature's violence.

She pointed vaguely towards the coastal path: "Are those people over there?"

The image disappeared into a horizontally driven, smoking squall, then reappeared closer, shaping into a caterpillar of eight heavily laden men and a dog. Caroline's anxious voice left no excuse: "Go and tell them we'll give them a lift to the pub. They can all squeeze in the back."

The storm snatched the van's door. Sweet wrappers, maps, travelling debris tornadoed around inside. Hail pitted my face as it pushed against my weight.

Squinting faces walked towards me. I pointed back up to the van: “Want a lift to the pub?”

The lead shook his head: “No, we’re fine thanks.”

The wind tore away other words, leaving me stupidly still pointing as they passed into the grey turmoil.

“Ben!” The collie chased after them.

Caroline looked confused and annoyed; a combination she specialised in for those occasions when I screwed things up: “Didn’t you ask them?”

“They said they were OK.”

“You’re mad. How could they be OK in this? Anyway what about the dog?”

“He said he was OK too. They knew what they were doing, had good kit and didn’t need help. What else could I say? C’mon Cuddles, let’s go for a pint. That’s what I am going to call you from now on, Cuddles Caroline.”

I’d received a friendly nudge, a reluctant smile and: “I love you, Steve.”

“Yea, I know.”

“You’re supposed to say something too.”

“Yea, I know.”

“Bastard.”

Chapter 2

THE WARM Durness pub gave immediate sanctuary: heavy red curtains, black polished wood and whisky optics queuing along a mirror-clad wall, reflecting our vain smiles.

Caroline was first: "I'll get the drinks."

I went and stared out of a window into the storm. Hail dissolved as it tracked down the Georgian panes; a street light caught its swirling vortex. I refocused on Caroline's reflection as she chatted away to a couple of local blokes. She had an Italian animated way of talking that brought out smiles in the most casual meeting, drawing men like bees to honey. I could predict the next move from past experience: walking towards me, concentrating on not spilling the pints, half way across, lifting her face, knowing the blokes at the bar were staring at her tight-jeaned arse, and knowing I knew. Trying to wind me up.

As we nestled up at a corner table, I squeezed her hand.

"That's nice Steve. You were going distant on me. You always do before you go away. I hate it when you do that."

"Sorry, I was thinking of the storm."

"I miss you when you shut me out. Stay with me; we're a good team."

I hadn't thought of us as a team before. It seemed a strange thing to say; an intrusion into our cosy world, reminding me of previous times when I went 'distant' and she became 'needy'. The clash annoyed both of us, so why couldn't she just enjoy now? She had to look for omens; I looked for solutions: clash, clash, clash. Her implied question was: 'Where is this relationship going?' My implied answer was: 'Why can't we stay the way we are?' Twisted, unemotional logic said it would be easier if we split up. I'd half decided to end it in the easiest possible way when it was too late for recriminations, tantrums or emotional blackmail. I'd have my freedom and she could get a decent, settled bloke. The problem was it was a brilliant set-up that many of my mates would give their right bollock for, and I was going to just chuck it away. She broke into my thoughts, more annoyed this time: "Come back, you're doing it again."

"Well, I'm sorry again then."

There was an old enamel AA map on the wall. It gave an easy excuse: "I was just working out how long it's going to take to get you back home."

"Liar, you were thinking of the storm. One day it could be you out there if you're not careful."

I didn't say I'd love to be out in it, tabbing through the natural wilderness.

She leaned over resting her hand on my lap with just enough pressure, her laughing eyes daring reaction. I kissed her ear: "Just wait till I get you into bed tonight."

My reward was more pressure and a meaningful: "I love you", adding more doubts to splitting up. Why not get married and put up with her drunken dad and nympho mum; get a civvy job?

The bar menu was good enough to blank relationship thoughts, confirming what I already knew – that I was a 100% selfish bastard designed to chase some vague life of freedom.

Chapter 3

TWO DAYS LATER we were sitting in Caroline's parents' suburban living room with their labrador, watching her dad try to light the fire. Frustration at his performance prompted Caroline and her mum to disappear to the upstairs bathroom and her dad to slink off to the downstairs toilet, to wash his smudged face. I was left bursting for a piss and nowhere to go. Outside was like Piccadilly Circus, so I half filled a handy vase and emptied it at the back of the fire grate. Noises from the stairs and dad appearing, still with a sooty nose, gave no time for checking the crime scene. I had overestimated the absorption factor of the ashes and underestimated my bladder capacity; seepage flowed onto the carpet. If nothing else I was good at improvisation. I lifted the labrador, stuck his bum in the fireplace and loudly blamed him for the mess.

Mum's shocked voice – "He's never done that before!" – was echoed by dad: "Don't blame him. I should've let him out."

An old-fashioned look from Caroline and the labrador told me I hadn't got away with it. Helpfully, the labrador started licking its bits, so as dad mopped up, relieved not to have to light the fire, mum put on the kettle for tea and I put on my innocent face, which only confirmed my guilt in Caroline's eyes.

Distractions came as we sat with our tea and biscuits. Mum licked her handkerchief and helped to get the remaining soot marks off dad's nose, while managing to rub my foot with hers under the table.

I intruded into the uncomfortable silence by pointing at the labrador: "He's got a black nose too." Heads turned but couldn't add anything to my observation, so forcing a laugh I said: "I'm always rubbing my nose in something, aren't I Caroline?"

My nose was now the centre of attention. Caroline panicked: "Yes, he's always doing it!" Helpfully, I rubbed my nose again, but she couldn't stop burbling: "That's what first attracted me to

Steve." My incredibly attractive nose came under more scrutiny. Mum's frozen smile released, she blurted out: "More tea?" We all grabbed the social lifebelt… thank God for tea.

My confidence returned: "I had a cat when I was eight."

"Really?" said her dad.

"Yes, it used to sit at the end of a log and use the hearth as a litter tray; of course he was smaller than your labrador." The innocent dog shifted uncomfortably as our focus returned to him. Helpfully dad mentioned: "Cow pats are used in India to cook on."

I thought Caroline was going to cry, but in a desperate attempt to rescue the evening, she demanded we have a winter barbeque, just as mum's foot found mine under the table again. "There's a wheelbarrow in the back garden full of wood, Steve. Mum and I will get the sausages." Her voice was too loud and too controlled.

I lit the logs in the barrow so if it rained I could move it into the garage – brilliant. From the garden I heard the downstairs bathroom door slam. It must be Caroline; she needed cheering up. I grabbed a pair of knickers off the line, wrapped them round my hand to form a puppet, crept over and waved them through the partially open window: "Hello, hello, who's a pretty boy then?" A satisfying squeal from inside was followed by the window opening to reveal dad, shocked and damp.

I tried to explain: "It's a puppet. You should be Caroline!"

He stared at the knickers flapping in my hand, his red bulbous nose swaying from side to side: "Are you mad?!" I stuffed them in my pocket and dashed back to the wheelbarrow, where concentrated heat had set the tyre alight. No problem – I pushed the barrow in circles to cool it down. Unfortunately it only encouraged more flames. I aimed for the puddles in the front road, passing Caroline and mum bringing out the sausages.

When the fire had quietened, I returned with the barrow and a bucket of water, just in case. Mum was concerned: "Are you sure you're alright, Steve?"

"Fine thanks" – and pulled out a handkerchief to wipe away my sweat. They stared in disbelief. Mum reacted first: "My knickers!"

Caroline's mouth moved without words; unexpected rescue came from dad: "It's all right, Steve made a puppet." Caroline and her mum looked at him incredulously. "Yes, Steve stuck the knickers on his hand and waved them through the bathroom window."

Helpfully, he grabbed them and mimicked the unforgettably obscene image.

"I was having a pee, so he caught me by surprise I must admit, but I understood when he explained that it was a puppet and he thought it was Caroline in the toilet."

All eyes were now on their very flustered daughter as she tried to drag her sanity back to normal. In a toneless voice, she responded: "Steve is always surprising me with his puppets."

We all nodded, as if everything made sense. Winking at me, mum felt the need to contribute: "You should see what Roger does with my knickers, Steve."

The line had been crossed; too many questions hung in the burnt-rubber scented air. The rain held off, giving no excuse to end the torture, until my limited social skills kicked in: "Well, now we know each other a bit better, can I get the drinks?" Receiving no reply, I poured two jumbo brandies. Mum and dad downed them in one and held out their glasses for more.

I thought the surprises were over, but dad made a suggestion: "Do you want me to say Grace?" Caroline, still clinging to the family wreckage, grabbed at the flotsam: "Yes please dad, we'd love that wouldn't we Steve?" I nodded cautiously.

"For what we are about to receive... Do you know you can tell a good brandy by spitting it on a hot fire? If it is poor, it will hiss and smoulder." He paused and made a long hissing noise between his teeth. "But if it's top notch, it will explode in a brilliant blue flame."

It was like watching a 'car crash' in slow motion. He took a huge swig from the bottle and violently sprayed it onto the red-hot wheelbarrow. The ball of flame surprised everyone. Triumphantly, he jumped up and down: "Plonkers, plonkers, I told you."

Fearing a blow-back, I hurled the bucket of water over him, mum screamed and for some reason slapped his face. Amid the carnage, Caroline was trying to understand the surreal destruction of her family. Mum started an insane giggle and dad joined in as they staggered off in alcoholic hysteria to bed.

"You know this is all your fault don't you?" Her accusation broke into angry tears and then to an open rant: "You're a first class bastard. What's the matter with you? You piss in the fireplace and blame our dog; you scare the shit out of dad, literally; you set light to the wheelbarrow; steal Mum's knickers and wipe your face with them; then you get my dad drunk, set him alight and chuck a bucket of water over him; the only thing you haven't done yet is shag Mum!" Instinctively, I looked at my watch. Caroline didn't see the joke: "You dare say anything about mum and we're finished."

On cue, mum came out in a tarty dressing gown, leant over, breasts heaving, and kissed my cheek: "Night-night Steve. I expect you and Caroline want to 'talk' for a while, since you're going away tomorrow."

Caroline butted in, voice brittle: "No mum, we're not going to 'talk' or anything else. Go back to bed and look after dad."

So, no farewell nooky and the morning shag seemed odds against. She emphasised the sour mood: "You can sleep downstairs by the fire. At least you won't have far to go for a piss."

I wouldn't have wanted it like this, but at least it would make it easier to end the relationship. In fact the way it was going, she might even dump me.

* * *

I woke groggily in the morning with a large pair of lightly veiled tits inches from my eyes. I smiled back, knowing Caroline wouldn't waste my early morning hard-on. Then two things happened at once: first, I realised the tits belonged to Caroline's mum and second, the cat-like growl coming from the doorway, was Caroline.

Mum broke the silence: "I just brought Steve a cup of tea dear."

As Caroline's white face turned away, I heard a gritted: "We're leaving now!"

I suppose it was good of her to drive me to the barrack gates – many wouldn't. Probably most wouldn't. We didn't speak until the handbrake came on: "I know what mum and dad are like. It wasn't all your fault, except the pissing in the fireplace and scaring dad with mum's knickers and…" She managed a real smile at the evening's disasters. This was when we both should have cracked up laughing, kissed and made up: not this time. She put her hand on mine: "I'll write. I love you Steve." This was it – how to be a number one prize bastard. I was going to throw away a solid gold relationship. My hand was on the door, ensuring a quick, cowardly escape: "Don't write, don't wait, find someone decent."

Her sideways look of shock searched for a joke and then for a way to wind back to the fun holiday… holding confusion, denying anger, her shoulders slumped in resignation. One last look of appeal, a chance to pump back the joy, but I turned away and took my bag from the back seat, making the mistake of catching her eyes in the rear-view mirror. They were the sad eyes I'd remember, not the laughing, teasing, loving eyes of only days before.

My immature selfishness made the responsibility of loving someone a weakness. It was easier to leave than to love. Adventure and the search for freedom awaited; inwardly I was smiling. Half way to the gates I heard her drive off. I didn't turn and look.

I hadn't shagged her mum, but if I'd had half a chance I would've done. They were both better off without me. Being a bastard could solve a lot of problems.

Now I was free.

Chapter 4

BRIEFINGS followed briefings, summarised by Mick as: 'Bollocks' – or in his rare thoughtful moments as: 'A load of bollocks!' There was one exception, an anonymous looking lecturer: short, brown, to whom Mick gave his five-star praise: 'Not bollocks.' The hour lecture was full-on from the start. No preambles, no 'put your comics away', no patronising 'good morning gentlemen' crap, just straight in.

"OK, head stuff, don't make notes. If you can't remember what I tell you, you shouldn't be here and you shouldn't be going there. On patrol, put your mind in gear, think hard, balance that with down time back at base: music, books, anything to put it somewhere else; resting the mind is as important as resting the body. If you have problems, log them in your brain before you go to sleep. When you wake, they'll be solved. Your military skills are now as instinctive as driving a car; that leaves space in your head for other jobs when the shit hits the fan."

He turned and wrote on the whiteboard: I – B – T – A.

"I = Instinct. Immediate response, like your foot on the car's brake.

"B = Breathe. Don't forget air is fuel.

"T = Think. Options and solutions. The bigger the problem the greater the opportunity for you to use your skills.

"A = Act. Just do it. Implement the plan.

"Back here in ten minutes."

No lame jokes or asking for questions. He just walked out as quick as he came in. Mick was looking thoughtful, so I belched in his ear and informed him: "Your brain is in your knob end so you can only think about pissing or shagging. There's no room left for anything like IBTA." I was pleased with that one and waited for some equally obscene response.

"Look, Dickhead, if you had half a brain anywhere in your body, you wouldn't have dumped Caroline. It was a twat thing to do. She was a good woman, and if you had any sense, you'd have married her." He was serious; it was unexpected and it pissed me off because I knew he was right. He then went and spoilt it by asking if he could have a crack at her on the next leave. I said no. It was against mates' rules; still it was good of him to ask.

The short brown bloke came back in, didn't wait for silence, just straight in: "Remember I – B – T – A? I -INSTINCT. Put your hands palm down on the desk, index fingers and thumbs touching, forming a circle. Now keep them touching and bring them up so the sign on the wall behind me is sitting in the middle of your aim… and fire! Everyone got it? That's instinctive aiming.

"B – Say to yourself BREATHE, out loud if necessary.

"T – THINK about what's happening, obvious, but not always done.

"A – ACT on what you see, hear, taste, smell and touch. Don't freeze. Remember, instinctive actions leave space for you to decide on reactions. And lastly, say to yourself what you want to be, for example: 'switched on', 'efficient', 'calm' or whatever… The CO will give you the final briefing now… Stand up."

He held the door open as the CO plus flunky came in. "Good morning gentlemen. Mission: to eliminate the threat to the Queen, the UK, our Allies and our High Streets, from the Taliban, Al Qaeda, their cohorts and fellow travellers."

Mick whispered: "Who the fuck are the cohorts and what have the travellers done now?"

The CO continued: "Or, if you prefer Chaucer's language – to hammer the bastards!" He paused with a meaningful look at us lot, for a cheer or a laugh, we didn't know which. It was hard to know what he expected. Why couldn't public school 'Ruperts' be more clear?

"You've been fully briefed and trained to the highest degree, so it only leaves me to sum up concisely." … Cue waffle… "This regiment has always been in the thick of it. Others have Balaclava, Omdurman, Cressy, we have today, so remember."

Mick whispered again: "Is Cressy in North Wales?"

"We're always at the sharp end, spear-head, in harm's way, in danger and we've paid a heavy price at times. Macintosh and Jackson 85 will always be remembered by us." The only reason I remembered Macintosh was he wrote a love letter to his girlfriend and one to his wife and put the wrong letters in the wrong envelopes: pillock. "They were lost on the last tour." He made it sound as though they had gone AWOL or on a walk-about somewhere in Afghanistan. "We had also lost two in the previous tour." It was impossible not to speculate which two would be lost this time. A few even glanced around. "So let's make sure their lives were not given in vain. We'll go there again, we'll do it again and we'll come home again." All except two unlucky sods, I thought. "We'll stop terrorists, drugs and bombs getting to our High Streets." He made it sound like we were going to stop Marks and Spencer selling them on special offers or bogof's.

He was away again: "It's been a heavy cost in blood and treasure." Where the fuck did 'treasure' come from, Long John Silver? "It's up to us to see it's not been wasted." He paused and stared for effect: the effect was a meaningless silence.

Mick hissed quietly: "Some bloody Ruperts don't have a clue, do they? Where did they learn to speak like that?" I shrugged. Underneath the waffle was a clear mission statement: stop drugs and bombs getting to the UK. We knew what we had to do; the strategy was someone else's job. Shit, he hadn't finished. "We are fighting the major threat to her Majesty's Realm." Another pause while he adjusted his glasses. All I could think of was how does he map read or fire a rifle in the pissing rain with those on. "You are the spearhead in protecting my lady wife, your wives, your women, your partners, on our high streets." He was certainly worried about Marks and Spencer: obviously had shares. "They are counting on us and we are counting on you. Go for it. Give them a black nose." Fucking idiot, a black eye or a bloody nose would have done. I thought of Caroline's dad and the labrador and coughed a laugh away. The CO scanned his notes and put his glasses away; looked at us again as if waiting for applause or three cheers or something: he'd have to wait a fucking long time.

"To conclude, keep your heads down and watch your backs." It was too much for Mick. He hardly bothered to whisper: "What does he think we are, fucking contortionists? How can you fire a rifle with your head up your arse?" I had to stamp my feet and cough again. The CO strode out, stopped half way, returned looking for his glasses, tapped his pocket and left reassured, triggering a general chuntering and a thirst for beer. Mick echoed Lady Shagnasties comments in *The Times* on Wimbledon strawberries: "A load of bollocks." However, underneath it made sense, just the mission a squaddie wants to hear: 'Kill termites.' It's what we're paid to do. Mick rounded off his comments: "Look Dickhead, if bullshit was white, that fucking Rupert would be a champion skier."

And that's how we left Brize Norton, cynical, aggressive and ready for action.

Chapter 5

Afghanistan

SOLDIERS look for the patterns nature doesn't make, things that don't fit in, like half a dozen stones in a straight line. Senses switched on for clues: shape, shine, shadow, sound, silhouettes and the speciality of suicide bombers, smiles. Our patrol was respecting the farmer's crop of heroin poppies, as if walking in a barley field at home. Shots from the tree line, three hundred metres away had become predictable and routine: "Bravo One. Contact. Wait out."

"Go right Mick." We dived into metre high poppies. The remainder of the patrol went left into a drainage ditch. The Taliban's latest scam was to take a few pot shots and, as we took cover, a generous IED would be waiting. The boss shouted to us from the ditch: "Air strike in five, don't move, you'll give them target practice."

Mick was not happy: "Fuck this for a game of soldiers! Next time you say go right, I'm going left." I could see his point, but the obvious place for an IED was in the ditch, not in a field. "Stop whinging! If they can't see us, they can't hit us. You know poppies are bullet-proof." Mick shouted across: "I've just remembered what IBTA stands for: Idiot Bastards Talk Arse."

I adopted a resigned acceptance of the situation, mind in neutral and focused on the ground inches from my face. A tiny spider was starting to climb a poppy stem. I dug around its roots with my fingers, then turned carefully onto my back, watching the spider make it to the seed pod: one of millions waiting to be milked for London druggies. I pulled the roots, the plant toppled, the spider scuttled off and one nano-irrelevant victory against drugs had been scored : mission accomplished.

Mick was about four metres away, rifle at his shoulder; he looked across: “Hey Dickhead! Getting a bit casual eh?” I couldn’t be arsed to reply, so stuck two fingers up and focused on a high con-trail chalking across the furnace blue sky. Civilian passenger aircraft still used the corridors above the war-zone, content that thirty thousand feet of air protected them from heavy metal; a clean tube of cool peace winging its way to beer and girls in Oz.

“When I get out of this shite-hole, I’m going to get one of those big iron birds to the Med and get rat-arsed for months and I don’t mean a ‘Cyprus debrief’, I mean permanently.” Mick looked skywards. He had one ready: “Don’t be so fucking stupid. What’s left of you will go back in an ammo box with sand to make up the weight. I’ll take your head and bollocks as hand-luggage, for the piss-up.”

“Cheers mate! How long have you been saving that one up?” Mick was on a roll: “I bet the Russian ambassador and his wife are on that plane.” It was a cue for the long-standing and endlessly repeated sketch, which travelled with us from exercises to operations all over the world. Every time it got funnier and funnier, at least we thought so. With contrived seriousness, I asked: “What’s the ambassador’s name, Mick?”

“His name is Colonel Buggeroff.”

“And what’s his wife called?”

“His charming, well-endowed wife’s name is Titya Onyerbakubitch!”

Suppressed anticipation released spattered laughter as Mick warmed to his forced accents, all sounding Welsh to me. “Hey Mick, was the Japanese ambassador there?”

“I’m glad you asked Steve. Yes, he was.”

“I thought he might be, what was his name?”

“His name was the Honourable Itchy Arsole, where the sun never rises!”

We were raddled with tension-releasing laughter; everything became mega- funny: “Was anyone else there Mick?” He’d lost his Welsh accent and could only just speak: “Yes, there was.”

“I hoped there would be.”

“It was the new North Korean ambassador.”

I dribbled out: “And what was his name?”

Mick regained his Welsh accent: “His name was Fukutoo and he didn’t have a wife… anyway, the German ambassador, Cunt von Farter, came over to our Foreign Secretary and said, ‘Herr Willy, in my country it is rude to laugh at other people’s names. I do not laugh at yours even though, in Germany it means, a head like a turnip.”

“I don’t get that one Mick.”

“That’s because it wasn’t funny. It was a German joke!”

I was now trying not to piss myself laughing. Fuck it, I wanted a piss anyway, so I pissed myself.

* * *

Nevada, USA. Drone Central:

“Looks like two wounded Brits out in the open, rolling in agony, Sir.”

“Leave them Costa, their casevac is nearly as good as ours.” (Casualty evacuation.)

“Shall I tag them, Sir?”

“Sure, why not?”

“78 and 79 tagged. Airstrike imminent, Sir.”

* * *

Grey explosions – heavy double thump – pressure waves rippling the poppies – deadened senses – black snow gently drifting towards us – silence, stillness – and worst of all, the smell. Had the aircraft passengers seen a puff of smoke as people’s lives vaporised far below – terrorists killed, we were alive – did they go back to their lunch tray and order another beer?

Into my surreal thoughts Mick chuntered: “When I get home, I’m going to buy a fishing boat and call her the Crack of Dawn.”

It was a gift I couldn’t resist: “I knew a girl called Dawn once.”

“What do you mean?”

“Dawn’s crack… Crack of Dawn , get it?” ...pause…

"You bastard! It took me a week to think of that. You've just ruined it. I've got to think of another one now."

"How about Fuck-u-Too? And the next one could be Fuck-u-Three."

"Tosser! That's pathetic".

It still didn't stop us cracking up laughing 'til my jaw ached.

Sergeant 'Gibbo' Gibbins shouted across from the ditch: "All right you two wankers, stop pissing about and come over here, NOW!"

* * *

Nevada:

"UK troops moving out Sir."

"OK Costa, return to wide area. Were those two, casualties?"

"I don't know Sir, 78 and 79 were separated, they have rejoined the patrol."

* * *

The compound was smoking rubble, a few recognisable pieces: kids' red T-shirts always seemed to survive, or maybe we recognised them because of their tragic implications.

"What do you see Mick?" He didn't answer. I saw violent waste.

"Don't go there, Steve. We kill them before they kill us – job done."

Chapter 6

A **PATTERN** of action and reaction, mistakes and luck: tactics predictable to both sides. We would 'advance to contact'; they would fire in our direction to collect a small bounty; if it lasted for more than ten minutes, we'd call in an air strike. The Taliban knew our response times and we knew theirs, so by the time we'd entered the compound, weapons would be hidden in a wall. After an initial shock to the enemy, the war developed into asymmetrical attrition. Invader, plagued by established strategies from red tabs; the invaded strengthened by the day-to-day observation of the invader's habits. (The opposite of military surprise.) 'Taking the fight to the Taliban' was the only strategy we had, even though it achieved little but casualties.

At the FOB (Forward Operating Base) we cleared our weapons, went for tea and a chunter about heat, fantasy crumpet and iced lager. I tried an idea on Mick: "How about setting up an OP (Observation Post) in the village we keep getting zapped from, so we can laser an accurate air strike before they get a chance to disappear. Drones can't see everything."

Mick was not impressed: "Did you get that idea when we were taking cover behind those bullet-proof poppies, while our muckers were safe in the ditch? You come up with some crap ideas at times and that's one of them. Any more like that and they'll make you an officer."

I kept going: "We could use an armoured wagon to back up our patrol, and when there were no eyes on us, we'd go through the 'top cover' hatch onto a flat roof. When the Taliban appear, we call in air support before they can hide their weapons. Simple!"

"Look Dickhead, even if we could get on a roof without being seen, there are dogs, kids and evil bastards moving around day and night with eyes like ferrets."

"Eyes like hawks, Mick," I corrected.

“Bollocks whatever, it’s not our job to plan ops. Leave it to the Ruperts with birdshit on their shoulders.”

“Fuck ’em – we have to get in close. They’re too wised up about drones. It could be a ‘game-changer’ in this sector.”

“Yea, you’re right, a game-changer for us, riddled with bullets if we’re lucky; our heads stuck on You Tube if we’re not. Forget it, it’s not worth it. Remember Joe 90? You are getting as bad as him. He took stupid risks just to see if he could get out of them. He was good, but he didn’t realise how much was luck. He thought it was all skill; never got a scratch. Steve, it was all luck. I just hope your luck is as good as his.”

Chapter 7

HQ took on the idea as their own and we were told to volunteer.

After three days on the roof, Mick was chuntering every hour on the hour that I owed him big time, even though he had to admit it might work. We knew we were incredibly vulnerable, but since we were not overlooked and since the Taliban didn't have an air force, logically we were safe.

* * *

Nevada:

"UK troops 78 and 79. Close reconnaissance rooftop, Sir."

"Weren't they the wounded in the poppy field a few days ago?"

"Yes Sir. They seem OK now."

"What can they do that we can't?"

"Get shot Sir?"

"Right again, Costa."

* * *

Roof debris gave us enough cover to observe the compound. We had decided to call it Ahmed's Farm… Ahmed's wife, Ahmed's sons, Ahmed's goats… I had grown fond of Ahmed's self-sufficient lifestyle. Early on the fourth morning, Ahmed was joined by six black hats, no weapons seen as yet, but when we did all would be vaporised. "Be a shame to destroy his set-up, eh Mick?" He wasn't moved: "It's what we're paid for. Collateral damage goes with the job."

A clear still night sky, interrupted by high planes, a dog barking, muffled family voices, a crying baby, all strangely peaceful, 'same-same' all over the world, except for us.

On the fifth morning, Ahmed had the six black hats round for tea again. We were both concentrating so hard on spotting for weapons that a flapping noise behind caught us off guard. Instinct: I spun, safety catch off, bead on a moving face just above the parapet… a kite jiggled at us. The kids could see it, we could see it, but only the kite could see us both. "Fucking Taliban air force," hissed Mick.

* * *

My earpiece clicked onto life: "Patrol deployed."

I pressed twice to acknowledge. It was as if the Taliban had heard the same message. They stood up, finishing Ahmed's tea, and became more animated; mobile phones but no weapons.

Mick whispered: "Where's the weapons?"

"Dunno, could be anywhere. Air strike's on standby. Come on you fuckers, just pick up a gun and you're dead… be a shame to waste Ahmed's family and goats."

Mick stared at me: "It's your idea; it's worked. Don't knock it."

"Shut the fuck up. Keep looking for weapons."

My earpiece clicked again: "Delta One. Alpha One. Confirm target. Over."

"Delta One. Wait, wait, wait, out!"

Mick thumped my shoulder: "OK Steve, there's six of the bastards. Just do it." I stared hard through the binos, willing myself to see an AK, a muzzle-loader, anything.

"Come on, come on, where are the weapons Mick?"

"Fuck 'em, confirm target, we've got the bastards."

"Mick, I can't see weapons."

"What do you want – a fucking display team and band?"

"No weapons, no strike. I'm not destroying Ahmed's family for nothing."

Mick was fuming: "We've risked our necks here and it's worked. Your stupid idea has worked. We can zap six termites and get a gong – job done. Now, just do it."

My earpiece cut in: "Confirm Target Red Seven. Over."

It was my decision: "Negative. Abort. Over."

“Alpha One. Abort. Roger. Out.”

*   *   *

Nevada:

“No confirmation from 78 and79, Sir.”

“Goddam Brits! We can see six in the compound. What’s their problem?”

*   *   *

Sickening regret spread immediately to my guts as I repeated the mantra: ‘No weapons – no strike.’ Mick was shouting: “You thick bastard. We know they had weapons somewhere. It was a perfect kill.”

An eye for an eye – a leg for a leg – a hotel full of tourists for a family compound – what did 9-11 justify? Collateral damage – no rules? It was too late to change my mind. Could I salvage something? Out-flank the Taliban when our patrol swept through the village? Could we find anyone in the alleyways? Risk of green on green?... If, if, if… Our suppressed adrenaline, which had built up over days on the roof, exploded. A confirmation thumbs up from Mick and we were away, leaping the parapet ten feet to the ground. The kite-flying kids stared open-mouthed as we raced the alleyways, past Ahmed’s farm to the intersection.

“Delta One. Our position Red Five. Over.”

The boss came on: “Roger, we’re sweeping north. Deploy orange smoke if our fire gets close.”

“Delta One. Roger. Out.”

So long as the boss knew where north was, we’d be OK; a Rupert with a compass could be more deadly than an IED.

Two shots from Mick kneeling – nowhere to go in the passageway – thirty metres ahead a foot sticking out from a doorway – ‘Instinct’: I fired once – a scream and a rifle falling out onto the ground. I ‘breathed’ hard, ‘thinking’ of options. A child, aged four or five, ran from a doorway, picked up the rifle by the barrel and started to drag it back slowly, like pulling a pram.

Safety catch off, I shouted: “No Mick! Stop!”

He held his aim on the kid – milli seconds – "No Mick, let her go."

We watched the little one and rifle disappear into the doorway.

"Delta One. Contact. Over."

"Roger. Be with you in five. Over."

"Roger. Out."

More shots. Closer now as our blokes hammered something. Game over.

* * *

We rejoined our patrol and helped with the follow-up search of Ahmed's compound. I walked up to his hostile stare: "Salaam Aleichem." Nothing but hatred from his eyes. I wanted to tell him I was the reason his family and goats were still in existence.

Mick came over with the interpreter and filled in the blanks: "You're very lucky. If it was up to me, you wouldn't be here." One of his sons, who looked about seven, came towards me and threw a stone at my leg. What did I expect, tea and buns or maybe: 'Drop in and see us on your next tour. My family are truly grateful…' I don't think so.

Later, we found out that some of the Taliban had escaped, they could go on to kill. Ahmed's sons could kill our blokes. My decision may have allowed that to happen, but I was a soldier, not a murderer – it was the right thing to do. Mick disagreed, he would've blasted the lot. Afterwards, there were times when I would've done the same. In the future, at three in the morning, I would replay the situation again and again, sometimes confident my decision had been right, sometimes smarting with regret. Either way, I couldn't rest in peace.

Chapter 8

A YEAR LATER I was in civvy street, developing an unhealthy drinking habit and spending more time in pubs than looking for work. I was pissed most days before lunch. Consequently my faith in humanity was curdled, rancid and self-inflicted. Toilets to me were now shop doorways, backyards, wherever. Dustbins and rubbish bags seemed made to urinate on. I stared down at my piss; one of the bags moved, two eyes from an unshaven face looked up blankly as I kept pissing. A wave of revulsion triggered reaction – I pulled out ten quid and chucked it at him. No words. His eyes said: 'Why piss on me, why give me ten quid?'

I mumbled: "Sorry… sorry… OK….. I'm sorry."

Back in the pub I tidied up, my reflection disgusted me. I was split in two: one a superficial drunken arsehole, the other the real me, whoever he was.

Automatically, Spanish George put another pint on the bar in front of me. I couldn't tell him to take it away and I wasn't going to drink it, so I stared, then looked around to see if my confusion registered on others faces. No one cared – I was just another drunk. Only George acknowledged my existence with the nod of the universal barman. I don't know how long I watched the condensation slide down the glass. I would've gone on staring until kicked out if my mobile hadn't started to whine. I would never admit it, but Mick saved my life that day.

"Hello Dickhead, doing much?"

"Mick! It's good to hear your voice! Yea, plenty on, bits and pieces, this and that, you know what it's like."

"Lying shit, I've heard of a job on a film set, might suit you – interested?"

"Might be able to fit it in; anyway, you still got a dose?"

"No I haven't, fuck off. Have you had a skinful already? It's only just after lunch."

“Bollocks to all of that. How are you?”

“I’m good. I’ve bought a twelve-metre trawler. Needs a bit of work, but I’m sorting it out. I’ve called her Dawn Rising and if you try making something of it or say anything about a girl called Dawn you’ve shagged in your dreams, I’ll hang up.”

I was pissed but still had enough sense not to antagonise him. “Mick, what’s this job?”

“It’s in London, where you are, four hundred a day.”

“Four hundred quid?”

“Yea, now shut the fuck up and listen. It’s on a film set – all you do is advise the actors on military procedure and all that crap, and stop them making pricks of themselves.”

“Right, give me the info. I might be able to fit it in.”

“Bullshit! Now listen, mostly you just stand around looking hard, once or twice move alongside the director, shout something in his ear and point anywhere, got it?”

“Yea, got it.”

* * *

The set looked like a surreal military ops room from hell: cables, screens, prats with clipboards, prats with headphones, prats from parties and even work experience prats; all looking for a reason to be there. I was determined not to be like them, so as soon as my position registered as: ‘a prat out of water’, ‘a spare prat at a wedding’ or ‘a prat ashtray on a motorbike’, I’d point meaningfully and shout in the director’s ear the first thing that came into my head. Satisfyingly, he took notice and eventually put his hand on my shoulder: “Steve luv, come and meet Alex, he’s our little soldier today. Make sure he does it right.” Instant contempt was mutual: to me, Alex was a lefty poof and by the look on his powdered face, he was a fascist bully.

* * *

Director: “Quiet! Airstrike Take One.”

Alex did his best: “Target confirmed. Destroy. Over.” I winced.

Director: "Cut! Alex luv, good, very good, but more intensity, INTENSITY."

Alex appealed: "I'm doing my best, war is shit."

Director, patiently: "Yes, I know, that's why we're making this film. Now try again and remember, with INTENSITY."

I looked around; a sound track started in my head. (Mick's voice: 'Confirm target, we've got six of the bastards.') My mind raved at screaming pitch. I crouched low, sprinted across the set, jinked across open ground and grabbed the handset:

"Alpha One – Delta One – Stand by."

Alex: "Are you going to kill people?"

"Shut it ponce!"

Alex persisted: "Your decision."

Why did he have to say that? I stared at the handset – Ahmed's family, his goats, – milliseconds of mind film – decision – a visceral urge: "Alpha One, Delta One. Target confirmed. Vaporise the bastards, women, children, goats, all the fuckers, make them black snow."

Alex was pulling the handset away: "Let go, let go!"

My contempt turned from red mist to blind hatred, to my fist. I slammed it into his guts, he dropped like a bag of shit: "We did save lives!"

He gasped: "Do you really believe that?"

"I've got to believe it."

Director: "Cut! Wonderful Steve luv, you're a natural, we must get you an Equity card."

My anger diffused quickly, red mist turned grey. I went over to Alex and apologised: "Don't believe all you hear, Alex."

"Or you. I believe nothing I hear and only half what I see."

I shook his hand and walked out, trying to ignore the mirrors in the passage reflecting a sick face. Acting was not for me. I returned to base – the pub – for a liquid lunch. The downhill, out-of-control spiral beckoned again, and again a guardian angel appeared, this time in the form of Mr Bert Harman.

Chapter 9

THE PUB'S small TV was high on a corner shelf, far enough away so only the bass notes of the Remembrance Day bands and odd words of the commentary could be heard. Above was a large, red 'No Smoking' sign, which Spanish George and the two druggies in the corner, obviously thought didn't apply on Sundays, judging by the smouldering ashtrays. An elderly gentleman, holding an unlit pipe, contributed nothing to the fug, but stared at the screen, occasionally looking round as if to comment. It wasn't the sort of pub where friends were made or where people complained of smoke.

Vaguely, I muttered something about: "You'd have thought the world would have had enough of war by now. Poor sods."

The pipe man observed: "A waste of good men on both sides."

It was the, 'on both sides', which made me respond. Germans didn't get much coverage on Remembrance Day. I didn't feel like a discussion, but needed to say something: "Were you in the military?" His eyes stayed on the screen: "Only once,1943 to 1945, that was enough for me."

The film job had failed, so my fallback position was booze, not chat. Try to forget, not remember. I'd have three more pints, crash out in my gungy pad, then start again when I woke up: lovely. No boring war stories. As I picked up my glass to walk to a table, he passed me a creased black and white photo: "That's the crew in 1943." Seven young, smiling faces in front of a huge Lancaster bomber, staring at me from a long-forgotten English summer: "We only lost one, that was Jimmy. He's circled in the picture – rear gunner. Apart from that we had the same crew and skipper all the way through. It was bad luck to change. We wouldn't have lost Jimmy if they hadn't sent us back. That's where Ted got his shrapnel wound."

As I passed the photo back, he pointed: "That's me on the end." His mind now focused on that distant summer.

"Where did they send you back to?"

"Arnhem resupply. They knew it was useless, but we were sent anyway. By then the poor buggers on the ground were either killed or captured. Germans had what we dropped and that's when Jimmy bought it. We didn't see much on the return, just a few thumps. The skipper said he'd lost rudder control. I made a lash-up and pulled the cables to steer, and that's how we landed. Skipper got a medal, said it was for the whole crew. Jimmy was dead, got nothing."

I pictured the desperate fight to get the plane back to England: "What happened to Ted?"

"We had a ribbon specially made up for him." Alongside his polished baccy tin was a small brown bear, ribbon on chest: Ted, the mascot. "You can see where the shrapnel hit, didn't say a word, tough little bugger." He wasn't the only one, I thought. We both stared at the Cenotaph on the TV. Too many memories like sand, blood-soaked paths carrying grief, pride and tons of pain.

"My name's Steve."

"I'm Bert Harman."

He pointed to the TV again, letting a comment fade before continuing his story: "Of course, I nearly didn't go." I picked up the chance to show interest: "Why not?"

"Well, there was a young lady in the village and I was going to be late getting back to camp, so I borrowed a push bike. The local bobby found out and I was up before the CO. Skipper saved my bacon, said he couldn't fly without me, not true, but it was good he said it. He was one of the best, only ever lost his temper once."

His lined face reflected the worry over half a century ago, about a poxy bike, when it was more than an even chance he'd be burnt alive thousands of feet up.

Both of us paused to sip our pints. He glanced at me to see if I was still interested.

"When did Skipper lose his temper – on the Arnhem resupply?"

"No, it was another show altogether, much worse than that. We all knew there was something wrong from the start. Geordie, the navigator, had a funny look on his face after the briefing. The course took us past every Nazi fighter station in the Low Countries. Geordie thought we must be some sort of decoy for a major op somewhere else. In a funny way, we were. It didn't seem right. They knew we were coming. Hun night fighters like bees swarming – you know what it was like."

"No Mr Harman I don't. I was born long after the war." He hadn't heard. Documentaries on TV gave me reference to the actions he described: "Planes peeling off slowly, in flames, sometimes black dots of crew baling out, incinerated in the firestorm they'd created. The course back was marked by a flare path of burning Lancs, navigation easy – so I thought of mum and dad's house and my shed in the back yard. The same house I live in today. Do you know what saved us?" Totally absorbed, I shook my head. "Skipper broke formation, against orders, cool as a cucumber: 'Hold on, going down.' I thought we'd had it, burnt alive, screaming for our mums, but he levelled off just over a railway: bridge, dykes flashed past, and that's where we stayed till the Dutch coast – then wave height to Blighty. The Skipper had saved us."

He sipped his beer then continued: "The Lanc ahead was signalled a red flare from the control tower. He went round again, crashed and burned in a field. They were home: dead, but home. It was our turn next. We were also signalled red. Skipper never swore, he did then: 'Fuck 'em!' More red flares, another Lanc, undercarriage gone blocking the runway. Skipper and co-pilot hauled back, bounced over and slewed onto the grass. We'd made it home: alive. Skipper said nothing, stormed to the nissan huts. That's when he lost his temper. He had the debriefing officer by the throat and we wrestled him off. He should have been court-martialled; they didn't because the Nazis knew we were coming. We'd been sold out; someone had told them course, timings, everything."

"What do you mean Mr Harman? Who told them? You mean a spy?"

No answer: a scruffy London pub years after the pyromania – Cenotaph memories – poppies – red flares – skipper and crew coming in on a wing and a prayer, all thinking of mum and dad.

I tried again: "Who told them, Mr Harman?"

"Years after the war, Geordie the navigator, reckoned he'd found out. We had a reunion in 1967 and all turned up including Ted, and Skipper from Canada. Geordie was writing a book on Bomber Command and he'd interviewed an ex-intelligence officer, got him pissed. We were the sacrifice, so a double agent would be believed that D-Day landings would be Calais. Lives lost, lives saved. I couldn't have done it. Geordie said he couldn't. Treachery or loyalty? It was for the greater good."

A compound in Helmand, lives could have been saved if I'd killed Ahmed and his family, his goats, the Taliban… turned them into black snow. Maybe Mick should've shot the kid; maybe lives had been lost because I hadn't called in the air strike. If all the money spent on weapons was spent on good stuff, what a country Afghanistan would be? What a world? Bollocks to all war. It's good for nothing.

I'd been staring into my half-empty glass: "Like another one, Mr Harman?"

"I won't thank you and Ted don't drink. Better be getting back, bye then."

He put Ted and his baccy tin in his pocket and patted the poppy flat on his lapel. I shook his hand: "We appreciate what you and your mates did, Mr Harman."

There was sudden anger in his voice: "We weren't heroes all the time, Steve. It was easier to keep going than stop. I'm not proud – I wouldn't march. How could anyone be proud of killing all those people – cats, dogs, families, homes destroyed – madness. We had to do it; it was wrong… but I am proud of the crew."

As he left, Spanish George came over: "Good gentleman Mr Harman. Can you watch him home Steve?" His eyes flicked towards the pair of druggies stashing roll-ups in a tin.

"Thanks for the tip, George. Look after my beer."

* * *

They stalked him like hyenas, stopping because he was slow and like hyenas never looking back to see who was stalking them. They closed in when he turned off the High Street into a terraced side road. As he put the key in the lock I shouted across: "Mr Harman! Good to talk. I live nearby – call me if there's any problems."

I couldn't tell if he'd heard, but the low-life had. Uncertain, they lit a rolly, so I leant against the house wall, just close enough to be in their comfort zone until they slunk off.

* * *

George topped up my beer when I got back: "Bonus Steve."

"Thanks George."

Mr Harman had made me think. My brain was hurting with the weight of betrayal – pure treachery.

I decided to give Mick a call: "Hi Bollock-chops. How's Dawn's crack?"

"Dickhead! Her name's Dawn Rising, so don't ruin it, because she's now a registered fishing vessel."

Dawn Rising was a gift. A few hours' work and I'd have enough obscene slander to really piss him off: "Nice girl, Dawn!"

"Fuck off! Look Dickhead, did you call just to wind me up or do you want something?"

"Did you see Remembrance Day on the telly?"

"No, I'm fishing. Did the two minutes though; knocked her out of gear. Makes you think, doesn't it? It could have been us two worthless hooligans they were remembering."

"Yea, I know what you mean. Remember Paddy from C Company?"

"Yea, went mad. We had to shoot him."

"No plonker, I'm serious."

"Yea, I remember. Left leg Sangin and head stuff."

"Any idea where he is?"

"Yea, Surrey rehab I think."

"OK, cheers Bollock-chops, good fishing."

"See ya, Dickhead."

Chapter 10

Surrey Rehab

IT WAS MODERN, high-tech, well-equipped and had a sense of cheerful determination. I soon established Paddy had moved on. Gone to CP a couple of weeks before, wherever that was. So I wandered back the way I'd come in, thanking my lucky stars it wasn't me, then feeling selfish survivor guilt.

"You look lost."

"No I'm OK… A friend of mine was here, but he's moved on. How's it going?"

A decent face in a white coat gave me a look which said: 'How the fuck do you think it's going when young bodies are shredded by high explosive and what's left riddled with goat shit?' Instead he smiled: "Progress mostly. Some hanging on day to day; some minute to minute; some take it as just another challenge; some are doing things they never would have done with two legs."

At a nearby desk a sergeant interrupted: "Excuse me Sir – Corporal Roberts – decision time."

The MO rubbed his forehead and picked up the notes: "Broken arms, burns, couldn't get his mate out, survivor guilt, sleep disruption."

"So what now sergeant?"

"CP would be worth a try… that's up to him."

I was very much aware of my intruder status, but interrupted anyway: "CP?"

The MO made a circular hand motion.: "Coastal Path… fancy a brew?"

I wasn't used to officers making me tea. He chatted away as he lined up three cups by the kettle.

"Coastal Path… instigated by a bloke called Dinger, wasn't it sergeant?"

"Legend has it an obese alcoholic, I believe Sir."

"Yes, in a Pompey pub – a trouble maker – 1982 – Falklands War just ended. The returning ships were berthing at HM Dockyard; two Marines walked in and settled down with their pints; five minutes later in came two Paras and did the same – this is not a joke by the way. Dinger saw a golden opportunity for a wind up. He made comments about 'who won the war?'; 'who got to Stanley first?' etc, etc – no one bit. They knew what had happened – bullshit was not on the agenda. In desperation, Dinger said it had never been proved Paras could 'tab' faster than Marines, or Marines 'yomp' further than Paras. At last a reaction, then a discussion that evolved into a challenge to race around the UK Coastal Path..

The MO was squeezing compo ration milk into the tea: "Never put the milk next to the toothpaste sergeant."

"And never put the toothpaste next to the haemorrhoid cream Sir."

(Standing jokes essential for institutional sanity.)

I tried to bring it back: "Who won the race?"

The MO blew over his tea. "Nobody, it became a ramble, 'walking and talking.' Perfect therapy, perfect R & R, perfect antidote to PTSD. (Post-traumatic stress disorder.) Soon military gossip of deserted cliffs under stars, long summer beaches, dramatic winter storms, encouraged others to join."

(A distant memory of Cape Wrath: a storm, eight men and a dog called Ben.)

My prompt: "Have many been all the way around?"

"Over the years probably thousands. Some twice, some continuous, making it their home. Some died with their boots on: peace in movement. The funny thing is, officially the Path doesn't exist, except in the West Country and a few other stretches. In the beginning we by-passed restricted areas and fenced property. One day it will be completed, government cuts not withstanding."

I prompted again: "What effect did it have on the blokes?"

"Some kept military habits, others went native, grew long hair and beards; some meandered, intoxicated by changing skies and seascapes; some racing snakes, sweated the mind pain out through their muscles – exhaustion gave quietness; some found a spiritual dimension, meditating on a purity of purpose or praying in coastal churches, or worshipping pagan nature, or challenging violent storms: shouting at the devil. Some planted clandestine gardens of kale and blackcurrant cuttings for the future. Amputations and wheelchairs didn't bar movement along the Path. Small teams would sometimes make no more than a mile a day. It was a challenge."

"Did the cure work?"

"Cure would be the wrong word. It helped most. Suicides were rare, traumatic memories would be eased by mates waiting with a brew. Everyone became fitter; drug and alcohol abuse were minimised. A few couldn't be repaired – bombs and bullets had been too invasive. The agony for one only ended when trying to rescue a fisherman's dog. Tormented mind stilled permanently by knife-cold water.

"A WW2 veteran escaped from an Eastbourne 'waiting room' in slippers and dressing gown. He soon got chatting to the blokes. In no time they kitted him out with boots and waterproofs. At last he was free out in the fresh air. Six months later he died with his mates. His last wish to be buried on a cliff top, so that's what happened: thirty foot inland from the path, six foot down, three large marker stones and a perfect view.

"Angst sweated out poisonous obsessions; death was a choice easily available but rarely taken. Locked away, their spirits would have died; they would have been scheming to kill themselves. Some had pets – adopted dogs – loved and fussed. A few had cats carried on their shoulders or in adapted bergens. One bloke carried his mate, without legs, in a modified pack. Two heads greeting startled passers-by."

I interrupted: "They must have got on well?"

"No, they argued all the time. Kept threatening to leave each other, just like an old married couple!

"Television was not missed; news avoided; stock markets could scheme and fret without them. Women were part of the walk as ex-military, or as girlfriends, wives."

I was totally absorbed – tea cold, forgotten. The facade of white coats, needles and antiseptic smells, concealed a genuine healing secret. The MO changed the angle to himself: "My first week on the Coast Path, I didn't speak, then the dam burst. Blokes listened – they were brilliant. Incidents relived in cathartic rhythm, putting them in the right place, not into obsessional memory. The walking pace gave punctuation and flow, preventing the harrowing incidents disintegrating into monosyllabic hate. Everyone helped each other. I would go into medical mode when required, as did two blokes who helped deliver a baby in a remote car park – proud as punch. Previous work involved killing in industrial quantities."

This was more than an explanation to a passing ex-squaddie. It was consolidating memories into a healing force that needed to see the light of day.

"There was a colonel… tried to get the blokes to call him Brian – everyone still called him Sir. He'd lost his wife and his reason to live… got sorted out.

"There was a padre who confessed to being homosexual – everyone had known for years. It was irrelevant when bodies and souls were mashed. He cared and said the right words. The blokes shrugged and got him another brew. There were always new headlands and bays to lift the spirit; coupled with natural black humour, we got through dark days."

The story was becoming random, making it even more compelling. It was a homily to the Path.

"Some left notes in dead letter boxes, to be read next time round the Island: 'Well done pillock – now do it again'."

I felt privileged to listen. Other white coats and some of the blokes had joined us. The MO seemed oblivious. His voice quieter and smoother, on a peaceful plane of generous understanding: "But mostly it was the beauty , the grandeur… the shapes of things, colours, lights and shades, the sacred junction of sea, sky and land that inspired… 'Look while life lasts'… There was something about being part of such a vast natural system that put personal suffering in its place: days were magical, nights were another dimension to the enchantment."

The faces around me were wrapped in the Path's evolution. We could all see what he was getting at. Something beyond ourselves, an eternity, a lack of death, perfect peace, understandable spirituality.

He searched for conclusion… "After each conflict, emergency, hostility, trouble or whatever euphemism was being used for the mindless violence caused by politicians failures, more war-weary sought out the Coastal Path. The imprint of hideous experiences in the most dangerous places on earth was eased by nature: a peregrine falcon's power dive, basking seals and pups, nesting birds, dolphins racing the bay. The beauty once recognised was so pure, no artist or musician could come close to copying… it had to be experienced. In consequence, we all felt instinctively affronted by the smallest piece of litter. To some it became an obsession, descending difficult cliffs to clean up plastic-covered strand lines."

The MO was looking weary now… "Wild storms on remote cliffs paradoxically offered safety. The Path rejected none; no qualifications or rank required. It gave not only solace and independence, but the greatest gift of all: freedom. My happiest memories are of driftwood fires, cooking mackerel on deserted beaches, talking of Bristol Channel tides, Scottish inlets, East Coast sand… not war, never war… Via Sacra… The Sacred Path."

And that was it. He stopped. Story finished, silent, staring at the floor. I stood quickly and shook his hand: "Thank you Sir."

"No need to call me Sir. Call me Brian."

"Yes Sir."

The sergeant cracked a smile. My smile disintegrated into a chuckle. The MO joined in with a gutsy laugh, then the whole crammed office cracked up, faces registering the truthfulness . The MO had opened his heart; we all knew. He looked around: "Sorry, went on a bit."

"No problem. Shall I tell Corporal Roberts about the Coast Path?"

"I think that would be a very good idea. He's a guardsman, is he not?"

"Yes he is".

"OK, emphasise the sea to his left, and sergeant... clockwise."

"I'll emphasise the clockwise bit."

"Good man."

* * *

I was inspired. Someone had a plan to deal with the madness of war by using the greatest power on earth: nature. Brilliant, top man. I left the MO with a load of respect and gratitude. But if I ever bumped into him again, I'd still call him Sir, not Brian.

Chapter 11

AT THE RAIL STATION my mobile buzzed: "Hi Dickhead, how's it going? Still getting pissed on your own? Still paying fifty to get your leg over?"

"No, I'm giving up booze."

"Oh yea, and I've just seen a flying pig."

"No, I'm serious; priorities have changed. Anyway Mick, what do you want? I'm busy."

"No you're not, cut the crap. Fishing is up and I need a hand. I've tried everyone else I can think of and they all said no, so you're my last hope."

"Thanks, you certainly know how to sell a job."

"Look, you can sleep on board and keep the vandals off, plus all the dogfish skins you can eat, and there's a bit of diving to do for R and R."

"OK, so you're looking for cheap labour and a night watchman on your Dawn Rusting."

"DAWN RISING!"

"Whatever – knowing you I'll be working from arsehole to breakfast time for peanuts and diving into god knows what freezing polluted soup to rescue your precious trawl when it gets fouled in Planet Fuck-up."

"Yep, you've got it in one. See you at the end of the week?"

"Yea, I'll be there."

"Good – knew you were desperate. One other thing, can you collect two oxy-arc underwater cutting torches from Felix and Wright off Bermondsey Road? I've got the hoses. They're ordered and paid for – might be useful in Planet Fuck-up."

"Yea OK. Do you want me to bring a decompression chamber and a couple of strippers as well?"

"No need mate. The cold will kill you before the bends kick in, and there's plenty of healthy young ladies here to keep even you satisfied. And you won't have to pay as much as you do in London. See you soon Dickhead."

"Yea roger. Fuck off now Bollock-chops."

Chapter 12

MY OLD GRANDDAD used to say: 'Always leave a job tidy, so you can go back if you ever have to.' So I went back to London to tidy up. The pub was empty, but from the grunts below the bar Spanish George was having trouble cleaning the pipes.

"No rush George."

I'd perched on the same seat on Remembrance Day, talking to Mr Harman.

The optics stared like sad crystal balls without a future – some never used. Obviously Green Chartreuse and some blue stuff didn't sell well in this post code. Out of nowhere I felt a surge of optimism. Coffee would do just fine. Fate was saving me from an early alcoholic grave: Mr Harman, MO Brian, and now Mick's trawler had conspired with the Gods. It would be criminal to throw my life away when so many others had theirs violently taken from them.

Pub still empty; Spanish George still plumbing. Self - consciously I dropped to the floor, did five press-ups, then another five. The PTI's mantra had been: 'Come on you crap-hats. Your dicks are going to rust out before you wear them out. Move faster…' I flipped over, tucked my feet under the brass foot-rail and did twenty sit-ups. I'd still got it, whatever 'it' was and I was going to use it. I just didn't know how or when.

Without a glimmer of surprise – English customs were still a mystery to George – he looked over at me on the floor: "All pipes clean... fresh beer for you Steve?"

"No thanks George. Coffee black, when you're ready."

Plan A: Tidy up my London life. No women to say goodbye to, or rather none that wouldn't charge me fifty for the privilege. Ditch the cynical shell, then a new healthy, low-alcohol, fat-free, sea adventure… no-one trying to kill me, safe offshore: just the job – everyone needs mates.

I collected the cutting torches from Felix and Wright and dropped in to see Mr Harman to wish him well. Sometimes you get a feeling a house is empty; nothing obvious, but you just know. Always play your hunches. A neighbour looked across: "Bertie Harman is in a home now. Are you a relative?"

"No, a friend. Which home is he in?"

"St Isaac's by the crematorium." (Obviously the council wanted to save on the transport budget for end-of-life care.)

I decided to check the back of his house to make sure everything was tight. A covered side alley led to a small yard, a shed and a stack of broken plant pots. The back door had been forced. Inside: draws, tins, boxes, cutlery, photos littered the floor. The two druggies I recognized from the pub came haring down the stairs and froze. I dropped the first one, then grabbed the other's throat and shook. He was a bundle of bones in a bag of rags. No resistance; no weight or flesh; meaningless eyes.

As I let him fall to join the mess, a rage surged into my throat: "You useless scum-bags, this home belongs to good people. They looked after it for years and you've trashed it. He risked his life for you useless swamp donkeys. The Nazis would have had you as fertilizer. That's all you're good for – fuck all else. You're not worth a monkey's toss."

Each word I spat out, hyped my anger. They were still on the floor, blank stares, searching eyes, looking for escape from a madman. I kept shouting to stop myself kicking their heads in. "Didn't they teach you fuck all at school? If people like Mr and Mrs Harman hadn't done their bit you wouldn't be here. THIS IS THEIR HOME YOU'RE IN."

One of the ragbags mumbled… "Sorry, it wasn't us; the door was open... we'll help clear up."

It defused me a little. "Right, make a start. I'll get a broom from next door."

It was less than a minute to the smell of burning. The druggies had done a runner, leaving a newspaper and cardboard fire under the stairs. I grabbed a coat from behind the door and smothered it – all faith in humanity knocked to zero.

I made a sad attempt at tidying up. What would Mrs Harman say if she could see it now? The country owed them a lot. I collected the mail and screwed the back door shut. The shed in the yard that had survived WWII, was also trashed. Someone had crapped in the corner. Illogically, a dozen tobacco tins still sat neatly in line on the shelf; obscure engineering labels: '3/8 Whitworth, Taps and Dies, Spring Head Washers.' A powder of rust had formed on the hand-polished steel; beside them a sharpening stone and above a job sheet pinned to the wall with ten items. Four crossed off; six never to be completed. Symbolically I put a line through them and wrote: 'Job done,' crossed it out and wrote: 'Job well done.'

I gave the neighbour her broom back and asked her to report the break-in to the police. Her attitude didn't give me much confidence anything would happen.

Mr and Mrs Harman were in hospital, so their home had become an easy target for the feral community. First in, steals the goodies; second in, trashes it. What evil mentality! I hated them and the culture that spawned them. Standing – looking at the sky, missing my army mates, missing Caroline – too late now. I also missed being treated as someone. I wanted a badge that said: 'I'm a good bloke: you can trust me.' Selfish and vain maybe, but that's how I felt. OK, enough self indulgence. (Someone… a voice in my head: 'Walk on.')

Chapter 13

A FLOWER-DECKED HEARSE led me to the crematorium. Across the road was St Isaac's Retirement Home. What bureaucratic genius decided that it would cause anything but fear to the residents? I bet the old timers dealt with it with a huge dollop of black humour: 'Home for the baffled and bewildered; the deaf and daft; the confused and constipated; the fed up and fucked up.'

A fat-arsed pseudo nurse took me along a hundred-metre corridor with white crouched faces staring out from small boxes.

"We call him Bertie; no trouble at all; completely harmless. I'll leave you to it."

"Hello Mr Harman. I'm from the pub. I saw you on Remembrance Day. Do you remember?"

"Are you a doctor? They don't know what they're doing here."

"No, I'm Steve from the pub. I've brought your letters from home."

There were a couple with Canadian stamps and another marked RAF Aircrew Association. No need to mention the break in. "Do you have anyone to look after your house till you get back?"

"Enid always washed the front door slate on a Monday."

He reached across and held my arm tight; back in the present: "There's a suitcase upstairs full of RAF photos. They should go somewhere; mustn't be lost." We chatted softly about Chelsea football, pubs and weather, until he fell asleep. He'd said what he needed to say. As I was leaving I stopped at the desk: "Can you tell me where Mrs Enid Harman is, please?"

"Sadly she died a week ago. We haven't told Bertie; it could damage his health."

If it was me, I'd want to know, so I went back. He opened his eyes as I walked in.

"Steve!"

"Mr Harman, I have some very sad news about Enid."

"I know."

"Did someone tell you?"

"No, I just knew. When you live together for a long time, you talk to each other, not just with words. After the war I said I'd never leave her on her own again and I wouldn't go till she did."

He was peaceful when I left.

Chapter 14

THIS TIME I sincerely hoped the druggies had got in again. I'd drop the bastards permanently this time. The front door was open; voices inside; Radio One bass thumping. Renovation work had started.

They were decent blokes and just assumed I was another 'surveyor' getting over- paid for doing fuck all. A skip outside was filling with the family history. The armchairs sat either side of the fireplace. Indentations in the carpet where their castors had settled in the austerity 50s, when on freezing winter nights Enid and Bertie had stared at the coals… glowing roofs of fire-bombed Dresden and London… and both had looked up for comfort, and found it.

But now modernising for a profit: damp course, re-wiring, new plumbing, new bathroom en-suite, re-plastering. Selling features, like the slate threshold and tiled fireplace would be saved. Everything else in the skip. Five layers of wallpaper from 1940's mottle, to 60's stripes, to 70's squares, to mock stone. Carpets rose patterned, covering two lino layers and old newspaper.

The suitcase! I hared upstairs two at a time. Under the bed, untouched, no value to thieves or druggies, photos of young 1940's air crew… and a small bear surrounded by his mates. The history of our country summed up in souvenirs more precious than gold; saved by minutes from the skip's oblivion. No one asked why I took the case. One of the builders was dragging out an armchair: "Be careful with that mate, it's valuable." He looked at me as if I was mad. I couldn't look round as it smashed alongside the other one – together to the end, side by side: dumped.

* * *

It didn't surprise me, when I phoned St Isaac's the next day, that Mr Harman had died. He had decided to join Enid. I called Mick and explained I was hanging on in London to go to a funeral. He picked up my tone and was surprisingly understanding.

I was glad I went. The three remaining crew; correct in blue blazers, RAF ties and decorations, smaller than I imagined. I thought they'd all be over 6-foot.

I went over to them: "Mr Harman asked me to give you this case." I held it open.

The service was very moving, even for a heathen like me. At the end they played a scratched recording of 'Coming in on a Wing and a Prayer'. More than a few handkerchiefs snuffled. Then on the coffin, amongst the wreaths, I saw Ted, ribbon and shrapnel wound. I didn't care who saw me. Tears ran down, crying not just for Mr and Mrs Harman, but for all the suffering of the Second World War – and the First – and for all the bastard wars since. They were tears of anger as well as deep sadness. How could humanity let it happen? One family's suffering unbearable, then double it then multiply by millions: madness, sub-human madness. Sanity extinct.

* * *

In a small Lincolnshire RAF museum, run by volunteers, there is a display of WW2 memorabilia. Ted has his own hand-written card: 'A mascot from a World War Two Lancaster Bomber. Damage believed caused by enemy action.'…

If they only knew…

'Any questions please ask at the desk.'…Yea right, I'll ask at the desk. I'll ask, why is there fucking war? I'll ask, why were all those people killed? I'll ask, WHY?... FUCKING WHY?... Someone is bound to know. I'm sure they'll be able to find out for me, at the desk.

* * *

It had been a wake-up call. Use life wisely – respect is earned, not bought. Live right, die right. Mr and Mrs Harman had lived right.

They'd paid their way and they'd died right. I said a prayer. I didn't know who to – for their lives, for their inspiration and added: "If any God has an idea how to stop war, now would be a good time to let us know."

Learn; walk on. Next Remembrance Day, I will remember them.

Chapter 15

I MET MICK at the Nelson's Arms near Gosport on a cold, rain-swept quay and told him how the funeral and other stuff had gone. He got it – only criticising me for not slotting the two druggies when I first had the chance.

He bought a round and introduced me to Harry, ex-Chief Petty Officer and pub owner: short, with a flat cap. Mick said, 'Never smiled but had a heart of gold': obviously well hidden.

"Handle or straight glass?"

"Handle please, Harry"

"Good, I don't have straight. You another pongo then?"

"'Fraid so. Working on Mick's trawler."

"God help us. Shouldn't be allowed… pongoes should never go anywhere near boats."

I tried to lighten it up: "Why pongoes, Harry?"

"Because wherever the army goes the pong goes… get it?"

He didn't smile; more like a self satisfied smugness with a point scored. He wandered out the back.

"You're right Mick. Not a bundle of laughs, is he?"

"He's O.K, but tight. Makes a duck's arse look like the Blackwall Tunnel. Anyway, the long winter evenings just fly past thinking how to twist the pub's name: Nelson's Farm, Nelson's Armless, Nelson's Army, Nellie's Fanny and on and on."

"Bloody hell Mick; not exactly Ibiza is it?"

"True, a bloke came in with his wife last week and all Harry said was: 'Not the same one as last night then?' She got upset, the bloke got upset and they both left arguing. After closing time the bloke came back and changed the pub sign to Nelson's Arse. That's why it's always quiet in here."

Harry's ears were wagging like bats' wings. He came over again: "I can always tell what someone is like by the way they look." No answer needed. Observation left hanging in the air.

Mick had to say something: “Your wife is going to miss your jokes when you’ve gone, Harry.”

“No she won’t; she’s deaf. I clean the chimney with a shotgun.”

* * *

The fishing went well from the start. Dawn was a good boat: forward wheel house rusty, but gear solid. Engine noise prevented much chit-chat, which suited me. So universal hand signals, modified and speeded up for hairy situations, suited fine. Trust was essential and taken for granted. Deck speakers blasted out Santana and Dire Straits… a day of white horses; surfing on a following sea; heading home with a good catch; the mood always got me. I braced on the stern gantry, playing air guitar like a pillock. Mick indicated with his right hand, I should probably get out more and find a girlfriend.

It was also working well financially. One share of the catch for the boat, one for Mick and, over generously, one for me. Life on board settled to the rhythm of tides and weather. And if a south-westerly hooligan was blowing up the Channel, there was always maintenance with the added attraction of fishing gossip at Harry’s. Life had moved into a satisfyingly productive state, resulting in my fitness and bank balance improving drastically. I should have remembered what my granddad said: ‘Nothing lasts. If it’s good, it won’t last. If it’s bad, it won’t last. So why worry?’

It was a day when mottled cumulus raced the showers, giving a lively feel to everything, except the stranger in a grey suit and matching Lexus. Mick seemed to think he was O.K. I didn’t like him from the start. He invited himself onboard and the three of us sat in the wheelhouse drinking tea. Mick must have known him from somewhere. Taylor, the guest, sipped at it. I felt like saying: ‘Just drink the bloody stuff, you won’t catch crabs.’ He had the aura of a fishery inspector or a taxman. So I went below to check the bilges, while Mick and Taylor moved to the stern for a chat.

When I came back, they were still talking: "Taylor has a job for us Steve. Ditching a container full of scrap on Klondike spoil ground. Well paid, simple."

Taylor slimed in: "Can I expand on what Mick has said? I'm employed by DEFRA to dispose of non-hazardous waste and we like to give the work to local boats."

He looked me in the eye for the first time, leaned back satisfied with his rehearsed piece and smiled. I'd never seen a snake smile before. His voice a touch too high; his credibility a touch too low.

He waited for my comment: "It's Mick's boat. I'm just the crew. It's not what I signed up for but if he says O.K, I'll back him."

Taylor jumped up. I'd loved to have seen him crack his head on the gantry – no such luck. "Right lads, job's on, good. I'll be in contact. You dive, don't you Steve?" It wasn't a question. He slithered onto the quay and drove off.

Mick forced a smile: "What do you think, good eh?"

"No, not good. How did he know I was a diver? The job stinks. What do you know about him? I wouldn't trust him with your barge pole, let alone mine. If he's from DEFRA, I'm a French condom on a Chinese dick."

"C'mon Steve. It's a challenge. It's what we do."

"No, it's not what we do. What we used to do was fight, fuck, make money then piss it up the wall. Now we go fishing and save money. Just think, Mick: One – what's in the container? Two – why don't the 'wavy navy' do it? Three – where does the diving come in? And Four – why does he carry a gun?"

"You sure about the gun?"

"Well if he wasn't, he fancied you something chronic and his erection was sticking out of his armpit. Now, before we get into serious shite let's go and see if Harry's got any warm rat's piss left."

Whatever I said was not going to change his mind. I knew I'd have to tag along to prevent fuck ups. Rule One, again: 'Don't leave your mates in the shite.' As granddad used to say: 'Everyone makes mistakes. What matters is what you do about them.' Thanks granddad. I had a feeling I'd be needing more advice before this particular job was over.

Harry begrudgingly left the preparation of the evening's menu – which consisted of putting salt and vinegar crisps in one box and cheese and onion in the other – and pulled two pints. On Fridays, packets of peanuts were available from a card which slowly revealed a naked woman. Mick and I had bought enough to feed an elephant. Whenever it got close to revealing her tits Harry would stick bags back on. It would have been cheaper if we'd bought the lot in one go.

"You pongoes want your usual or are you going to pay for it this time?" Was it a joke, a conversation starter, an insult, who knew?

Mick got in first: "Harry, it would be a lot easier to run this pub if you didn't have any customers."

He actually thought about it: "That's true. My pension is enough. I only open as a community service."

I had to stir it: "You'd miss us if we didn't come in. Your takings would be cut by half. I didn't know we were charity cases."

He pushed his cap back, showing a tide line across his forehead: "You two need a joke to cheer you up: the Admiral looks after the fleet, the Vice Admiral looks after the vice, so what does the Rear Admiral look after?"

It was a typical Harry non-joke: no punch line. I tried a chuckle to encourage him – nothing. For all his crotchety moods it was a cosy sanctuary. If he'd only light the fire it would be perfect. Mick did once, when Harry was out the back. It had been laid waiting for minus ten, so when he came back his face was a picture. Torn between putting it out with beer slops or removing the logs that hadn't caught. Mick had been banned for a week. Happy days.

* * *

Friday: I scanned the bar. A few early evening customers having a quickie before heading home to the missus, pizza and telly, and two smart office girls nattering at the furthest table. Harry didn't miss a thing: "No chance. Out of your league."

"Just looking, Harry."

Mick blimped over his shoulder: "Rather be in that than the Royal Navy, eh, Harry?"

My first pint hadn't touched the side. Since London, I rationed myself to a maximum of two an evening and felt better for it. Harry's comment had niggled. "O.K Harry. I bet a tenner I can talk to them for 15 minutes and get them to buy me a drink."

Mick jibed: "No way. If you do, I'll double it."

Their lack of confidence in my chat-up skills was unnerving – still, a bet's a bet. I hadn't a clue what I was going to say. Oh well – here goes: "Is this chair free?"

Eyes of the most beautiful feline darkness swamped my confidence. "Yes of course." I rubbed my knee and winced.

"Are you O.K?"

"I'll be fine if I can just sit for a minute. It must be Harry's beer."

How beer would affect my knee, I hadn't thought. I hadn't rehearsed. The beautiful eyebrows arched slightly, clearly saying: 'Chancer.'

"Anyway, my name's Steve."

"Look we don't want to offend you Steve, but it's been a long week."

It was a polite way of saying piss off. O.K, last resort, 'the truth': "Right, I give in. I have a bet with Harry and my mate at the bar that I can talk to you for fifteen minutes and you'd buy me a drink."

The eyes now fully hostile and even more beautiful: "So you come over here for a sordid bet. How much?"

"Twenty quid."

"Twenty! We're worth more than that!"

"I know you are. You must be worth at least fifty… each."

I realised the implication of what I'd said and so did their now fully-arched eyebrows. This wasn't going to plan. Then the dark-haired one exploded in a delicious giggle of mock disgust: "We usually charge at least a hundred, unless you want the special. Do you want the special Steve?"

God, I wanted the special and anything else that was going. A sensuous rug was being pulled from under my feet by beautiful female hands. I should have kept quiet – but no: "You're both so attractive you must keep busy." Why on earth did I say that? Plonker. The looks said I was now on very thin ice, so moved to go.

"Wait. How long before your fifteen minutes is up?"

"Another five." Inspiration – sympathy – get in quick: "I really am sorry to bother you two, but it's only because we've been fishing near Greenland for six months and we've just come ashore."

The polygraph eyebrows registered. I kept going: "We've been rescuing dolphins from nets and setting them free." Bingo, their weakness, gotcha! They were buying it. Softening faces encouraged me. I was even beginning to believe my own lies. Modesty helped: "We're volunteers, working for love, not money."

"O.K. you've won your bet. I'll pretend to give you money for a round. You tell Harry and your mate you've pulled, put a tenner in the lifeboat box, bring us two gin and tonics and we'll call it quits. And Steve, my name is Leila and this is Emily."

We shook hands elaborately and I did an exaggerated laugh to build the scam. I was enjoying myself: "So what do you really do?"

The teasing hadn't finished: "We really are high class escorts, having a night off and your fifteen minutes is up. If you require any more of our services, please pay in cash – up front."

I sat there, allowing the succulent taunts to flow around me while becoming more and more conscious of their very short skirts, until Leila gave me an old- fashioned look: "Can we have our drinks now, Steve?"

This could be awkward: 117 times 9 – erection busting maths. Crouching slightly, I shuffled back to the bar looking at my watch: "Close your mouth Harry; it's your round."

He chuntered to himself as the evening's profits were placed on the tray: "My bloody prices are going up."

Mick carried the drinks across and the introductions made smoothly.

"So Mick, you are both fishermen?"

Truthfully he said: "Yes we are."

"And you've just got back from Greenland?"

His face flicked a surprised glare at me: "Yep, it's a long way."

"And you've been at sea six months rescuing dolphins?"

He was looking deep into his beer for inspiration; unfortunately he found it: "Yep, six months, saving cuddly dolphins, except when we ran short of food. Little Stevie here had to eat one. I'm a veggie so went hungry. He got the taste for them: dolphin burgers, pies, you name it – couldn't get enough – could you Stevie baby?"

The girls' compassion twisted. I shook my head: "He's only joking."

But Mick hadn't finished. He was on a mission: "Of course he thinks dolphin meat will improve his virility and stop his inappropriate, anti-social sexual habits. I won't tell you what they are in case he comes out in a rash again."

Leila was ahead of him: "I love sensitive men. They make such comfortable lovers."

Mick tried another put down: "He still pisses the bed – rubber sheets and all that."

Leila crooned: "I love rubber, especially when wet."

Mick: "He's so mean his wallet looks like a duck's arse."

Leila: "I love ducks."

Mick: "He's got a dick like a rabbit."

Leila: "We've both got 'Rabbits'. It would save on batteries."

Mick: "He can't stop farting in bed."

Leila: "A man relaxed with his body!"

Exasperated, Mick played his ace: "He has to pay women to sleep with him."

Leila: "So generous – especially in our business."

Mick raised his hands in surrender: "O.K, O.K, he's not a bad mate." Duel ending in warm laughter – game, set and match to Leila. The girls stood up, both looking at their watches pointedly: "One hour, forty minutes – we'll take a cheque."

Mick was even more confused as we watched them leave.

"I enjoyed that, Mick."

"Trouble with you mate, is you see women through rose-coloured testicles. Anyway, they must be lesbians."

"Why? Just because Emily didn't beg you to shag her after one gin and tonic?"

"Fuck off! Back to business. What are we going to do about Taylor? I've said we'd do it."

A wet, grey fog seeped into the bar ending Happy Hour. My instinct said forget it: "Mick, we've a good set up here. Why risk it?"

"'Cos it would help pay off the boat loan and give you some savings – that's why. And you could afford a woman like Leila ."

I agreed, knowing things would go wrong, knowing it would be a fuck up and knowing when life was on the edge. I loved it.

Chapter 16

THE FOLLOWING FRIDAY the four of us sat at the same table – atmosphere relaxed until Leila confronted Mick: "Do you really think we are lesbians? Lip reading is so useful. We thought you two were chutney ferrets."

Mick looked at me for support: "Sorry mate, you're on your own. I'll get the drinks."

Harry was still brooding: "They're too good for you pongoes."

"I know, but if you've got it, you've got it."

Leila came over: "I'll get these, Steve."

"Why? Have you lost a bet?"

"No, we wouldn't like to be under any obligation, since we're lesbians."

Harry's ears were flapping red as he gave her the change. He couldn't resist a stir: "Has he told you about his wife and kids yet?"

"No, but he's told me of your adventures down Boogey Street, Singapore."

"I've never told anyone about that."

"I know Harry, but you have now!"

She picked up the tray and swayed back to the table. Harry puffed on his unlit roll-up: "She's a smart one. Watch what you say to her. Don't tell her about the Black Syph in Shanghai."

"Wouldn't dream of it Harry." ...Until the conversation goes a bit slack.

* * *

The four of us went into a phase of stimulating normality – Mick and Emily, me and Leila. Mick's customised euphemisms and old jokes about 'rocking the boat' wore a bit thin. But apart from that, life was good, fishing was good and I was enjoying Leila's company so much that we just let the emotions roll without constraint. I felt it could go on forever – but 'nothing lasts' – so I wasn't surprised when the good bits took a knock. Taylor slithered onto the quay. We'd just moored up.

"Hi Mick, you're looking well, and you Steve, good catch?"

He'd obviously just finished chapter one of, 'How to be nice to people when you've got a crap personality.'

After we'd iced and boxed the catch into the freezer van, we sat in the wheel house and drank tea, or rather Mick and I drank tea while Taylor moved his mug around the chart table like a demented chess player. If you spill even a drop of that, Mick wouldn't care if you were King of the Faeroes, he'd lump you big time. Eventually he took a patronising sip: "Really nice cuppa. The job's on, right?"

It was another of his vague semi-rhetorical comments, statements, questions which got up my nose. Mick got in quick before I could tell Taylor to piss off: "Yep, jobs on. We're ready when you are."

Taylor's response was businesslike: "Good, follow me. The gear is in the car."

I was seriously impressed: plastic wrappers, smelling newness, top quality dive kit and two more oxy arc cutting torches. I hefted one – identical to those I'd lugged from London's Shagnasty and Twatface.

Mick saw my look and smiled: "You can never have too many."

The way things were heading, I was going to be cutting acres of heavy metal on the sea bed, for some reason I'd yet to discover – one in each hand.

Taylor was still trying to build his authority: "Steve, you and Mick go and do a test dive tonight."

I didn't like him telling us what to do. I didn't like night dives on my own with no backup. I didn't like cold Channel water. I didn't like zero visibility, and I especially didn't like whinging to myself, because next came flapping, then panic, then dead, dead, dead. I needed a few answers: "Why dive at night?"

Taylor had rehearsed again: "We don't want any curious green eco-warriors checking on what we're doing, do we?"

That was bollocks, but I let it go. Negatives were piling up. What was in the container? No one went to this much trouble to get rid of scrap metal. Mick couldn't dive, and Taylor looked like he wore a hair-net in the shower to stop his comb-over disappearing down the plug hole. I was flapping big-time. Everyone knew some ops would be a cock-up from start to finish. Mr Harman and his mates knew and still they went. I knew and I suppose I'd have to go too. Getting control of my flapping was not easy, so I resorted to checking gear.

Taylor interrupted: "Tomorrow leave at 18:00." It was an order. Mick nodded. I gave a sarcastic,"Yes Sir", as he slid off back to snake central.

Rehearsals are essential but boring, so to Mick's surprise I said not to bother flashing up the engine. I'd go off the end of the jetty to wash the newness from the kit. It wasn't thirty metres deep, more like three, but it would do.

* * *

Taylor was on time and full of shit. He must have finished chapter two : 'How to get what you want by smiling at everyone.'

"Lads, I've bought pasties to keep you going."

I could picture him at school, trying to snivel up to the football team on the way to a match. I was breaking another rule: 'Don't let personalities get to you.'

We cast off. Time to focus, turn professional and start work. Shipping forecast: '...south west, force three to four, showers.' O.K. this was not going to be a pleasure dive so the only thing I had to look forward to was seeing Taylor spew up over the side. Most people don't like someone looking over their shoulder when they're working – Taylor knew it: "Getting nervous Steve?" I felt like saying, 'Yes that's why I'm mentally preparing for as many things that can go wrong as I can think of, which is why I don't want a prat like you standing behind me.' Instead I quietly replied: "No I'm fine thanks." Disappointed, he went back into the wheel house to bolt more gizmos to his computer. My revenge was to follow him and ask about every bell, whistle and coloured dot on the screen. A real fascination formed as rapidly changing data gave projected vectors, co-ordinates, ETA's and extra squares clogged up with obscure warnings: 'Release tow only at exact position.' Amongst it all, somewhere in the dark, was an infra-red flashing light from a transponder beacon on a big fat steel box saying: 'Come and get me suckers.'

In the loppy sea the forty-foot container showed with its top awash. Where had it come from? Of the thousands lost at sea every year, collisions are inevitable and boats disappear. Mick brought Dawn carefully alongside. I jumped the two metres with the tow line and shackled on. Mick took up the slack and I pulled myself back on board, hand over hand – cold sea biting hard through the wetsuit – and payed out thirty metres. We were now in the tug business.

Taylor was still in the forward wheelhouse obsessing over his laptop, so I stood irritatingly close, looking over his shoulder: "All secured and ship shape … Sir."

"Fug orf Steve, I'm busy."

Why can't public schools teach correct pronunciation: it's Fuck Off not Fug Orf.

Considering we were towing a flat-faced steel box, we were doing O.K. Chugging along at four knots, plus the three-knot flood tide, gave us seven over the ground: a rough ten mph. Mick waved me over, leaned on the wheel and pointed to a pencil mark on the chart: 'Klondike Spoil Ground, Hazardous, No Anchoring.' It was the first time I'd seen the exact position. It gave me an involuntary shiver. Spoil Grounds were bad news for divers and fishermen. All kinds of tangled jetsam layered the sea bed, fouled in a deadly candy floss of nets, silently ghost fishing. And it was night, and spring tides, and I was alone, and no buddy, and no reserve bottle, and there was a dirty slop on top of a long swell: Situation Normal All Fucked Up… brilliant. I don't know why but I loved it. It wasn't bravery. If I'd been scared and did it that would be brave, so mental deficiency seemed the only answer… whatever. I was smiling, confident, ready for anything and full of elitist arrogance.

Taylor came over holding a notebook and pen: "Steve, when we get in position, the depth will be thirty metres. I'll signal a red light. When it goes green, open the valve alongside the transponder. It has been designed to slowly sink with you on it. Secure yourself. There will be turbulence. You will have a shot line and a marker buoy with auto strobe. When you have ensured the container is sitting level on the seabed with doors accessible, you will surface – DO NOT OPEN DOORS. We will pick you up, recover the gear and return to the quay. Any questions?"

"Yes, why do the doors have to be accessible?"

"I can't tell you that."

"OK, what if they are not accessible?"

"We will use the trawler's deck winch and reposition it. Any more?"

I said no, but there were dozens of them. I'd have to sort them out myself, so I blanked him, and went into checking phase. No decompression tables, no more 'what ifs?' – it was time to get on with the job. 'Scrap metal' – who was he trying to kid?

Taylor shouted to Mick: "Hold her on station there."

I went backwards over the side into thick black turbulence. Tow rope slack – it was easy to haul across. Standing like a surfer, all I needed was a green light.

"C'mon twatty snake. What are you bloody waiting for, Christmas?"

There it is: Red on – Green on – Go – towline released – shot line clear – torch on – valve open – dust jetting out – sinking slowly – a couple of vicious wave slaps, then into the quiet peaceful underwater world. I was home again.

It must be like this on a sinking ship – poor sods. I was standing on a steel box, gliding into god knew what – but I had air: squeeze nose, equalise pressure, ears pop. It was like driving a car in fog; the torch beam hitting a wall.

Rate of descent increasing, air bubbles streaming faster. 'What ifs?' came in a rush: what if the depth was more than thirty metres? What if we landed on some evil contaminated explosives? Questions ended on impact in a cloud of silt.

The current cleared visibility to about four metres. Container stable and upright; doors accessible – 'DO NOT OPEN' – yea right. I levered off the seal, eased one about two feet and went in. Why was Taylor so keen to dump this cargo? Surprise, surprise, the torch beam showed rows of five-gallon plastic tubs – no scrap metal. Fuck Taylor, lying bastard. The colours were difficult to gauge, but appeared as rows of black, white and red, all stacked to within a metre of the top. I opened one of each colour, removed a small plastic packet and stashed them in my grab bag. If Taylor was trying to take us for a pair of cunts he'd eat his bollocks for breakfast.

Check time – tide turning – get out.

There is one thing divers fear more than Great White sharks and that's monofilament drift nets: invisible to fish and other forms of life, especially divers.

The flood tide had set in hard, bringing a cloud of the deadly stuff fouling the doors.

Panic bubbled – keep it back – keep still – count breaths slowly. Heart thumping in my ears. I tried to weave my way through – stay cool. Something snagged on the bottle – I reached for my ankle knife and felt another snag on my fins. The torch beam couldn't penetrate more than a few feet, then shapes appeared: a rotting jelly of dead fish: ray, skate, doggies, and further, hanging vertically, a wet suit, lifeless arm waving. I pushed it away, forcing a cloud of vomit to jet from the skull where his mouth had been. For me vomiting would be fatal. I grabbed at what I thought was the shot line, feeling plastic tendrils hardening their grip, pulling me back. Don't panic – don't panic; I repeated over and over.

Now I had to do something. I slid the bottle off and held it in front; trying to reduce snagging; steadily cutting at the net; weight belt fouled; more netting wrapped around me.

The watching dead were hoping for company. Panic is death – don't panic.

My face mask flooded. I was going to have a very calm, unpanicked death. An involuntary spasm of fear hit me... trembling... I panicked. All control lost.

Insane thrashing for release – to claw to the surface – clawing for death – reason gone – end guaranteed.

Some detached part of me was watching as I growled, fought, slashed blindly, biting, gasping gallons of air.

It shouldn't have happened. The rules said I should have drowned. I didn't. I broke free. The shot line controlled my mad ascent to the surface just enough. God, I'd never dive again, ever – ditch bottle, weight belt – wait – shaking with fear – hugging the strobe buoy, coughing, spewing.

Mick didn't waste time. In less than a minute, they were hauling my body in. My mind was somewhere else.

Taylor – the inconsiderate bastard – spoke first: "Where's the bottle and valve? They cost a fortune!"

I kept my jaw clenched, pushed past, headed for the forward cabin, and started pumping my arms until warmth returned. I doubled up on jumpers, hid the grab bag under a bunk and went up to the wheelhouse. Good old Mick stuffed a cup of hot sweet tea in my face.

Snaky Taylor was studying me closely: "Problems?"

"Na, piece of cake."

"Container level?"

"Yep."

"Doors accessible?"

"Yep."

"No obstructions?"

"No."

"You sure?"

I gave him a look which said: 'If you ask any more questions, I'm going to rip one of your arms off and let you swim ashore with an anchor tied to your bollocks, and a blunt fish knife for company.'

I could feel the shakes starting again so, before anyone noticed, I went below and crashed out. Job done, yea, but done badly. Panic rule broken. Mick's whisky bottle nodded against the fiddle rail: five minutes and the craving would go. I should be dead. Only luck meant I was staring in a mirror. It had been luck, not skill. As a wreck diver I would make a fucking good banker. I decided no one would ever know I'd screwed up.

(A voice, sounded like MO Brian: 'Live and learn. You made it. File it away. Everyone gets good and bad luck. Learn from the bad. Keep on the Path.')

"Thank you, sir."

Carefully, I took the still dripping bag from under the bunk, checked the three packages and re-stowed it.

*   *   *

Nevada:

“Container in position Sir. 78 and 79 leaving site.”

“Let’s see if the Brits can screw this one up Costa.”

“Yes Sir.”

Chapter 17

TAYLOR disappeared with his precious computer as soon as we got back to the quay. He didn't even leave the pasties. Mick tried to be helpful. It didn't suit him: "Get your head down. You look knackered."

"Bollocks, we've got to go and see Harry."

"He won't be open this time in the morning. If you're busting for a drink, help yourself to the whisky."

"I don't want a drink. Just follow me and play along."

Harry was his usual welcoming self: "What do you two tossers want? I'm closed."

I asked respectfully: "We need advice. It's important."

"I saw you moor up earlier – not much fish."

"Can we come in?"

"Alright, but be quiet. The misses likes a lie in since her operation."

The back room was full of rugs, armchairs and tobacco smoke clouding his morning comic. He didn't ask us to sit, but went straight in: "Mush Jones reckons he saw you off Basset Point as it was getting light. No fishing there, only Klondike Spoil Ground. Hand lines and rods get fish on the edge, but they lose gear."

It was the opening I needed: "We thought we'd trawl the east side on the flood Harry."

He re-lit his roll-up: "Don't even think about it. There's plenty of fish alright, but no one goes there, for good reason. Klondike is bad news, evil. There's stuff there that would sink the Isle of Wight if it went up."

Mick played along: "What sort of stuff?"

Over the fireplace hung a framed, tobacco sepia'd chart of the Western Approaches. He pointed vaguely at it. Chief Petty Officer Harry Baker was shuffling his thoughts: "Right, listen hard, don't piss about and try to remember what I tell you. I don't want to see you lost, even if you are pongoes – takings would go down – understand?"

Mick: "Yes Chief."

He looked at me…

"Yes Chief."

"When I joined up, I was on *HMS Resource*. It was just after the war and us nippers got sick of hearing about it. Officers had the official version but the old hands knew what really went on. The stuff you never read about."

He paused to relight his dried rolly, tilted his cap back showing the tide line on his forehead: brown, weather-etched below, dough-white above – then pointed at the chart again: "We were on the Frenchie side of the Channel, off Ushant, homeward from Trinco, Ceylon. Everything went by sea in them days except some army brass. Anyway, course laid for Pompey – just as Nelson, Frobisher, Ironclads, Dreadnoughts – all the same course. The compass don't change. Anyway, us crew got the nod. Certain equipment had to be sent 'deep six' – over the side – 'just to see if it floated', get me?"

"We get you Chief."

He tried to re-light the dead rolly. It stuck to his bottom lip. Mick stared: "Is there any baccy left in that thing?"

"Cheeky bugger. Best Pussers shag. You want me to finish this tale or not?"

I got in quick: "Ignore him Harry, keep going. It's very interesting, really."

"Anyway, where was I? Right – we were given the nod just inside British waters – hove to – all crew and Royals (Marines) formed chains – passing shells, ammunition boxes, weapons: all sorts of nasty stuff. Heavier boxes were winched over the side – one was dropped – the powder burnt two crewmen badly – their skin fizzed as we sluiced them down – the scuppers smoked for hours. Anyway, listen carefully you two farmers. We found out the dumping ground had been used for years – centuries – same area – from Oak Walls to Iron Clads. You don't know what I'm talking about, do ya?"

"We do Chief. It's making sense, fascinating."

"Anyway, for centuries, our ships, same course, same distance from the coast. It don't change – you won't find it in any pilot. Orders were: 'When Albion in sight let Neptune keep your secrets, right!' I haven't told you this – you haven't heard this from me."

Mick: "No Chief."

Me: "No Chief."

It was like something out of Treasure Island, except his attitude baulked any fiction. Me and Mick were kids mesmerised by tales of the high seas; the Spanish Main, timbers shivered... deadly secrets from accumulated nautical heritage. Harry's voice became conspiratorial: "Navy ships throughout history did the same in the same place. Radioactive material was only banned from dumping at sea in the 80s – 'out of sight, out of mind.' Get me? Do you know what PCB's are? They were banned from dumping on land so what did the bastards do? Dump them at sea!" He paused, looking carefully at both of us: "You've heard of the Official Secrets Act? Good, so you know where this hell hole is?"

Mick said it: "Klondike?"

"Yes Klondike. It's covered in poisonous crap from past wars: chemical, biological, radioactive and god knows what else. A lot has been covered by dredgings from Pompey and Southampton – a lot hasn't. At the end of the war some vessels were too dangerous to unload – booby trapped. No one then wanted to risk it, so they were sunk to rot away on the sea bed. No one knew what the cargoes were."

Mick was taking it all in: "Surely nowadays there are strict environmental laws. It's more controlled."

"Rowlocks, it is not. It's made things worse. Toxic material like asbestos is too expensive to dispose of on land. Where do you think it goes? There's always plenty of rust buckets and greedy crews waiting to dump anything, and I mean anything."

Mick stared at the carpet uncomfortably, and scratched his ear.

A long pause, then Harry added more from his memory chest: "After the Falklands War, 82, officers read the riot act to returning troops. As they steamed slowly over Klondike: Argie pistols, bayonets, showered over the side, plus more gruesome souvenirs – even the padre's porno collection – all went 'deep six'. Now you have been warned. Not everyone gets warnings. And one more thing, I don't like your posh mate Taylor. He asks too many questions and never answers any himself. Talks a lot, says nothing. Pen pusher, is he?"

"Yea."

"I knew it. If you want to catch him out, give him a bag of money and make sure he never spends it if you know what I mean." He unlocked a cupboard beside the fireplace and took out a shotgun.

Mick winced: "Bloody hell Harry. Let's prove the bugger's guilty first."

"It's not for him, though one day it might be." He loaded a barrel, stuck it up the chimney and fired: "Best way to clean it. Cheaper than a sweep."

"What about your missus?"

"She'll be alright. Deaf now anyway. Remember what I've told you."

Mick: "Yes Chief."

Me: "Yes Chief."

Chapter 18

THE NEWS from Afghanistan was about the legacy of our involvement, not its 'success.' And this coupled with warnings of terrorism and increasing amounts of heroin on the high streets, convinced some people the war had been a waste of time.

If I'd killed Ahmed and the rest, maybe bombs and druggies would not be such a threat, the world would be a safer place and there'd be free beer every weekend .Yea right… It still bugged me.

(M.O Brian's voice – 'Let it go Steve – move on.')

* * *

Two weeks of good fishing and good loving with Leila kept Klondike at the back of my mind. Occasionally Mick would ask about the dive and I would keep repeating: 'Visibility nil, no problem, job done.' He didn't believe me, but left it at that.

Things began to change, innocently at first. Leila and Emily went on a computer course for a week. Harry told them he'd keep an eye on us. Not difficult since we sat at the same table moping into our beer, summed up by his 'spare pricks at a wedding' comments.

When he was out of earshot, I opened the subject I'd been stewing over: "Mick, I want to dive on the container again." I didn't tell him I wanted to blow it up.

"Bollocks, no way – you're mad. We'd never find it again."

"Yes we would. I took GPS coordinates off Taylor's laptop. When I was down there I opened the container's doors. There was no scrap metal; it was full of plastic tubs. Outside there's fouled nets everywhere. I was lucky to get back. Good job I didn't panic and thrash about."

"What was in the tubs?"

I lied: "Don't know, but I want to find out what Taylor has to say. I don't trust him."

Mick countered: "He's genuine. I've seen his I.D. from DEFRA. I'm not risking my neck or yours, just out of curiosity."

"Look, he could get an I.D. saying he was the bloody Queen of Tonga. His I.D. is worth as much as a cow's fifth tit. Now get him over here. I want to ask him a few questions, that's all."

"O.K. O.K. if you're that worried."

I didn't expect Taylor to turn up an hour later, irritated, confrontational, no 'hello mates.' We all stomped back to the boat.

"What do you want to know, Steve?"

"What's in the container and why does it have to be accessible?"

He stuck his head forward aggressively: "What and why? You're outside of your pay grade, so forget it!"

It was the cue I needed. Thoughts I'd bottled up for too long surfaced. "Look snake shit, I don't like you and I don't like being set up. I opened the doors and went in, so now tell us what's going on."

He uncoiled on his chair: "Your orders were to make sure the doors were clear, not to look inside."

"I couldn't check they were clear without opening them, so I couldn't help looking in, could I?"

"What did you see?"

"Enough." It was a weak card but it worked.

"You both have signed the Official Secrets Act, so if you divulge anything to anyone, you will be sanctioned, understood?"

Neither of us wanted to be sanctioned, whatever that meant, so nodded, watching his scheming little snake brain race.

"Right, fact one: ninety per cent of U.K. heroin comes from Afghanistan. We don't use napalm because it would destroy the local economy and empower the Taliban. Our government's plan is to buy the total annual crop and use it for medicinal morphine in Africa. Demand is huge."

I was waiting for Mick to get the implications. He asked: "What has that got to do with the container?"

Taylor waited, I waited.... one and two and three... and...

"Shit, you mean the container is full of heroin?"

Taylor ignored the question and continued: "Fact two: the three main routes out of Afghanistan are through Russia, the Balkans and the sea route to the U.K. Containers with false bills of lading transit Karachi onto U.K. bound vessels, to be jettisoned at pre-arranged co-ordinates off Greece, Spain, France and the U.K. Since thousands of containers are lost overboard every year, it is not considered suspicious. Operators working for dealers tow them into shallow water, sink them and remove the drugs when required – just like a bank. Cash goes to Switzerland via any of the branch offices: Gib, Jersey, Cayman, B.V.I, from where it's invested in the London stock exchange and property – all legit. All laundered, all accessible to finance more terrorism and corruption."

Mick's hands were clenched on the table, knuckles showing white, matching his face. Taylor moved for his check mate, raising an index figure for theatrical emphasis: "We track the drugs when they are accessed with our tech gadgets and eliminate the bad guys. And here's the good bit. Not only does the morphine help Africa, but we destroy the terrorists' funds, and at the same time U.K. gov. institute a drug user rehab programme. Everyone's happy except the dealers: three birds with one stone – win, win, win. You two have played a very valuable part in ending this evil trade, Q.E.D: Quod Erater Demonstratum."

Taylor was now out in the open. I fired back: "What happens when heroin prices go through the roof in London because the supply has stopped? Crime will increase proportionally to match the cost, Q.E.D: Queer Error Dummy."

Taylor looked irritated: "The antidrug programme will include T.V. ads, counselling and more."

I didn't believe him. Mick was still floundering. He repeated the question: "So our container is full of heroin?" Taylor raised his eyes heavenwards and repeated his answer: "I can't tell you that."

I had to keep him talking: "Are there more containers coming to U.K. or are there some here already?"

"I can't tell you that either."

"Well, can you tell us why you didn't get RN divers to do the job?"

His smile widened. What a bundle of laughs he was: "We needed unconnected operators, who had basic skills and were disposable – like a pair of ex-squaddies."

Disposable! I wanted to stuff my fist down his throat. Stay cool, keep him talking: "Have you arrested anyone yet?"

"No, we don't plan to make arrests, as such."

'As such!' We were in deep shit without a shovel and with more information than was good for us. The snake was pleased with himself. We were now complicit. Fuck it – I'd tried to be too clever.

He reared up: "Must go. I'll be in touch. Your pay will be with you soon. Tax deducted at source, so you won't have to declare it. Bye, bye."

Chapter 19

MICK got the whisky from the bookshelf.

"Put that away; get the kettle on. We need to think."

I wanted to get a bergen on my back and head off to the Coastal Path.

(Rule one: 'Don't leave your mates in the shite.' And rule eight: 'Shorts is a mug's game.')

"O.K Mick, we've got to prioritise: primary and secondary actions." I was bullshitting, but it helped.

Mick slopped the mugs on the cabin table. He was also looking for a way out: "What's the worst that can happen? We've finished our part of the operation, so let's go back to fishing and the girls and forget the other crap, yea?"

I quashed it: "No way. You heard what he said, 'I'll be in touch.' Not well done lads, forget you've ever seen me."

Mick was flapping big time, which in his case meant staring hard at his tea: "What if we just tell him to piss off?"

"We can't."

"Why not?"

I reached under the bunk and pulled out my grab bag, still salt damp, and let it dramatically thump on the table: "I didn't tell you. I opened three tubs in the container."

I reached inside: first rabbit a pistol; second rabbit a 200mm black slab; third rabbit a 200mm white slab; all vacuum packed. Mick's eyes alternated between me and the rabbits. Methodically, I pointed: "First: Browning 9mm, oiled, sealed, ammunition, spare mags, cleaning kits. Second: black heroin, ready for use, uncut, evil. Third…" I picked up the white slab, turned it over to show the imbedded detonator and held it under Mick's nose.

"Marzipan!"

"Yep, enough marzipan to blow up all the Christmas cakes in the U.K. Just when you thought it couldn't get any worse."

"Shit."

"Exactly – in one."

I leant back with a sense of dull satisfaction and took a swig of tea. Mick had seen all the stuff before in the military – not on his cabin table, not in his comfort zone. Out of context they stirred ugly memories.

"What now?"

"I haven't finished yet, there's more."

"More! Fucking hell, don't tell me you found Harry's false teeth down there."

Good old Mick, he'd recovered. He was back in the game, doing what he was good at, keeping it real, taking the piss.

I told him nearly all I knew: "The sea bed around the container is covered in military debris, just as Harry told us, plus a candy-floss of snagged fishing nets with a bye-catch of cod, ray and divers."

"Divers! What, dead bodies?"

"I saw one close up. He didn't say much; there's probably more. I would have joined him if I hadn't stayed calm and not panicked. I didn't panic, just stayed cool and professional. Now you know as much as I do. If Taylor is from DEFRA, I'm a flying pig. And we don't even know whose side he's on, but we do know he's a liar."

Mick stared at the pistol: "How much ammo?"

"Thousands of rounds, sealed, 9mm parabellum."

"Damn, bugger, arseholes, bloody, bollocks, shite."

"That's exactly what I thought, Mick."

"Taylor said they'd catch them when they came ashore. Get the lot before any damage is done."

"You reckon? How many cock-ups have we seen? Correction, how many ops worked out as planned? None, right? They all go ape shit after the start. Imagine when things on this job go wrong. We've just delivered enough weapons and explosive to start U.K.'s own insurgency."

I picked up the pistol, removed the mag, pulled the slide back, checked the breach. Mick was a natural soldier in Afghanistan but here and now, he was a fisherman: "What are we going to do with this stuff?"

"Deep six it, next time we go out, except the pistol. I've a nasty feeling we might need it."

Mick was still looking for way out: "Can't we go to the police?"

"And say what? We've smuggled in a container full of explosives, drugs and weapons and now we don't know what to do with them. Can we give them to you please? Yea right, it would be a minimum of twenty each if we lived long enough to get to court – which I guarantee we wouldn't."

"Alright Steve, let's get rid of this stuff tonight."

"Not yet. Hide them in the forward bilge for now. I'm taking Leila to London for a dirty weekend. It will give me a chance to think, then we'll corner Taylor, blow up the container and him as well if necessary."

Mick looked desolate. He wasn't happy. His tone accused me of desertion: "The only thing you'll think about this weekend is your knob end. You and Leila are getting serious, aren't you?"

"We are Mick. That's why I want to sort Taylor out, before he screws up our lives."

* * *

Leila looked fantastic, and seemed pleased with the way I'd scrubbed up too. A shop window reflection on the way to the station made us pose contentedly, mentally photographed.

We sat opposite on the train, so when I looked up she looked up, pure pleasure in each other's company. With my captive audience, I turned into a crummy magician. I tore a hole in my newspaper, and stuck my finger through. Her indulgent giggle bubbled into laughter; trying to stifle it to appease other passengers.

I mouthed: 'I love you.' Her face softened and silently echoed it back, leaving us gazing at our vows.

I'd have preferred Exmoor; she'd chosen London – it didn't matter. The important thing was a weekend together, away from the Taylor crap. The train's sensual droning movement lulled me into false optimism: terrorists would be caught coming ashore; Mick would pay off the loan on his boat; I could spoil Leila rotten, knowing I'd done my bit for Queen and Country… quiet satisfaction.

I refocused on Leila. Dramatically I took out a handkerchief and wrapped it around my hand to form a puppet. Her ravishing mouth opened in stage admiration. We were now miles away from the suspicious fencing of when we first met. The other passengers concentrated on ignoring us, so I kept the show going until she satisfyingly dissolved into an orgasm of giggles – with more apologies to her neighbours. God, she was great.

* * *

The hotel she'd booked, near Earl's Court was our base from which we could explore the city; except going out was the last thing we wanted to do. We could have been anywhere, so long as we had each other. She test bounced the bed, short skirt riding even higher. We became serious and lay together full of concentrated longing. Our plans for bright lights and food were shelved. We just whispered and loved, fearful a jealous spirit would take our happiness away. We were soul mates, lovers, cuddlers, confessionalists, everything. I couldn't believe I'd found my other half – what were the odds . This was it.

Chapter 20

"**GOOD MORNING** my gorgeous lover woman. It's a beautiful day."

"Good morning my gorgeous lover man. No it's not, it's raining."

"Well it's beautiful to me 'cos I'm with you."

She slapped a full, juicy, wet kiss on my lips and danced naked to the shower. When she returned: "Do you like what you see? Do you find me irresistible in this fluffy white towel? Does my body drive you wild with desire?" She let the towel fall, jumped into bed and pulled the duvet up under her chin in a tease of false modesty: "Let's play a game."

Anticipation of an erotic surprise sent a flow of chocolate salivating into my taste buds. I nodded enthusiastically as she continued: "Well, let's pretend I'm going to die."

The room temperature crashed as I waited for an unfunny joke… nothing…. She kept going: "We say goodbye forever and you leave. We both feel awful, then after twenty minutes you return and we make up. There, what do you think?"

I thought, where the hell did that come from? Was she trying to tell me she had a terminal illness? No, no, no. I thought I knew her so well. This was way out of character. Why pretend something so appalling? It wasn't funny, it wasn't erotic, it didn't make sense – like coming into the middle of a conversation – something was missing. I didn't like any of it.

Appealingly she added: "Steve, my friends always say making love after making up is the best."

We didn't need games. It was the best already. I adored her, so I said: "Right, O.K, you're staying here?"

"Yep, keeping it warm for you."

"And this is just a game?"

"Of course it is."

Grey thoughts were turning black, surrendering commonsense which screamed NO!

"Bye Leila my love, see you in twenty minutes."

"No Steve, that's no good. Say goodbye forever, I don't love you anymore. Say it."

I'd never seen her like this before. Her face looked different – my throat dried. It was a bad film; something was drastically wrong. I was off balance; body in love; mind fracturing.

"Say it Steve."

"I'll love you forever. Goodbye forever."

She groaned: "I suppose that will have to do. Now my turn: I'm going to die. I don't love you anymore. Goodbye forever."

It was perverted madness. We loved each other so much – it must be a cruel test. Confusion wouldn't let me think. A gaunt dread shrunk the room; walls pressing in.

Time: five minutes past eight. That makes return twenty-five minutes past eight. Never again, I'd play this game, then never again… never. Searching her dark eyes gave nothing away – same eyes, no beauty.

"I'm leaving, my love."

Her reply was from someone I didn't know: "Go forever. I hate you."

Chapter 21

I COULDN'T REMEMBER going down in the hotel lift or out into the street. (A voice found me – 'Keep calm. Walk on.') Consciousness and breathing restarted as fresh air pushed sense back into my mind.

The bakery and newspaper shop had friendly faces and normality – Time: fifteen minutes past . No, I wouldn't wait, game over, she loved me, we'd get married, have babies, meet her family, whatever. I'd never leave her again. That was the explanation. She'd engineered this hiatus to seal our relationship. That was it, obvious. It was a test – a stupid cruel test. Sorted.

The smell of newly baked bread warmed my soul: the newspaper headlines froze it: 'Terrorist bombers target London.'

Turning – a slow film: explosion huge, jetted foam of concrete, glass, vomiting from our hotel windows – frontage moved out yards – gravity taking over – collapsing – a smoking shock wave of tumult, fear and death – a channelled avalanche, shredding cars, people – a hail of shrapnel ricocheting off walls. I began to fall… not here, not London.

Hands pulled me back into the bakery, door closed, a dam to the blast… fine dust jetted under.

Vibrating silence, breathing stopped, one voice crying in the street: 'Jamie! Jamie! Jamie!' Quiet seconds, then came the screams, groans, angry shouts.

I wasn't a soldier any more. This wasn't Afghanistan; training didn't kick in, anguish did. I saw Leila's grave, the flowers. I was choosing them. I knew which music.

Tears of grief clotted the dust into a blinding paste. Leila's 'game' had saved me.

The hands that pulled me in had a voice: "You're safe now. I followed you. I couldn't let you die. I love you Steve. God is great."

She was alive, real, solid… Leila! We lay sobbing in the dust, rocking, touching, kissing, holding. Her eyes moved close: "I couldn't go to heaven without you."

"What do you mean? What heaven? How did you know?"

"It was my duty to kill."

The words came with a choking sickness, sawing dust in my throat, ripping denial into madness: "Please no! Say it wasn't you. Say it, quick. Swear by God, any God it wasn't you. Please. Please."

Nothing. I compelled my body to stand. Needles rashed the side of my face, concretions matted my hands, pain cancelling the search for 'a nightmare'.

I thought she was going to kiss me. She stopped inches away, repeating: "My duty."

Outside the torn grey street – like 911 TV – a dust cloud hovering where our hotel, staff, guests, me and a woman I once loved, had been. Just seconds – lives forever changed in seconds – reverse time in only seconds – it could be changed back in seconds – a God could do that – any God, please any God – why aren't you listening God? Why?

I recoiled. Her outstretched hand pointed an oily, black Browning pistol at my head: "We go to heaven together."

"Why rescue me and then kill me? You could have killed us both in the bomb. Why now? Why like this? You don't know, do you? You're insane. You don't understand what you've done. YOU DONT UNDERSTAND DO YOU?"

Stepping towards her, I pushed my forehead hard against the muzzle, my voice rasped: "Game over. You are evil. You have lost. You will not go to heaven. You have listened to the Devil, not your God. This is an aberration of a great religion. He rejects you for what you have done. Islam is great. You have betrayed your history – betrayed humanity. God is great."

I pushed my forehead harder. She tried to push back, her eyes changing from insane conviction to raging doubt. Pressure easing, pulling away, leaving the ugly pistol rocking, too heavy for her small hand, red painted finger nails curling the trigger, safety catch off.

We were statues, time contracted to stop – flashing lights flecked our faces. Dust blinded and distracted me for an instant. The pistol fired. I waited to fall, waited for oblivion. It was not written. When I looked down, I saw the flowers I had chosen, heard the music we both liked: my other half was dead. She had died twice. Now I'd grieve for who she had been, not for who she became. It was release from an unforgivable evil. She had betrayed Islam; betrayed humanity. The placid face I'd loved had returned, surrendering imprisoned blood like lava flowing from a cave. A dusty meniscus. Images never to forget. I wanted to squeeze life back into her, just for a few minutes so she could explain.

The pistol lay beside her, inviting. No stupid games. I felt a resolve growing in strength – a cause. She was wrong. I had to find out why she had created such terrible suffering? There was a war we had to win. I tucked the pistol in my belt and went outside to the mayhem, trying to separate what she had done from the woman I'd loved.

"Goodbye Leila forever. I don't love you anymore. Game over."

* * *

Running medics with stretchers – grey confused walking wounded – the helplessness of badly injured supported by human spirit – ordinary people knowing what they had to do – that woman still calling for 'Jamie' – an office worker looking for his glasses – parasitic photographers already scavenging.

I tried to get back to the hotel. I needed to look, but the area was already a sealed crime scene. Someone said Bicknell Street police station was the emergency centre. In less than five minutes I was queuing at the desk amid the first responders, shocked faces and organised chaos. I had always been amongst the ones who helped, now I was being helped; it was appreciated but took away my power… swaying, trying to expel the tinnitus of hate-filled adrenalin.

A shout: "Steve! Steve! Over here. We've been looking for you."

Taylor the Snake. What a surprise!

"How the hell did you know I was here?"

"Mobile tracking. Are you O.K.?"

It was like a thick sea fog clearing on a hot day: Klondike – container – explosives – pistols – pub – Leila – tracking. I launched myself at his throat, spitting to kill.

His minder fired: "Tazer! Tazer!" Fifty thousand volts of agony. Thrown in a van – cuffed and hooded – pistol pulled from my belt – injection. Sleep full of targets. Snake smiling, pointing: 'Steve, you're still firing too high and a touch left.'

Then painful, grey, mind sponge, mental scarring: healing time unknown.

Chapter 21

A **BAD HANGOVER** was nothing like this. White paper overalls, hard metal chair, cuffed hands, hood pulled off catching my nose. I went straight into surly, grey man mode. 'Try not to antagonise your interrogators.' Yea right. I wanted to wind the fuckers up.

Three of them sat behind an office table. In the middle a small woman, black hair, thick black rimmed glasses and a black hostile face. On her left a bloke with a beard; on her right, baldy. Something about him said 'American'. The triumvirate were not there to tell jokes.

The Black Witch spoke first: "You are under arrest for being a terrorist and a traitor. You planted a bomb in London which killed seven civilians and maimed twenty others – more may die. Your normal rights and due legal process will be suspended until we decide otherwise. You are not within the U.K.'s jurisdiction. The option of silence is not open to you. We have to act quickly to stop further atrocities. Intelligence indicates a large quantity of weapons, drugs and explosives have recently been smuggled into the U.K. You smuggled them in; you planted the bomb. The more you co-operate the less you will suffer. Forget about anything you have heard about enhanced interrogation techniques. We will torture you brutally. You will suffer and be deformed permanently until you answer all our questions."

For some reason the threat sounded worse coming from a woman. I leant forward to speak. Someone behind painfully twisted my cuffs.

"Don't say anything until we tell you, then answer clearly: yes, no, don't know or explanation. Do you understand?"

I suppressed the urge to shout: 'I'm not a terrorist or a traitor!' and answered, "Yes."

The Black Witch was having trouble with her anger management, so Beardy bloke took over: "Were you at

Portsmouth railway station last Saturday morning at 08:00 hours?"

"Yes."

"Were you with Leila Yousef?"

"I don't know."

"Cooperate. Look at this photo. Do you know her?"

"Yes."

"Was she part of your terrorist gang?"

"No."

"So you used an innocent woman as cover. We don't believe you acted alone. Who was in your gang?"

"I am not a terrorist. I am not in a gang."

The cuffs twisted.

"Steven, we cannot waste time, lives are at risk. These are photographs of body parts from the scene of your atrocity."

One of the guards held them in front of my face, his hand shaking with visceral loathing. Detached rounded legs contrasting with the angular rubble – and hands – always those hands reaching out of the debris, appealing in death.

"I did not plant that bomb."

"Steven, everyone fears something worse than death, we know yours from the file. Let's try again. Did you know Leila was a terrorist?"

The angle of the questioning had changed. Did they think she was a terrorist or not?

"No. I want to explain."

The cuffs twisted: "Steven, say 'explanation', nothing else."

"Explanation."

The Black Witch nodded: "Good, explain."

"We were in love and going for a weekend break."

"Who booked the hotel?"

"She did."

"Doesn't the man usually do that for a dirty weekend?"

"I don't know."

Beardy raised his eyes from his notes: "Not a very convincing cover for bombers is it?" Another angle, another trap, he didn't wait for a reply: "The photos you have seen do not show the full legacy of a lifetime of traumas you and your girlfriend inflicted on innocent men, women and children. CHILDREN, Steven. Do you feel proud for your cause or do you feel like the hideous coward you are?"

His face seemed to enlarge as he generated more hate. I found it hard to believe I was being spoken to like this, by people on my side. I was one of the good guys. The pain of injustice could never be matched by physical torture. Terrorists would be physically violent, but my own side's accusations hurt more,.

He continued his hate filled rant: "I. Me…" He was jabbing at his chest. "…would like to torture you. I would enjoy it. Unfortunately they won't let me because I would kill you before you talked – like Rwanda and Columbia." His laugh was a slow cough. "However, we now have people better trained than me." He jabbed his chest again. "If you are expecting gentle hypnosis, betraying kindness, psycho babble, truth drugs inducing verbal diarrhoea, think again. We use the same techniques as the Russians, Chinese, North Koreans, Americans, Argentineans, Tajikistanis, Turkmenistans, Afghans, Australians, and everyone else. Water boarding, fingernail extraction, castration, electric shocks, drugs, relation killings, character assassination, blinding, deafening, dentistry and the one I particularly like, unnecessary medical procedures. One of our foreign assets sent back a living trunk in the diplomatic bag: eyes, nose, arms, legs, ears, all gone… all gone. I can't even remember who he or she was or what he or she had done – you couldn't tell the gender, all gone, all gone. They left its tongue. In the end only one word came out, over and over again, it sounded like EL-EF-THERIA. We never found out what it meant – code obviously – GCHQ worked on it – nothing. Took the secret to the grave – still on file. The skill of the torturer is not to kill. Understand? Do you understand?"

He'd lost it and ranted on. Chuffed with his own eloquence, he couldn't stop: "A large area of skin had been flayed and painted blue… still alive."

He didn't make me proud to be British – or even human. Black Witch and Baldy were looking embarrassed, hoping he'd finish. He was trying to, but the right words wouldn't come for closure. Eventually he repeated himself: "Understand? DO YOU UNDERSTAND? Understand…"

I wasn't going to do him any favours: "No."

"What? What? What? – You What?"

Now I felt sorry for him: "Yes I understand."

He was psycho. The others knew it.

"O.K., thank you, not thank you. Three votes and you're a trunk with a tongue, eh, eh, get it?"

"Yes I get it. Explanation."

Black Witch rescued him: "Go on, explain. But if you fuck us about, we'll fuck you about." She seemed to think swearing gave toughness.

I now had a chance: "I served in Afghanistan to stop terrorism in our country."

Beardy's forehead bobbled with sweat trickling down. Black Witch put her hand on his arm to quiet him, and then she attacked: "Ah Afghanistan, let me tell you what happened in Afghanistan. You saw civilian deaths and developed sympathy – 'Croydon Syndrome' – for the local population. You refused to call in an airstrike, even though Taliban were there, because of your misplaced sympathy. You recruited Leila youself for revenge bombing here in the U.K." That meant I was still in the U.K. "Your sick corrupted mind thought it was right to attack your own country. You are a traitor."

'Traitor' hurt more than anything. Beardy slapped both hands on the table satisfied with the Black Witch's attack, nodding admiration, not knowing when enough was enough. She quietened him, then struck again: "Did you abort an airstrike on the Taliban to avoid civilian casualties?" If she knew, why did she ask?

"Yes, explanation."

"Go on."

"There was a compound with a farmer and his family – children, goats. I decided the collateral damage was too high a price to pay. We could not see any weapons."

A screen on the wall behind them flicked on; drone footage showing two men on a roof in an Afghan village, tagged 78 and 79: me and Mick. Nearby a compound with eight figures and a herd of goats.

She was trying to stay cool: "From where I'm sitting it looks straight-forward. You are on the roof; the Taliban are in the compound – tagged alphabetically. Why did you not call in an airstrike?"

"I decided not to because, as I've said, I couldn't see any weapons."

"You decided on your own, did you?"

"Yes, I was patrol commander."

"Did you see the whole family in the compound?"

"Explanation."

"No – No explanation. Did you see the family in the compound?"

"No, but I knew they were close by."

Beardy was shaking his head, tutting and rolling his eyes.

Black Witch: "Had previous air strikes you'd witnessed killed civilians?"

"Yes."

"So why was this different?"

"It was my decision. I decided it was too high a price to pay."

"You decided, did you? And what was your rank? Major? Colonel?"

The triumvirate smiled at each other as the ball hit the back of the net.

"I was a Corporal."

Her smile twisted into a sneer: "Outside your pay grade sonny. You do what you're told. How many of our troops were lost because you didn't confirm when you had the chance? Your decision cost U.K military lives and now you have killed civilians in London. You are a traitor, a terrorist and a murderer."

The condemnation was clear but her delivery, though aggressive, waivered.

Baldy took a turn. American accent, spoke fast, too much information, too little time: "You left the British army – couldn't hold down a job – violent homophobic behaviour: hit a gay actor – March 9: got drunk, visited a hooker – March 11: drunk again, hooker again, vomited and urinated over a tramp in an alley – March 15: drunk again. You see a pattern here?"

I saw a pattern: 100% surveillance of a squaddie on a bender, so what? I'd miss it off my next CV for air traffic control. The Bald Headed American Eagle had a ton of data to tell everyone. A black hand silenced him. She had more points to score: "Where did you get the explosive and the pistol?" She lay the Browning on the desk. "You had this on you after the bombing. Where did you get it from? You killed Leila Youself with a single shot to the head. Why? Your DNA, fingerprints and samples of her brain tissue, all match – conclusive evidence for conviction in a U.K. or U.S. court. And enough for us to play with YOUR brain any way we want."

I'd been dreading seeing the pistol again.

(Mick's voice in my head: 'You're in deep shite now mate.')

She continued: "Swabs from the lab confirm you'd had sex with her that morning and you'd handled explosives within 48 hours of the bombing: that is confirmation you manufactured the device. We are not going to kill you yet. We will leave just enough blood in your body, just enough sanity in your mind to feel, and of course your tongue for you to explain how you suffer. Now, explanation."

An image of Mick's cabin, explosives, drugs, pistol… I'd been playing a weak hand from the start and I'd run out of cards. Desperation: "I did not plant the bomb. I did not kill Leila. I am not a terrorist. I'm not a traitor. What does your polygraph say now?"

Black Witch, Beardy and Baldy leaned forward to the screen.

Black Witch looked up: "You are either a very good liar or telling the truth. I believe you are a liar. We are convinced of your guilt. You will now be passed on to the dentists and I can assure you that you won't get tea and biscuits." Sadistic smiles. These people were supposed to be on my side and yet they were malicious bastards. Their job was not to reduce pain but to increase it. I decided a more thoughtful comment was appropriate: "You're all talking a load of fucking crap."

Surprisingly all three looked at the polygraph again and shrugged. Black Witch looked into one of the cameras filming the proceedings: "END."

They stood like judges, but they hadn't finished. Handcuffs forced me to my feet, paper overalls ripped off – bollock naked. Humiliation has always been a weapon, but only if you let it. The Witch pointed and laughed – too theatrically: "You can't believe Leila wanted you for your body? She used you."

She was reading from a script: "The next stage will be physically very painful; permanent damage is possible. A dentist tries not to hurt. Here we try to hurt – intentional pain. What happens to your mind, we cannot predict. Terrorism has no rules, no Geneva Convention – nor do we."

It was still only words. If they were going to kill me, they would have done it by now. Where the fuck was Taylor? He could explain.

The process was too well rehearsed to be as fearful as they intended.

Next phase: strapped in a wheelchair, ripped overalls dumped on my lap, hood on, sensing a corridor, a lift, another corridor, a sliding door, antiseptic smell, heat, hood off, nose snagged, blinking brightness. Again, it was more like a stage set or amateur dramatics than a real clinic. Several small cages on a side bench held rats. Four androgynous staff, white coated, face masks, stood around holding props: syringe, scalpel, clamps, hose. The script obviously called for muted discussion, squirting syringe, flicking of rubber gloves. After posing long enough, they withdrew to their ratty friends – again, too theatrical. My gay film mates would have called for: 'More INTENSITY.'

Behind me a female voice soothed: "Put your head back please." I didn't move. Sticky rubber-gloved hands forced compliance; head phones clamped on; a restraining strap keeping my eyes on the ceiling, showing a moving picture of a garden, clouds and flowers; then horrific scenes of decapitation – then the garden – alternating, shocking – pleasant. I closed my eyes – a painful scream jarred the head phones. I opened them and it stopped. The message was clear: 'We are in control. You are being conditioned. Do what we say.'

I closed my eyes again and rode the scream for as long as possible. Was it predicted? Is this what everyone did? If I tried to beat it, would it enforce their brainwashing? Where were the questions? What did they want? I had no way of judging the effectiveness of their technique or of what they were trying to achieve. If they had said: 'Did you plant the bomb?' I could have said 'No.' But this was not inquisitive – it was confusing. Why don't the bastards ask me something – anything?

I shouted: "I'm on your side!"

I might as well have said 'sausages', so I concentrated on remembering the M.O.'s story of the Coastal Path: 'Even with no legs the Path can be walked.'

Got it, thanks Sir. I imagined cliffs, beaches, headland, seagulls, Mick's trawler butting its way into a south-westerly.

Head phones came off. I could move. I would only be vulnerable if I accepted I was vulnerable. I would accept nothing. So far no physical pain.

The four dentists stood in front with their props – a female walked behind me carrying a stainless steel dish, a scalpel clanking. I sensed movement, braced for pain, here it comes, seconds dragged. A gloved hand gently pushed my head forward and softly stroked my neck. A violent punch would have been easier to bear – the shock of tenderness brought a burst of vomit to trickle down my legs. One of the dentists, talking like a consultant to students: "They always do that – interesting, isn't it?" I had become part of a contemptible 'they.'

Another shock – a rush of activity – hood back on – another injection – empty sleep, still alive – hang on to the Path – hearing is the last sense to go – footsteps – then nothing.

Chapter 22

FIRST sense to come back, the smell of polish. Second, pain – a fracking headache.

I awoke in a yellow painted room, no windows, a pile of new clothes on a chair, labels still attached. Nothing fancy, just jeans, sweatshirt, no shoes. Above the chair, a hangman's noose stuck to the ceiling with duct tape. Useless except as a crude joke.

The door wasn't locked. It opened to a long corridor: left or right? I went left, bare feet, doors on both sides, numbered randomly. I tried one on the right: 79.

Inside: "Morning, morning, take a pew. I'm Major... Major... It doesn't matter who I am, except I'm a Major."

Why had I chosen this door? Were there other prats in the other offices waiting for me? He wore no badges of rank or unit and seemed nervous, like his first day at work. Famously, there had been a Major Major and a Sergeant Sergeant in the British army. It didn't matter, to me he was a Cunt Cunt.

He placed a set of trainers on the desk. "You are free to go. Do not mention to anyone what has happened. Delete, expunge, erase, redact. Understand?"

It was like being threatened by a rabbit. He made Bean look like Bond.

I was in survival strop: "And if I do talk?"

"You will be off the ladder and facing a snake: sanctioned."

"Can I have my own clothes and mobile back?"

"No, we need them for further tests and if necessary, evidence."

"What am I supposed to do now?"

"We have arranged that you won't be missed, even from the fishing boat. With your track record, it won't surprise the few people you know that you've gone walk-about. Here is your new passport."

I flicked it open – Steven Hurst: "That's not my name."

"Steven is. We chose Hurst. We're thinking of the future, your future. Here are euros, sterling and condoms... (Condoms must be a local currency where I was going.) "…and a plane ticket to Athens. Go to an island called Hydra, pronounced 'Edra' and wait. Don't come back until we say."

He stuffed it all in a brown A4 envelope and pushed it across the desk towards me: "Everything for a perfect holiday."

"Does this mean you think I'm innocent? Do I get an explanation?"

"No and no."

If they thought I was a terrorist they wouldn't let me go – maybe. I didn't push my luck with any more questions in case the Black Witch materialised with a wheel-chair.

As he stood, Major Major's face contorted into a grimace. He rattled change in his pocket, which for some officers substituted for a handshake. It was like finishing a course without getting a grade or knowing if you've passed or failed.

I walked out onto a fire escape, down steel steps, along an alley and out into an English suburban high street, complete with post office, charity shops and a bus signed Croydon… Freedom.

A car pulled up on double yellows. Two bulky black suits ran towards me, eye confrontation, veering off at the last second: "Tossers." They'll have to do better than that: walk on.

I leant forward; stretched my legs; increased the pace. Movement generating energy, shops gave way to urban sprawl then hedges and green fields, rusty muscles loosening, the Downs showing between trees. It was my cue for a shout of release: "Chelsea, Chelsea, Chelsea." An embarrassed silence followed by a blackbird chinking off. Picking up speed into a jog, smelling the English green spring powering the countryside. Bollocks, life was good.

Chapter 23

A FEW HOUSES appeared, and a church. I was ready to sit quietly, get centred and work out a plan. The ancient, studded oak door advertised: 'Modern Zumba Dancing on Wednesday.' It opened to dust fissured light, freshened by the church ladies' flowers. Centuries of sanctuary, rows of pews and a cross, combining to create peace; same as underwater. Another world demanding unconditional awe and respect. I was alone, a heathen bowing to an altar: heritage engendered feelings.

A door catch by the transept rattled; my heart thumped. I searched for cover – the vicar walked towards me: "Good morning. You are welcome."

"Thank you. It's peaceful."

"Peace helps to solve problems. Are you a Christian?"

"Sorry, no."

"I have my doubts at times; didactic, dogmatic, diatribes of damnation turned a lot of people away! To me it seems as if only grey haired old ladies are not put off."

I smiled. First impression, he was a good bloke: "Do you think your church is still of value then?"

"I do. A lot of people say it's enough to know the Church is here, even if they only come at Christmas. If all religions said, 'try to do good, try not to do evil', the world would be a better place."

He had hit a nerve in my conscience: "But what if you have to do evil for the greater good?"

"A common dilemma I grant you, but if one has a good basic set of commandments God will give the answer. We just have to ask the right questions.

"I believe the words God and Good are inter-changeable – everything then makes sense. The theme for my sermons recently has been about helping others with their problems, and then your own problems are miraculously solved too. Good, don't you think?"

I agreed with him in a non-religious, common sense sort of way, although the 'dentists' would have been a challenge to his ideas.

He allowed a silence in our conversation without unease, then continued: "The person you help is a reflection of yourself – we are all one – even a concentration camp guard, a terrorist, they are us. Treat them as you want to be treated."

I was uncomfortable. It was too much to ask: "Even if that person is evil?"

"No one is evil. Only deeds are evil."

My mind hung on to his words, willing an understanding: "But if evil is not stopped good people suffer."

"True, we are human, not angels. We have to learn to use the gifts we have to solve problems."

"I feel we are back where we started, vicar."

"No, time has passed since you came into this holy place. When you leave everything, including you, will have changed – sky, trees, people, all changed – you can never step into the same river twice. My job is to hatch, match and despatch: to commemorate change. Outside the clouds have changed; never the same pattern to be seen again – ever. The 'Law of Non-Repetition' – like a snowflake, unique – like our world never repeated or copied, like problems changing, solutions changing as you move. But, but, but… basic values of good don't change. They are the consensus of humanity. Aberrations of evil change – absolute good does not. Travel well on your Path."

He made the sign of the cross – a blessing to a heathen. I felt blessed, and bowed respectfully to a vicar who had doubts, but was still a good man.

As we shook hands: "If you are ever lost, stop looking and you will find your way. May God and Good go with you."

"Thank you vicar. You have helped."

It was another step on the Path. Walk on.

Chapter 24

OUTSIDE in the car park a grey BMW. Obviously vicars' wages can run to a new Series Four, full spec, tinted windows. It hadn't been there when I arrived; he probably needs a high-powered engine to get to funerals on time; probably needs three aerials for his satnav and on-board comms, probably... or probably not… Unprofessionally, I waved.

As I jogged off down the lane, I remembered the 04:00 Athens flight from Gatwick. By luck, fate or whatever you want to call it, I was meeting guides: Mr Harman, the M.O. and now the Vicar. All had talked sense, because they cared. All I'd done was ask questions and listened. It was still a shit world but not everyone was a bastard: 'Just get on that flight pillock.' Optimism irrationally flowed.

* * *

Out of the plane's window, dawn's first light showed the Dalmatian coast to port and the distant Italian coast to starboard; heading south in a big iron bird; memories of an Afghan poppy field looking up at con trails. And now I was up there; clean food, beer and hosties. (I wonder if the Russian Ambassador and his wife are on the flight.) It was a pity Mick wasn't here. I could have used the Crack of Dawn joke again. He never laughed, miserable sod; still, he was a good mate. I wonder how much he knows?

The ferry port of Piraeus gave new sights and smells. The strangeness demanding curiosity even from a traumatised cynic. Everything looked beautiful, not superficially but in a deep fascinating way, like a woman whose faults, imperfections and scruffy times you love unconditionally. It was love at first sight – with a country – and I didn't know why. Queuing was anarchic, road signs ignored. In fact all official signs seemed to demand the opposite: 'No Parking' – there was double parking; 'No Fishing' – an angling competition; 'No Ball Games' – football and basketball twenty aside. Total contempt for authority – it made me smile. I loved it.

Three hours later the Flying Dolphin Hydrofoil turned back into boat and glided into Hydras' small harbour. Everything was external – introverts and sulkers had nowhere to hide. Real life was unavoidable – the opposite of English suburban twitching curtains. No secrets, life confronted – I wasn't ready for Greece. I didn't deserve the sun and friendliness.

First Greek lesson: walking purposefully is wrong – dawdle, meander.

Second Greek lesson: time is measured by the senses, not by clocks.

A ferry's siren blasted alongside me – viscous acid explosions, instinctive hatred. I spun, dropped to one knee, looked around, crouching – and met the face of a small cat. She became my excuse for taking cover.

(A voice: 'Get centred, move on pillock.')

There was a lightness of being, reflected in the crisp sky, red tiled roofs and lime washed walls. Along the back lanes, shade gave thoughtful respite, then emerging into hot glare. No grey or vague evasive mediocrity. It was full on hot white or cold black. A clear choice, duality, Yin Yang – doubt lost.

Third Greek lesson: it is not necessary to go from 'A' to 'B' by the quickest route; it is not even necessary to have a 'B' to go to; 'A' is quite sufficient to wander around.

I was getting lost in a paradise of narrow, pirate deceiving lanes, pleasingly disorientated, ubiquitous bougainvillea and jasmine scenting in waves, open, accepting faces giving firm eye contact and warm smiles. Someone was playing a piano in English, totally accepted, in strange harmony.

I found rooms referenced by a small blue and white church. No deposit, no security check, no passport retention, just a kindly round woman in black head scarf with no conversation.

I dumped my bag and left to explore, navigating by selecting uphill tracks until I caught glimpses of the harbour far below and a clear view opening to a sweep of sea; so pure and blue, the beauty took my breath away.

"Kali mera!"

"Good morning"

"Ochi 'good morning' we say kali mera."

"Hatymara?"

"Bravo, perfect."

His robust greeting rolled into a broad stubbled smile: "I am Manoli!"

He said it as if I should recognise him. Logic said he was mistaken.

Fourth Greek lesson: everyone is a friend until proved otherwise.

"I'm Steve, from London." My revelation changed nothing. He continued clinking his worry beads. Suspiciously he had a flower behind his ear.

"Ah bravo Stephan, sit, look at the sea, beautiful, yes?"

I didn't reply. I couldn't. It was too beautiful. I wanted to just stare and stare. Not to see it every day would be a crime against my eyes. English caution of friendliness, together with a class conscious concealment of needs and wants, masked a fear of unmanaged emotion . Under a Greek sun, it was little more than arrogant rudeness.

Fifth Greek lesson: 'Don't hide what you are or what you want. In Greek light you are mentally and physically naked – literally and metaphorically.

Two small metal tables and a cluster of chairs fronted Manoli's Taverna. He needed five: one to sit on, two to rest his arms on, one to rest his right foot on and one to occasionally flick with his left foot. All were painted blue. The sea and the sky were blue, and they were beautiful, so why not furniture, windows, doors and all? The other colour in this dual chromed world, was white: eye squinting white. Walls, floors, ceilings, paper table cloths, shirts, the cat's paw, waves stroking the ravishing sea – white waves on blue. At one end of the wall, the Greek flag. It matched everything. I was in silent, repressed, ecstasy.

The perfect harmony was dappled by red geraniums sprouting from olive oil tins. It was perfect. Why was it perfect? But nothing was perfect, or level or upright – as if an earthquake had moved things years ago, only to let them settle again, without damage, just slightly skewed. I scanned back to the sea; it induced a feeling of deep contentment – beyond art.

A ferry arriving drew my eye to the amphitheatre of the busy harbour far below. For someone so keen on hustling for customers, Manoli's service was tortoise slow. Occasionally he'd point at boats as we sat in companionable silence. In London a waiter would have pounced or moved me on – here it was different. It was like… what? It was like being home – that was it. I'd come home to a land I'd never been to before.

"Can I have beer please, Manoli?"

"Yes beer, of course, over there. Bring two."

He pointed to a dust covered, glass fronted, fridge. A chair wedged it closed and worringly, a spaghetti of bare wires dangled alongside. Maybe two was a minimum order, maybe a 'bogof,' a sales con. It didn't matter. He brought out two glasses from the shaded interior, opened one bottle, flicked the top over the cliff and filled both. He was going to drink my beer! I've seen fights for less. I'd been in fights for less. He thumped his glass on the table; a cool head frothed: "Yia mas."

"Cheers."

"Ochi cheers, yia mas: to us."

('To us' seemed over friendly, bordering on gay. It bothered me.)

"Yia mas."

"Bravo, you speak my language in one week."

The beer was good – 'Ice cold in Alex' condensation . A small flotilla of ten metre sailing yachts were queuing to enter the harbour. The lead boat, flying a huge New Zealand flag, motored in, sails neatly furled, a bikinied figurehead, breasts pointing the way. Twenty metres from the quay, the anchor splashed from the stern; the bows nudged in, lines secured to a bollard and anchor chain tensioned: easy, smart.

"Stephan, you watch the show!"

The next flotilla yacht came in much too fast. Helmsman frantically going astern at the last minute. Two women took over, demoting him to the foredeck, where he hopelessly knitted the bow lines, resulting in being decommissioned below. When a boat's engine is running, it is necessary to shout to make anyone hear on the foredeck. However in the tavernas around the harbour all was as clear as a goat's bell: insults, marital problems, physical peculiarities, were listened to with relish.

Manoli shook his head: "Poh, poh, poh."

He opened the other bottle, filled my glass and helped himself to more of my beer, again without asking. It was getting past a joke – rip-off prices were guaranteed with such a superb view – that's why no one else was here. Disregarding my frown, he enthusiastically pointed to the harbour : "Look, another one!"

Everyone was in confident control. Unfortunately, the anchor was let go too far out so the chain was not long enough to reach the quay. The helmsman realised his mistake, stared, let go of the bitter end, then inexplicably dived in after it, leaving the yacht to glide into the fat-arsed transom of a plush 'gin palace'.

Manoli was clapping ecstatically and rattling off in Greek something about Boubalina, Nelson and Trafalgar. He pointed to the fridge – "Two more beers" – and disappeared inside, returning with a saucer of five olives and some stale bread. It spelt rip off, big time – nouvelle cuisine in London was mega bucks.

"Yia mas Stephan."

"Yia mas Manoli."

To hell with the cost, H.M. gov were paying. If it was cheap, the place would be heaving, plus I was beginning to seriously enjoy it. The glare was going out of the sun. The walls were radiating heat instead of absorbing it. Yacht crews were mooching about the harbour-side bars and souvenir shops. They didn't explore much, which was why Manoli had been so keen to grab any passing tourist. I felt sorry for the unshaven, ageing, lonely, gay Greek, in a heterosexual, patronising, uptight English way. I didn't mind being ripped off... What did I know?... Nothing.

His face turned serious, pointing seawards: "Eleftheria!" The view was waiting for a focal point. The picture now complete. There she was, out in the channel, a fully rigged schooner, powering in, bit between her teeth, catching the evening breeze. What a sight! A mind photograph I would never forget. It didn't take her long. On a beam reach she surged through the entrance into the calm harbour – no engine.

"Poh, poh, poh!" Manoli whistled.

She needed a crew of six; there was one balanced at the wheel. She could never stop in time. His arm moved, releasing combined halyards, sails furling neatly; now in the middle still carrying too much way; he left the wheel, walked steadily forward; the bow anchor broke the quiet; chain looped over port guard rail lashed astern with increasing speed until brought up taught by the aft cleat; a slot between two plastic charter yachts was just enough; bow closed to within a foot, jackstay kissing the quay. In one smooth movement he stepped ashore, looped the mooring line over a bollard and strode up a side lane without looking back…

"Wow!"

I'd been standing, holding my breath. Now I looked to see who else acknowledged this Olympian skill, but the bars were still occupied with gossip and souvenirs.

I turned to Manoli: "Poh, poh, poh, Manoli?"

He shrugged: "Yes, very special, very good."

"Do you know him?"

"He is Eric, a Frenchman. They as mad as English."

It was my turn to shrug: "True."

"He sails from here all summer, goes on mainland in winter. Last year his wife drowned off Spetse. Jack, his son, blamed him and went back to France. He is Buddhist – believes she is now dolphin – he keeps looking for her. Greeks understand."

Sixth Greek lesson: Love life, take death when it comes, full on.

I stared down at the schooner. Her functional beauty eclipsing all the mega plastic gin palaces: she didn't need make up.

"What does Eleftheria mean, Manoli?"

"If you stay here long enough, Stephan, you may understand – but only if you want to."

There seemed to be eight empty bottles and four plates crowded on the small table. Who cares – I'd be generous and pay for six, and split the food fifty-fifty. It had been worth it, so long as he didn't ask me to dance or stick a flower behind my ear.

"How much do I owe you Manoli?"

He looked at the table: "Poh poh poh"… he shrugged. Here we go.

I asked again: "Beers, food, I want to pay. How much?"

"You owe me nothing. You cannot pay."

"I have money. I pay."

He explained slowly: "You owe me nothing. You cannot pay because my taverna is closed. You have been my guest."

I stared at the euros flapping in my hand. Greek music played inside. I shook his hand in an over-exuberant, gushing English way. As bad as the retarded suspicious mode at the other end of my social spectrum. I had been guilty of irrational prejudice coupled with patronising over-reaction.

"Adios Stephan."

"Adios Manoli."

He went back to his lonely five chairs, beer, view and worry beads. I knew nothing.

Now I had to get back to my 'rooms'. All I had to do was find a small white and blue church. Unfortunately, there were dozens of them, so I tried re-tracing my route – impossible. So 'I stopped looking', sat on some steps and there breaking the darkening sky line was 'my church' pointing to 'my rooms'.

'Thank you Vicar. Man of God – Man of Good.'

Chapter 25

SLEEP HEALS like medicine and bandages, turning pain into peace, exuding festering puss-filled memories.

That night it worked overtime, purging thick and fast: exploding faces, Leila in a blood-red wedding dress; ships sinking, leaving thousands of containers bobbing about; me searching constantly for explosives, asking everyone, asking fish, gulls, anyone, shouting, sweating. The subconscious releasing my soul back into the dark room. Disorientated, I forced calmness, combing the walls; 'find a corner' then a window. Then, gasping air, a panorama of stars. My friendly Plough pointing north.

'I'm still here. Not dead yet.'

It was four a.m. and I had no intention of revisiting those fearful nightmares, so I grabbed a water bottle and headed inland, walking uphill, cresting the central ridge until the black southern sea showed flat towards Crete, then on to Africa. Apart from a few fishing lights a mile or so out I could see no signs of life. I was alone, unarmed, not hunting or being hunted. An 'escape and evasion' exercise with no one to escape from and no one to evade. T-shirt, jeans and trainers were all I had and wanted. Warm air contradicted the morning gloom. Looking back at the village, three lights came on signalling the first cock crow, then a dog, a donkey, a complete orchestra – a lone caique motor providing the bass drum – now more joining: cement mixers, motor bikes, goats, a full breakfast symphony on longitude 30 east.

A clump of resonated pines gave a bed for requited, dreamless sleep till past midday when wafts of insects on baking air, invaded my safety; too late to prevent the healing process of positive rest the island had started. Greece had made me an offer. There was just enough sense left in my raddled brain to accept.

My feet were still light when I got back, but despite a shave, shampoo, shit and shower, the new-found elation waned. The grey mould wouldn't let go that easy – no problem – walk on. A new Chelsea blue T-shirt, watch, wallet, spectacles, testicles and I was ready for anything; heading for the quay.

Glowing specimens of healthy young ladies, smelling of coconut oil, wandered smiling past the waiters' banter. Things were looking up. At the far end, where the small caiques moored, hand-written signs for discos and tavernas were arrayed. Manoli was advertising: 'Sun Downers, Fiends Welcome' – (Fiends had to drink somewhere I suppose), and 'Best Pig' and 'Pig of the Day' – (Port chops for the Fiends?) A special was added in chalk: 'Manoli's Cock in Red Wine' – (Coq au vin for a new Carry on Film?) I know it pays to advertise, but this seemed a bit too obvious or perhaps he really did put his cock in red wine for the Shirley Valentines. He'd certainly gone up in my estimation. Maybe he wasn't gay after all.

Idiosyncratic translations, scattered in unlikely places made me laugh out loud: on a shower cubicle – 'No Smoking.' It was the only sign I ever saw obeyed. No need for obscene graffiti; the taverna crews had got there first.

* * *

I wandered back up the hill and found Manoli's easier than I thought. He was busy pushing tables together for a large Greek family who had just arrived. Several strings of bare light bulbs bobbed in the dusk, lighting a mum lovingly scolding baby Yanni... then smothering him in kisses.

"Yas sou Stephan. Greek men go from mother's boobs, to girlfriend's, to wife and back to girlfriend's boobs: Greek man never without boobs." Passed around throughout their lives smothered in boobs – sounded good to me.

He pointed me at the ten-strong family: five generations; grandparents, uncles, aunts, teenagers, all the way down to baby Yanni spoilt rotten, never without boobs. Already the nearest auntie had him hugged in massive mammaries. The look on his face had a strangely mature contented smile. I could swear he winked at me. A lifetime ahead of wonderful warm female cuddles, and he knew it. Lucky little sod!

"This is my English friend, Stephanos." He whispered: "Say, kali spera."

Self-consciously: "Kali spera."

A nodding multi-generational choir returned the greeting with cries of. 'Bravo','Yia mas','Kali spera'.

He slapped my back: "You know where the beers are. Go see Angelina. She will show you the food."

Inside were lime green, noisy, five-way conversations. TV on, CD on, shouts, laughs and always the same loving arguments. What were they arguing about?

"Hi, I'm Angie. Manoli likes you." A sun-burnished blonde fresh from the shower, sawn-off jean shorts and white T-shirt, stood behind the bar smiling. In cool Oz she asked: "You want a glass for that beer?"

"Yea thanks. I'm Steve. I had four here yesterday. He said I couldn't pay because he wasn't open. What do I do?"

"You're English, right?"

"Yep."

"Well just say thanks. Don't make a big deal about it. What goes around comes around." She pointed at my Chelsea T-shirt: "You like footie?"

"Yep, and you?"

"Best game in the world, apart from Aussie Rules."

Her T-shirt said 'Life Saver'. It gave me an excuse to stare at her tits.

"Are you a real Life Saver?"

"Yea. Do you want to be saved?"

Before I could say, 'Do I ever', Manoli came in with an order for the kitchen. "Ah, Stephan, you have met my beautiful mistress."

Angie didn't blink: "If Maria hears you, she'll have your balls for souvlaki tomorrow."

"It would be worth it, eh, Stephan?"

I couldn't say yes. I couldn't say no. It just came out as: "Whooaa."

She paused mid-step, put her hands on her hips, tilted her head questioning and smiled, so I said "Whooaa" again. Why had

I said that? I didn't want her to think I was a lecherous, pommie perv!

And that's how it went on, teasing, shouting, drinking, eating from different plates – full on humanity. No embarrassed silences or constricted sniding, no tables for one, no loneliness, no artificial crap, no waiter saying 'have you booked sir?' or 'we have a table free in two hours'. None of that bollocks, just bish, bash, bosh – get in there. Manners and humour perfect – no one left out.

Seven, eight, maybe more, sat round a table, leaning over, digging into different plates as they appeared. I was having a great conversation for about fifteen minutes with a fisherman, before I realised he couldn't speak English and he realised I couldn't speak Greek – fantastic.

The taverna got busier, people spoke louder, social interaction moved up a gear. Baby Yanni was thriving, nesting in a loving bowl of humanity. As I looked across, he fell asleep, safe and content. Tables got pushed together like dominoes. My greyness was squeezed out into the night. Angie brought over a Greek salad, a plate of chips and two more beers. As they landed, several forks dug into the feta and poured my beer. Sharing was good but I needed my own grub. Was there a set price menu?!

Angie came back: "Don't look so worried Stevie mate. This pork chop is just for you."

"'Best pig' or 'pig of the day'? I hope it's not 'Manoli's cock in red wine.'"

Her laugh cleaned my scowl: "How's it hanging now, Stevie?"

What was she talking about – my knob or what?

"I'm fine."

"Good. You're in for a treat if you like dancing."

I thought: 'If I can get hold of you, I certainly will be.' The trouble was I hated dancing. I felt her hands rest on my shoulders as she jostled away. O.K. just one dance. A haze of faces, accents, languages, came and went, till around midnight, I asked her for the bill.

"Stay. It's early. Don't be a pommie fader – dance."

So I stayed, to play more table dominoes, to slide more chairs, to talk in languages I'd only just heard, to top up others glasses, to adjust paper tablecloths, to take plates back for Angie, breakages celebrated not charged for.

I wasn't drunk; I wasn't tired. Life had levelled out onto a plane of companionable, blissed out, ecstasy. I was getting a grip on life. Life was getting a grip on me and I felt at home... no, I was at home.

* * *

A small elderly Greek lady I hadn't noticed before leaned over: "Are you German?"

Seventh Greek lesson: direct questions are not rude. They just cut the crap so real conversation can get on, like: 'Are you married?' 'Have you any children?' 'How much do you earn?'

"I'm English from London. My name is Stephanos."

"I am Eleni. I like English... and Germans, some I don't."

We shook hands. Baby Yanni's family had left; the taverna settled into a more mellow mood.

"Otto was a good man."

Not for the first time I felt I'd missed something: "I'm sorry, who was Otto?"

"A German soldier who came here during the war, part of the occupying force." Her English was clear, accent-less, from UK academia, full of intellect.

"It must have been a terrible time."

"For many yes, but not all. We were lucky here. The German soldiers succumbed to the island's magic in weeks. They had no idea what subversion our ancient land could create. It did more damage to the Nazi military than any partisans."

I sipped my beer. Where had World War 2 come from? Her voice beguiled, the taverna noise faded to a low buzz. Angie was serving behind the bar; all was well. But a story had begun and I was travelling through time.

Eleni continued: "Patrolling this island soon turned into rambles, where sun and swimming corrupted Hitler's ideology. Troops in observation posts stayed on duty to see a sunset or watch migrating birds. Teutonic efficiency was replaced by a new-found wonder for nature: war corrupted, the island healed."

I was hooked, protectively pulling my chair closer to exclude interruptions and nodding occasionally to encourage more.

"Otto often took his patrols along the island's central ridge to the western end, where there was a small stone farm occupied by two sisters and a herd of goats. He would stop and politely ask for water. Natural hospitality still existed. Reports of atrocities had not reached that remote corner. The patrol would rest and he would take time to gaze across the gulf to the snow-capped Peloponnese mountains, then let his eyes follow the coastal cliffs south towards Monemvasia."

The taverna lights hazed. It was 1943. I could feel the war in Greece. Otto had found somewhere quiet to think.

"The sisters lived far enough away from the main village to be outside its daily consciousness. Apart from Otto and his patrol, no one had reason to pass. The war decimated towns and villages across the mainland, but our island was lucky. The sea acted as a fire-break to the insanity.

"Otto was told of imminent withdrawal, so he decided – against orders – to go alone on one last patrol, to thank the sisters for their hospitality. When he reached the farm, he realised he was too late to save his loyalty. The island had won. It had tipped the scales. The ancient environment invited him to stay. The sisters didn't fuss, just drew him in to their daily rhythm of farm life: feeding goats, collecting olives and the usual myriad of rural work.

"In the confusion of a retreating army soldiers disappeared, casualties of revenge, accidents or love . Otto was posted missing; believed killed by partisans. I have been told there is a war memorial in Austria with his name on. There are many names where bodies were not found. He tried to bury his war with his uniform, badge and rifle, but sometimes during a meal, acrid thoughts would stir. He would apologise, and seek out a muscle aching job to cauterise the mental scars. Both sisters would wait patiently for his return."

I'd forgotten my beer. Herb scents from the kitchen were now from the sisters' farm. Eleni continued, quieter now, so I had to lean even closer:

"As the allied capitals celebrated the end of war in Europe and Axis troops crammed POW camps waiting to go home, for Otto, the sisters and the goats nothing changed: 'All was well, and all would be well.' Occasionally a shot from a hunter in winter or the wake of a fishing boat far away intruded lightly, but these only reinforced their contented solitude."

Eleni's tone gathered emotion: "The sisters loved blue-eyed Otto and he loved them. Beautiful days flowed into beautiful seasons, flowed into beautiful years. Their diet of wild herbs, greens, fresh fruit and sun-filled air ensured perfect health. History, death or the future were never mentioned, except in terms of when rain might come, when olives would ripen, when a goat would kid."

I was now with Otto in the magical land. Her tone changed again, darker, sharper: "I don't know when Otto died. It was probably in the early sixties. The pain the sisters felt was so intense they could only bear it by denial. They couldn't let him go. Don't be repulsed or condemn what I tell you, Stephan. They embalmed him and sat him by the window overlooking the sweep of sea he loved. They would sit together as before – grieving and black would be unnecessary. Are you repulsed?"

"No Eleni. There's too much love to feel anything but compassion."

She smiled warmly. I'd said the right thing, but the darkness came back: "In the fiercely dry summer of 1968, fires swept along the island's central ridge faster than the sisters or the goats could run. All that remained were blackened bones and stone walls – potash fertilising the spreading bougainvillea, nature's shroud protecting the sacred site.

"I think it was 1973, a group of multinational, archaeology students – Greek, English, German, Arab, Israeli, American – from an Hellenic dig on the mainland, walked the ridge. Their trained curiosity spotted the charred walls. They scraped a shallow trench revealing shards of plates, cutlery and a German infantry cap badge from World War 2. Logically, they deduced that there had been a skirmish between German troops and local partisans and unanimously decided to respect the site as a war grave, bowed their heads, each saying a few words in their own language. Time and youth helped their compassion. Several believed it had been a reprisal burning – logic again. They saw no evidence of the many loving years of paradise the sisters and Otto had experienced. Why should they? If only they knew."

I felt cold and drew a deep breath, letting the warm taverna surroundings back into my consciousness: "How do you know all this, Eleni?"

"We all have to choose what to know. The logical is not always the truth. Understand, Stephan? Knowledge does not give wisdom. We have to decide in other ways."

Slowly, so slowly, I was beginning to understand: Mr Harman, the MO, the Vicar and now Eleni. I felt blessed. I was blessed. Instinctively I asked: "What year were you born, Eleni?"

Her clear blue eyes looked kindly at me: "Otto was a good man, both my mothers said so."

I hesitated. A raft of questions I couldn't ask. I kissed her cheek: "Thank you." Her sun-dried face scrunched into a smile.

I went over to the bar and asked Angie for another two beers: "Snogging on your first date, eh? You prefer older women?"

"Eleni's fantastic."

"Yea you're right. She's great. Reminds me of my gran. Try this ouzo."

I sipped it. She looked disgusted: "You poms. That's just how you live – sip, sip, sip. Get a grip, fill your boots, life's too short – be nice to yourself."

Tables loaded with debris were being pushed back to the wall. Sound levels were rising again, a Greek bazooki skittering. Tiny Eleni was now dancing with two hairy-arsed fishermen twice her size. Angie had said 'life's too short', so here goes – both feet: "Are you with anyone?"

She squealed with laughter: "Why, are you interested?"

"Well…"

"Are you for real? Why not send a written invitation to my chaperone and I'll get back to you in a week or two!"

I looked at her face, her hair, boobs, tight frayed shorts: sex on legs. “You asked for it.” I grabbed her hand and waist and lurched onto the floor. Manoli started clapping a rhythm. Yourgos, the grizzled baker, cig in mouth, leapt and circled. An elderly English couple rose sedately and started to waltz. A donkey driver swept a table clear, plates smashing and picked it up in his teeth – then it all kicked off – sound to club level plus. We hung on to each other as the floor crowded. For a second, I looked skywards through the open doors and caught the Milky Way. Here humanity concentrated, raw, delicious. Greek culture shared with a cosmopolitan diaspora. All mixing, all the same, all unique. A surreal blend of dance styles: disco, waltz, twist, middle-aged Euro shuffling , jive, Greek Hasapiko, U.S. line dance...

A group of trendy, Nordic teenagers, wandering back from a late night disco – 2 a.m. closed – couldn’t believe it. Drawn in by thumping feet to a circle, forming, spiralling. A life of its own; another concentric circle. Becoming one human expression of free-flowing joy. Bacchus at the U.N. Individualism lost in a dance. The circle made up of individuals – we became one animal called Dance.

The place was full, then more arrived. Northern Europeans released from correctness, found exuberance channelled into laughter and movement. Good messages indestructible, and Manoli not controlling but guiding. A Surrey bank manager making a prat of himself, until he left his class-conscious props behind and joined the circle. Manoli showing him a few moves until he got it.

Angie leant to my ear: “You’re not scowling now.”

I turned as if to reply then kissed her cheek. My greyness trodden underfoot. I willed her to hold my stare. Lips too close not to kiss.

“I’m going to have to watch you Stevie.”

“I hope so. You’re gorgeous.”

The circles grew, compressed, then spiralled outwards again. This was it – the meaning of life. Not money or war, but dancing in a circle, blanketed by warm sugared stars and bare light bulbs.

The music smoothed, keeping its power, circle edging out to the walls. Yourgos, short, wide, muscled, cig in mouth, moved into the middle – a young man again, leapt, spun, arms balancing, knelt – then a change: slowing, twisting, swaying, pain drawing in – a spasm racked his body, back arched, legs contorted – he fell – a sponge diver's death – he tried to rise, again, again – pushing up with knotted arms – death scented rictus, fighting the traumatic end. Our circle holding its breath, aching to help. The music stopped. He leapt to his feet – alive, life affirmed – relieved applause, more music, off again. Fantastic.

But now chairs and tables resumed their use by the sated circle. The Nordic teenagers wandered off into the night, looking back over their shoulders wondering what they'd just experienced. Maybe life was more than fashion, exams and the latest pop. They would have learnt even more if they'd stayed a little longer. Manoli moved centre stage. Standing still, staring at his feet, barrel chest filling, arms outstretched, muscles corded by distended veins, fierce concentration, power exuded, sweat damp shirt. This was not death. This was man as supreme immortal power – unhindered by changing technology or money. It was extreme male pride, contemptuous of rational customs or authority. His movements – invidious to call it dance – surpassed structure and form. He had become Man as God – it was a statement of total arrogance – impossible not to admire…

He returned to our world and to Maria. She ruffled his hair as if he were a child. Laughter defusing hubris.

Angie had been standing too close for too long. My brain was in my balls. God, I wanted to shag her senseless. She saw the look on my face and responded.

"Old Oz saying: woman with skirt up, run faster than man with trousers down!" Humour made rejection kinder – no problem. She lightly side-stepped my next moves and crass hints by suggesting I should come sailing with her and a friend. Obviously a medallion swinging kamaki stud. Ah well, it was another kind put down, apart from the irrational jealousy it churned.

"Eric is looking for a crew, eight a.m., if you can get to the harbour in time."

I had a hard-on I could polish my boots with, and now I was going sailing. Sort it out pillock.

"I'm looking forward to seeing more of you Stevie."

I knew a prick-teaser when I saw one. The trouble was I was more than willing to have my prick teased.

"I'll be there at eight. What's the name of the yacht?"

"She's a schooner; you can't miss her. Her name's Eleftheria."

Something stirred deep inside. The Path was drawing me in. Walk on.

Chapter 26

THE MORNING HARBOUR was full of easy smiles, fresh air, and white sails, so I smiled back – just couldn't help it. The bowsprit swept up to overhang the quay by several feet and just below the rubbing strake, her name: 'Eleftheria.'

"Bonjour! You are Steve – come aboard."

So her knobbing friend was not a Greek kamaki but a French smoothie git. We shook hands; inadequately I said: "Beautiful boat."

"Yes, I was lucky to find her. She is pitch pine on oak, copper sheathed, laid teak deck, built by your Camper and Nicholson in 1939. She spent the war without masts ferrying troops in the Solent. Afterwards she had a big box put on her deck and was used as a house-boat. I took the box off. I rescued her – she rescued me."

I removed my trainers and walked aft, stroking the oiled mahogany hand rail: "What a beauty."

The casual 'merci' could not conceal his extreme pride: "She is still as tight as a drum. She has dust in her bilges." I was seriously impressed. "An English archaeologist had her built. He was killed fighting on Crete during the war. It is honourable that his yacht is here now, is it not?"

"Yes it is. Why did he call her Eleftheria?"

"It means beyond freedom. With us French it is joi de vivre and liberté but more, it's like when Greeks dance, like Chelsea when they score." He pointed to my T-shirt. "It's what Greeks say when they live, when they die. It is in their national anthem."

* * *

Angie's voice came from the quay: "Give us a hand with the goodies, guys."

There were two of them, sex on legs times two. Two lots of blonde hair, two sets of boobs, two sets of white smiles: porno fantasies were queuing up in my grubby little mind.

Angie introduced me: "Stevie, this is Kim, she's Eric's bimbo." Kim stuck her tongue out. I leant over and shook her hand: "I'm glad you're not a bloke." Angie gave me a gotcha look as Kim gave me the once over: "Angie told me you weren't the screwed up, repressed, arrogant pommy bastard she first thought – almost a ten."

"I'll take that as a compliment. She said she was bringing a friend. I thought you were her bloke."

"Blimey Ange, this guy's eyesight is better than the last one and he still has his own teeth."

Angie scratched back: "Well, your last one couldn't even read."

Kim was quick: "I didn't want him wasting time reading when I could be shagging his brains out."

How refreshing female honesty can be.

Eric interrupted: "We go mes amies."

As we motored past the end of the harbour wall a rod fisherman shouted: "Kali mera Chelsea." I smiled, gave a thumbs up and pointed to my T-shirt.

Kim shouted: "Best not give that sign in Greece sport, it means up your bum here."

"Sorry"

"It's O.K. He knew you were a pommy 'malaka'."

"Malaka?"

"Wanker." Kim illustrated with hand gestures as Angie came back on deck: "My my, you two are getting on well. You're learning fast Stevie."

Eric finished stowing fenders: "Take the wheel Steve. When I wave, steer her towards that island."

He moved forward with the two girls to hoist the main and a huge genny. I remembered watching Eleftheria arrive from Manoli's; now I was at the wheel. Looking back, a figure at the taverna was moving chairs. Manoli was starting his daily life of warm comfortable repetition. What technological breakthrough or mega bucks could improve the sun, friends and good food?

Where do politics and war come into it? They are not required. He'd be sitting with his five chairs and iced coffee in a minute, watching Eleftheria complete the picture.

Eric waved from the bow. I put the wheel over, sails filled, she lifted to the light wind, an accelerating surge. The girls came back into the cockpit, T-shirts billowing. It seemed pointless to have them on. The God of sex must have heard; unselfconsciously they both pulled them over their heads; the wheel keeping my hardening knob in check.

Eric went below and killed the engine, leaving a shocking silent tranquillity; senses overloaded with peace; dappled patches showing where the morning breeze stroked the oil flat Aegean.

Angie dropped into the cabin to do grub. She shouted up: "You O.K.?" I was more than O.K., but grinning too much to answer. A small caique was chugging back to our fading harbour; apart from that we were alone in a world of endless warm blue. A rush of joy filled my heart. Skywards I roared: "Chelsea! Chelsea! Chelsea!"

Angie stuck her head out of the hatch: "You sure you're O.K.?"

"Never better."

"Here, have an orange juice."

I swigged half of it: "Wow, tastes like vodka."

"Yea, morning punch."

"Bit early isn't it?"

"You poms, do you have to do everything by the clock?"

I looked at her; I was going to say yes. It was Monday; grey computer commuters would be blandly processing crap. I looked at my watch, took it off and hurled it into the blue. One glint, then gone forever. A piece of freedom regained – tracker functions would confuse them for a few hours.

Angie and Kim went on the coach roof, chatting softly, unselfconsciously smoothing sun cream on each other's backs. Angie looked over, daring me to stare, whispered something in Kim's ear, then sensually kissed it. This was sexual provocation bordering on cruelty. She came towards me, smiling: "Who's got the nicest tits Stevie? Would you like us to 'les' it up a bit for you?" I shrugged, hopelessly lost in lust… "Whooaa"… I'd have to stop saying that.

"Give me your arm – slip, slap, slop… now the other one."

I changed hands on the wheel, trying not to show how erotically saturated I was. Her breasts, shiny, oiled, strokeable, just inches from my hand.

I whispered: "Kim said you think I'm a ten."

"Yea I do – out of a 100!" She stuck her tongue out. "Are you advertising Stevie?"

"No, yes, no, no, yes."

"That's good. A girl always likes to know where she stands."

Luckily Eric came on deck with a distracting chart: "There's a small uninhabited island here where we can lunch and swim. We have not been this year – perhaps see a wreck somewhere."

…or perhaps chests of treasure, or mermaids… anything was possible – all believable. The popple flattened to a mirror as we entered the bay, our reflection disappearing as the sea bed showed gin clear: air and sea of equal density. The anchor redundant, chain hanging vertically, weight alone holding us in place. Eleftheria grazed contentedly.

Eric looked down: "Our minds are like water. When disturbed we see nothing. When still, we see clearly – our choice."

We all dived in naked. Weirdly I wondered if such clear water would hold our weight. It was more like flying than swimming. Sea-bed troughs giving feelings of vertigo. Around me swam real mermaids; the beautiful female body supported in crystal sunshine. I dived to the anchor, lightly tucked my foot under and looked up at the mermaids playing around Etheftheria's copper sheathed hull. Eventually my lungs reminded me I was not a fish and took me gently to the surface.

Kim whistled from the cockpit for lunch: bread, olives, feta, honey melon, retsina, orange juice, satsiki. Eric had collected a dozen spiny urchins, adding to the simple perfection. He put some classical music on. It couldn't match the music of silence, so switched it off: "Make your thoughts the music."

There was no wreck, just a timeless deserted island. A trireme crewed by ancients could have anchored nearby and I would have raised my glass without surprise.

After lunch Angie dived in again to cool off – I followed: "You look like a ravishing mermaid."

"Thank you sir, and you look like a horny pirate. Are you going to kidnap me and have your wicked way ten times a day?"

"I'm a horny pirate, not superman. How about five times a day?"

Laughing, she pushed my head underwater as she swam past in a languid curve of streamlined feminine beauty – pure carnal sensuality. I watched her climb the boarding ladder on the transom... such a beautiful transom. Back on board, she turned and smiled. A sun-drenched mermaid skipping below, dripping crystals.

(Mick's voice: 'Stop pissing about, go and give her a good seeing to. She's gagging for it.'… 'Get lost Mick, you crude bastard. This is different.')

Much too soon, we hauled in the anchor and headed back. Eric and Kim disappeared below. Angie said: "Siesta, they're shagging friends."

This was where the Gods came to play. We now had the whole beautiful world to ourselves. The afternoon sunwind freshened and Eleftheria surged from walk to canter. Under full sail she seemed to go faster than the wind dictated, leaving hardly a bubble in her wake. She moved more like a fish or a...

"Dolphin!"

Angie pointed astern. We were doing a good ten knots. They caught us easily, leaping in arcs of joy. A pod of twentyish, questioning, smiling eyes. I couldn't help it, I leant over and called to them from my new-found heart: "You beautiful darlings." Their clean, lithe shapes skimmed the keel to surf the bow wave.

It had been love at first sight with Greece, Eleftheria and now dolphins. I moved back. Angie was there, nestled in front of the wheel, hair scent, coconut oil, warm sun, a sea woman, mixing, moving, the taste of spray – a rhythm of cresting waves.

Her face was serious : "You beautiful man, hold me."…

"I'll hold you."…

Hugging, a tender power, then release turning to sweaty salt tasting kisses and contented smiles. Picking up a towel she turned on the companion way and posed – my mind photographed her, recorded forever. She raised a beautiful arm heavenwards, glistening, salt glazed – “Eleftheria! Eleftheria!” – our mantra; the world’s mantra. I would have died for her there and then if it didn’t mean missing out on all those future shags.

“Eleftheria!” I howled my ecstasy. God, I was happy!

* * *

Nevada, USA. Drone Central:

“79 is a lucky son of a bitch, Costa.”

“Yes Sir. Shouldn’t we censor that bit?”

“Hell no. It’s going up in the bar.”

Chapter 27

LIFE settled down to more than a routine: a rhythm had taken over of sailing and swimming, laughing and talking, shagging and shagging – all with a newly discovered passion, spirit and heart: 'We can do anything, Stevie.'

A long hot summer lay before us. We didn't plan the future or dwell on the past – except once – it was my fault and came from love. We'd just got into bed for an afternoon 'siesta' when Angie suddenly sat up: "Let's play a game!"

(Leila's voice, the London hotel.) I had no control, no check, too hard, too loud, shouting: "Never, never say that again!"

She stared incredulous, trust and love crumbling in fear, a pause, then tears, pushing me away. I tried to re-wind: "I'm sorry, sorry, you said 'play a game'. It's a bad memory. It wasn't you, never you."

I was shaking. Traumatic images buzzed inside: explosions, a pistol, violent death, blood on dust, red on grey. Angie's compassion came as sudden as my anger. She cradled my head, kissed my hair. If she'd shouted back, I could have dealt with it, but she didn't. She gave me love and that cracked me up. We hugged our tears away, repairing and deepening our feelings: "Do you want to tell me?"

"Not yet, no. I want to say I love you."

It was the first time I'd said it to her and she responded: "I love you too."

We squeezed more tears out of each other. My pretence of being a controlled hard case, emotionally impervious, disappeared along with a bucket of false ego. The positive reaction elevated our relationship to a new level in which it thrived....

We made love...

"Do you have a ferry to catch, Stevie?"

"No."

"Well slow down then!"

Chapter 28

(Track 9, Very Best of the Eagles. 'I can't tell you why.')

ELEFTHERIA was not just a beautiful boat but a spirit from an age of miracles, myths, and sacred deities. Her status was accepted easily, without question, by everyone who met her. She was spoken of with reverence and would welcome all beliefs and ideas comfortably, except violence and abuse.

Our endless summer drifted on, just as it had for Otto and the sisters. Life's good music, impossible not to dance to. It had been stripped of superficial crap: no computers or mobiles, no ties or suits, no socks or coats, no gales or tides, no news of financial disaster or wars, no fear or worries, no debts or savings – life decluttered – minimalist – leaving room for maximum thought, understanding and love.

It was just T-shirt and shorts in the day. T-shirt and jeans at night; everyone was equal, fishermen, millionaires, billionaires, crooks, tourists, bankers, bonkers, spooks, students, working girls, mafia, top sportsmen, politicians, donkey drivers, farmers, doctors and even screwed up ex-squaddies. All the same, all different: respectful anarchy. Entourages of film stars found exclusive isolation impossible. They were absorbed into the tavernas milieu like everyone else. Minders and heavies shoved aside for tables and chairs. Social tricks, snobbery, intellectual arrogance, sexual bad manners, were dismantled and replaced by real friendliness.

The best food and the best wine were for everyone: Manoli and Maria's goat, chips, Greek salad and retsina were always the best – and so it was – no problems – social equality.

The confusion of the mega rich, looking to spend their vast wealth and seeing that love, fun and sun were free, was a revelation. Their faces implied: 'I have worked, schemed, cheated, stolen, killed, to get money. And now I realise what I really want costs nothing.' The sight of con-men realising they'd been conned, (suppressed bitterness turning to enlightenment), was a joy to behold. Eric's humble and wise harmony really worked. He often sang: 'Everyone has to learn sometime.'

Initially I felt out of my depth, overawed by famous names, faces and pretentious intellect; that changed listening to Eric's gentle humorous clarity of thought and compassion for idiots. Above all it was his courtesy that made people respect him. I learnt that polite patience and good values were universal ways of solving problems. Simple – so fucking simple – where had it gone wrong?

Occasionally, we came across animals from another part of the forest that had irrational evil festering in their guts. Eric would treat them the same. I knew my way had to be there as back up. Snakes were not intrinsically evil, but they were poisonous. Survival priorities sometimes demanded they were killed. His Buddhism wouldn't stop them, I could. When evil comes, it's too late to work out a strategy. My way worked. If a snake was a threat, I killed it – Q.E. D.

* * *

I didn't always get things right – far from it. A smart-arse criticism of Australian culture and a piss-take of her accent caused Angie to respond with aggressive pride. I had been stupid. I'd got it wrong, so apologised and changed. I'd also changed to a new kind of health, from the ten-mile run and multi-press-ups, to a more sensual, fluid fitness, free of muscle ache, eating good food, singing, swimming, shagging.

We slept six hours max. We got up to live, not to work. Sleep came with not a single cc left out of ten. Angie was brilliant at sex, nudging ideas: 'It's not a race Stevie – why rush?' I didn't say: 'Because I used to pay by the hour.' She said stuff like: 'Love making is making life. Why count time? Time is a drag – love is not time.'

(Eric's voice echoed her words: 'Live in peace. Do not force change, but change.')

So I changed.

I was knee deep in love, sinking fast, drowning in a sensual overload of sun, coconut oil, wine, boobs, and a wonderful salty, blonde, fanny. Why was I still trying to stay afloat, in control? 'Let go, sink into real life.'

* * *

Everyone who came out on Eleftheria seemed to like us. They may have gone ashore and slagged us off afterwards, but it never seemed like it. Another thing was how disparate groups became infatuated, not only with the magical environment but with the stories we'd accumulated; stimulating their own extraordinary tales.

Eleftheria rocked at anchor with multi-accented laughter...

–The voluptuous young lady, told to shower behind a taverna, confronted by granddad watering his courgettes. She stripped, soaped up and waited to be hosed down: poor old granddad!

–Yanni, the tripper boat skipper, who gave each new girlfriend a T-shirt with the boat's name: 'Neptune.' The qualification for ownership was well known, except to the many and varied ladies who proudly paraded the quay. One particularly energetic season, over fifty 'Neptune' T-shirts were awarded. Advancing age meant he had to give baby ones to returning mums: stubble chins confirming his responsibility.

–A top model, mentioning suicide, painfully thin, ate with her mouth open, then forced herself to be sick, not always in private – cameras looking for saleable shots. Angie and Kim put her on the right lines with some good OZ common sense. I don't know exactly what they said, but a couple of days later she was proudly wearing a 'Neptune' T-shirt and tucking into goat and chips! Sex here wasn't obscene, dirty or illegal. It was an option, not a perversion – just one of life's choices.

('Angie, did you ever get a Neptune T-shirt?')

('No Stevie. I got ten from the USS Kennedy when it docked in Pireaus!')

–A female London string quartet paid a fortune to play naked on a reinforced glass ceiling at a famous politician's birthday bash.

–And Nigel, who worked in the female pleasure industry, trying to have a rest on the island, but only managing to accentuate his magnetism.

–An old yachtie couple, who financed their wanderings by panning for gold in an Albanian river, protected by a Cold War mine field. They'd found a way through. It was as good as money in the bank.

Some tales were so far off the wall as to be dismissed as retsina induced bollocks…

–A Russian spook, caught in the U.K, because he'd learnt his English from porno books: 'I am very excited to be in your huge throbbing country.' Once the source of their language education had been established, several more K.G.B. were indecently exposed. I didn't care if the story was true or not but it rocked the boat with laughter again.

Not all the stories were as funny:

–One-armed dynamite fishermen.

–Drug smugglers financing hospitals in Lebanon.

–A big game hunter boasting about adding to his 'African Five' with a human trophy from Sarajevo: What a Big Stupid White Hunter.

–A writer whose latest book told of Swiss Banks financing Nazis, before, during and after World War 2. The plundered wealth of Europe from titanic atrocities, stored under clean mountains, accruing even more wealth and power from dead accounts for elite ruling families. Loot chugging away, generating vast amounts for morally blind oligarchs.

–And Eric, who never got pissed, casually mentioning that Silex B would create world peace one day.

–And an ex-squaddie who was being educated by just listening.

* * *

Eleftheria sailed on; we sailed with her. She was a beautiful horse guiding us; knowing the way. Everything was good, even the bad bits were good: a guest cutting her foot, being made a fuss of, a chance for her to know people cared. She cried not from pain, but from the realisation she was loved unconditionally and she would only be lonely if she pushed people away.

Past ghosts exorcised; future demons ignored – why worry twice? Deal with it when it comes, not before. There were no Monday mornings, no work days, no weekends, no bank holidays – every day was to be enjoyed full on. Surrogate living in films or TV was ignored because real life was more interesting.

Sometimes a full moon said spring tides or a half moon neaps. Here in the Mediterranean there were no tides – a sailing paradise. Every day we took out small groups of artists, writers, musicians, photographers, to secluded bays for inspiration.

After twenty minutes, sometimes less, with pen, brush or camera, they became entranced with the natural environment and just sat or talked quietly in a state of meditative bliss. It was uncanny to see it happen again and again. Different languages, ages, religions – same reaction. For us crew, repetition of scenery and food never became monotonous. No one asked if we got bored. Eric and Eleftheria managed it all with their gentle Buddhist wisdom. There were times when, in any other context, he would have been laughed at – not here. This was as close to reality as anyone could get.

And more wisdom casually surfaced: 'Choose your Path. The choice is infinite.' 'You will never die because you have always lived, even before Earth was formed.' 'A true artist brings out the rhythm of a subject, not its likeness.' 'Humans are governed by the same laws as the universe, so we should understand those laws.' 'Koans with logic, a paradox of ancient sunlight.' 'Calming opaque water to clear, with enlightened thought.'

"Eric, I thought koans were unsolvable riddles designed to confuse?"

"Buddhism, Steve, is changed by your thoughts, not the Buddha's. We are all Buddhas. I find logical koans more useful. Buddhism is not a dogmatic God religion. It is a way to think, based on universal values of good. There are universal values of evil too. I fight them with good."

We all sailed on: Angie and Kim dished out drinks, food, coconut sun oil, and appeased lecherous husbands. My responsibilities were sails, engine, listening to secrets they couldn't confess to a deaf priest, and appeasing lecherous wives. What a job. So by the end of each day, I'd heard every melon and cucumber joke going in at least four different languages.

Occasionally I'd get a dig in the ribs from Angie if things got too flirtatious. And I'd do the same to her if she was paying too much attention to a horny speedo trussed bloke. Blackmail could have netted us millions, but secrets given in those situations demanded integrity. Anyway once the 'big thing' in their lives had been confessed everyone felt better: just like having a good crap.

A coded socio-sexual language at 'Carry On' level was well developed in the U.K. contingent: 'My husband played hide the sausage with his secretary last Christmas.'… 'Maybe I wouldn't have done if my wife had been at the party, instead of at the tennis club hiding someone else's sausage!' On and on it went, until a German woman announced: 'We eat more sausages in Germany than in any other European country.' There was a pause, then an eruption of spilt drinks and incontinence as the poor woman wondered why her immaculate English was being laughed at. I felt so bad for her I had to dive over the side, underwater laughing. When I came back on board, I was pleased to see she was being spoilt with warm censored explanations by the eclectic group, until she added: 'But I can't get a good sausage anywhere in Greece.' I dived in again, trailing bubbles. Unfortunately that wasn't the end of it. In Manoli's that evening, she asked him: 'Is the refrigerator for ice-cream in the front side of your taverna or in your backside?' I held my breath, coughed once, ran up the track 100 metres and pissed myself laughing. To be fair, it made me wonder how many mistakes we all make when learning a foreign language: Greek for beautiful and fat is the same word with the emphasis in different places. Humorous tolerance of my Greek, I could now admire.

Music was integral to Eleftheria's life – 'French Pops Greatest Hits' – or more usually International Classical Orchestras. I listened and started to get it. Once a guest stuck on a Dire Straits C.D. We were goose-winging south of Spetse. I couldn't help it, I made a right prat of myself on the air guitar. I didn't care. It couldn't have been that bad – I got a round of applause. Angie covered her eyes. Kim translated malaka by hand. But the greatest music was silence; (as koan or paradox) there never is silence. Each note is gold dust, layers of sound reduced to single notes… perfection.

I watched and learnt and saw how beauty in all its forms – music, sunshine, islands, sea , sky – affected people, sometimes to tears. A dead dolphin on a beach was not treated with disgust because of the smell, but with respect as if human. We stood, prayed and buried it because it was the right thing to do. All nations, religions, creeds, colours, all 'same same'. When Eric saw people heading the right direction he'd back off and let them generate their own enlightenment, or if wrong he'd gently react. We were talking in a cafenion on how he believed animals have personalities. A heavily tattooed English drunk nearby butted in: 'Are you queer?' Eric smiled: 'No, but thanks for the offer and if I ever change my mind, I'll let you know.'

* * *

In the middle of our summer, it could have been July, Eric told us he had to spend five days in Athens with his son Jack. No explanation why his son couldn't come to the boat, but his mother's death seemed to have something to do with it. We never asked how she'd died.

"Can I have a word Steve?"

"Yea, sure Eric."

"Can you look after Eleftheria while I'm away? The life rafts are inside the cabins – one lashed to the forward bulkhead, one to the engine bulkhead. They are not to be taken on deck. If she is holed, pull the cords. They will inflate in the cabins and they will keep her afloat even when full of water." Genius.

I couldn't believe he'd trust me with Eleftheria, even though we both knew she would really be looking after me. It was impossible not to treat her as human. She had a spirit of her own; passing yachts, caiques, even ferry captains waved or hooted to acknowledge her charisma. They'd point and stare wistfully at a thoroughbred from a past generation – the way yachts used to be.

The honour of Eric's trust had a deep positive effect on me. He wasn't a teacher who told you things. The right information was just absorbed. Things got done properly; it was always going to work out when he was around. He never preached. He became our mentor without a hint of superiority. I'd known a few patrol commanders like that – officers and NCO's who had a way of behaving that instilled confidence: 'When Capt X or Sgt Y were around, all was O.K.'

Eric was of that mould. I admired him and copied his ways. Who had he copied? Who had copied who through history? Nelson had copied someone.

(Mick's voice: 'Shut up now Steve. You've made your point. Eric's a good bloke. I get it'.)

I'd learnt where monk seals had their pups. I knew remote island beaches where turtles left eggs and footprints, fighting gravity to go back to grazing the sea. And dolphins, always dolphins. Eleftheria and Eric seemed a magnet for them. It was uncanny. I'd stopped wondering why. I had a good idea, but that was too spiritual for me to accept. Maybe his dead wife really was a dolphin. Out here all was possible. Back in U.K. it would be dismissed as being 'un-scientific'. Humans pre-frontal lobes give us the ability to experience happiness, creativity, idealism... dolphins have similar brain development – some say it's more developed. (I do – now.)

I took my responsibility much too seriously, so when Eric returned from Athens it was a relief. Angie could stop calling me Captain: 'Yes Captain!' 'No Captain!' 'Whatever you say Captain!' 'I'll do anything for you Captain!' 'It's huge Captain!' 'Is that all for me Captain?' Heavy duty, piss-taking Oz style.

Life flowed on without effort – everything good. If someone was late or forgot something, it always worked out one way or another. Happenstance, serendipity, fate, whatever, all would be well and all was well. She was a happy boat and chuckled along with amused acceptance at our antics.

Angie and me felt like a golden couple. Commonsense said we would never grow old or get sick. She was beautiful; I was good looking; all was perfect forever. Hubris and mortality vanquished, we were indestructible. The Gods couldn't touch us.

The defining moment came on a day of strong Meltemi. Eleftheria loved it. I was hogging the wheel on cloud nine. Roy, an elderly American, was sitting contentedly in the cockpit taking it all in. As we tacked, he neatly coiled the jib sheets. Half a mile off our starboard beam a 42' Jeaneau, fast charter yacht. I asked him if he wanted to steer, handed the wheel over and stood resting on the back stay. He balanced himself, sighted the Jeaneau and we were off, charging after it. Eleftheria scented her quarry. He gave me a glance as if to say, 'This is something special.' I smiled and nodded. Eric looked back from the foremast and gave a lazy French salute. Roy returned a clipped U.S. Navy reply. The crew caught the mood. They weren't on holiday any more – this was serious.

At certain points of sailing Eleftheria went faster than her displacement water- line length said she should – just like a dolphin.

Our new skipper pulled out a few feet of worn flag from his beach bag. No problem – I hoisted it on the aft courtesy halyard. All thirty foot of U.S. Navy battle pennant, snagged once, cracked and flew clear. A frisson of recognition on keyed faces: it was Roy's flag.

The Jeaneau's skipper kept looking over his shoulder. I heard him shout something. Seconds later their genoa was smartly replaced by a giant rainbow spinnaker. They were good, bollocks, we'd never catch them now.

I stayed hanging to the backstay. Angie and Kim were working hard, no longer 'hosties' but tough Oz sailors. She caught my eye – one message – somehow we've got to win. Eric was by the foremast exuding calm confidence, directing the deck crew. But their spinnaker was making all the difference. They were pulling away.

Roy eased Eleftheria down wind. She slowed, pennant sagging; we lost more ground. I started towards the wheel to correct – no need – Roy shouted: "Gybe-ho!" Eric and crew ducked. The twin booms whacked across – now she had wings, not sails. She creamed onto a broad reach; her fastest point – pennant straight out. We were gaining – she loved it – then magic on magic, four dolphin outriders appeared.

The Jeanneau skipper was shouting more orders – more faces turned towards us. Roy held his course, surfing a couple of useful waves – our bowsprit aimed dead centre of their transom – the last second – "Gybe ho!" Booms whacked across again. We sailed right through to windward, blanketing all their sails, spinnaker collapsing, spiralling their forestay, mainsail screwed to a chinaman. We'd flattened her all standing, like a rolling broadside from a man of war. The Jeaneau was dead in the water. We roared a cheer. Roy was still focused – steering us just feet from their stern. A gust surging our victory and cracking the pennant. I could have pinged their backstay as we passed. Their skipper's face said it all. Cursing, he acknowledged Eleftheria; took his cap off and bowed. His crew lined the side deck cheering, applauding, cameras going.

An old lady, who'd been heaving ropes like a good'un with Angie and Kim, caught the moment, pulled her top off over her head and waved her glorious tits at them: more photos, more cheers. Priceless. I'd give a lot for one of those photos now.

We pulled away fast, leaving them staring at the stern of ELEFTHERIA. I knew they'd be asking what it meant. They could have asked any of us. We all knew. The dolphins had done their job.

Their fading three cheers, softened by distance, sealed the occasion: yep, job done. I roared my battle cry "Eleftheria!" Angie, Kim and topless gran were doing a war dance on the coach roof. Eric broke out the champagne, called me an anglo-heathen for drinking out of a mug, and we all toasted Roy – a tired, very contented, quiet American.

When our adrenalin slowed, Eric lowered the pennant, folded it respectfully and handed it to Roy. He took it, patted the wheel and presented it back to Eric. A simple act; huge meaning. I'd have waffled; Eric accepted it with a slight head bow, and stowed it carefully in the flag locker – no fuss. Angie, Kim and gran could see the ceremony, wiped salty eyes and bounced on again with their war dance.

God I loved that boat. She was the Holy Grail. She enabled stuff like that to happen – brilliant – if only it could be bottled.

I concentrated looking astern, wondering how a boat could leave no wake, just a low bubbling tune. Eric came and stood beside me.

"I wish her first friend – the guy who was killed in the war – could see her now, Eric."

"Ah mon brave, he can."

"You believe in reincarnation?"

"I believe Eleftheria is a spirit in all of us. It does not depend on age or looks. It has been here forever – it will last forever; it is the spirit of Tao. Newton's Law says energy cannot be created or destroyed, and so it is. It is what energy we put in the cup, or Grail, that makes us special and enlightened. So if I am damaged – face, legs or something – I am still me. If you lose everything, your self remains – you are still you – Eleftheria – freedom – understand?"

What had the Greek Jew from Salonica said walking to the gas-chamber? The only word he could: 'Eleftheria.' The word he chose.

"I had a friend. He was old when I knew him."

"Was he your mentor?"

"Mentor? *Oui*. He was a man who planted trees; very many in the south of France, inland from Cannes, where soil had been lost, mountain sides washed away, trees had been cut down in WW1 and 2. He told me, old men plant trees, young men cut them down. If young men planted trees, they would have a better life, and their children would too. I listened to him and learnt because I had always known, but it needed real actions to make it true. His idea was to plant a type of oak that didn't burn – it would if logged, dried and put in a hearth – but not free standing in a forest. Pine trees burn easily and spread fire, especially in a hot dry climate like here in Greece. Oaks grow very slowly. He said everything has its own time. I said he would be dead before his oaks matured. He said his bones would help the trees grow and small oaks were beautiful and he would come back to see them. I said, what if the trees are all cut down again? He said, then a free man will plant them again.

"Steve, there is no need to understand everything. The more science explains, the more we realize how much we don't know.

My friend died twenty years ago. His trees keep living. Their acorns are growing; his children are growing. New life, reincarnation, simple.

"When I go back to France, I thank his spirit for the beautiful trees he planted. They use thousands of litres of water; he planted them on dry, barren mountain sides. Do you know what happened? The water-table rose, streams chuckled again, and with it came deer, butterflies, fish and brave woodsmen and women. They renovated the old stone houses, had families and joie de vivre, liberté, and Eleftheria. His secret was to see beauty in an acorn as much as in a giant oak; also to realise the space between the trees is just as important as the trees. In the winter I plant acorns, from a Greek oak, on one of the uninhabited islands without goats. When I'm dead, my son will see them and his son and I will see them, understand?"

"Yes I do."

* * *

A few days later Eric was just finishing sanding the new cabin table top made from ancient olive wood found on a beach. We all stood around, stroking the precious swirled grain. Disaster! Kim got overexcited and spilled her red wine right in the middle – stained – ruined – bad feeling – shouting – recriminations – clumsiness? There was none of that. Eric spun his white T-shirt over his head onto the table, took the glass from Kim, emptied the remainder on to the wood and polished it in, giving it a golden lustre, highlighting the grain violet. He stood back to admire it, gave Kim a kiss, and polished in some more. Angie and I burbled words of admiration. It looked fantastic. Eric couldn't have known. His reflexes were too quick. An accident turned positive; disaster to triumph – job done. He hadn't cursed; his clear mind had changed negative reaction to positive. It was now an even more beautiful table – the day had been saved – we were laughing instead of moaning. I logged it firmly in my hard drive. It was the fast version of cognitive behaviour therapy or as he called it, the aesthetics of enlightenment: changing preordained negative reactions to positive outcomes and solutions. How about conflict resolution, anger management, turning bad to good? Alchemy wasn't turning base metal to gold, it was changing evil to good and then keeping it in the Holy Grail. Not a physical cup, but a mental cup of ideas: books, computer... I was getting the hang of this.

(Mick's voice: 'Bollocks, you can't eat or drink ideas mate.')

('You're wrong Mick, you can.')

We were all standing around the table admiring it. And the way Kim was looking at Eric, he was in for a treat later. He put his wine-sodden T-shirt back on; left-hand side in small letters M.S.F. What else? When you do things right, you keep doing them right.

Later, I wrote secretly, under the same cabin table: 'Kim and Eric – Angie and Steve, lived and loved here. Date…' I put the pencil back on the shelf and noticed the comments book. There were loads of nice stuff…

– 'The pennant couldn't have a better home. Thanks for reminding me what it's all about. Roy, USN ret'd.'

– The best time of my life, love Angie x.

– Same as above and double it, love, love Kim xx.

– I wrote: 'Eleftheria – you are the spirit of white waves on blue. You hold our hearts and ideas. You are the Holy Grail.' A fear shivered my soul at the responsibility given to her, so added: 'You can't sink an idea, you can't sink a rainbow. Love and thank you from all your friends.'

Indiana Jones had been looking in the wrong place. The Holy Grail is something that holds ideas, like a church, a mosque, a university, a library, even a beautiful boat… not a golden bowl.

Chapter 29

ANGIE was so beautiful when asleep. I wanted to wake her up and tell her; not a good idea, so I left quietly and went to the harbour to fill Eleftheria's water tanks. People unused to living on boats, could never understand that as we circumnavigated the island, we didn't have a hose connected to the shore.

I passed Manoli on the way back: "Kali mera Stephan."

"Kali mera Manoli – ti kanis?"

"Poli kala efharisto. Bravo, your accent is perfect. I am the best teacher in Greece and I have made many children. In Greece we live long and die quick.. In your country you live quick and die long time." I'd long ago stopped being surprised by conversation changes. It was all part of the charm.

"Stephan, listen, there is an Englishman looking for you. My daughter said ugly, but nice."

A cold draft stirred the early morning warmth. Taylor was ugly but not nice, so it wasn't him; probably one of the guests wanting to book another trip – so why was my gut demon niggling?

* * *

In the evening Angie went to work at the taverna as usual, while I went for a jog. She'd left me a few olives. I rolled them around the plate like a fortune teller staring at tea leaves, unease niggling.

After a shower, I wandered down to see her. A big bloke was chatting her up, his back to me. I recognized him as he turned: "Dickhead! Found you at last."

We shook hands: "It's good to see you, Mick."

Angie was bubbling: "Mick's been telling me all about your sordid sex life back in the U.K. I didn't know you were into goats. You should have said – I'd have dressed up for you. And your stripagram job sounded real neat. Go sit outside and I'll bring the beers."

Mick gave her one of his twisted smiles women seemed to find attractive, so as we walked out I gave him a heavy slap on the back: "Don't even think about it mate. We're together and it's working well – get it?"

He held up his hands in feigned innocence: "She's got a nice smile."

"Yea, that's only because she's too polite to laugh at your pug ugly face."

"Good one Steve. You've certainly got your feet under the table here."

"How did you know where I was?"

"Taylor."

Parts of my brain I hadn't accessed in months buzzed: "That snake shit. I hoped he'd be dead by now. So why are you here?"

"I needed a holiday, so bingo."

"C'mon, I can read you like a book. What's real?"

"Well you know how Harry tells the woman you're with she's a different one from the night before?"

"Yea."

"Well he did . She was and she didn't like it."

"What a twat. So you were making a pig of yourself and got found out. I knew it would catch up with you one day."

"True, but the boat had to go into Burgess Marine for a new prop and antifouling, so here I am."

Angie came over with more beers: "It's great to see you two muckers getting on so well."

"I'll tell you later what a bastard he is, so you can warn all the women you know."

"Cheers Dickhead."

"Cheers Bollock Chops."

He stared at the view: "Good here in'it. You certainly landed on your feet Steve."

"It is good and I wouldn't like anyone or anything screwing it up, understand?"

He then started to screw it up: "Taylor told me Leila had dumped you, and you'd come here to recover."

"That was nice of him. Anything else?"

"His tooth fairies took me to Croydon for interrogation about the container job we did."

"Don't tell me, Black Witch, Beardy, Baldy, Four Dentists and Major Major?"

"Yep. They kept asking me why you hadn't called in the airstrike in Fagan."

"What did you say?"

"Nothing, except you'd done the right thing at the right time, so they stripped me bollock naked. The Witch laughed and pointed at my prick; so I told her she must have a cunt like an elephant's arsehole; so they stuck a gag in my mouth and took me to the 'dentists'."

I chuckled: "Good old Mick. What happened?"

"Usual. You remember Jackson 85?"

"Yea, did a tour with Int. Corp."

"Yea right. He told me some techniques, so I had a good idea what was coming. Everyone spews when the creep strokes your neck, so I spat it as far as I could, all down their lovely white coats. They all got a bit."

"Fucking brilliant. I've missed these intellectual discussions."

"Bollocks you have. What's for chow?"

"When she asks what you want to eat, say: 'Emai ena malaka.'"

Manoli's daughter, Sophie, came over; dark piercing eyes and twenty-two summers of glowing Greek femininity, conservatively dressed, very sexy and very 'out of bounds'."

"You have a new friend Stephan?"

"No Sophie, this is Mick. He is an old friend and a very big malaka. If you see him down the harbour, run back here to your mum."

Mick tried out his new Greek phrase: "Emai ena malaka." ('I'm a wanker.' His pronunciation was perfect.)

She scowled at me: "You need someone to teach you Greek properly, Mick."

He gave her one of his lopsided smiles, took her hand for an instant and for an instant she ruffled his hair before disappearing inside.

I groaned and stared heavenwards: “Don’t go there either. It’s against the rules.”

“What rules?”

“Rule one: she’s Greek. Rule two: her father and brother are very protective. Rule three: if you behave improperly – which is all you ever do with women – they will chop your cock off, slice it for souvlaki and give your testicles to the cats.”

He winced and held his groin: ”You’ve got too many rules.”

I hadn’t finished: “There are plenty of openings for blokes like you. Dozens of Swedish and German ladies to keep even you satisfied. Forget Sophie and any other Greek females. That includes cats, donkeys and goats. O.K.?”

“I get the message Steve. You want all the goats for yourself.”

I was about to flick a gob of beer at him when Sophie came back with the plates – Greek salad, chips, pork chops, satsiki, hummus. I didn’t like the way she felt the need to explain to Mick how she cooked the food or how it was prepared. And I especially didn’t like his new-found interest in Greek recipes, or the way she looked over her shoulder at him when she walked away. (Why do women do that? To see if you’re looking at their arse?)

I dipped my bread in the satsiki: “How long you staying mate?”

“Steve, I’ve only just got here, give me a chance. Two weeks should do it.”

“Should do what?”

“It’s a small job. I might need a hand.”

“You what? No. I’ll tell you now, no, no, N fucking O spells NO. Stuff the job up your arse!”

I stared at him hard :“Taylor?”

He nodded: “Only a small job.”

“Well in that case stuff it up Taylor’s arse – if you can find one on a snake.”

I was seething. “What part of NO don’t you understand? No, bollocks, no… Mick, it’s good to see you, but all that crap is over. Angie is great, life here is great and neither you nor Taylor are going to screw it up.”

My voice had got louder. Angie came out to see what was going on. Mick went into appeasement mode: "I get the message. Forget it. No problem."

I grudgingly tapped my glass on the table and lifted it to him: "To you malaka."

"What's malaka mean Steve?"

"Wanker."

* * *

Mick was more interested in the caiques than 'poncy yachts', so he naturally went out fishing every evening with Spiro, Sophie's brother. They'd leave about midnight, Greek time, and return at five in the morning. Catches were always 'light', according to Mick. A few barbounia, mullet and squid, but he loved it. They spoke the same language: fishing, hauling, gutting. Manoli saw the way Spiro and Mick worked together and adopted him as another son. Sophie would possessively fuss Mick when he came back from fishing. Her mum Maria watching them like a hawk. Most evenings we'd meet up for a beer before he went out:

"Remember I told you Greek women were 'out of bounds' Mick?"

"No I don't remember that mate."

"Bollocks you don't. Look, they are a good family. I wouldn't like to see anyone get hurt or lose their bits, O.K?"

"No problem. You worry too much."

"I didn't have a care in the world till you turned up."

It wasn't true, but I wanted him to think it was.

"Yia mas malaka." (Cheers wanker.)

"Yia mas poly megalo malaka." (Cheers very big wanker.)

* * *

About a week later Angie was bubbling with something:

"Stevie."

"Yea?"

"I've got some gossip. I can't tell you."

"Good. Don't tell me."

"It's about Sophie and Mick."

"Tell me."

"She says she likes him."

"Is that it?"

"She says he likes her too."

I groaned, staring heavenwards: "They haven't done anything, have they?"

"No, but she says she hopes they will soon."

I groaned again: "Do you women talk about everything?"

"Yes, so what? You're acting like an old pommie grump. It's romantic."

"I know Mick. He treats women casually. He shags them and leaves them. If he feels like it, he might kiss them goodbye. Sometimes he doesn't even take his boots off – that's not romantic."

"I thought he was your mate."

"He is, but Sophie is a good woman and Mick doesn't understand Greek ways."

"Am I a good woman Stevie?"

"Yes you are – very good."

I was having a powerful work out, explaining, shrugging, groaning, when Mick appeared from the harbour and Sophie appeared from the taverna with his beer. Now was my chance to sort it out. Angie and Sophie went inside: more gossip.

"O.K. Mick. Is there something you want to tell me?"

"Yea, the job's on."

"That's not what I meant. I was talking about Sophie and you. Anyway I told you no to the job."

"Alright I'll do it myself if you won't help."

"Good. I hope you drown and get shredded into fish bait."

He didn't give up: "It's a container, like the last one, only this time it's just cannabis. It's to establish a supply line, identify players then screw them. Plus Afghan farmers get an offer they can't refuse. Two birds, one stone – job done."

"Taylor cannot be trusted. Innocent people are dead because of him. I just hope the collateral damage was worthwhile and they know better than us. Who decides what's acceptable, Mick?"

"What the fuck are you talking about?"

"The U.K. container had pistols, drugs and explosives, right?"
"Right."
"The bombing campaign in London started after we set up the container. C'm on Mick, put your mind in gear. Did Taylor allow the termites to have explosives so he could roll up the whole organisation? Or was it just a cock-up? We were the ones who smuggled the stuff into the U.K., remember?"
"Fucking hell Steve, you're doing my head in. They've got intelligence we don't know about. It's their decision. They know more than we do."
"Do they? Is their intelligence intelligent or is it just spinning guesswork for promotion?"
"I don't know. We have to trust them."
I lost it: "Trust! Fucking trust! I wouldn't trust them with a dead goat's fanny."

* * *

My friendly stars in the canopy above the taverna had seen it all before. The madness of war was nothing new to them. Maybe that's what the politicians banked on. Humans only experienced death once. I rubbed my forehead in frustration.
Mick laid his cards out: "Taylor said if the Afghan economy is healthy, termites won't get back in control. McIntosh, Pearce, and all the other lives, limbs and treasure won't have been wasted. The Russians stop the northern route. The U.K. route is hammered, so that just leaves Greece and the Balkans. Pearce was shot in the Balkans."
"Fuck off Mick. That's not funny."
"Sorry, you're right. He was a good bloke. Taylor says this job will close down the last route. We can do it Steve."
"When is the job set for?"
"Saturday."
"What day is it now?"
"Wednesday. You really have gone native, haven't you?"
"So would you if you stayed a bit longer. It could be your life too with Sophie and the fishing."

I couldn't believe I'd just said that; must be getting soft. An ache spread across my chest as I scanned the harbour lights. I knew this place better than anywhere in the U.K. and I didn't want to lose it: "I wonder what the millionaires are doing now Mick, 'cos they can't be having a better life than us. I'm sorry Mick no, I won't do the job. I've too much to lose now. Let Taylor get another two 'disposables' for his shit jobs."

He didn't look disappointed, just came straight back with his ace: "O.K., I'll do it myself."

"Twat. You can't even dive."

"I'll learn."

"Pillock, by Saturday? Get real."

Sophie and Angie came over and lightened things up.

Mick chirped: "What have you two ladies been talking about?"

Sophie, casually: "Nothing much, just marriage and babies."

Angie couldn't resist it: "I want four and Sophie wants six."

My jaw dropped. I gargled into my beer. They dissolved into screaming giggles: "Your faces! I told you Sophie, they're all the same."

Angie stroked my shoulder. Thank God she didn't stroke my neck: "It wouldn't be such a bad idea, would it Stevie?"

I went into goldfish mode again. More shrieks of laughter.

Sophie stirred it: "Look, they're going to run for the ferry, Angie."

More shrieks. Manoli stuck his head out of the kitchen: "My children, please allow your hard working father some peace."

A big corner of my mind said marry Angie, live in paradise with four babies and teach them how to tie a bowline with one hand. How often had teasing and jokes sown seeds? I loved her, she loved me. If she was pregnant it would be great. Once it would have been a disaster… maybe she was.

* * *

Rare grey skies and a sloppy sea matched my mood. Mick and Spiro were chugging in after a night's lamp fishing. Eric and I were washing Eleftheria's deck. As they passed astern, Mick held up an octopus and signalled thumbs up or down for the job. I gave an indecisive flip flap.

Later I joined Eric gazing at his beloved charts and rambled on about friendships, duty, loyalty and making decisions. His comment made sense, as always: "Decide one way. If you feel happy it's right, if you feel sad it's wrong."

I tried it. Both premises left me feeling a deep sense of unease. I cursed the day I heard of Rule One: 'Don't leave your mates in the shite.'

That evening I found Mick helping Sophie in the kitchen: "Yep, I'll do it." He'd called my loyalty. I had no choice.

Mick was pleased: "Great. You'll get a gong for this."

"Yea, I expect I will. But from which country and will there be anything left to pin it on?"

Sophie asked: "What will you do Stephan, and what is a gong?"

Mick lied: "Nothing to worry about, just a charter job and a gong is slang for money."

We wandered outside. He already had it organized. He'd been too confident I'd say yes, so I decided to add a few conditions: "No one involved except us. The cover is we're taking a gang of American Cougars around the Cyclades, and if the job goes tits up and you don't make it, I get your new trainers."

"You worry too much."

* * *

Angie and Kim were not enthusiastic about the trip and insisted we'd been frightened off by talk of marriage and babies: we were doing a runner. Angie said she would defuse me good and proper before I left, so I couldn't have sex for a week. Shyly Sophie looked at Mick.

As we strolled down to the Poros ferry, Mick surprised me: "Why does anyone want to leave here?"

"I certainly don't. Why not cancel the job and blame me. You and Sophie are getting on well. Why risk it? We've both got stuff to lose now. Before we had fuck-all."

Mick repeated the reason: “Taylor says this job is the last piece in the jigsaw of ‘Operation Burnt Whistle’; a game changer; save the U.K. loads of blood and dosh.”

“Mick, some of those blokes are good but some are a waste of space: ’Burnt Whistle?’ Who the fuck thinks up operation names? I bet there’s a whole department buried in Whitehall dedicated to it. All with degrees from Magdalene and Fuck-Nasty Unis. All dribbling for their pensions and perks. Mick, I don’t trust Taylor and if I don’t make it, you’re going to have to slot the bastard yourself, O.K.?”

“O.K.”

Chapter 30

SAYING GOODBYE to Angie was difficult. We hadn't done it before. We'd always been within arm's reach since we met. This was different. The symbolism of me on the ferry and her on the quay had the poignancy of a long aching separation, even though it was only going to be for a week.

We picked up the charter yacht in Poros. As we headed out, I checked the dive gear. It was adequate for thirty feet off the beach, not thirty metres down in the dark oggin. The air tasted sour. If any bit failed, I'd be doing the Kalymnos sponge divers dance like Yourgos, only I wouldn't have an audience or music and the agonizing death would be real.

Mick put a laptop on the chart table, same as Taylor's, with all the magic giz'mos. He punched in a few numbers. We now had course, distance and time for an R.V. somewhere towards Cape Maleas.

Pitch black and approaching midnight, Mick gave me a shout: "On the bows in five, Roger?"

"Don't call me Roger."

And there it was, no nav lights, fresh from a giant container vessel, the invisible beacon calling: 'Come and get me suckers.' Tow line secured; two hours motoring to the site. Reluctantly I agreed with Mick it was good to be on a live op. again – challenges, team work, danger, trust, job satisfaction, thinking on your feet, brilliant.

A labyrinth of canyons and tunnels lay beneath the sea prairies, scoured from limestone by river systems that flowed from the snow-capped Parnonas mountain range east of Sparta. Melt water disappeared into giant sumps to reappear miles out in the Gulf, recognizable by the iridescent shimmering as fresh water hit the dense salt sea. During the Second World War, Nazi submarines used the phenomenon to deceive British destroyers' asdic, but it was a double edge sword. Miscalculating buoyancy sent U-boats plummeting, to implode in deep subterranean river mouths. Along the cliff-lined shore, caves gave protection from air attacks, but over decades, earthquakes had rearranged entrances, entombing Nazi gold and U-boats alike – evil buried.

I was now sitting on a forty-foot steel box again, ready to ride it to the sea bed. No back up; situation normal. How long would Mick wait if I didn't surface? What would he tell Angie? Wrong thoughts – cancel – but my mind still churned. Who else would do this, or could do it? Middle of the night, no recce, untested gear… It was a personality defect. Talking to Taylor was stressful. Here I was relaxed, confident, smiling. I loved it.

The echo sounder had shown a plateau 30 metres deep, surrounded by valleys disappearing off the scale. As we sank, phosphorescence showered around my arms and legs until we hit a layer of fresh water. I could feel the extra cold. It caused tilting and rapid acceleration until impacting the seabed, stirring sediment. Doors clear. I had no wish to look inside, for all I knew it could be booby trapped. My torch showed a deep abyss disappearing only a few metres away. Marine detritus, plankton and the stirred sediment welled upwards, vortexing in the fresh water current. The pig was now someone else's problem – job done. A state of cool suspension directed me – no faster than my bubbles – up the shot line, meditating on each marker tag.

No need for the torch, the phosphorescence signalled to Mick I'd surfaced. Like a rat up a drain pipe I was back on board . At that moment I didn't know or care who I'd done the job for, or why. I just didn't want to let my mate down. Now home to paradise and never again. Taylor could go fuck himself.

"Job done Mick, RTB." (Return to base.)

"O.K. Roger – O.K. Boss."

The lack of an adrenalin shaking overload didn't disappoint. All I wanted was Angie and the Island. Otto knew where he belonged and now so did I. I'd done my bit.

* * *

Nevada: "How's 78 and 79 doing Costa?"

"Job done Sir."

"Good. Trap baited. Let's see what we catch."
"Yes Sir. At least they do it cheaper than we can."

* * *

Mick was at the wheel, trying to coax another fraction of a knot, chuntering: "Couldn't pull the skin of a rice pudding. There's still a few days of charter left. How about heading down to Crete for a piss up?" It was the sort of thing we used to say and do. Now it just sounded immature:

"No, let's go home Mick and tell the girls we missed them and the Cougars got bored."

"Or, we could just tell them we missed them."

"You've changed. You're really a romantic old bastard aren't you? What's happened to the 'shag 'em and leave 'em, they're all the same'?"

"You didn't believe all that crap, did you Steve?"

"Na, of course not." I had, but wouldn't admit it."You and Sophie are getting on O.K. then?" Unintentionally I'd asked the right question.

"Yea, I've asked her to marry me."

I went into goldfish mode, then paused for the shock to wear off: "I hope she told you to piss off. You've only just met. Greeks are engaged for years."

"She said yes and we want you to be best man."

I pumped his hand: "Congratulations. What did Maria and Manoli say?"

"They're over the moon. We'll be living in the U.K., so they can visit when they like and stay during the winter. It'll work out. We'll get married in September and start making babies. She really does want six."

With Sophie and Mick it hadn't been stars and rockets. It had been a natural acceptance that they'd found each other. A simple recognition of their other half. Neither was surprised when they met. They just got on with it, like animals in the forest: 'You are perfect. I've no need to search anymore.'

Chapter 31

WE TOOK THE YACHT back to Poros then caught the Flying Dolphin to Hydra. Angie and Sophie were waiting on the quay to meet us.

"How did you know we'd be on this ferry?"

"Sophie has aunties everywhere. You can't get away from us that easily."

After giving Angie a long hard kiss, she eased away: "You'll have to go away more often if you come back to me like this."

Sophie teased Mick: "How was the sailing *agape mou*? (my love)."

Mick was on the case: "O.K., a couple of the Cougars wanted me as a summer stud." Sophie rattled off a Greek tirade as he stood there with a big smile absorbing all the scolding love.

Angie's kiss was still buzzing but I managed to turn back to the plot: "He's lying. They thought he was too ugly. They wanted me to go back to the States with them."

Angie frowned: "Would you want to?"

"No, I love you."

"Well don't play silly games then."

The four of us linked arms, singing as we strolled back. A golden time of happiness. Container forgotten. I'd pushed my luck for the last time. Indulgent smiles and greetings from tavernas and shops swelled our kefi.

When I'm old, when its pissing with rain, when I'm pissing the bed, when I'm pissing blood, a demented husk, senses fused… I'll remember.

Chapter 32

THE SUMMER of infinite contentment became finite, quantifiable: calendars, diaries, planners, once blank and irrelevant changed to imminent. I hated it. Several times at the wheel of Eleftheria I stared at the mast head and cursed the future. The repetitive beautiful life changed to a rush of 'things to do', lists, options, scenarios, all reluctantly discussed. Why couldn't this life go on forever? The sea and the sky could, so why couldn't we?

Friends were talking of where to spend the winter, who to spend it with, what was happening next season. Rocky relationships would hang on till October then they'd split.

Amongst it all Sophie and Mick's wedding plans sailed calmly on, guided by centuries old customs. Frantic U.K. crises of venues and menus were avoided. Food would be the delicious same, as for every wedding. The small, white Greek Orthodox church on the hill – one of 300 – nested in large, lime-washed boulders. Perfect from which to contemplate the zig-zag track to its door. It had always been perfect and it always would be.

By turning slowly, the mainland and channel coaxed the eyes to wander further to islands anchored in the vast harbour stretching to Crete.

As best man, I thought I'd give some advice: "Smile – shake hands with men, kiss the women – head down, mind in neutral – when it's over, get pissed." It wasn't needed. A look of total conviction on Mick's face and of glowing confidence on Sophie's, helped the preparations flow smoothly around them. From a standing start of being on his own with no family, he now had masses of relatives extruding from every island orifice. They were on cloud nine plus some. They deserved it. I was chuffed to bits. Then Angie went broody.

* * *

The procession was led by the Pappas and a scrawny dog. Sophie and Mick next, followed by family. Manoli had a 1930s style striped suit, which made him look even more like a gangster. Then came friends, babies, teenagers, grannies and a donkey. Then a bloke with a violin, who had to stop to play, so kept having to run to the front. All were blessed by the sun-wind swirling Sophie's dress; precocious maids catching it. All as it ever was.

In church, groups chatted, eyes flitted to friends, to potential lovers, to starring Icons. Widow's remembering, rustling disorder – Pappas steady as a rock – rings exchanged three times, until I felt I'd married Sophie myself. Flower crowns held over the couple, then the wine cup and finally the ceremonial walk. First steps together in sacred marriage.

Mick's Greek was better than mine due to Sophie's 'night classes', but I caught enough of the service to be deeply impressed. More villagers came in; no apologies for lateness. The Pappas held his status with smiles as he led us out into the divine blue. Jostling stragglers making their way up as some were going down. Rotation linked by Hellenic incense and thrown rice. Sophie and Mick, the church, ancient and modern Greece – all joined.

The hill top was like a disturbed ants nest, the couple carried like a leaf. In the crystal sunlit jostle, Sophie and Mick faced Maria and Manoli, all beaming, swelling with kefi. Manoli had shaved but his stubble seemed to be growing as his face alternated from smile to frown, suppressing tears of pride: "Ah Stephan and beautiful Angelina, you are next. Look at all the love here. Is it not good?"

"It is wonderfully good Manoli. They are made for each other."

Upon some unspoken sign Sophie and Mick – heads up – led the jostling gathering back down the track. Their witnessed union now part of Greek history.

I picked up a small stone and put it in my pocket. They would have children; Maria and Manoli would be grandparents; they would be proud to burst; the Church would hold their vows safely. And when the grandparents died, they would grieve, but mostly they would dance in thanks for lives well lived. Sophie and Mick knew all this. They knew they would grow old together; no fuss, loving arguments, dynamics of a good relationship. It is written:

What is better than love and laughter under the sun?

Nothing is better, and so it is.

* * *

Angie and I lingered by a boulder near the church. Middle distance; the wedding procession heading down. Far distance; a horizon of blue mountains, footed by blue sea, topped by blue sky. And central Sophie's swirling white wedding dress, all white on blue. Mountain herbs and church incense mingled in waves of spiritual light. They were over a hundred metres away. Mick looked over his shoulder and raised his hand. Angie started crying and hung on to me tight. She was supposed to be tough and carefree – what happened?

"Stevie I have to go back to Oz to see my folks, will you come with me? You'll love it in Perth. Mum and dad will love you. There's sea, boats, sun. You can even watch Chelsea on satellite. We're good together. I've never loved anyone like this before. What do you say?"

It was the lead to ask her to marry me. I'd been planning a long-term future for us on the island, while she'd been doing the same for us back in Oz. We should have talked. I stalled by thinking aloud: "Sophie and Mick are going back to the U.K.; Kim and Eric are wintering Eleftheria on the mainland; Maria and Manoli close the kitchen for the winter and he plays backgammon with his cronies until Easter; we could look after a holiday villa?"

She hadn't planned for anything but an exuberant 'Yes' and a big hug and my hesitation confused her: "Stevie, Australia is my home. My family live there – it's everything to me." She managed a hopeful smile.

This was it, crunch time, here goes: "Why can't we stay here and get married? It would be a great life for us."

She replied sharply: "Because this is not the real world. People come and go, fall in love, get drunk, move on. In five years or less we'd be alcoholic, expat wrinklies, having affairs, resenting each other."

She had just trashed my paradise. I reacted too fiercely: "Is that what it's been to you, just a summer of piss ups and getting a bloke to take back for breeding?"

Our passion flipped to a destructive force: "Well if you don't want to come – I've just been a holiday shag – I wouldn't have wasted my money on a plane ticket for you. It was meant as a surprise."

We both wanted to stop – we couldn't – the button had been pressed. I crashed on: "What about the money I wasted on you?"

She didn't look pretty anymore: "I earned that just being with you."

"Yea. I know. I was paying by the hour."

"Are you calling me a prostitute?"

(Just say No. Say anything. Don't say yes. Say beans on toast. Say West Bromwich Albion. Say cheese. Say sausages… but don't say yes.)

"Yes."

I didn't mean it and for the rest of my life I'd regret it. We were now screaming at each other, shocked by the sound of our own viciousness. I could hear myself. We paused; I calmed:

"I didn't say you were a prostitute."

"Yes you did."

"No I didn't."

"Yes you did."

"No I didn't."

"Yes you did."

We should have laughed and made up at that point – at the childishness – hugged and said sorry – we didn't. Our eyes searched for what had been there only minutes before. We'd never balanced our love with dynamic arguments. Life had been too interesting. Now we were paying for it. Suppressed annoyances turned to vitriol.

She went for it: "Without me you'd have been a sad, lonely wino. I felt sorry for you, not attracted. You didn't shag me – I shagged you. It was never a competition – it should have been about us – not one against the other. That's immature. Don't you get it? I'd have thought by now you'd have worked out your attitude to women. I hated the way you never made me feel equal. I could sail and swim as good as you. You never asked what books I liked. Remember when you read to me on the side-deck? That was one of the most erotic things I've ever experienced. You didn't care. You don't even know my surname, or my birthday – you don't know who I am, do you? I could have been anyone. Why did you choose me?"

(Say West Bromwich Albion. Say sausages. Say because you're a beautiful person. Say anything , but don't say…)

"Because there was no one else around."

I saw the punch coming. Her fist just catching under my chin: "You bastard. Never touch me again. You've just destroyed all the love I ever had for you. I would have done anything for you."

An elderly Greek couple walked past. Looks condemning our anger on the sacred day – making us pause. She was quietly crying: "We could have made it Stevie. I wanted a soul mate, not just a good time. I did love you."

We were now in the past tense and it hurt. Finished in just a few sentences – only words – all that trust and fun gone. I tried appealing. Last chance. I was begging her to stay. I began to realize what was happening.

"Please don't go Angie, please. We'll work it out."

"No. Come back with me to Oz. It'll be great."

Poisonous anger gone. If only we'd argued more in the summer and cleared the air, shouted at each other like Greeks. We should have argued like Sophie and Mick; sorted out stuff and made up. We hadn't because we were sure we would go on forever. Now we'd screwed it up. Greyness coming back. Last pleas… then a resigned slump.

"I'll miss you Stevie. Don't let me go. It'll break my heart."

I hated her calling me 'Stevie'. Now it was too late for stuff like that and for important conversations about needs and wants. We'd been surrounded by a love we thought was too strong to damage. We'd lived on a high for too long. We hadn't got it balanced and now we'd lost it. We walked down the hill together, separated by stupid words, just words. Once said, never to be unsaid; destroying so much. How did it happen? We acted normally at the wedding evening for Sophie and Mick's sake and later got into bed together, annoying each other with every movement and then worst of all, having bad sex:

"Have you finished yet?"....

* * *

In the morning everything became an unnatural rush. We were kind to each other; it helped: "I've got my ticket and passport. Take care of yourself. If you're ever in Oz come and see me. Say goodbye to everyone; I couldn't do it."

She was gabbling, trying to keep it together. At the quay, loads of friends suddenly turned up to see her off. We both smiled as the ferry pulled out. I was voluntarily saying goodbye to the woman I loved. Three feet, four. I could jump it easy. It wasn't too late. Everyone would cheer and wave, and we would have a new life in Oz. She read my thoughts. Her face tried to hold the smile as she shook her head. She'd gone.

It was half a mile to the lighthouse on the point. I ran the coastal track. The ferry was out in the channel. I could see her standing under the Greek flag. My shouts wouldn't be heard. I waved my T-shirt over my head like a loonie; her red jacket waved back. Distance hazed the ferry – then the horn sounded six – she'd asked the captain – and that was it. Angie had gone.

Loneliness kicked in immediately like grief. I looked around as if she was still with me and we'd said goodbye to someone else. Oldies spoke about companionship; now I saw why. The harbour signs said sun and fun. My head said desolation. I'd screwed it up again; chucked love away. (Some demonic voice twisted the knife: 'Better to have loved and lost than never to have loved at all.') No, bollocks! It was better to have loved and then go on loving forever. A joyless walk to the taverna didn't get any better when I saw Mick:

"You didn't let her go?"

"Yea."

"You stupid twat. What's the matter with you? You were made for each other. She loved you – God knows why. If you'd had any sense, you'd have married her. Didn't you get the message when you saw Sophie and me? Go catch her at the airport. Go to Oz."

"Fuck off Mick. Fuck off back to the U.K. This is my home."

But it wasn't – things had changed. We'd been a couple invited everywhere. Everyone wanted to be with us. It was odd now on my own. I got fed up with people asking if I missed her; was I going to see her again? Was she coming back next season?

Then a married expat started giving more than hints; flashing her tits as she leant over; goading her husband into some reaction; jolting a stale marriage. I'd become a prop for revenge used in silly games.

The final straw came when Manoli had a go: "Stephan, you are sad. Angie was beautiful for you. Many Greeks live in Australia. They come back every year. Why not?" For some reason he gave me a cigarette – he knew I didn't smoke – I took it and wandered up the track, puffing away. One of life's cruellest jokes is never to have experienced paradise, but what is far worse is to have experienced it and lost it.

My grieving was exacerbated by knowing it had been self-inflicted. Anger took over. I lashed out at Mick first: "I backed you up on those shit container jobs. I risked my neck for your bank balance. Next time get your snaky mate Taylor to dive into those black holes."

* * *

Unlike Angie, no one knew I was leaving; no one said goodbye. I jumped on the first ferry to the mainland and took just what I'd arrived with: jeans, T-shirt, some euros, and cynical greyness. I was moving on. I didn't want to move on. I wanted Angie, Eleftheria, dolphins, sun, sea, sex. I wanted the perfect life back.

* * *

I got off the ferry at Ermioni, no plan, just a 'Rent a Bike' sign opposite. The owner said he had a 'Style Bike', a 'Type Bike', or a '500 Kwacker' (Kawasaki) that was ready to go if I could be sure to bring it back in one piece . The 500 would do nicely. No crash-hat, I wheelied down the quay like the boy racer pests of summer. Now it was my turn. Riding fast used up my remaining brain cells. If the road straightened, Angie's memory came back. Was she telling her friends about sailing a beautiful schooner across a beautiful sea? Would she say how she made love with her soul mate as dolphins surfed alongside? Would she say she still loved him? Or would she say it was just a fling and he was a bastard?... or in years to come, if we met by chance, would we regret the loss and look at each other's aged faces and wonder?

On the secret sea shore
White like a pigeon
We thirsted at noon
But the water was brackish.

On the golden sand
We wrote her name
But the sea-breeze blew
And the writing vanished.

With what spirit, what heart,
What desire and passion
We lived our life: a mistake!
So we changed our life.

George Seferis – translated by E.Keely and P Sherrand.

Chapter 33

KEEPING THE BIKE wound up on bends, with random potholes and stones and racing cloud shadows along deserted mountain roads, distracted me until I hit the coast. Sea to the left, mountains to the right, I opened her up. It was what I needed. Signs for Kalamata showed . Tavernas seemed to know I was a miserable git, as if 'nil by mouth' was written on my forehead. I was left alone to mope. At one place I ordered two beers and two glasses. When asked 'where is your friend?' I replied: 'Australia.' Breaking the rules, I ate fast and drank fast. Circumnavigating the Peloponnese in three days was easy on a bike if you didn't have a beautiful woman to make love to. Nothing interested me. After a garrulous summer, the sudden change to being alone was unnerving. I needed a friend before I ran out of road.

* * *

Eleftheria was moored stern to the quay in Ermioni, not far from where I'd hired the bike. I skidded to a stop, grateful to see Eric's calm friendly face: "Come for coffee Steve. Tell me your adventures."

In the sanctuary of the saloon with the Crystal Buddha looking down from the bulkhead, benign and non-judgmental, my spirits lifted. Some people are the same whenever and wherever they are. Eric was like that, just chatting, letting me get centred: "Kim has gone to London for a couple of months. She comes back at Easter. Angie went back to Australia?"

"Yep. She's moved on and so have I."

He gave me a silence. It was that time of year when most tavernas closed. Usually one was left open in each village for locals playing backgammon and cards. Skies were sharp; visibility clear; sea Prussian blue; heat haze gone; evenings cool enough for jumpers and long trousers; yachts laid up; villas hibernating; a few expats relishing the empty shops; ferries on winter timetables; football on the TV; surf scouring summer beaches, pushing plastic bags higher.

"Steve, how can I help you?"

"Why do you think I need help?"

"Because of your face and your shoulders. Are you missing Angie?"

"I am, but that's not it. I need somewhere to think on my own. Not a boat; maybe a monastery."

Eric half turned to the Crystal Buddha, as if to discuss a patient's symptoms: "Show compassion to others and to yourself. You are safe. Live mindfully, breathe in peace, breathe out poison."

That was the advice and now the prescription was ready: "A friend of mine has a villa near Thermia which needs a caretaker for the winter, no pay, a few kilometres down the coast, doors unlocked – you can visit Eleftheria when you like. If you want to know the past, look at your present condition. If you want to know the future, look at your present actions. Look at the Buddha. He is Crystal Silex from Tibet. One day I will tell you how I found him. He is future peace."

I looked and realised my self-obsession was wrong. Eric and the Buddha were telling me to help others. It was another step, but I was still locked in to old feelings. Staying in an isolated empty villa staring at winter storms, gave my new life an appealing masochistically-themed tragedy. I could wallow in self pity thinking of what might have been and indulging the agony. Eric read my thoughts. He had no wish to cultivate immature self-indulgence with any form of sympathy. He seemed disappointed at how little I'd learnt in the summer: "Go to the village and turn right by the bakers on to a narrow track, then keep going as far as you can."

* * *

Serendipity played with my soul again. The phantom translator had worked at the bakers: 'Internal Bread' was on sale. It gave me the first smile for a week… and six cheese pies. The next sign could have been written by hippies: 'I Tembalakis Welcomes you to my Land – Requesting you Care for Me – With love, The Forest of Tembalakis.'

The trees opened up; a thin dog ran off . I switched off the bike and sat, letting the silence dominate, accentuated by a slow ticking as the engine cooled… like gran's clock when I was a kid. The cicadas started up again; a strong scent of pine spiced the air. It wasn't the dumb silence of a snowfall. It was a sea shell over the ear silence, reflecting the minds and gathering mush from ancient lives. It was the silence of a full auditorium as the orchestra paused. The atmosphere was as if something momentos had happened long ago and everything was stunned.

The villa was flat-roofed, single storey and would have been completely out of place if the builders hadn't used sea water in the concrete to cut costs. The resulting weathered corners and crumbling patches had softened its intrusion and given foot-hold to jasmine, hibiscus and bougainvillea. Glass doors led to a patio exquisitely positioned to stare southwards across a deserted sea.

Scattered ghosts of summer: towels, canvas chairs, coconut sun oil, (I opened it just to smell Angie's neck again); everything had been left as if they'd all gone for a swim. Next year they could continue without the interruption of unpacking: typical French. Unmade beds and a giant black centipede crawling away as I pulled the sheet back. Once I would have killed it; now it looked like company. Geckos and spiders scuttled for cover as I moved from room to room, feeling like a thief. Marble floors, minimal furniture, a few tins of tuna and half a jar of coffee in the kitchen, two chairs, two cups. Angie would have loved this. She'd have gone straight into nesting mode; cleaning, arranging – get a grip – everything I saw heightened my loneliness. What was she doing now? I sunk deeper into a gut aching nostalgia, until darkness and a bursting bladder encouraged me to move. I walked out on to the patio. The sensory deprivation of white noise wasn't there. It was a stage with an audience of ghosts, angels and devils – I bowed. This wasn't a midsummer night's dream of twinkling sugar. This was a tinnitus of hard crackling stars, intimidating, to be feared. I'd have to wait a long time for any sympathy from them. My mind empty, except for a bouncing ball, generating rapid eye movement, keeping an uneasy balance.

A sun-lounger gave the perfect space vehicle. A weightless feeling hypnotized. No one to care. A temporary cool breeze soughing in the pines, then a warmth not of the night, stargazing, flying , starbathing: Orison's Belt, Pleidies, my friendly Plough pointing to the Pole Star, ('You are not lost, I'm still here'). Then lights of a plane heading north. Perhaps Sophie and Mick U.K.-bound. I waved. A dog barked nearby and I'd landed back on Earth.

If I died now, who would know? Who would care if I did? Eric might come over at Christmas, but by then the packs of feral dogs would have chewed the marrow, leaving no clues. He would say it was karma and I was following my Path searching for Nirvana. No one would grieve or mourn. Mick would tell everyone I'd been shot by a jealous farmer, caught shagging his goats. Shuddering at death thoughts, then a feeling of release, drifting again, recriminations, senses redundant.

I blasted out: "Fuck everything!"

The impotent insult jarred my conscience, pulling murmurs from the audience. Who cares? I'd intruded into my own privacy. No religious zealots complained, so I stood and raved in a tirade of shouts, growls, rants. Daring the Gods, the Devils, the Stars, to punish me. My throat hurt, so I stopped. No sanctions, no neighbours, no complaints, no one to remember, just an irrelevant smudge in time.

Shooting stars! Beyond the Islands, beyond the Med, the Atlantic, beyond the Oceans of the Moon. They didn't care. Why should I? Or should I live, not in war and ego but in Buddhism? Kill to save your family or kill to save your country? Or become like Taylor the Snake and kill for other reasons: 'the greater good.' I should have called in the air strike and killed Ahmed, his family, goats and Taliban, kill 'em all. How many of our blokes suffered because I didn't? Mr Harman and the crew killed thousands, children, dogs, cats, grannies and he was a good kind man. They saw the same stars. They used them to navigate and decimate German cities.

I suddenly noticed there was no atmosphere between the Earth's surface and the stars, no barrier. It was clear – my Path was clear. The astral map above my head became three dimensional; some stars moved closer. I swear I saw a star stop breathing, disappear, die. Some moved further away creating a depth of field, so the Milky Way became a tubular writhing cloud closing to the horizon. My mate the Plough became three dimensional. Intimidating or inspiring, it was a choice. They could overwhelm with fear if you let them. Random thoughts formed logical sequences. I soared further into galaxies. Long dead ancient sunlight travelling towards us. Life existing in time-travel alone with origins extinct. We would be like that one day. Maybe we were now. Maybe we were just light travelling through space. We would be seen at different times of existence; some life forms seeing the light from Ancient Greece and some a future period. Which cosmic strata was someone on the Pole Star looking at? The light from Elefthevia would continue travelling for ever – never dying. The warm thought made me shudder with its cold implications. Perhaps everything had gone and there was only light left.

The dog barking grounded me back to the patio, to a grain of sand by my feet. Thousands of years ago a man stood here. Thousands of years in the future, same man, same spot. Evolution had made us the ultimate destructive creature. We'd lost our way. The only hope was an evolutionary branch, leading to become… dolphins? Man into dolphin. Obvious. That's it! Life is love. God is Good. I'd found the missing piece of the jigsaw. I shouted at the stars: "I've found the answer!" The equation of life: Man + Good = Dolphin = The Holy Grail = The Truth = A Lonely Twat going insane on a Greek headland, travelling at the speed of light.

Half a dozen steps from the patio led into the sea. I baptized my arms and face in its silky blackness. I wanted to immerse my whole body and sink peacefully. I also wanted to share my revelation.

(Angie's voice: 'I'm happy now. I hope you are too. Come back, Stevie.')

She was so close. I had to look around. A line of mauve expanded to the east.

(Mick's voice: 'If you make a joke about Dawn, I'll piss in your beer.')

I smiled. I was not alone. There was a team of spirit friends, hallucinations or what? Night had passed without sleep or tiring. Happy would be the wrong word. I was energized with a questing life force. Against the odds I was back on the Path.

It wasn't fully light, the slow thump of a distant caique, the same dog barking again quite close, a cock crowing waking his mates, new contrails descending to Athens airport. A brilliant new day… I knew the meaning of life.

I went back into the villa. Finding a pen, slowly I wrote: 'Life is love, Man is Dolphin.' I re-read it. Bollocks, it didn't make sense. I felt embarrassed – back in a sad world, nature didn't have emotions. The sea, the sky; they weren't sad – they weren't happy. They were the sea and sky.

The summer's social steam had long gone, along with arrogance and calculated false modesty: 'What a good bloke.' I wasn't looking in a metaphorical mirror but a real pit, where I happily chucked friendships, love and time: 'Shallow selfish bastard' didn't begin to cover it.

(Eric's voice: 'When you identify your problem, you have taken the first step. Walk on. You are never so full as when you are empty.')

(Mick's voice: 'Yea, full of shite. Get pissed. Get your head down. Get over it.)

Later, no wind, but surf-topped combers from a storm out deep, beyond Crete, capping a long swell… maybe tectonic plates shifting… a subsea canyon opening and closing to hide a poisonous container, forever.

Eleftheria had been a stage with a real audience, real actors, exchanging roles continuously. Now the theatre was empty, I could rehearse, rewrite any script that had gone wrong, like the bit with Angie, at the end. I was free of critics. A prat or a good bloke, no one cared. I could choose a word, any word and build a sentence, a paragraph, a chapter, a book… all flowing from one word. I could re-write history. I was ghost.

Chapter 34

INSIDE THE VILLA there were shelves of books. If no one hears a falling tree in a forest, does the sound exist? A book not opened; kept in darkness. Does the story exist? Or does it wait another year for a stranger to open it?

And what of music? Another shelf: CDs resting in silence: Borodin, Holst, Santana, Vaughn Williams, Johnny Halliday, Dvorjak, Eagles, Wagner, Carly Simon. The deal was, if the dusty player worked, I'd dance like a loonie. Randomly I stuck one in, turned the volume full throttle, went outside and waited, arms outstretched, feet together. Santana blasted loud. I leapt in a surge of kefi, copying Manoli, Zorba, Yourgos, Eleni, making it my own.

* * *

Nevada:

"79 dancing like a redneck Sir."

"Log it Costa, and get psydoc to have a look. I want a second opinion on this guy's mental state."

"Yes, sir."

* * *

I was not alone. The power of the music flowed around, stimulating, energizing. The last stars disappeared as our own began to dry the patio of night dew. Santana's elongated chords quietened my dance to slow power, like Manoli's constrained movements – sweating muscles screaming for release – wanting to fly – an audience of phantoms – bollock-naked Vitruvian Man. Leonardo da Vinci's image: everyman, reduced to one.

The music stopped… time for coffee and cheese pies.

* * *

Omens easily assumed the portentous weight of truth. The new domain told secrets as I explored from room to room: summer clothes, rackets, tennis balls, dozens of unfinished charcoal sketches of the same old woman, full of character, smiling eyes – the look of a grandmother to her artistic granddaughter.

The back door – or rather the door which faced inland – looked at olive groves, showing silver under-leaves in the wind. Not another building in sight, so I could be a slob, evil or kind, cruel or generous, no one would know. No one would criticize, except my self-respect. I needn't clean my teeth or eat. I could just lie down and rot if I wanted to. My brain had honeycombed into empty cells waiting for wisdom's pollen. It was a chance to know myself; selfishness replaced by giving to myself. My devils were leaving. Would my angels stay?

Loneliness was feeding my melancholia until after a few days of little food and introspective bullshit, I was rescued by a hairy, grey-faced bitch: the origins of the nightly barking. She stood ten metres away, sussing me out, occasionally looking round, making sure her escape route was clear, showing me her emaciated flanks and loose empty teats. My trainers were just in front of her. She picked one up and ran off – "Bitch!" One trainer was no good to man or beast so I threw the other at her. It missed and disappeared in the scrub. I couldn't find it, so now I was a barefoot miserable git.

Next day, same time, she reappeared with the trainer she'd stolen and put it down where she'd got it from. Why had she taken it away? Why had she brought it back? I still only had one trainer! A life lesson, a metaphor, a joke, a koan – I don't know. It didn't wind me up; it made me smile. I went into the kitchen, opened a tin of tuna, put it in a bowl on the patio and sat and waited. Her hunger overcame her fear. If I moved suddenly, she'd run off. But after a few days of routine feeding, it broke down suspicions.

Slowly the sad, exhausted look changed to a healthy leanness. Then one day she waited beside her water bowl as I refilled it; supped and haunched down to rest. But what really opened my heart was the next day. She fell asleep beside me as I dozed on the sun-lounger. From then on our relationship escalated into exploring beaches and jogging together along the miles of pine-shaded tracks. I'd saved her life; she'd saved my heart. Not a bad deal for either of us. She listened to my theories of how to end war… but as soon as I stopped, her chin would lower to the ground and her eyes would close. She preferred stories about dolphins and adventures at sea. It must have been the change of my voice, from strident logic to rounded, kindly murmurings. She told me: 'The thing you hate in others is the thing you hate in yourself.' She'd told me without saying a word – how did she do that? More thoughts streamed in and out. All assessed, considered or given quiet approval by her face, body language and occasional throaty growls. All based on my tone of presentation.

One evening there was an earth tremor. She came to me for safety and my heart opened more. She had turned loneliness and melancholy into peaceful solitude. I'd been calling her vague names like: 'good girl', 'you', 'hairy' – until 'Molly' got a rapid tail wag.

As the evenings grew darker and the year aged, she slept on my bed. I sang to her. She didn't like violence so I told her nice stories of a beautiful schooner called Eleftheria and of the beautiful people who sailed on her. And she told me of her puppies: 'You listen to me; I'll listen to you.'

Nearing Christmas, the sea and sky had days of lumpen iron grey. It seemed a suitable time to catch up with Eric. Deceitful bribery of food was the only way to get Molly distracted while I guiltily pushed the bike over the hill. She'd be fine for a few hours.

I'd hired the bike on a long term basis. It was useful for shopping every couple of weeks and a joy to ride; no helmet, no traffic, fresh winter sun. Before I reached Eleftheria, I stopped at the village *periptero* (kiosk) for choc bars: Eric's weakness. Semi-naked females on magazine covers reminded me of summer and Angie – I missed her. Headlines of politicians' scandals, footballers' wages and the same photo on four front pages: two men running towards the camera, supporting each other, one head up, a bloodied silent scream. The background was an Athens street covered in rubble. No not again, no no NO! – my mind saw Leila and London – physical pain was nothing compared to mental anguish. Translation was easy: 'Terrorist Bomb. Many Dead. We will not rest until this atrocity is avenged, said Prime Minister.'

A deep growl came from my guts. The kiosk guy looked startled. I spat out the venom: "Taylor you bastard. I'm going to slot you fucker for this." I was past anger. Now it was murderous revenge.

* * *

Eric was varnishing the forward hatch: "Bonjour Steve. You look like murder. Where are your shoes?"

No pleasantries: "We need to talk."

In the saloon he offered coffee: "No, just listen. There is a serious problem I have to deal with. I could ignore it and no one would know."

"You would know. Who would suffer?"

"Maybe a great many. If someone was going to kill innocent people, would you kill him first?"

"I would try other ways but if I had to, yes I would."

"Even though you are a Buddhist?"

"Yes I'm a Buddhist, but that does not stop me making difficult decisions."

A soft harbour popple slapped the hull. I looked from Eric to the Crystal Buddha bolted to the bulkhead.

Eric spoke first: "Let me tell you about my wife. She drowned off Spetse and I blame myself. If we had never met, she would be alive now, but we would not have had the happiness together, so was it good we met or not? We can only follow our Path, Steve. We must understand that every action has a reaction. That is not always in our control: karma. The Path is 'Now'. This point is on your Path and my Path. All is 'Now'. You know the butterfly in the Amazon and the hurricane? The skill is knowing what can be changed to create good and avoid suffering. Sometimes the butterfly causes the hurricane, sometimes it is in our power to stop it, sometimes we decide not to stop it, sometimes it is for the best not to stop it, sometimes we make a mistake and the hurricane kills people. We cannot always do good; we can only try to do good. That is enough to be a Bodhisattva (An enlightened being helping others). Our Greek friends say: 'We will do it avrio' (tomorrow). Firstly, it often works because there is time to think – for the water to clear – for the butterfly to settle. Secondly, it gives 'good' a chance. Thirdly, other problems become more important. Our northern latitude efficiency of doing things immediately, can lead to karmic suffering. If tomorrow never comes, the problem never comes. But if your problem is possible to solve, you must act."

Eric's ideas ordered my decision process: I had to destroy the Greek container – evil was evil. I wouldn't wait for good to come along.

(Granddad's song: 'If I can help somebody as I move along then my living has not been in vain.')

"Can I see your Argolic Gulf chart?"

"Of course, mon brave."

"Is your dive bottle full?"

"Yes, for sure."

"Can you take me there tonight?" I pointed to a position off the Eastern Peloponnese coast, down towards Cape Maleas.

"*Oui*, I can."

"Thank you. I owe you a lot."

"You owe me nothing."

The dice were rolling. I had only thought of the job, not the people who would be endangered. His unconditional help humbled my aggression – Operation Calm and Decisive was underway: not a bad name. It was better than Operation Burnt Whistle, Flapping Frog , Constipated Hedgehog, Demented Dung Beetle, Baffled Bewildered and Buggered or Mick's favourite: Operation Planet Fuck-up, as planned by General Fuck-up and his side-kick Major Fuck-up.

Chapter 35

I RODE THE BIKE fast back to the villa. Molly's wagging tail was waiting. I dished her grub out and sang her favourite song: "Molly, Molly, give me your answer do. I'm so jolly just to be loving you. Golly Molly I'm so jolly." But I wasn't jolly or loving. I was leaving her. She trusted me. I'd made her reliant on me and now I was betraying her like the other women I'd known. Should I desert her and let her search for me or knock her on the head for a quick end, with no suffering? Think, slow down, get a grip you callous bastard. Unplanned action was no good. Molly was still eating.

(Mick's voice: 'You're in the shite again. Write a list.')

"Fuck off Mick. I'm working on it…"

1. Feed Molly. Done – Tick.
2. Feed myself. I had the same as Molly – Tick.
3. Close all doors in villa. Kick out lower panel of back door for Molly's access. – Tick.
4. Give English lady, married to Greek garage guy, a wodge of euros to come out regularly and feed Molly.
5. Leave bike at garage.
6. Go to Eleftheria. Check air in dive bottle.
7. What the fuck is seven? Obvious twat – destroy Greek container.
8. Go back and destroy UK container.
9. The last and best one – kill Taylor. I'd enjoy that. What could possibly go wrong? Seeing it written down made it do-able. It also gave a glow of satisfaction, like finishing school homework:

('Well done Steven, you've improved since last term. It has a beginning, a middle and an end. B+ , your highest grade this term.

I especially liked the ending, where you rip Taylor's fucking head off and stuff it up his arse.')

"Thank you Sir, so did I."

* * *

I'd been kneeling on the patio writing the list, facing the fading light. Molly came over. We often sat together looking at the same thing, sharing the view without talking. Since she arrived I'd been anthropomorphizing her every action and giving her the love I should have given another human being. We shared the last of the day, not having to look at each other to know we were appreciating the same things. She'd been a focus for my caring; stopping my heart drying up: "Molly, I'm sorry."

Life was hard to work out. One minute I was safe and trusted by a loving creature, the next I was off on some weird self-generated mission. Then the 'what ifs?'started. What if the Athens bomb had nothing to do with Taylor's container? What if I'd called in the airstrike in Afghan? Would it have saved lives? And what if the container was just full of cuddly teddy bears?

(Mick's voice: 'Zip it mate, or I'll piss on your chips. Stop flapping.')

"Bollocks. I told you to fuck off Mick."

Molly looked up at my hands waving about, so I stroked her chin: "Molly, do you think they'd let innocent people be killed?"

(Mick's voice again: 'You know the bastards would. You know they have. They'd sell us down the river for promotion if they thought they could get away with it, and they can.')

(Mr Harman's voice: 'They told the Nazis our route, so fake gen would be believed.')

(Mick's voice: 'Seriously mate, get it right, do it and get the hell out of there.')

"O.K., thanks Mick. Fuck off now or I'll stuff an onion up your arse and call it a casserole – I'm working on a plan."

(Mick: 'I hope it's better than your other plans. They were all cock-ups from start to finish.')

"Thanks mate."

Molly lifted her nose, smelling the breeze, looking at me to see if I'd finished prattling on. I ribbled her ears; she liked that. Her eyes went soft: "I'm going to miss you darling." I loved her. Then again I'd loved Angie and Greece and Eleftheria and Dolphins. It hurt. When my nightmares came she'd make growly murmurs and they'd go. I'd do the same for her. That way we both got a good night's kip. If I ever I saw the M.O. again, I'd suggest prescribing cats and dogs instead of sleeping pills, as part of his PTSD cure. I told Molly I didn't know when I'd get back. I was explaining more to her than to the other women I'd left. Why was I doing it? I wanted to stay, listen to Santana, dance like a pillock, write, meditate, swim, play air guitar, jog with Molly… but I couldn't. I had to go and do evil stuff… Who said I had to?

The odds were not good. There was an alphabet soup of killers trying to put me away: FSB, CIA, SVR, SIS, NSA, IRA, ISIS, ISNCA, RAC, AA, RNLI, and now the provisional wing of the RSPCA. I had to get grounded.

(Mr Harman's voice : 'One huge comfort we had was a safe airfield to come back to. I also found that if I helped someone else, I was calm. On my own I went to pieces. Another thing, always tell those left behind you love them.')

"Thank you Mr Harman."

I didn't have a safe base. I would be diving on my own and the only one I could say I loved was a grey, hairy-faced bitch. Thank God for Eleftheria and Eric. They were indestructible.

I looked into Molly's face: "I love you Molly."

More food distracted her as I pushed the bike silently away. If she'd run after me and I'd seen those eyes, I'd have stayed and let the world fester in its own putrid excrement. Brits love animals more than people; Greeks love people more than animals. Garage lady would care for Molly.

Chapter 36

"LET'S GO, STEVE."
We hauled out quietly, letting the jib catch the offshore night wind. I felt something tacky on my hand: "What about the wet varnish on the hatch Eric?"

"I think this job is more important than varnish, Steve."

He hadn't asked why we were going. The fact I'd asked him was enough. He trusted me. I shuddered with the responsibility. His only motive was to help.

"Remember when you first came aboard Eleftheria eight months ago?" Eight months, it must be eight years. "Remember when we raced the Jeaneau, the American navy man Roy? I have the flag ." I ached with the memory, went below and found it.

"If we go to war, we fly the right flag Steve."

Thirty foot of US Navy battle pennant caught once and cracked free. Now everything was different. Eleftheria moved like a horse sent to war. Not the graceful summer beauty, but tough and functional. I patted the coach roof. We were standing into danger and she knew it. An immense pride in her and Eric made me straighten up.

North wind, light, bitter cold, from the snow fields of eastern Europe; close hauled, a long low swell, more like the Atlantic. She bravely butted into the increasing chop. Eric and Eleftheria were backing me up. I had to do my bit, switch on, operational mode: Distance divided by Speed = Time. Therefore, twelve nautical miles at six knots equals two hours. Action on site: check container's contents, could be empty – leave alone. Could be full of cuddly teddy bears for the Al Qaeda Christmas party – leave alone. Could be full of explosives, drugs and weapons, action – blow it into little pieces.

Way before time, I put on the wet suit, dive knife, weight belt, coupled the demand valve, borrowed Eric's watch, checked positions on the GPS and sat in the cockpit with the bottle balanced between my knees, tasting the stale air, and fiddling with straps… again and again. The GPS would take us close enough for the echo sounder to pick out the forty-foot steel box on the sea bed. Eric didn't question why I asked him to switch off the nav lights. Sordid, clandestine vandalism was not part of his experience. The 30-metre depth contour disappeared off the scale in a subterranean gorge from where a major river discharged. Nothing looked or felt right. If I'd seen a way to call it off, I would have done. Eric was coaxing Eleftheria. She was sensing danger – shying. I was nervous, no plan B, no dive buddy, no reserve, no decompression chamber… at least no one was shooting at us.

Why wasn't I with Angie on a beach in Oz?

The echo sounder started to look like the heart monitor of a guy with his dick stuck in a toaster. I was running out of aphorisms: 'If not me, who? If not now, when? If I don't fuck up, who will?' The feeling of dread grew: ('C'mon get a grip – just do it.')

Best scenario: container empty, surface, romp home as dawn breaks to a good fry up, Molly and Santana, job done… yea right – no chance.

(An evil voice I didn't recognize: 'Leave it Steve. Make an excuse. Let the bombs go off. Hundreds get killed on the roads every day – who cares?')

Eric looked over from the wheel : *"Ça va?"*

"Oui ça va."

But I wasn't a bit 'ca va'. Nothing was 'ca va'. I was heading for big problems. My intuition, my hunch said so: always follow your hunch. The trouble was I didn't know how to stop. Good voices were needed. Where were they? I didn't want the responsibility for Eric and Eleftheria. He had trusted me when he went to Athens during the summer. I didn't let him down. Now I was putting them in harm's way. Why didn't he say this feels wrong. Let's go home?

"There it is!"

Eric pointed to the echo-sounder. It stood out like a spot on grannie's bum. Why did he have to find it? Couldn't it have been lost forever in the U-boat graveyard? My breathing rate was too high. I was flapping like a dover sole. Skywards my mate the Plough reassured… then weirdly something changed. I was going to do it even though my gut and head said no. What a brave little bastard I was.

(Mick's voice: 'Yea, yea, stop pissing about like an old woman and get on with it.')

Down the transom boarding ladder, off to work, shot line down… Go! Quietness, bubbles clearing from the torch beam, a layer of cold accelerating the descent – concentrate, centre, count (CCC) – a layer of warm, then cold again, fish nervous, tails twitching warning of predators – a bad sign.

There it was. The big, ugly steel box. Doors opened easily. C'mon teddy bears where are you? I hung for a few seconds, checking depth, air and time. I swung the torch inside. Bollocks, it was the same plastic tubs. All 'same-same'. Bastards. I opened the nearest one. A moray eel disturbed, jolted me. Other nasty little hands had been there before. Self-contained bombs, detonators, timers: 'take-aways' ready for delivery, evil instructions in four languages. I set a timer for a thirty-minute delay; changed it to twenty, then back to thirty again; double check, minutes not seconds, air O.K., time O.K., sweep torch around, no nets, back to shot line. I gave a long out breath and followed the bubbles up, same speed. This was danger time. Imagination focusing on the explosion beneath me. I'd be gutted like a fish.

The vast canyon off the end of the container sent fresh water wellings from the snow melt off Parnonas. I hung on the shot line testing my mad desire to rush to the surface and stared at the plankton rising. A perfect project, if I lived, wandering the Peloponnese using dye and a drone to chart their outfalls.

I rose another ten metres and stopped, calmed. I'd been wrong; the fish had been wrong; Eleftheria had been wrong. The job was a piece of piss. I'd overcome irrational fear and done it. I was chuffed to bits. I was a hero.

Nevada:

"Yacht stationary over container Sir."

"Notify local assets Costa…"

"Yes Sir."

There were five minutes to go. Don't screw it up now. More mountaineers are killed coming down a mountain than going up. With divers it's the reverse. The torch picked out Eleftheria's beautiful copper sheathed hull. Ten metre depth tag – meditative visualization. I'd surface into July sunshine: Angie, Kim, Eric, Sophie, Mick, all in the cockpit waving, calling; Angie blowing kisses; Mick holding up a beer, all smiles and warmth: 'C'mon Dickhead, salad's hot, beers cold.' Faces so clear, friends, good people, Molly's face – how did she get there?

Reality returned, time up, keep it slow, follow the bubbles, Eric would see the torch. The boarding ladder drifted into my grasp. I passed up the bottle and fins.

"Eric. Let's go. Fast. *Vite. Très vite*."

"*D'accord mon brave.*"

He pushed the throttle to three quarters. I gave it an extra shove to full. Eleftheria leapt. She'd done her job. "Good girl." – I patted her.

All the worries, premonitions, hunches were groundless. A surge of elation. What a brave bastard I was – fears beaten.

"Explosion in two minutes Eric."

Maybe I should have told him before. It came like rolling thunder. A luminous column burst the surface; a crater in the sea, a mound of white froth domed. Pressure waves banged our ears.

"*Merde* Steve. It is war!"

"No, we're trying to stop one. Now we go back to see if everything is destroyed."

(A strong voice. It sounded like my dad: 'Never go back. Don't push your luck. It's all used up. Hubris, arrogance is fatal. Leave it son. Come home.')

I didn't listen. I never listened to dad.

We turned back on the reciprocal course and met the tsunami bows on. Dead fish everywhere in the churned up soup. Eleftheria was shying again. She wanted to leave – US pennant cracking – I was over-confident. I'd conquered my fears. Premonitions were wrong; intuitions wrong. I'd won!

Air bottle on again, just to make sure. Engine off, all sails hoisted, shot line to hang on to, we quartered the area, breeze light. Apart from feeling like bait on the end of a 20-metre line, it was very relaxing being towed along, torch beam showing clouds of debris, rapidly clearing by the fresh water upsurge; canyons giving feelings of vertigo, knocking back my cockiness.

(Mick's voice: 'Well done Dickhead, got a job right for once.')

"Piss off Mick. I'm busy."

My concentration had slackened for seconds. It was long enough for the faint clicking of a prop to go unnoticed. It wasn't Eleftheria. The volume increased rapidly to whining high intensity.

"Shit. Who the fuck's that?"

The line went slack, then multiple tugs from Eric. I began to fin quickly up. My torch picked out Eleftheria's hull – shouting to myself: "Contact, contact." – Violent imagery; red flaming shrapnel lacerated the water, turning green, drifting down, staccato of tracers, two grenade thumps – whining, jetting prop louder, torch off – more red fireworks.

Eleftheria began to sink.

Hand over hand I frantically raged along the line – 'Pull the raft cords, keep her afloat.' This was it, it would work. I shouted into the water: "Pull the cords Eric." The bows were under, thirty degrees, bubbles streaming from multiple wounds, mutilated planks bleeding, groaning in pain, war horse battle wounds.

Sinking faster – "Pull the life rafts Eric!" – Sails filled by water, keeping her on an even keel. Shot line tightened, dragging me as she sailed past. My torch picked out Eric, rope around his waist, tying bowline, gripping the wheel, one arm trailing useless in a macabre cloud of blood, waving… steering Eleftheria into the ebony abyss. The fully-rigged schooner still beautiful, still sailing. US Navy battle pennant flying straight. Eric was with her, together on another voyage, going deep.

I was hanging on trying to get closer. I spat out the demand valve and shouted into the sea: "Let go Eric, you mad French bastard. Pull the cord. Let go!"

He didn't let go. The crushing pressure increased. He knew their wounds were too great. They sailed on, 30 degrees trajectory, down 20 metres… 30; past the cliff, past the container's evil debris into eternity, accelerating down to 40 metres… 50. I let go, lacerating my hands. Anger and pride, witness to reincarnation, transom name fading: 'ELEFTHERIA.'

I put my hands together in prayer; body and mind racked: "*Kalo tuxidi* (travel well) Eleftheria and you Eric, be with friends. Going to miss you both – take care. You were true 'Bravehearts'. Bless you."

The whining prop got louder again. Fuck they were coming back, looking to chop up anyone surfacing. I held my breath, bubbles stopped, torch off, finning slowly, hanging in the blackness. Mind pixillating options. Kill the murderous scum. Prop spiralling phosphorescence cruised overhead, no identity. Suddenly full pitch, jetting away, fading, clicking… gone… Eleftheria gone. Eric gone. Killers gone.

I was alone, three miles from land, 30 metres deep, at night, in winter. Couldn't go up, couldn't go down, air gauge zero. A last hard pull on the empty bottle… I waited.

Instinct said race to the surface… and die in agony from bends: a sponge diver's death without music or audience. Never give up: think, think, think. A mate of mine once used air from his buoyancy cartridge to give a dozen life saving breaths – Action – I cracked it open. This was not a good time to experiment. There might just be enough if the penetrating cold slowed my metabolism without sending me into terminal decline. Three shallow breaths, hold… slow exhale, hold, calm meditation, soft counting, soft images, another three, hold… slow exhale, count. Mind and body in a very dangerous place where everything was peace and death would be warm.

The reason to live outweighed the reason to die. I was witness. If I let go, no one would know. There would be no one to exact revenge. My life was in the balance. It was my choice – minutes passed. I survived because I sent my mind on a journey and when it came back my body was still there… just.

I floated up. Part of me regretted surfacing. Why not wander down to Eleftheria's cabin for a coffee? Underwater was gentle.

The surface was harsh, murderous. I gasped fresh air, waves jostled. My friendly Plough gave position. I now had north, so the mountain range was west. I knew where I was and where I had to go. The problem was I was deeply knackered and deeply lonely; only rage kept me afloat and that would soon drain my strength.

Death nudged. In the end, the thing that saved me was luck, simple million to one luck. Not an ounce of credit to me or my mind. My arm bumped into a dead fish killed by the blast. Instinct, bite the side, fresh fluids and confidence pumped in – think, think, think – deep breaths – action: ditch weight belt, bottle, knife, torch – keep fins, mask, snorkel. Another bite, more energy, more protein, more breathing.

Not dead yet. Land was still miles away. The nearest people would kill me if they came back. A voice would be seriously appreciated, but not the Black Witch: ('That's it Steven, just let go; join your friends. You planted that bomb; now it's your turn to die.')

I shouted at the night sky: "I did not plant that bomb."

Her malicious voice helped the drive for revenge. I bit into the fish again, more energy, more revenge.

(My own head voice: 'C'mon, think, it's just another job. Swim westwards. You've done it before, you can do it again.')

Side stroke conserved energy; the Plough on my right shoulder; a couple of village lights in the mountains. Distance – three nautical miles, speed one knot, rest every 20 minutes, estimate 4 hours. It was do-able. Morale needed a boost, body needed a rhythm, so I sang in my head: 'Rolling down to Rio with my best girl by my side; Rolling down to Rio all the stars to guide; Rolling down to Rio with Angie by my side… we'll swim all the way.' I wasn't hallucinating but I could feel it coming, mind drifting pleasantly from body.

A distant big splash woke me up. Imagination creates emotions – this was fear. Sharks are rare in the Med, but they do exist, following ships through the Suez Canal. Dead fish always attract predators, especially at night. Now I was part of the food chain, swimming through 'rubby dubby' from the explosion. It hadn't taken them long to find me: four large killers, circling, leaving comet trails of phosphorescence. One detached from the pack and rocketed in to attack; terrifyingly only bumping and pulling away. Spinning defensively only heightened my fear. I shouted to Mick: "Look wanker I'm going to get eaten alive here. Got any ideas?"

(Good old Mick came through loud and clear: 'Dickhead, go to plan B.')

"Mick, I haven't got a plan B."

(Well sorry mate, you're in the shite again.')

"Brilliant! Fucking brilliant! Is that the best you can do?"

Fuck, here they come, two killers broke from the circling pack. I braced, shoving fists out in front. I hope I choked them… both creatures leapt skywards, over my head trailing luminous fins into the stars – DOLPHINS! – eyes staring, faces smiling, chittering.

I whooped for joy – "You beautiful, beautiful darlings, I love you."

I grabbed at them with relief. They were friends, reincarnated friends. Their appearance spiritualized the whole situation. All would be well: nudging, swimming alongside, relaxing my body and mind, energy generated – fear turned to energy.

Dolphins move faster than science says they should. Their muscle mass doesn't explain the high speeds they attain. I was carried along by their close escort, relaxing my fight for survival to a gliding flow, more in the sea than battling to stay on the surface. I was at home, not in a monster infested nightmare. There was no rush to make landfall. Evolution had jumped. I was Dolphin, flying in a fluid vortex, fins together, impelled without pain, streamlined… distance, time, irrelevant… islands, seas, oceans, all accessible. I was among friends. I'd stay and live with them, forever.

* * *

Suddenly the lift stopped – they had gone; their lessons forgotten; a beach; a cliff 100 metres away. Floundering in the water, exhaustion and empty muscles returned, so close, don't die now. I fought for the shore. My feet found sand. Like a mother turtle I inched my way up the beach on my belly. A rocky outcrop gave cover and release from the responsibility to stay alive. A gratitude to my dolphin friends, then nothing but uncaring sleep. Except for the obituary.

* * *

Obituary. *The Daily Goat Breeder*: Corporal Steven Bracken, known to his friends as Dickhead, lost somewhere in the Aegean Sea while trying to save the world from bombs, bullets and bastards (BBB). Leaves a huge bar bill at the Nelson's Armpit, but remembered for his generosity to 'working ladies'.

Achieved distinction in Afghanistan as the only member of his battalion to get his end away while under fire. The goat survived but was later treated for PTSD and STD. (Sexually transmitted disease.)

No flowers, donations only to Busty Bertha, Bermondsey Goat Farm.

Author of best seller: *How to Fight, Fuck and make Money with Goats, When you're Fed-up Fucked-up and Far From Home.*

Signed editions available in Norfolk, at Shag Nasty and Ball Breakers Publishers Ltd. Has been translated into five languages – fortunately none of them English – by a dyslexic feminist, resulting in a surge in value as a collector's item. Paperback versions available with absorbent index.

Nominated for RSPCA Book of the Year, Pornographic/Farming category.

Chapter 38

"**DAD!** Is it a big fish? Is it dead?" From comatose exhaustion voice filtered in: "Are you alright?"

A young man and his small son were staring down at me. I whispered: "Have you water?"

He handed me a plastic bottle from his beach bag. I took a swig and splashed my salt encrusted eyes.

"Thank you, are you on holiday?"

"No, we live here now. My son speaks Greek better than I do."

I halted any more chat by giving him my face mask and snorkel. As they wandered off, I heard dad explaining the gear to his son. Angie and I would have had a son. I'd have taught him to dive properly and tie a bowline with one hand.

The beach was at least a mile long. I could just make out roofs scattered behind clumps of scrubby broom. After burying the wet suit, I strolled the shore line getting my head into gear. T-shirt and shorts drying salt-stained in the fresh morning air. The usual plastic litter despoiled the sand, so within 100 metres I had an unmatched pair of flip-flops, a belt and a towel.

Achingly, I stared out to sea, willing Eleftheria to cruise in and pick me up – then back home to Molly. Pointless, but I had to search. If I reported the loss, they'd know I was alive. Eric's murder would have to go unrecorded for now.

Close by, a small taverna, surprisingly open this time of year. Only two tables under a vine covered pergola. An elderly gentleman sipping Greek coffee.

"*Kali mera.*"

"*Kali mera. Ti kanis.*"

"*Kala efharisto.*"

I could see the service was going to be slow even by Greek standards. Who cared? I was alive in a ravishing landscape: a refugee, a survivor.

"Are you German, Italian?"
"No English."
"Ah, my son has peed on English sheeps."
"Your English is good; better than my Greek. Did you hear thunder last night, out at sea… or fireworks?"
"No, I sleep well these days. I heard nothing, only my wife snoring."
A small round elderly woman came out with a tray of bread, a few olives, a small coffee and a glass of water. It's usual to receive un-ordered food in tavernas so I mentally shrugged and downed the lot.
"You are hungry?"
"Very. What are you cooking today?"
"My wife will bring you soup."
I was looking forward to goat and chips with a Greek salad: "Have you a menu?"
"No menu."
It didn't matter. Any food would do. Above my head the last vine leaves made the grapes stand out. I stood and cupped a bunch: "They're plastic!"
"Yes, its winter. You could not tell until you touched them. They gave you pleasure?"
His wife bought out soup and more stale bread. I ate fast and stood to leave: "Can I pay now?"
He looked disappointed: "No you cannot pay."
I thought back to when I first met Manoli at his taverna on Hydra. He had been closed so I couldn't pay. I smiled indulgently: "It's because you are closed, isn't it?"
"No, it is because this is not a tavern. This is my home!"
His hard brown face creased to a gentle smile. I had been caught again by the unconditional generosity of Greek people to strangers. It was the key to release the night terrors in an eruption of laughter. I couldn't stop. My eyes filled. I'd walked in and sat at his table, in his home and he'd fed me… 'No menu.' Of course private houses don't have menus!
The sea, the grapes, the soup, the life… I stood, arms held out, kefi surging, thumping heels. I danced, swooping, sweating, crouching, stamping, forward, back. They were both clapping the

rhythm. She beckoned me over. We lifted her husband, arms linked supporting his weight. I roared: "Eleftheria." He whooped, she sang. Our feet thumped bass in unison. The coast wind gave melody.

Kefi sated, I helped lower him back in his chair. We shook hands. His wife rummaged in an old box and gave me an unmatched pair of salvaged trainers. That's what cracked me up. Not the bullets and hatred – I could deal with those bastards – but the kindness of this wonderful couple – tears came: "Sorry."

"Why sorry? When we happy, we laugh; when we sad, we cry. It is normal. Greeks sometimes cry when happy, laugh when sad or laugh and cry together."

They had stabilized me, antidoting the poison of the night.

"What is your name?"

"Stephanos."

"I am Andrea and my wife is Yenia."

"Thank you for your hospitality. I'm sorry for entering your home uninvited."

"You English always saying sorry. Sorry for what? For dancing, for food, for sun? We give to you and you give to someone else. In many years time perhaps. Why would you not be welcome? Do you mean us harm? You were a stranger seeking food. That is an honour for my house. Once I had no food or home. A good family gave me food and home. It is the way, the good way."

"Who helped you?"

"Yenia and her father."

"When?"

Before he could answerYenia brought over cut honey melon and more retsina.

"*Yia mas.*" (To us.)

"*Yia mas.*"

(I translate his story): "You asked when, Stephan? It was during the war. We were winning in Albania against the Italians. Try and stop any young man when he is winning. There were four of us, full of victory, advancing too fast. We were captured unharmed. They took us to a hospital and cut off our legs: healthy legs. They wasted anaesthetic so we wouldn't die of shock. The doctor was crying, but an officer held a pistol to his back. All around real casualties. They left us on stretchers when they retreated. They could have shot us, but that would have been kind. The officer said no – he wanted to cause pain. If you kill someone the pain stops; they let us live so the pain would go on. Greeks love to dance. He knew the pain."

I could see Yenia squeezing his hand white.

"Our troops found us. None of us said what happened. Later, one killed himself, one died of gangrene, that left Spiro and me. He stayed in Athens begging near Syntagma. I asked to be put on the first train… it was heading for Kalamata. A farmer started talking, offered food and a house for no reason. I refused. I bless him for ignoring me. I said I could not live with anyone. I had to be a hermit. There are caves up there." He waved at the mountains behind us. "He sent food once a week. Food was scarce, and for my pride he said I would be a fire watcher over the forest. He carried me on his back. The caves were dry. There were goat skins and spring water nearby. I could see the Argolic Gulf up to Nafplion, across to Spetse and Hydra and a long way south towards Monemvassia .You know these places?"

"Yes, I know where you mean." Just names but they gave such an ache.

Andreas continued: "I saw German bombers attacking British troop ships as they tried to get to Crete. Ships burning, men dying, for what? Italians, British, Germans, now together in tavernas. Why fight? It is mad."

"Was the officer punished for war crimes?"

"No, I wanted to kill him. Cruelty causes revenge. More revenge, more cruelty, more vendettas. I didn't care. I was going to hunt him, kill him and find my legs for burial when I died. As you can tell, I was going mad.

"At night, I would watch village lights go on, taverna fires glowing and fishing lamps strung out in lines at sea. Greeks are not meant to be alone. We love families. I suffered, looking down like a wounded eagle that couldn't fly. I stared out to sea for hours every day. Sometimes I could see where the rivers boiled up like oil. I couldn't sleep. I was getting weaker.

"Every Sunday the farmer sent his daughter with a food basket. I was deliberately cruel and growled without thanks. Eventually she just left it by a rock without speaking. I collected mountain herbs. You English think we are not gardeners. That is not true. The whole of Greece is a garden.

"The day that changed everything and saved my life, was about a year after I'd arrived at the cave. The weather was dry and hot. The smell came before the flames: low scrub was burning towards the forest. The food basket became a sledge. I skidded down the gulley, dragging burning clumps of grass, firing a break to stop it spreading into the trees. I was in the smoke, tired, black, choking, bleeding stumps, but the forest was saved and I was a man again. Do you understand Stephan?"

"Yes, I do."

He tapped his knee hard with a knife: "I made a wooden leg and a crutch from an olive branch. I was getting better. When Yenia next delivered food, I was polite. She said the Pappas had prayed for the forest and she had prayed for me.

"It was easy to explore the caves without legs. I found a giant cavern filled by a river which disappeared out under the sea. I believed that if I could block it, the water would flow to the surface and feed the valley.Yenia joined the secret work and bought dynamite from a one-armed fisherman. I crawled in the caves, through small gaps, placed the dynamite, like in war. Yenia waited at the entrance."

Like me Andreas had been using explosives.

"I was exhausted. She pulled me out. She was brave. I lay on her to protect her from the explosion and we fell in love."

Yenia lovingly stroked his hand.

"The river was blocked deep underground and the water flooded out into the dry valley. A new river finding its own way. A week later, she came to tell me the Pappas was the village hero because his prayers had been answered. He was drinking more and had two new widows. I told Yenia to turn away. I put on my new leg, hoisted myself up on a branch, walked towards her and asked her to marry me. We hugged and fell over again."

A polished olive crutch rested beside his chair.

"You see Stephan, I live a free man with Yenia and our family - Eleftheria – you know what this word means?"

"Yes Andrea I do… So if you met the officer with the pistol, your good life would be your revenge?"

"No, I would kill him. I am a man, not a saint. But if his children came here, they would be welcome. They are not guilty. Vendetta poisons everybody. The next generation must be clean."

The three of us sat looking out to sea. Flat and solid enough to walk on. Clarity of thought, keep the plan: go back to the UK, destroy container, kill Taylor and come back to Greece to kill the terrorists who murdered Eric.

I stood to leave. Andreas knew about English confusion with hospitality, so we shook hands quickly. Little Yenia's face said it all in her contented smile: "*Kalo tuxidi* Stephan." (Travel Well.)

"*Adio* Yenia .*Adio* Andrea. *Poli agape sas*." (Much love to you.)

Chapter 39

THE SUN still had enough heat to keep the roads dusty. A mile from Andreas and Yenia a path broke away, offering a hermit's life in a cave of safety with views of beauty. I hadn't expected my resolve to be tested so soon. Looking up to a sanctuary in the cliffs released any doubts: I had to get back to the U.K.

On the main road the sign said Argos; no bag, no spare clothes, no mobile, no passport or documents – flying back to UK was out. Creeps and spooks would have the routes covered. It was possible that a yacht needed a delivery crew even so late in the year. Levkas on the west coast was a yachtie wintering hole and as good as anywhere to look for a lift.

I planned and plotted, chewed and schemed as kilometres disappeared along the quiet road; legs freeing enjoying liberation. A road-side church, smaller than Sophie and Mick's, prompted a need to say something spiritual for Eric and Eleftheria. The blue door was locked, so I walked on.

"Ela! Ela!" (Come back.) A black clad lady was waving a lime brush from behind the church. Proudly she unlocked the door and let me in, crossed herself and returned to painting. The smell of incense and the cool shafts of vapour made the painted icons move. I bowed, made the sign of the cross and tried to think of suitable words. One icon had its eyes scratched out. The distraction made me leave.

* * *

A car slowed down alongside, offering a lift. I waved no thanks. I needed movement and metronomic rhythm to think. Several more vehicles passed, then an engine quietened behind me. Danger combed by neck. I spun, dropped to one knee, scooped a stone. A large hound, bigger than Molly, grinned from behind the wheel of a Toyota pick-up. His friend pointed to the back. I was ready now, so flopped in beside nets of water melons. Zigzagging higher, more of the Gulf opened up like a chart. Eric and Eleftheria were out there somewhere... resting.

I'd fallen asleep to views of the Argolic Gulf and awoke disorientated, to views of the Gulf of Corinth. Three more lifts and I was looking at rafts of modern charter yachts filed away for the winter. The privately owned stood out by their customized deck gear and red ensigns.

Cards on the information board in the yachtie bar, revealed several going back to the U.K. through the French canals. One sounded more vague: 'Yacht Lizcol. 36ft Contessa. Leaving for UK soon. Crew wanted. Non smokers. L. Armsworth.'

I found the 'Lizcol' and assumed the owner would be a bloke, not the 60+ lady looking confused as I asked for Mr Armsworth.

"He's not here anymore. He died in the summer. I'm Liz Armsworth."

Not a good start: "I'm sorry. You advertised for crew?"

"That's right. No pay, no alcohol, no drugs, no smoking, no girlfriends."

"And no fun!" I added with a smile that was not returned.

"Have you done much distance sailing?"

"Yes, some." I should have added, the last yacht I was on was sunk by terrorists and the skipper killed, but decided to leave it off my CV. She accepted me on the basis of a five-minute chat, which meant she was either a very bad judge of character or desperate. If I'd been her, I'd have reached for the nearest barge pole.

We went below into a neat, clean saloon; family photos pinned to the bulkheads. One showed a couple walking along a busy U.K. street in 70's flares, long hair. The beautiful people looking for life. She seemed at a loss what to say next, so I asked her about the yacht and suggested the Bay of Biscay route via Gibraltar as being less hassle. Which was true only if there were people trying to kill you. But for a widow with family crockery stacked in the galley, the barge pole would be useful again. Storms could last for weeks in the North Atlantic at this time of year, and even when they'd finished, enormous seas remained.

Innocents put at risk for the greater good by a caring, sharing patriot – collateral damage. I was beginning to think like Taylor, and it made me sick.

Liz was always pleasant but there was an absence of warmth and humour, so our relationship was based purely on sailing efficiency. That was fine by me.

No fireworks or farewell parties as we left, just a pickled expat saying we were going the wrong way. We soon settled down. Lizzie navigated and did some watch keeping. I did sail changes, cooking and steering when Toby Tiller – the auto helm – needed a rest. Each day we ran the diesel engine for an hour to charge the batteries, and for added miles if the wind was light.

We snacked and dozed through daylight hours, but at night kept strict four-hour watches. Her lack of curiosity in my personal life seemed strange after being used to the unashamed Greek noseyness. I got nowhere with my questions, so we restricted out chat to boats and weather,

On the second day, we sighted hazy Sicily to the north, giving me a lot of confidence in Liz's navigation. Her late husband had taught her how to use a sextant, so GPS was dismissed as techno-cheating. 'What happens when the batteries run out?' That clinched the argument for me.

The undisturbed night watches on moon-gladed seas, with meditative rocking, were just what I needed for head repairs. My mate the Plough, off the starboard beam, gave perspective to earthly traumas. However, 'what ifs?' continued to become more extreme… only punctuated by Liz passing up cups of coffee at the end of a watch. We'd sit companionably for five or ten minutes while her eyes adjusted and I pointed out nearby shipping.

The option of the French canals came up once, but I managed to nudge the decision back to the Biscay route. What an evil Machiavellian navigator I was. Taking advantage for my own ends, correction, for my country's ends. I dissuaded her from stopping in Gibraltar, quoting a fake weather forecast as reason to press on, even though a walk on solid ground would have done us both good. There's up to an eight knot current flowing into the Med sometimes, so we took ages to get from Gib to Cadiz. It was there the sea changed from garden scenery to high moorland. Waves were bigger and the long underlying heave smelt of storms. I told Liz about Eric's theory, keeping the life raft in the cabin ready to be inflated and the dingy up in the bows so if we were holed we'd stay afloat with all gear accessible, even if decks were awash. Surprisingly, she agreed. If it worked, we stood a better chance of survival than in a rubber raft. Also, blocking the limber holes in the bulkheads effectively formed watertight compartments, potentially giving more buoyancy. My paranoia still dominated since having watched Eleftheria sink.

Wet weather gear was now essential permanently. I'd sit in the hatchway like a tank commander, just head and shoulders out, surrounded by towels, letting 'Toby Tiller' do all the work. Respect for Liz developed. Not only for her navigation, but for the quiet way she carried her grief. It meant I could get my head down with confidence.

We were in sea area Trafalgar. Reassuring and poetic when tucked up ashore in bed, but at sea it could be a horror story. The more gale warnings were broadcast, the more guilt I felt. We could have been lunching in a French canal-side café if my obsessions hadn't persuaded otherwise. I lowered the main and fore sail, hoisted a storm jib and set a course further offshore. In a good boat, storms are only dangerous when they meet land. I kept thinking of Eleftheria. She could have dealt with it easily and do whatever you asked – more guilt, more hatred, more 'what ifs?'. My mind was better, but it still wasn't right.

Eventually 'Toby' was overpowered by the gale and a quartering sea, so I steered, spending hours hanging onto the tiller in metronomic meditation, replaying past scenes – right or wrong, yes or no? Taylor, good or evil? Leila: could I have stopped her? Should I have gone back to Oz with Angie? Should I have destroyed the Greek container?… on and on. It was now a full-blown storm. Paradoxically it calmed my mind.

A couple of times Liz asked if I wanted a break, calling me by her husband's name Col. She didn't correct herself so neither did I. All things must pass, and we were left with a washed out seascape, quiet enough to hoist the main and a working jib. Our morale high after coming through the battering.

"I'll steer for a bit now Steve. You have a break." Then out of the blue: "Are you married?"

I saw Angie's crumpled face on the ferry: "No, I always manage to run too fast Liz." The flippancy didn't fool her. It certainly didn't fool me.

"Your face is saying something different."

I acknowledged her perspicacity with a shrug: "How long were you married to Col?"

"Forty years. Forty is gold. From virgin to widow in forty wonderful years. Faithful to him alone. We met at teacher training college. The kids were great but eventually we had enough. Col loved sailing. I learnt to love it too, so we took early retirement and sailed to Greece. It was the best thing we ever did. Friends and family came out. We were still fit, healthy, sexy... golden years. I replay them in my mind to stop them fading." Her gaze shifted to distant breaking crests. We sat quietly: "Have you had someone special?"

"Yep, she went back to Australia."

"Why didn't you go with her?"

I wanted to tell her about bombs, bullets and bastards but just said: "Because I'm a selfish idiot."

"You could still find her."

The conversation was getting uncomfortable so I crassly asked: "How did Col die?"

"Heart. He had chest pains for years. Greek doctors were good, and we thought our way of life would be the best medicine: laughter, love, family. In the end he had to go back to England for an operation. He knew he would never see Greece or our boat again. By the cruellest of fate we flew in daylight over our islands. Like a chart we worked out where our boat was. That was the worst moment of our lives. Holding hands, crying, feeling like deserting angels. I spent the remainder of our savings on private care, but didn't tell Col. This boat was sold on condition it came back to England: that's what we're doing now. They say most people who have heart attacks die either on the toilet or making love... yes Steve we were making love. Are you shocked?"

"No of course not Liz."

(Mick's voice: 'On the job or having a crap. Not exactly a tough call, is it mate?)

She continued, unaware of the disrespectful bastard in my head: "The soulless crematorium, jeering flowers, pantomime curtains. Later the urn and endless paperwork... the will. He'd left the boat to me but I'd already spent it on his treatment. I held it together till it was all over, then collapsed and sobbed for days. Col spoke to me, comforted me. You don't think I'm mad hearing his voice Steve?"

"No Liz, it's a sign of sanity, not madness. I hear voices. They can be comforting, inspiring or occasionally extremely irritating."

"Col's never irritating. His ashes are in a coffee jar by the chart table. He had to come on the last voyage."

Jeez, that was close, several times I'd nearly made a cup of Nescafe, *à la* Col. She was crying from a beautiful, lined face. I wanted to hug the pain away.

"I would give the remainder of my life for just one more hour with Col. That's how much I loved him. Just to say things; hold each other quietly. Can you understand love like that?"

"Yes I can Liz." Thoughts of Angie again.

"Col always called me Lizzie. The boat should have been called LizzieCol, not Lizcol. Is Toby Tiller O.K. for an hour?" I was going to say no.

"Yea, Toby's fine."

She went below and turned in. I checked the sails and followed.

"Is that you Col? Come and get warm."

I could have pretended I hadn't heard or said 'I'm Steve not Col'.

"Yea, I'm coming to bed now Lizzie."

A blissful cave of feminine warmth. Cosiness, heightened by the cold, hostile sea outside, enveloped me. I hadn't held a woman since Angie left. She wrapped her body around me and sighed with safe contentment. I played my surrogate role, envying their love. She wasn't being unfaithful – I was Col.

"Goodnight Col my love. Sleep tight."

"Sweet dreams Lizzie my darling. Remember our golden years and sunny days."

Her finger quietened my lips and she slept. Admiration and jealousy mixed, for their long relationship as I pressed my body – Col's body – against her. Lives simple and true, death impossible to end it. Now it was my turn to sigh. I eased out of her bunk and sat in the hatchway. We'd been joined by a ghostly silver galleon: the moon sailed alongside, fading between shadowed cumulus. Sky, miles high – sea miles deep – land, miles distant. The boat's compass the intersection of infinity.

(Mick's voice crashed my reverie: 'Well done mate. You are now a fully paid-up member of the granny shaggers club.')

"You pathetic, callous bastard. You and your voice can fuck off for good. You're terminated, as from now."

('I think you'll find my voice is not that easy to get rid of, Dickhead.')

* * *

I didn't call her for her watch. She eventually surfaced mid-morning, looking rested and smiling:

"Like a cuppa Steve?"

"Great, thanks."

I was at the tiller, giving 'Toby' a break, feeling the light turbulence flow over the rudder blade, juggling thoughts and congratulating myself on being an all round good bloke. A certain acknowledgment of the previous night's caring-sharing would have been welcome. I didn't want flowers and chocolates, just a kiss on the cheek. Instead nothing but a cup of tea and back to the friendly status quo. Col had been with her, not me. I'd been used in a very loving way and learnt how much two people can mean to each other, in life and death.

* * *

The boat got into a comfortable groove. She wasn't Eleftheria but still sailed well, making a clean eight knots with the stiff westerly on her port beam.

Singing weather:

"Rolling down to Rio with my best girl by my side

Rolling down to Rio with the big flood tide
Rolling, rolling… roll on Geronimo, strolling, rolling on…"

* * *

Two days out from Lizzie's home port, conflict coloured our thoughts. Wanting to get there, but not wanting the decisions and struggles that waited shoreside. Plan A was to find Mick, destroy the container and kill Taylor… end global terrorism and world poverty, plus free beer at weekends… easy. Plan B was the same as Plan A only with less fuck ups.

Off Ushant, an ultra large container vessel passed within a half mile, furrowing the same centuries-old course Harry had told us about. I scanned the boxes through binos. Thousands of them, anonymous, no clue which held cuddly toys and white goods, and which held the terrifying violence of bombs, bullets and drugs.

Memories of a school atlas in geography lessons, pencilling voyages and getting a whack round the head, held my thoughts until Liz passed up another cuppa. This one coffee-laced with whisky.

"I thought we'd celebrate."

I wouldn't have called last night a cause for celebration, but still it was nice to be appreciated.

She lifted her cup: "Here's to entering the English Channel."

Of course. I'd nearly said thanks for the cuddles or thanks for making an immature bastard like me aware of what a real loving relationship can be.

I said: "Cheers, to you and Colin."

* * *

Sea and sky melded into one washed-out grey. Horizon gone, impossible for midday sextant shot, dead reckoning would have to do. The rhythm of the voyage would soon be over and Liz would go back to her grandchildren, with granddad in the coffee jar. Her bedtime stories would be of kind loving people and glorious sailing. Granddad as brave as a lion, rescuing Italian tourists from an overloaded dinghy; taking them on board, their sunken boat surfacing astern on a line, as they steamed off to ecstatic cheers – unplanned success.

Another story she told me several times: as a teenager on his uncle's 40ft sloop, left to sail it home single handed, approaching the mooring buoy too fast – dozens of Sunday yachties watching from the club house. He should have overshot into the crowded moorings under full sail; instead she grounded accidently with the buoy on her bow. He dropped all sails, took his luck and moored up to applause of the club house. His reputation forever secure, a story retold all his life.

He was the batsman, when dropped at five, goes on to score a century: his pattern for life. Having done it once, he would do it forever – until his heart ran out. A man brave and ambitious, who knew when things fell into place and was admired because of it. Bad things were ignored or dismissed with jokes. That mooring incident had set the tone for his life. Even when chance or luck had been the reason for success, he took the undeserved credit, modestly. Liz had seen his way soon after they met and wisely steered him to more luck when times got difficult, carefully cementing their love. They'd been a good team.

She wouldn't tell the grandchildren about someone called Steve, who tried to do the right thing and ended up getting friends killed, or of global, corrupt imbeciles who made money from wars and drugs, or of Snakes and Taylors who fought using any weapon they could find.

Surreal thoughts agitated as we approached the U.K. coast. Somewhere thirty metres down, was my container, surrounded by other festering remnants of war: 'When Albion in sight, let Neptune keep your secrets right.'

If only there was a plug to pull out and drain the English Channel, then people could walk around and see the poisonous, leaking detritus of the First and Second World Wars, Korea, Falklands and all the rest – army surplus, chemical surplus, failed projects, embarrassing projects, archives of colonial crime, biological conundrums, nuclear scrap, nerve gas, radioactive widgets, weapons from wars won and lost. Anything that couldn't be incinerated. Trash for cash from friendly countries, a padre's porno collection and Harry's false teeth. All out of sight – out of mind.

What if I blew up the container and started a chain reaction of explosions, releasing toxic sea clouds into harbours and estuaries? What if I did nothing, and terrorists blew up shopping centres?

Answer A. Go to the authorities. Negative. Taylor was the authorities.

Answer B. Deal with known active threats and take the risk.

I had to destroy the container, even though I was not going to get paid, laid, promoted or pissed-up. It was serious shit to ruin a vital U.K. intelligence operation and kill the controller, all because tiny synapses had linked in my head.

Fact: evidence was zero, so confidence in my deductions ranged from 50% to 90%. Do I kill someone on those percentages? Taylor does with less and gets paid for it. Fuck this for a game of soldiers. I wanted to be in Oz with Angie, worrying if the beer was cold .

* * *

Underneath Lizcol's hull was the evil container. Liz gently interrupted: "You look miles away."

"Not miles. Closer than that. Have you ever wondered why we can see stars light years distant, yet we can't see 30 metres below us?"

Her reply surprised me: "I don't want to know. It makes me shiver when I think of it. Let sleeping dogs lie."

She passed me an empty bean tin to punch a hole so it would sink… no, not a single can… All rubbish had to go ashore.

* * *

Nevada:

"Estimated Time of Arrival 04.00 Sir."

"Thank you Costa. Share U.K. eyes only."

"Yes Sir."

* * *

Solent nav lights and neap tides made landfall easy; shipping sparse and distant, no cross bearings needed. Except for one vessel directly astern, less than a mile away. Masthead lights in line, port and starboard both showing. She was bows on. Probably a coaster or dredger taking a short cut on the rising tide. I altered course 90 to cross out of the main channel into shallows. Our nav lights showed port with white masthead. Her masthead lights stayed in line – she was following us round.

I shouted: "Liz start the engine now."

"Can't we sail a little longer Steve?"

"Start the fucking engine NOW!"

I'd shocked her into action. Then when you need it most, the dreaded click of a flat battery.

"Forget it – come here – we'll have to tack – one chance – stand by."

She was on us. Lights disappeared behind her rusting hull. Bow wave bearing down:

"This is it Liz – Now! – Leigh ho!"

I whacked the tiller hard over: "C'mon you fucking bitch, turn!"

Liz's face was a mixture of fear and pain. We were getting dirty air but she was turning: "Back the jib Liz. Hold it, hold it... now, sheet in tight." I held the tiller with my foot and helped Liz winch in. The bow wave hit us; green water swamped the deck, but it also pushed us away enough to clear the wall of rusting steel, just feet from our paint. The thumping prop passed close. Stern lettering gave nothing away. A clean gust filled the sails and we gently grounded on good English putty. The first land since Greece. We'd arrived.

I dropped all sails, cursing the coaster's captain and crew, and their lack of fathers. I was in no mood to accept accidents. The captain could have been pissed, or been taking a short cut on a rising tide, or he could have been under orders to cut us in half. Whatever, it was not the sort of welcome either of us wanted. Someone had been at the wheel and they must have seen us... Bastards!

Chapter 40

THE BLEAK, early morning marina matched our mood. The goodwill and respect Liz and I had built up had gone with the near collision. Now there was no time for repairs.

"Col would never have sworn at me."

"I know. I'm sorry. I'm not Col. It was an emergency."

Trying to salvage something only resulted in strained smiles and awkward platitudes. Fleeting warmth returned as we hugged goodbye.

"Do you have any money Steve?"

I'd forgotten the bleeding obvious from Plan A, but pride didn't stop me asking for twenty: "It doesn't seem much for saving me and the boat, even if you did have to swear." I was pleased she conceded that saving her life was more important than swearing.

"Col was a lucky man."

"I hope you find someone to love, Steve."

"Yea, one day. Are you staying here?"

"Only until the marina office opens, then I'll do the paperwork for my single-handed, non-stop voyage from Greece. I'm assuming your passport was stolen?" She gave me an old-fashioned look.

"Yes. You assume right."

We were strangers now we'd touched land; different people, so we shook hands.

"Whatever is bothering you Steve, try and deal with it soon."

"I'm planning to Liz, very soon."

The sea had given us boundaries, routine, purpose, respect, affection. Now too many options crowded in, clouding the new day.

* * *

The early coastal bus carried half-asleep night workers going home and half-asleep day workers going to offices and factories. I wanted to wake them up and tell them of a parallel world of terrorism and corrupt governments; of killers for good causes; killers for bad; killers for money; killers who got it wrong; and killers who didn't care. Maybe bovine ignorance was better than knowing.

The transition had been so sudden from sea life to commuter bus that my senses were still tuned to the boats roll. There had been no customs, no passport control, just a bus driver who was pissed off having to change a twenty and a searching face reflected in the window's darkness.

(Mick's voice: 'You pretentious prick. Get back in the real world')

('Yea alright, I know, save it. I'll be with you in ten, real time.')

* * *

Nevada:

"Looks like 79 heading for 78's trawler, Sir."

"Get U.K. liaison now, Costa."

"Yes Sir."

* * *

MFV Dawn was moored in the same familiar place, along the quay from 'Nelly's Arse' (Harry must have pissed off another customer). The net box on deck gave enough leg room to crash out with the lid closed.

I was rehearsing what to say when boots thumped on deck, followed by a tuneless whistle. Wheelhouse door opened, radio on, hiss of gas stove for his first cuppa – so predictable. I eased the lid an inch, scanned an empty quay and quietly made my way into the wheelhouse: "Make another one Mick."

"Jeez – shit! Where the fuck did you come from? I thought you were dead."

"I'll tell you later. Have you seen Taylor recently?"

"I saw him about two months ago when me and Sophie came back from Greece. He said you'd disappeared out to Oz. Couldn't you find Angie?"

"I didn't go to Oz. Forget what that lying bastard told you, we have to destroy the container."

Mick was looking over my shoulder. Something nasty had slid aboard.

"And why do you want to do that, Steve?"

As I rounded on Taylor, I saw the pistol: "What the fuck you doing here snake shit?"

"We knew you'd return if you lived. You're in very serious trouble – sit down."

He kept his aim on my chest: "This is how it looks to us. You were paid by U.K. government to put a container on the sea bed, off the Isle of Wight. You opened it against orders and stole weapons, explosives and drugs. You became a terrorist because of your sympathy for Afghan civilians: 'Croydon Syndrome' is sympathy for the enemy. It originates from Betjeman's poem: 'Come friendly German Bombs and fall on Croydon."

"What the fuck are you on about Taylor?"

Mick interrupted: "Slough. It was Slough Betjeman wanted the Germans to bomb."

Taylor's intellectual arrogance made him look a prat; Mick's surprising poetic knowledge muddled his flow. He was confused, floundering: "I know it was Slough but the analyst who named the syndrome came from Croydon."

Mick was on the case: "So what's that got to do with Betjeman?"

The Snake's blood pressure was rising nicely: "Now where was I?"

I stirred it: "FOFO."

"Meaning what?"

"Fuck Off and Find Out." And added helpfully: "You said not to interrupt or you'd shoot yourself."

Taylor tried to regain dominance, pointing the pistol aggressively: "You gave Leila explosives. You betrayed your country."

"No I didn't. Anyway I've never been to Croydon."

"What?"

His pistol waved like a mad conductor's baton. "Croydon, I've never been there."

Spital appeared on his chin and his sadistic eyes squinted as he searched for his narrative: "At the interrogation your answers were ambiguous and guilt laden."

He wiped is mouth with the back of his hand: "We sent you to Greece to test your loyalty. You agreed to help Mick with the container operation there. When you realized your terrorist friends would be trapped, you used a Frenchman to help destroy it, then killed him and sank his yacht El Faria, just as you killed Leila when her usefulness was over."

I'd had enough of his crap: "Look, you snivelling gob shite – the yacht was EL-EF-THERIA – even a perverted little fuck wit like you should understand what that means. And that Frenchman was an incredibly wise, brave man. Now put that pistol away before I stuff it down your slimy throat and pull the trigger so you'll need a broom to wipe your arse. Get it?"

Mick gave me a round of applause. Taylor was scared. He tried to salvage some credibility: "I don't need a gun. I have back up on the quay. You wrecked two years of intelligence work in Greece. Now you're trying to do the same here. Your motive is revenge against the U.K. for civilian deaths in Afghanistan. How does that sound to you?"

"It sounds like a load of bollocks, which even you don't believe or I'd be dead by now."

(Eric's calm voice: 'You're doing well Steve, but remember the answer is compassion'… 'Thanks Eric, I hope you're right, or I'm going to look a right pillock.')

I stared at Taylor: "You have forgotten the most important factor in winning a war."

He twitched: "Which is?"

"Compassion… Compassion for humanity, for country, for dolphins, for life, for Eleftheria."

Taylor was scratching his neck. Mick nodded and smiled: U.K. thumbs up.

"I went to London with Leila because I loved her. I worked on the container jobs because I love my country. Do you really think

I'd go out to that godforsaken shite hole Klondike for the good of my health?"

I leaned forward into Taylor's face: "Just pretend you know what I'm talking about for one second, then re-run your theory. Do you have reasonable doubt? Couple me up to any polygraph you like. It will confirm I am not a traitor." It was like pissing into the wind.

"Can you prove you are on my side?"

"I'm not on your side. I'm on my country's side and what it stands for: humanity, truth, justice, tolerance, compassion, freedom… Eleftheria."

"And which country is that Steve?"

Very wisely he backed away: "Funny thing is, Steve, we agree with you now. The container has to be destroyed; it has served its purpose. We can kill two birds with one stone. London is being rolled up, so as long as no one warns them. You destroy the container and it will help your case, or if the terrorists kill you, it will also help your case – either way you win." His self-satisfied smile and constant suspicion was getting on my tits. "One option we considered was rendition – not to a U.S. black site of course – but an Al Qaeda base. I'm sure they'd believe you were loyal to the U.K. The job is tonight, 18:00, yes or no?"

"Yea, why not? What have I got to lose? What could go wrong?"

As he walked away he gave a warning: "When I come back I'd advise you to improve your attitude to authority."

"Fuck Off Snake Shite." I knew now I was valuable, for him to put up with that. The problem was, why?

Chapter 41

WHEN we were sure Taylor wasn't ear-wigging at a porthole, Mick opened up: "Now it really is shit or bust."

"Yea ,whatever. Put the kettle on if it fits."

"Could you smell his aftershave fumes?"

"Yea, shame he doesn't smoke. I'd love to see his head go up in flames."

We had a good chuckle, just like old times. All was well with Manoli and family. Sophie had a baby on the way: a beautiful girl or an ugly Mick.

Experience said it was likely Taylor would try to write me off as collateral damage, so it was good to have Mick as back up.

* * *

I crashed out for the afternoon, until Mick 'flashed up' Dawn's big diesel, waking me from a surreal sleep: WW2, flying over Berlin in a Greek fishing boat; Mr Harman dropping exploding fish; Taylor attacking us in a U-boat; dolphins killed; parachutes going up, coming down burning; nets dragging everyone into an undersea cavern; giant lobsters, breathing air from their claws, biting everything.

Not enough air, fighting my was out of the bunk, thumping on the floor, flapping like a landed cod, diesel roaring… not exactly restful.

* * *

Taylor turned up just before 18:00 with new Walt Mitty yellow, waterproofs, a small backpack and a comb-over hairstyle – blowing 'up-hill'. I lip read Mick's reaction: 'Twat.'

I went below to try to catch up on rest. Last time I got exhausted fighting lobsters: sleep is gold dust before a dive. Two hours later, U-boat commander Taylor was shouting for me to get kitted up, nervously flattening his hair. I couldn't take him seriously with Mick's impersonations behind his back.

"Steve, the timer is set for twenty minutes – *minutes*, O.K.? Place it inside the container, then surface. We pick you up and we all go home together." He made it sound like a holiday. "Oh, and Steve, good luck."

The look on his face said something different: 'I hope you screw up, to save me the trouble of getting rid of you later.'

Almost as an afterthought, he pulled out an underwater, battery powered saw from his pack: "A present for you, so if you get caught in nets this will sort it out; very expensive, used in the oil industry."

What did he think it was like down there – landscape gardening, hedge trimming? I was using other tools: mind visualization, meditative breathing, counting – they helped – but didn't change the fact I was going into a black, cold, ghost netted, polluted, diver's hell. on my own again…

Taylor kept looking at my eyes for signs of fear. I'd evolved a squinty smile, supposedly to indicate confidence but which Mick regarded as madness. Shaking was inches away. If something had caused a cancellation, I'd have grabbed it. A resigned attitude can develop and if it takes hold, blokes get careless, slump and give up. I had to get a grip – I pogoed and thumped myself in the guts. Mick looked over, so I stuck my thumb up Greek style.

It was now very cold. We were on site, danger time had begun, explosives packed around my waist – ready. The old feeling kicked in as I submerged, mind focused, doing stuff, drifting calmly down the shot line. Visibility was surprisingly good. My spotlight picked out nets and the dead bye catch. One door was open. I hung to it. Explosion twenty minutes – loads of time. I scanned inside. The beam picked out the drums; half had gone.

Check, double check – arming pin – 20 minutes, check – shit! 20 was right but seconds, not minutes; barely time to reach the shot line before my swim bladder was gutted. It didn't make sense – panic crawled my back. Resetting was straightforward. It was the kind of mistake that was difficult to do... unless you were a

Snake. Check again – 20 minutes – timer on – pin out – place in the middle drums – 'job done home to mum.' I gave a quick all round scan, floors, walls, ceiling… Involuntarily I spat out the D.V. Bloated faces of four lifeless divers, hovered above me – air bubbles jiggling their arms in macabre salutes.

I stuffed the D.V. back in my mouth – rapid gasps locked it up as I finned to the door. The current had pushed it closed. I pulled frantic, looking back at dead faces; my own death; terror accelerating.

(My own voice: "You've got a minute to get sorted out – use it.")

Count, breathing controlled – think, look. How can I open the door? Simple twat, I'd pulled instead of pushed at the wrong door – I was out – shot line grabbed like a lost friend – ascend 10 metres, wait – ascend another 10 metres, wait – another 10. I followed the bubbles to the surface.

The swell had picked up – no sign of Mick – I'd never swim out of the gutting zone, so I fired a mini flare. Immediately the whizzing prop. Before she'd lost way, I was up over the side like a rat up a drainpipe.

"Mick, give it full throttle or we're dead. Go like hell." I took the wheel as he went below and cranked the engine a few more revs. Dawn had never been so fast. Taylor was flapping, comb-over sticking to his fear sweat. No time for silly games: "Keep out the way snake-shit."

We were putting useful distance between us and the big bang, unless there was a chain reaction, in which case we'd be with the Isle of Wight floating in Bordeaux harbour. Nearly safe. Then I saw the dolphins: "Mick spotlight!" There was a pod of a dozen or more, heading up channel, straight into the killing zone: "Mick head them off."

"Steve NO!" We were fighting over the wheel. Taylor hit me hard on the back of the neck – I twisted – now I'd kill the scum. The rolling deck sent us sliding on fish guts into the scuppers. I compressed his throat. His weakening hands pummelled the air. Mick's voice came through the red mist: "Tazer! Tazer! Let him go."

Good old Mick – back up – zap the bastard and we'll deep six him. Extreme pain – full ten, hit the middle of my back. He couldn't have missed. The stun allowed Taylor to cuff my wrists and ankles. Uselessly I bellowed to the dolphins as I wallowed in the sludge of weed and slime… betrayed, shot in the back.

Shocks of blasted air first, then a double crump. Mick spun the wheel to meet the tsunami bows on. I was still raging as Taylor tried to stuff a rag in my mouth, so I bit a chunk out of his hand, getting a satisfying scream of agony. Grief for the dolphins fired inside my body. Taylor tried to avoid my thrashing and pumped a full syringe into my leg – no dreams, no voices, no fight – no dolphins to rescue me… no dolphins to rescue.

Chapter 42

"HE'S COMING ROUND."

I was on the cabin floor – Dawn moored up – hands and ankles cuffed. I managed only a low growl and spat in Mick's direction. He tried to pacify: "We couldn't go back Steve. We'd all been killed. You'd gone berserk – I had to do it."

I wasn't interested in reasons: "You killed dolphins – they're sacred. Only yellow scum shoot their mates in the back. I expected it from snake arse, not you." They let me ramble on in a hate-filled rant, then I focused on Taylor: "The timer was set for 20 seconds, not 20 minutes."

He was looking way too confident, even with the blood soaked bandage: "It's the diver's responsibility to check his equipment."

"Bollocks! Diving is a team game, and you fucked up deliberately. There were four dead divers in the box stuck to the lid, before I blew them to pieces. Who the fuck were they? Whose side were they on?" Satisfyingly, I saw him press his bandage to stop blood dripping out but he still had an answer for everything: "They knew the game, and lost."

His girlie pistol waved about. "Put it away. You won't shoot me you deluded fuck wit. I'm too valuable and I won't kill you because I want some kit."

He acknowledged with a nod and released the cuffs. The problem was, I didn't know why I was valuable. They'd killed for a lot less than the points I had on my CV. I decided to push my luck further: "Equipment. Make a list."

He tried to hold the pistol in his bandaged hand, gave it up as a bad job and got a notebook and pen: "You will get what you want as long as you keep your mouth shut. If you don't, you will be sanctioned."

"Stuff the sanctions up your arse and write…

"Bergen, 98 pattern x 1.

"NATO bivvy bag x 1.

"Gas stove, plus cartridges x 8.

"Craig boots, size 10.

"Full Nevis waterproof suit x 1.

"French compo rations x 10 day packs.

"Water bottle x 2.

"£10,000 cash." (His pen didn't waver.) "Passport: not one with secret etchings. A new clean one." He was nodding like a Pompey hooker on the first night's gobble. The scam was working, so I pushed my luck:

"Rechargeable radio x 1.

"Dutch Asparagus, tins x 5.

"Tin opener, left handed x 1."

His pen wavered. His smile of gritted acquiescence soured into white knuckled subjugation. I pushed again.

"All by 16:00 today. Delivered by you."

I got the feeling I wouldn't be on his Christmas card list this year. Before I could extract any more urine, he got up to leave. Unfortunately, he didn't feel safe enough to turn his back to me, so reversed up the companionway. The contortions bringing out bulging veins.

The wheelhouse door slammed, releasing tension. Mick's face was a picture as he laughed himself to tears: "You should have asked him for a dozen Himalayan duck eggs and a pineapple from Tierra del fucking Fuego. You can't learn it mate."

Our banter eased as night memories came back: "I don't know why I'm laughing Mick, that Tazer was bad news."

"I know. I'm sorry. I had to do it to save your poxy life. If you'd killed him we both would have been dead before reaching Harry's."

"Maybe. But if you ever see me with a Tazer in my hand, run like hell. When I said 'watch my back', I meant watch it, not shoot me in the fucking back. Now, get the kettle on and do one of those burnt rubber egg breakfasts you're so good at."

Sophie must have been teaching him. He managed to talk and cook at the same time: "Taylor's crap has finished now Steve. Go off to the cuds for six months, longer if you want, then come back here fishing and find a decent woman. It'll be great."

"It's never finished Mick. There's always another war, another atrocity. Blokes like me get dragged in. You're O.K. You're out of it now, so stay out. I don't like loose ends. I'll draw a line under it when I'm dead."

"If you say so. Now debrief – who were those dead divers?"

"Don't know. Standard kit. Just hope they were termites."

"Did they have air left?"

"Don't know. I was shitting myself trying to get out; vests inflated; no visible wounds." I took another bite of burnt toast.

"Has Taylor said if anyone has been arrested?"

"He's told me fuck all, anyway debrief over. How's Sophie?"

"She's brilliant. If it hadn't been for all this crap, I'd never have met her, so something good's come out of it. You should have gone with Angie. You were made for each other – you know that."

Mick was right but for now I was more comfortable with bitter cynicism, as I continued to chew over ideas and black toast.

Three hard knocks on the trawler's side – 1600 – Snake time: "You wouldn't think the slime ball could make so much noise."

I shook Mick's hand: "Watch your back mate, it's not over yet. Next time I'll buy you a pint of Harry's rat's piss. Give my love to Sophie and Bumpy."

"I'll do that. See ya Dickhead."

"See ya Bollock-Chops."

Chapter 43

TAYLOR was waiting in his grey Lexus; a pile of boxes on the back seat, stacked around a fat bodyguard. He didn't look at me as I got in. The bandage had been changed.

"Where to Steve?"

"Ramsay Point car park, by the Coastal Path. You and your boy friend can have a cuddle when I've gone."

"Roger matey."

Everything he said wound me up. Why didn't he just say O.K.? Thankfully he shut up. In the car park three empty cars and an old guy walking a poodle. A set-up was still on the cards.

Taylor seemed proud of his acquisitions, emphasizing the French compo rations. The fat BG passed me the parcels like a pissed-off Father Christmas. I ripped out the stuff I wanted and chucked the wrappings back on fatty. With a gut like that he'd have a job finding his cock, let alone his pistol. Taylor waved a Dutch asparagus tin under my nose. I casually ignored it. Pathetic and childish, but it would give me a laugh later.

The weight of the bergen felt good as I hefted it on my shoulders: useful, purposeful.

"Got everything you need Steve?"

"Yep."

"You could have the company car if you wanted it."

"Na, I wouldn't like to spoil your date. Anyway now you've got him in the back seat, it'd be a hell of a job to get him out."

He was doing well on his personality course. He managed a sick smile. I faced up to him, turned and walked towards the Coastal Path.

"Steve, stop!"

It was intentional, rehearsed. He reached into his jacket, slight crouch, feet shoulder-width apart. He knew the reaction it would cause. The 'pistol' was a black mobile phone: "I nearly forgot Steve."

I hissed to myself: 'No you didn't, you slimy bastard.'

"Your mobile, £10,000 in cash and a new passport: "Steven B-------."

"That's not my name."

"It is now. Take it or leave it. Passport office wouldn't validate Dickhead."

The Snake had almost made a joke and I'd almost smiled. I didn't check any of it, just walked away, leaning into the slope. I was about a 100 metres before their engine started. Don't look round – walk on.

* * *

(Brian the MO: 'Keep the sea to the left. It's the island you've fought for, enjoy it. It's beautiful and remember, clockwise.')

"Clockwise it is Sir."

I had joined the proud ranks of the Coastal Path Regiment.

* * *

Nevada:

"79, he's on his own Sir."

"O.K., log it. Name?"

"B------- Sir."

"Why didn't the Brits eliminate him?"

"We don't know yet Sir."

Chapter 44

THE M.O. was right. Physical and mental peace was immediate. Each step savoured, breathing easy, meditation, concentration, mindfulness, short strides up the slopes, long loping down; ignoring everything, except the two-foot ribbon of Path encircling our island. An endless Path: leave a message under a stone and pick it up coming from the other direction. 'Beating the Bounds' – an affirmation of ownership; a confirmation of history and geography; a recognition of lives lost in war and work done in factories and farms. Good old M.O. Good old Brian. Good old Britain.

Several miles on, the grass turned to tarmac – railings, waste bins, ice-cream sellers, bus shelters – then out again into sweet peace, clean sky; breathe, push, lean into it, flow, hope. The whole body working hard, pumping arms and legs, conscious spirit, soul cleansing… *Anxiety turned to energy.*

I kept the pace up through twilight into dark, eventually rolling out my bivvy bag by a hedge for a few hours. No tea or food, just a safe fasting tiredness soothed by shingle waves and the warm scent of a southerly. No timetable, no target, no fear.

For five days I pushed hard, stopping for fish and chips, but mostly snacking on the hoof. If I eased, dead dolphins appeared.

(Eric's voice: 'Let it go. Anger destroys you. Thank your enemy for making you confront your demons. Stop hating and the hating will stop. To destroy your enemy make him your friend.')

"Don't ask me to forgive. I want revenge. I am human."

A mind film started: smoking blood, arm waving. Eric steering into a black abyss. 'Let go you French bastard.' No to forgiveness. Yes to revenge. I am human. I have ghosts to kill.

*   *   *

I woke very early each morning in the dark, rolled up the bivvy and walked a few miles, then brew, oats and a crap – not necessarily in that order. On the sixth day I repacked the bergen, found the mobile and posted it in a car boarding a French-bound ferry. They could track it out at sea for a while.

* * *

Nevada:

"79 discarded mobile, Sir."

"Why do they always do that? He may react now he thinks he's free."

"Yes Sir."

* * *

I kept to the Coast Path. Friendly voices called my name in the night. I considered their origins: schizophrenia, obsessions, hallucination, delusions – I got it. I'd just been incredibly lucky to meet good people: Mr Harman, the M.O., the Vicar, Manoli, Eleni, Eric, Angie,Yenia, Andreas, Liz and Molly. Kind generous mentors for solving life's paradoxes in sensitive, non-cynical ways, and sometimes I thanked them for their help.

(Mick: 'Hey Dickhead, don't forget me.')

("Mick, I said sensitive, not bull in a china shop.")

What to do with the advice? 'Don't kill': but to save your family – kill.

'Don't steal': but if your family is starving – steal.

(Manoli: 'Stealing gold is theft – stealing bread is not.')

(Mick: 'I can help you out Steve: don't commit adultery, unless you can get away with it.')

"Fuck off Mick. I knew you'd say that."

* * *

Every day I swam, masochistically accepting the cold as a cleansing penance. On the Path I rudely ignored 'good mornings' and 'nice days' until driving rain pushed me into a bus shelter on a sea front. Across the promenade was a war memorial – names remembered and what else? Freedom yes, but what would they want for us now? I stared and thought: Sgt Smith, Corporal White, Smudger and Chalky. Their duty done, our duty still to do. I stared, five minutes, ten, twenty – our duty is to live well; to show what they fought for mattered. It was a start but there was more to think about. Walk on.

The mind is more important than the body. Ideas turned to actions. The key to the Coastal Path was not only 'walk and talk' but 'walk and think'. Miles were 'thought miles'. The wonderful environment a meditative backdrop.

Sometimes the 'elation of revelation' kept me walking all night. The Greek villa had given me the means to explore space and time. The Coastal Path was giving human connections. Sometimes it was so black, I couldn't see my boots. It was like flying without reference to land, sea or sky. That was when the subconscious moved to the conscious, then dived back to continue beavering away in the personal hard drive. Access meant pressing the right buttons. Daily life changed from, 90% physical – 10% mental… to 90% mental – 10% physical.

Painful memories dissolved, good memories flourished and filed away. 'I think, therefore I am' changed to: 'I think, therefore I am free to choose.'

A paradox: the vast coastal beauty encouraged deep introspection. Miles would pass with no conscious memory of the route. My mind had been somewhere else as I filled it with shelves of information, neatly labled from A1 to Z100.

* * *

The sight of dolphins, way out, brought intense bitter-sweet feelings. The smell of seaweed, sand, the waves murmuring mush, gulls mewing: delicious sensory overload. I bought coconut sun oil at a tourist shop to complete the sensual rainbow. 'Kefi' peaked as I crested a cliff top. The air sang in post-rain purity. My bergen dropped to the grass. I danced for the joy of life – circling with arms outstretched – linked with loving ghosts. "Eleftheria!" I roared a challenge to the gods. Answering thunder came from mountainous cumulo nimbus ploughing up the Channel. I didn't seek shelter, instead searched for the highest point: "Come on you bastards, I'm here. Come and get me." They grumbled away into the distance, spitefully chucking their lightning into the sea.

* * *

Nevada:

"What's 79 doing Costa?"

"A Greek dance Sir."

"On his own?"

"Yes Sir. Greeks do that."

"He's not Greek."

"Affirmative Sir."

* * *

Dance as if no one is watching. Don't look at your feet, just dance. Consciousness of self gone. Giant splattering rain, boots off, bare feet on wet grass. I rubbed coconut oil in my hair and let it wash down. I spun, leapt, taunting evil, any evil, death is life, life is eternal.

(Manoli: 'Sing Stephan, sing like you have never sung before. Sing as loud as you can, then louder. Shout at the Devil.')

(M.O: 'I approve. The experience is a physical expunging of traumatic events by challenging a greater threat, not as fatalism, but as liberation. 'Havening' is a contemporary term for an old Viking therapy: Norse legends. Read when you get a chance… if you live long enough. Unfortunately the therapy does not guarantee survival.')

Boots back on, bergen hefted and a new resolve to say, 'Good Morning! Beautiful Day!' I overdid it. The bloke stumbled and grasped his wife's arm. Their bemused look didn't match my shining elation.

He managed to rasp: "Do we know you?"

"No, just being friendly." I repeated: "Beautiful Day!"

Wariness hadn't left their faces. I realised I'd have to be more selective who I shared my newfound joy of life with. Walk on.

Chapter 45

INSTEAD of fighting against everything negative, I was going with a flow. It made life simpler and generated energy, instead of wasting it. *Turning trauma to energy.*

I recycled a rod, line and feathers from a beach waste bin and set it up near the high water mark. Beachcombing turned up barnacled driftwood, dry enough for a fire. Half an hour later mackerel set the rod twitching.

Seven rugby types and a dog mooched toward me along the shingle ridge; hands in pockets.

"Hi there,' I grinned, 'alright then?"

"Yea fine. See you're into the mackerel."

"Yea, too many for me. Want some?"

"Thanks, appreciate it."

"Are you a rugby club or stag do?"

"No, on leave, military. I'm Bob."

"Good to meet you. I'm Steve."

He came over, shook hands and pointed to his mates straggling along the tide line: "That's Dasher, Tinker, Buster, Ginge, Digger. Lofty's the one with the bucket. The dog's called Ben." Each gave a nod or a wave as they continued combing the beach. Dasher started gutting fish while Ginge pissed in the sea. "More than two shakes is a wank Ginge." He saluted two fingers back.

More firewood appeared, then bread and cider from Lofty's bucket. Everyone got stuck in, poking the fire, turning the fish – good crack. Bob explained that every year they did a section of the Coastal Path 'on plastic' – credit cards. Comfortable B&Bs, fried breakfasts and liquid lunches: "Any fool can be uncomfortable."

"Yea that's true. You lot RAF then?"

"Cheeky bugger – Marines. What's your line?"

"Ex-squaddie 3rd Foot and Mouth. Stretching my legs for a few months. Where you going next?"

"We've had our three weeks, so tomorrow we head back to wives and girlfriends."

Dasher got in first: "Hope they never meet!"

After that it got better: old jokes, standing jokes, stories told a hundred times, fractionally changed each time. All, however lame, greeted with cheers and jeers. A cracking evening by a drift wood fire; laughing till my jaw ached. Ginge took a jar from his back pack.

"Coffee?" I asked.

"No, medic Jill. She had more balls than any of us."

Maybe black humour, then I remembered Col's ashes. Why always coffee jars?

The piss-taking stopped as Bob picked up the jar: "She used to talk about coming with us after the last tour. Ironic really – medics aren't supposed to get hit. We did our best. She told us what to do until she lost consciousness. We couldn't save her so we brought her with us. A toast to Jill."

We all raised our cups, tins, glasses: "To Jill."

Digger: "Remember when…" And they were off; recounting more stories, sadness levelled, warm laughter, more raised cups, tins, glasses.

"She'd have loved this."

Digger was getting tired and emotional: "To Jill."

More speeches of genuine sadness and respect. "To Jill," we echoed again.

The rod flicked, more mackerel, wind picking up on the rising tide. Dasher or Digger, or was it Buster, went for more booze. I'd forgotten what good crack getting pissed on a beach and talking bollocks was.

Lofty was helping me gut the fish: "You can't help being a crap hat Steve."

"Fuck off! I wasn't a crap hat."

More cider, more bread, more fish, more jokes – nearly high water. Bob bashed a tin for silence and picked up the coffee jar. We all stood to something resembling attention.

"All the best Jill. You're home safe now. Your mum's well. Padre got it all sorted. We were proud to have you with us."

We all lowered our pissed heads as he undid the lid and her ashes swirled out into the waves: "Three cheers!"

"Hip ray, hip ray, hip ray."

The cold lonely beach held death and I shivered. There followed a few emotional coughs and kicking of pebbles. The service was impressive. It couldn't have been done better. It honoured her. I went round saying goodbye, shaking hands with Dasher, Nasher, Shagger, Nobby, Lobby, Bodger, Grumpy, Dopey, Twitcher, Tosser and all Snow White's other mates. I'd lost count. Ben the collie was the only one sober. As they moved off, I picked up the coffee jar.

"Do you want this Bob?"

He came back: "Yea, better had. It'll come in handy for the next one!"

An eruption of cheers and jeers, buffeted by the rising wind, and they were gone. Part of the world I'd left behind and missed – comradeship. Blokes and women you could trust with your life. 'Back-up' when you needed it. Where was my back-up? A Snake in a grey Lexus who made Machiavelli look like Bob Geldof.

I crashed out in the bivvy bag. Drunken sleep immediate. Vivid dreams of waves and coffee, drowning, air running out, trapped – wet face, shock, zip stuck; waves rolling me like a beached seal, choking… what a prat, tide still coming in. It was a shame the Marines weren't there to see a squaddie ripping the zip out of his gonk bag – it would have rounded their holiday off nicely.

I cleaned the site and walked on, turning once to see a small tough woman in combat kit, happily beachcombing.

Chapter 46

IT WAS A DAY of noise: running sheep, slamming gates, grass like surf, rolling clouds. By afternoon the movement stopped, except for a stray dog walking alongside and refusing to leave. Memories of Molly made me baulk any responsibility. I tried throwing her sticks to chase. Eventually she got the message.

Caroline's words from Cape Wrath ages ago: 'Those blokes in the storm could be you one day.' I hope her new bloke hadn't shagged her nympho mum, though he'd have to be a saint not to.

Autumn days matched my mood: blanket fog alternated with cold rain so I cancelled the daily swim. Passing near a rail line, glimpses of faces staring out reminded me how easy it would be to give up and get a warm B&B. For the first time I was sad, lonely, wet, cold and hungry. I'd been one or even two at once but never all five, plus a new feeling of homesickness for a home I didn't have.

At furthest north, the same car park, I thought of stopping at the pub near Cape Wrath where Caroline and I had rested up, but it seemed like more pathetic self-indulgence. I walked on. Later I came face to face with a phone box. I knew Manoli's number in Greece by heart. There wasn't a chance in a million I'd get through. Manoli answered. There was shouting and laughter of the tavern – all was the same. I lowered the phone slowly, cutting the thread.

* * *

Down the east coast my mood changed – everything changes – the weather changed. All good, except for a sudden raging toothache. An Arbroath dentist took me on as an emergency. White coats and needles brought intense paranoia. The Black Witch was waiting somewhere. I dealt with it until, near the end, a nurse said: ‘There, nearly done,’ and stroked my neck. Vomit hit the floor as I apologised between retches.

How much remained from the interrogation? I knew now there were malicious implants ready to hatch on key words my precious mind the Coastal Path had been re-building, was not as free as I hoped. What techniques had they used? They knew I'd ditch the mobile. I bet they were laughing all over their poxy drone monitors.

* * *

It was a week or so before the paranoia solidified into the shape of a grey Lexus parked up on Bridlington harbour front. A snake coiled on the bonnet. Whatever ‘hackles’ were, mine went up.

“Steve!” He had the good sense not to try and shake my hand. “Five minutes Steve, that's all, then walk away if you want.”

I lowered my bergen and phased him by jumping in the driver's seat and flicking switches at random.

“We didn't think you'd stick it for so long . You and your Marine buddies had a laugh, didn't you? Mackerel were good, eh?”

“Fuck off Taylor. What do you want?”

“I've a job for you.”

“Huh, you've got a nerve. Unless it's to blow your brains out, I'm not interested.”

He was impervious as ever to my contempt: “Just listen. We know who killed Eric and sank his yacht.”

“So you know it wasn't me. Who was it?”

“His name is Malik. I persuaded U.S. you'd be best for the job. You have local knowledge and motivation. He is based in Athens. Every weekend he takes his motor yacht to Poros Island. On completion you will receive cash and a clean record.”

“I didn't know I had a dirty record.”

Silence. I started flicking indicator and light stems. Noticing his annoyance, I broke one off and let it dangle on the wires.

Quietly I asked :“Has the U.K. operation finished?”

“As far as we can tell, yes. We rolled up their network with acceptable losses and minor collateral damage.”

"Acceptable losses? You mean innocent people were killed?"

"Omelette, eggs – well known saying."

"You complacent little shit."

He was still smirking: "I'll take that as a yes, you'll do the job?"

I got out of the car: "Take this as a yes."

A road-work sign opposite was just the tool, I smashed it through the windscreen. He covered his face from flying glass. Methodically I smashed each window. He was trying to get out and brush glass from his hair. A traffic warden stared in disbelief. I shouted across: "I bet he won't park here again."

I grabbed Taylor's throat: "That is not even a fraction of what you call collateral damage. How do you like it? Now, I'll do the job, not for you, not for revenge, not for money, justice or even my country but for something called Eleftheria." I picked up a shard of glass and scratched ELEFTHERIA on the bonnet.

"You don't even know the meaning of the fucking word – look it up."

He nodded warily as I shouldered my bergen: "Where are you going?"

"You tell me Snake shit. You're the one with the magic trackers."

I cursed myself as I walked away: 'Sorry Eric.'

I was also apologizing for the buzz I felt, for the anticipated hunt and kill. Deep inside revenge and anger vied with hatred. And deep inside I knew I was no better than Taylor.

* * *

That night I slept on a nearby beach: images of flowers and body parts. World leaders shaking hands after years of war made me sick. Why couldn't they have done that at the beginning and saved the suffering? (McGuinness and Paisley.)

* * *

Heavy metal chopper blades, strobe lights and a viscous down draught brought rapid consciousness. The winch man gave me a helmet and lifejacket. Here we go, back to work. I loved it.

Chapter 47

THE BRIEFING was at a Lincolnshire air base: "Mission: kill or capture Malik. Delete capture. That's just for the office. Photo attached. Habits, medical history, sexual preferences, blood group, favourite food, favourite books, favourite music."

"For fuck sake. I want to kill the cunt, not take him on a date."

"Comment ignored." I didn't care. I didn't want to join their club.

"Every Saturday his motor yacht goes to a small bay on the north side of Poros." Looking at the chart, I could picture the bay. "He eats at the beach taverna with his family. They stay at a nearby villa. He returns to his shipping office in Piraeus on the Monday morning – alone. Method: floating rope from headland; 100 metres out; prop fouls; you go to help in a small dinghy; you untangle rope for him; place charge under hull; leave area; target destroyed – your record clean."

"You mean I kill him, you won't kill me."

"Correct."

'What ifs?' were queuing up: "What if he sees the rope?"

"It's monofilament, invisible to fish and humans. I believe you know it?"

"Yea I know where there's tons of the stuff. What if he doesn't want help?"

"Pretend you don't understand and do it anyway."

"What if he sees the explosive pack?"

"He won't. It will be in a dive belt round your waist."

"What if he's not on his own?"

His look said, I can't believe you asked that question: "He's a high value target. Take him out anyway."

"Why this way? There are easier ways to kill him."

"True, but current operational procedure dictates an eye for an eye. If he kills your granny, we kill his granny. They don't like that." What depth of depravity meant killing grannies? (Louis Armstrong : 'And I said to myself what a wonderful world.')

"We've customized this hit for you. He killed your friend and sunk his boat. You kill him and sink his boat – global law. We like to send a message as well as kill."

Customised killing. I was ashamed to be human. But I'd do it.

"What if it all goes tits up?"

"You have orange smoke. Someone will react."

"That's not back-up. That's pissing in the wind."

"Listen corporal, we want him exterminated and we also need to re-instate your loyalty. This op is designed to satisfy each criterion. We have spent a lot of money training you and so far you have not killed anyone. You've got to start paying your way."

"Well, fuck your luck, I'm sorry about that. If you just hang on a minute, I'll nip down the golden oldies rest home and slot a few grannies so the cash hasn't been wasted."

"Comment ignored."

"Yea Yea. I assume I don't take the explosives as hand luggage on the holiday flight?"

"No. When you exit Athens airport, turn left, walk 100 metres. There will be a taxi, get in, there will be a holdall on the back seat, don't talk. He will take you to Piraeus. You take the ferry to Poros and hire a dinghy. Anything else?... Just for your interest the U.S. wanted to drone Malik. I persuaded them you were right for the job. Don't let me down."

I gave him a big thumbs up – Greek style.

Chapter 48

ATHENS AIRPORT: smell of aviation fuel plus herbs, all baked at 30C; taxi driver leaning out smoking. Game on.

"*Kali mera.*"

Flying Dolphin ferry from Piraeus – easy; dinghy hire – easy; 100 metres of monofilament rope, set – easy; waiting – not easy. Routine means death to a terrorist. Acres of hard drives spend their existence searching for routines and anomalies without getting bored or needing holidays.

* * *

Nevada:

"Whose doing the Greek job Costa?"

"79 Sir."

"That guy again. Ain't he got no home to go to?"

"I don't know Sir."

* * *

Malik's routine had been established. His flash motor yacht slowed to stop as the prop fouled. I could see him leaning over the transom as the exhaust panted white smoke on tick-over.

It was revenge time. I waved in a friendly fashion, pointed at the drifting rope, pulled alongside in my dinghy, ready to go over… too keen, no eye contact.

"Wait!"

Malik had a pistol like Leila's and I was looking at the wrong end again. This was the man who killed Eric and Eleftheria. I'd last seen his boat from 10 metres down: "Who are you?"

"I'm on holiday, fishing. If you don't need help, I'll go."

"Come on deck, now."

Bollocks, that didn't take long to go to rat shit. I held my hand out to be pulled aboard. He stayed three metres away, out of range. He was tall, lean, dark and had the look of a diplomat. A young boy, about ten, stood by the wheelhouse door: "Father, what is wrong?"

Malik didn't take his eyes off me: "It's alright. Go below, my son."

I'd been sloppy. Now all I had left was talk and orange smoke.

"Take your belt off and empty it on the deck."

Here we go. Shit or bust: "No."

"If you say no again, I will shoot you."

"You won't because you don't want your son to die. This belt contains sound detonated explosives. Even a head shot would blow us all up. You understand?" Good, always end on a question. I wouldn't have predicted his next move in a million years.

"Are you telling me a jihadist, that you an infidel, has a suicide belt on? You are the same as us!"

He couldn't control his smile turning into a Tommy Cooper chuckle. The situation didn't feel like a bundle of laughs, but he had a point. GSOH hadn't been mentioned at the dating agency. (Good Sense Of Humour.)

* * *

Nevada:

Costa had first seen 79 in Afghanistan on the house roof OP when the attack was aborted. The U.K. and Greek containers came next, then the routine on the Coastal Path. The sea and cliffs made it a priority for his next leave. He just hoped there'd be no one to watch him crap each morning. And now Greece again – Malik was six on the kill list… Good job."

"What gives Costa?"

"They're still talking Sir."

"Goddam it. What's 79 trying to do, bore him to death? Give him five minutes then destroy whole target."

"What about our man Sir?"

"He's not our man, he's a Brit, not one of us, not one of U.S., get it ? They always make it more complicated than it need be. Malik is a major player. Collateralization has unavoidability written all over it. Lose one, save ten – understand?"

"Yes Sir."

* * *

"So infidel assassin, what shall we do? I would die for my cause; you would die for yours. I would go to heaven with my son; you would go to hell. I support Bristol Rovers. Who do you support?"...

Surreal words to die with: "Chelsea."

"So you know what a no score draw is?"

He had a son, a Tommy Cooper laugh, now football. We stared at each other, calculating options.

* * *

Nevada:

"Time up Costa. Totalise target. Lose one save ten."

"There's another boat closing fast Sir."

* * *

I could see past Malik's shoulder: full sails, white bow wave on blue, bit between her teeth, half a mile off, a schooner on a broad reach, closing fast. I knew her... a ghost. He thought I was trying distraction.

"Malik, a yacht will be coming alongside in seconds. If we stay a drone will kill us and your son. I have orange smoke. When I pull the pin, count to three, get your son, move to port side and do what I say. Your decision. We all die or we all live. Inshala."

His pistol didn't waver – smoke grenade ready – pause – I pulled the pin – orange cloud hissed – it rolled on deck – he turned for his son – schooner 20 metres – explosive belt laid on deck – armed 30 seconds – visibility nil – I crashed into Malik – schooner's sails noisily luffing, a bowsprit, a name EL...... a side deck "Go. Go. Go!" I cleared the metre gap. Malik threw his son and followed. Barely registering the helmsman, we hammered below. Orange port holes cleared to blue. I knew the cabin, the companion way. I knew the grin at the wheel and the French tricolour.

"*Vite, vite, très vite*. Explosion in seconds."

A bright flash, a shock wave, a double thump, black smoke, debris splashing nearby. A secondary thump of gas bottles and fuel tank, boat gone… flames on the water.

* * *

Nevada:

"Orange smoke. Schooner moving away. Nice boat Sir."

"I don't care if it's the president's golf buggy. Totalise now. Lose one save ten."

"Too late Sir, target exploded. I bet that hurt."

"Good old 79. He did it after all. Ethical assassination at work. We owe him one. Record schooner's name Costa."

"It's Greek. My parents are Greek Sir."

"O.K. I want its name, not your ethnic origins."

"Eleftheria II, Sir."

"What's it mean?"

"It's what we're fighting for Sir… Freedom."

* * *

The young man at the wheel was still grinning: "Is there a war on?"

Malik and his son sat wide eyed across the saloon table. I couldn't kill him now. I should but I couldn't. Maybe in a few weeks' time, in a rubble-strewn shit pit, but not now, not after I just saved his life.

He looked at his son: "The future of my country."

"There is no future without talk, Malik."

"Agreed. We can talk."

"I'm a squaddie, not a politician."

"Squaddie?"

"Foot soldier. All I can do is pass on intelligence. If they find out you are alive, they will kill me. If you talk to U.K., something might change: 'You don't bomb us, we don't bomb you.' Basic stuff, simple, try it – deal?"

He held his hand out. If I was naïve, I could live with that. Killing was easy, making peace was difficult. Revenge for Eric would be easy. Someone had to start somewhere. Any twat can make enemies. It takes a genius to make peace.

(Mick: 'Dickhead, kill the fucker and his son. He's a termite. He'll kill again. In a few years his son will kill too. Get revenge for Eric, Leila and the rest. It's your job, just do it. You aborted Afghan strike. Get this one right. Your piss-pot ideas don't work. Kill them.')

(Me: 'I kill him and his son; what's left of his family kill me; you kill them; another kills you; your kids kill them and so the suffering goes on. Someone has to break the cycle.')

(Mick: 'You'll regret it.')

* * *

I was sitting in Eleftheria's saloon. A photo of the Crystal Buddha was pinned to the bulkhead. This was a sister yacht, newer, sharper, teak hull, not pitch pine but with enough of the sameness for grief to ache my guts. The saloon table was stained with rings from coffee cups and wine glasses, leaving a mosaic of circles. Eric would have loved the beautiful multi-olympics.

I was staring at the man who had killed Eric and sunk Eleftheria. But he was a man, not a rabid devil. My anger wanted to kill him. He sat opposite me.

I asked: "Why do you kill people?"

"To defend my faith, my family, my country. Why do you?"

"Same reasons, plus one: Freedom. The most important."

* * *

The young skipper came below – French accent, Eric's smile: "Wheel's lashed. Where do you want to go?"

Gratefully I said: “Can you take us to Anagiri beach, south side of Spetse?”

“*D’accord*, no problem.”

“Why did you rescue us?”

“Text message, from someone called Mick. He knew my dad. Said go to Poros north bay. I saw orange smoke and here you are. I am Jack.”

I held my hand out and looked into Eric’s eyes: “I’m Steve. Your dad was a very wise man – one of the best.”

“He wrote to me Steve, about life on the island: you and Angie. He said you were on a difficult path.”

My thoughts stalled at the mention of Angie. Malik stood and reached across to shake Jack’s hand.

“NO! don’t. Put your boat on course now.”

Jack shrugged and loped up the companion way.

I hissed at Malik: “That’s the son of the man you killed. If you ever come to my country, I will kill you.”

He responded: “And if you ever come to my country, I will kill you. But if your son comes in peace, I will protect him.”

I looked at his kid: “If this war can be ended, the next generation stands a chance. I will not kill your son.”

(Mick: ‘What a load of airy fairy bollocks. Slot the fucker.’)

(Mr Harman: ‘If only there’d been a way not to bomb German cities.’)

(Eric: ‘If the same amount of money had been spent planting trees in the Middle East as on weapons, it would be one giant, green ,peaceful oasis. Honour my memory.)

(John Lennon: ‘Imagine.’)

When they found out Malik was alive, I’d be a: ‘Terminate On Sight Anywhere.’ What a prize TOSA I’d be. I’d get it in the neck, or back, or guts, unless Plan B worked. What was Plan B? I was working on it. Walk on.

Chapter 49

IN THE BAY on Spetse I helped Jack drop the sails on the fore deck so Malik and son could slide underneath into the water, unseen. I could still kill him, then what? Kill his son? There is a difference between a soldier and a murderer and I knew what it was.

All the gear on Eleftheria II was similar. She had been built in Thailand to original Camper and Nick plans. The original showed a giant Bermudan rig of almost 'J' Class proportions. Eric had her re-rigged as a schooner and the balanced beauty was complete. Jack explained that rumours in the yachting community were that his dad and Eleftheria had been lost to pirates off Somalia. Guilt raddled my conscience as we hoisted sails together.

"You have done this before Steve."

"Many times Jack. Your father was a brilliant sailor."

"Do you know what happened to him?"

"No, not exactly."

I did know exactly. I knew the co-ordinates. I knew where Eleftheria and his dad were and who killed them. And who rescued their murderer and set him free.

He stared, until he realized I wasn't going to say any more. I concentrated securing the halyards. Jack returned to the wheel, standing just like Eric, completely in his element. Eleftheria II took off like her sister. You can't kill freedom's spirit.

"Where to Steve?"

I pointed: "Hydra harbour – Manoli's. Do you know it?"

"Are you kidding me?! It's our home port. Manoli's is our Club."

I went forward, rested on the pulpit and looked down at the bow wave. I wished I'd swam ashore and killed Malik and his son. I wish I hadn't seen those four shapes gliding below. Please God, not dolphins – I'll crack up . They broke the surface, silver surfing with joy, guardian angels. I cracked up – tears dripped.

For a hairy-arsed squaddie I was certainly doing a lot of crying these days, disguised only by staring at my friends.

Eleftheria II cleared the island's fluky air. We gybed the aft sail, goose-winging. Accelerating away; both of us whooping with elation. Dolphins stepping up a gear, racing ahead – eight, ten, fifteen knots. Working my way out on the bowsprit holding the forestay. Flying only feet from their backs. Free spirits. I wanted to join them. Just dive down; live forever; become a dolphin.

(Angie's voice, so real, called me back: 'Stevie! Cold beer, 'cos I love you.')

I could see her face full of sun and fun. I could smell the coconut oil. Fine bow spray misted my vision. She was gone. Sadness went too. Only joy of good times remained.

Jack pointed to the wheel. I took it. He went below and chucked me a new T-shirt, 'MSF', same as Eric always wore. I pointed to the motif. Jack shouted back: "Medicin Sans Frontiers. Dad worked for them once, didn't you know?"

Eric was already my hero. Now there was only one level above that: Dolphin, swimming off the bow… he was already there.

Jack brought Eleftheria II into Hydra just like his dad. Figures wandered in front of Manoli's tavern. I couldn't see who but I knew they'd be watching. Maybe I'd been forgotten or not welcome.

A new 'No-Smoking' sign at a trendy bar had at least half a dozen locals puffing away for Greece. I loved it. A healthy contempt for authority. I was waiting for some bastard to put a sign saying, 'No Shagging.' They'd be a grunting and rutting from the quay to the light house! My anarchist nature bought a packet of Marlborough. I tucked them in my T-shirt sleeve – not to smoke – just to say 'bollocks.'

* * *

"Stephan! *Ela! Ti kanis! Bravo!"* It was hugs, beer, everyone talking at once, food, stories, laughter, music, loving, scolding, banter. All generating unstoppable kefi until Manoli couldn't help himself. He leapt and danced in a sublime state of joyous exuberance. It was Ma and Pa Larkin on retsina. Any excuse to raise the flag of happiness.

We all joined him. Arms and shoulders linked in a line, moving to a circle: Jack and his girlfriend, fishermen, little Eleni, grizzled Yourgos, expats and a new generation of young lovers discovering the meaning of life. Feet sliding on spilt beer, harmony, three breaking away to the centre, cigarette smoke swirling. If I could bottle this, wars would be extinct, the UN redundant and defence budgets used for planting trees.

The dance circle moved back to random chairs. On the wall behind the bar, where Angie had dished out drinks, were dozens of postcards and photos. There was one of six smiling faces. I can't remember who took it. We were a couple then. She looked good but it didn't show the real beauty I loved – photos couldn't catch that.

I felt a hand on my shoulder: "Did she ever come back Manoli?"

"No Stephan, she never came back. She sent us a card from Australia. She is married; she has children." I hadn't expected that – it hurt. He unpinned the card and gave it to me to read. I wanted it to say: 'Give all my love to Stevie when you see him. I miss him so much. He was the love of my life. I hope he's happy now.' It didn't. It said: 'Love to all from Perth. Hubby and kids fine. Going sailing now. Love Angie xx.'

"I'm happy for her Manoli."

"You and her were good together, you know."

He then went on to tell me the latest hilarious gossip: how Yourgos, the baker, had got drunk and burnt all the village bread, so he threw it in the harbour – hundreds of black loaves drifting around. He then spent the day hiding with many and varied widows, until his tortured libido crashed and he had to give himself up to the Port Police. He was told he was not a suspect. It could have been anyone!"

I loved it. The thought of Yourgos drained by his exuberant concubines and surrendering to the police, cracked me up laughing again.

All was well. Sophie and Mick had a baby, so life went on as always.

I couldn't sleep, just talked, danced, drank. Time here was too precious for sleep. A lot of old faces I remembered and some new ones: lifelong memories being made.

* * *

The early morning ferry to Piraeus was full of homeward tourists, sheepdog reps and Angie's face. I was even more tempted to stay and go over to see Molly until a too-friendly American offered me a lift in his Boston Whaler, twin Johnson 85's. He was too tidy, too clean, buzzed haircut, white vest under light blue club shirt. It would have been less obvious if he'd worn a CIA baseball cap.

"No thanks." The U.K. debriefing was going to be interesting enough, without being renditioned, reprogrammed and redacted in some U.S. black hole.

* * *

Nevada:

"Did they pick up 79, Costa?"

"No Sir, he's on the ferry…'

"No crap. We'll have to sit in with the Brits."

Chapter 50

BACK IN THE U.K., the same grey six, plus Taylor, watched the drone video of Malik and me on his motor yacht: orange smoke, a schooner rescuing me, then presumably Malik and his boat blown to pieces – end – job well done. Video proof: clean, professional, unequivocal. Taylor shone. As operational controller he could expect an MBE, enhanced pension and slimy approbation from his superiors. As the operative who actually did the job, I decided to piss in his beer: "Malik got away."

Faces whitened, looked at each other, then at Taylor, then back at me.

I piled on the agony: "Malik had a gun. We talked. He said some Jihadists wanted to talk. I set off orange smoke. We jumped into the sea. Malik swam away." Let the polygraph pick the bones out of that.

"I was rescued by a schooner."

It was like being caught shagging the gym mistress – or so Mick said. Taylor's face turned sickly red with blotches. He groped for straws and stopped breathing: "Shit, shit, shit, shit! Is it possible he's dead? The U.S. need DNA, body parts, his head, anything. They trusted me not to screw up. Malik could be anywhere now, shit, shit,… shit."

His anally-challenged panic seemed to be upsetting the six, so he tried to salvage something with a show of decisive action. Pointing at me: "Right, you! Go to the trawler. Stay there. You've screwed up again, not me, you, like Afghanistan… Go. Go… Now."

The 'trick cyclist' sitting at the back was now focusing on Taylor. I'd gone from hero to zero in one minute. My bonus would be used elsewhere. Even so I was chuffed to bits. Not only had I pissed in Taylor's beer, but he'd drunk it too.

Chapter 51

I PAUSED on the wet pavement, dark puddles reflecting 'Nelson's Fart'. Harry had offended yet another customer. It gave me a smile. Inside I could see Mick at the bar nursing a half: "Dickhead! Good to see you. How's Greece?"

"Fine Mick. Thanks for calling Jack. How did you do that?"

"I didn't. Someone's pulling your pisser mate. Manoli phones us every week. He said you'd had an accident; Jack rescued you and you were O.K. but still danced like a malaka."

"O.K., doesn't matter now."

Harry's welcome had been used before many times: "Usual, or are you going to pay for it this time?" He hadn't changed. After all the madness, he was still reassuringly grumpy: "On your own then Steve, not married?"

"Can't afford to and drink as well at your prices."

Mick and I chatted, which meant taking the piss out of each other – but things had changed. He'd never been happier – Sophie, baby Bumpy, and fishing all good if you fiddled quotas and landed discards.

"Do you want your job back Steve? Sophie doesn't like me going to sea on my own."

"Is that the same job where people try to blow me up then shoot me in the back with 50,000 volts?"

He didn't reply, so I said yes.

* * *

It wasn't like old times. We got on and the weather was comfortable but inside I was restless for something. I couldn't settle; I needed danger spikes. Even Taylor turning up with a job would have been welcome. Mick wanted the opposite and he'd found it, so most evenings I'd prop up the bar with Joe, the Nelson's resident alky. He never looked drunk, never violent or abusive, in fact he was a decent bloke, ex RN, a mate of Harry's. He just continually drank beer with pusser rum chasers.

For Mick, Fridays were the exception. We'd have a pint each. I'd ask if he wanted another one, he'd say no, I'd get one anyway, he'd drink it anyway, then return to his cosy nest with Sophie and Bumpy. This routine was interrupted one week by Harry calling from the cellar: "Steve, phone call."

Mick jeered: "Busty Bertha caught up with you mate. You'll have to pay her now."

"Piss off Bollock Chops."

I tried to stand out of range of Harry's wagging ears: "Hello."

"We have a job for you."

The voice was whining, female call-centre estuary, laden with bureaucratic boredom – a typical sales pitch.

"Who are you?"

"I represent a government agency. We are contracted to assist in non-routine programmes. We record all calls for legal and training purposes. Okaaay?"

"What do you want?"

The hypnotic resonance didn't change: "Listen this is important. Do not hang up. We want you to terminate someone."

The joke was wearing thin: "Who?"

"You. We want you to kill yourself. SIT." (Self Inflicted Termination.)

I tried to hang up. The phone was stuck to my ear.

The tone didn't change: "Listen, this is important. Everyone fears something more than death, like pain or reputation destruction. Last week a drug dealer, his daughter at uni. ….we persuaded him to jump under a train. There was not enough evidence to convict, but enough points to terminate. He loved her more than his own life. We saved the government Effort, Paperwork and Cash (EPC), especially since the new EU legislation means suicides are cheaper than assassinations. It's all down to Treasury cuts."

Taylor was playing silly games; I wanted more clues: "If you want me dead, there's plenty of sub-contractors who would do it, or is Health and Safety an issue?"

She loosened up, off script: “Partly H&S but mainly cost. All budgets have been slashed and we have to reduce the cost of terminations.”

It was like discussing the month’s sales figures. I looked back at Mick, Harry and Joe, just to make sure the beer hadn’t driven me into La La Land.

“O.K., so you want me to jump off a cliff?”

Added crispness came to her voice; she was ticking boxes: “No. ‘This is important.’ Go to the car park behind the pub. Red car. Under driver’s seat, a revolver – use it. Your resources, reputation and relationships (RRR), will be respected.”

I’d had enough: “Listen you sick bitch, go fuck yourself.”

“This conversation is being recorded. Obscene language can result in prosecution. Go to the red car now. This is important.”

The dial tone held me for a few seconds. With senses as brittle as ice, I walked back into the bar.

“You O.K. mate?”

“No Mick I’m not. They interrogated you, didn’t they?”

“Yea, so what?”

“Did they try to hypnotize you?”

“Yea, Jackson 85 did an int. course; said ignore the psycho babble, just keep adding seven to any number you can think of. What did you do?”

“I didn’t. I was sure I didn’t go under – now I don’t know.”

Mick switched on: “Who was the call from?”

“The Black Witch friendly customer call centre.”

“What did they say?”

“I’ll tell you in a minute… Joe, want a pint?”

I didn’t have to ask twice: “Do us a favour Joe. Go to the red car in the car park, look under the driver’s seat, don’t touch anything, come back and tell me what you see.” He really did lick his lips.

Mick was serious: “Tell me what they said Steve. Now.”

I didn’t get a chance – four loud fireworks popped outside. Mick reacted first; I followed. Two armed police were staring at Joe slumped in the driver’s seat holding a revolver. A civilian was standing behind them. I leaned close and shouted in his ear: “Taylor, you murdering bastard. You’ll pay for this!”

He stared in fear: “He’s not you. Who is he?”

“Don’t you even know the names of the people you kill? This is, or was Joe – Joe, this is Taylor, your murderer.”

I grabbed his head and started smashing it into Joe’s shoulder: “Go on, say sorry to Joe, go on, say it, say it!”

Mick pulled me away: “Shut up, cool it.”

Taylor followed us in a daze: “How did he get in the car?”

“Don’t you know snake shit? It isn’t me, so it must be some innocent bastard you call collateral damage.”

“It was a mistake. It wasn’t meant to happen. I’m sorry.”

“Don’t say sorry to me, say it to his family. What was meant to happen?”

“After the debrief, we decided to terminate your contract. The new head of ‘D’ section is a ‘fast track graduate’. He thought we meant ‘kill you’. I was too late to stop it.”

“I don’t believe you, you pathetic little shit. Are you telling me Joe has a tight group of four bullets in his chest ’cos you toss pots can’t speak fucking English? Death by twatting euphemism. Why not say ‘kill’ or does it offend you? Use simple English like: ‘couldn’t organize a piss up in a fucking brewery’ – simple, understand?”

I was shouting and shaking: “Right, we’ll go and see those six prats before they blow up the only fucking brewery left in this god-forsaken country.”

I couldn’t stop ranting: “How many cock-ups happen ’cos you can’t get your words right? Intelligence is supposed to be intelligent. Get it?”

Mick finalised it by hassling Taylor into his car: “Go with him Steve. Sort the fuckers out and come back.”

* * *

Taylor phoned ahead, so after the thirty-mile drive, the least I expected was hood, cuffs and needle. Self protection had gone out the window. I was dead in their eyes, so now I’d go down fighting.

The same six. Guilty averted stares. Their only defence, a paper file: “Joseph Birket – ‘Joe’– Alcoholic – Labour party –

Drink driving – Nine years Royal Navy… a revolver, loaded, one round…"

If they were expecting some acceptance of the murder, they were mistaken. I'd been silent in the car; now I exploded: "Look you stupid fuckers. Capital punishment has been abolished for left-wing pissheads, so get your act together before there are any more fuck ups."

Taylor held up his hands in trite appeasement. The young, RAF type spoke . He looked enough of a pillock to be head of D section: "We've decided to take you at your word."

"What fucking word was that?"

He ploughed on: "Comment ignored. We make difficult decisions every day. Sometimes we get it wrong, for which we apologise. Our new back office has calculated we only have to be right 25% of the time for successful outcomes. So far we are on target."

"You are not making sense – 25% of what? You're talking bollocks."

He gave me a patronizing look over the top of his glasses. I thought: don't smile, please don't smile. If you dare smile, your pen is going right up your fucking nose.

He continued talking bollocks: "It doesn't matter how we got here or why; alarm bells have been going off. Suffice to say, we have to do the right thing now. I think we are all in agreement on that."

I tried to make my look of contempt as obvious as possible. It didn't stop his own twisted logic: "Malik is alive and leading a clan of jihadists in Syria against Assad. Assad is our enemy. That makes Malik our friend, so now we do not want to eliminate him. We want to talk to him."

His laboured didactic tone didn't help his argument. I incinerated the implications with his other waffle and tried to understand the point. I had a good idea where it was going: "How does he know you don't want to kill him?"

"Ah, here's the good bit. You could have eliminated him and his son, but didn't. His code of honour dictates he respects you. We need to talk to him, not negotiate. We don't negotiate with terrorists, we talk – understand?"

He looked around for recognition of his use of the approved semantics, so I decided to shake the tree: "Fucking JC. How do you tossers sleep at night? If you did English at uni, you should go and ask for your money back. I thought snake shit here was bad enough. I wouldn't trust you lot with a donkey's dick, so why should he?"

If it had been an interview for officer training, I'd failed. They regarded me with the same detached superiority as the white coats had when I spewed up. The female 'trick cyclist' at the back, silently mouthed the words as she wrote: 'Comment ignored.'

RAF twat went on: "We won't go into whys and wherefores. But if there were alternatives, we would consider using them. You are the key to peace talks."

I burst out laughing, but he kept going: "Forget your contempt for officers and our modus operandi. We ask, and it's a big ask, to do this in the national interest. U.K. and U.S. lives depend on you getting Malik to talks."

He was laying it on thick. I got the message. I just didn't trust them. But it was exactly what I had talked to Malik about: stopping the suffering of war by discussion, cease fires, safe havens, UN peace keepers, et al.

There was more: "If you say no, you can go back fishing or chasing Australian girls or whatever you choose." Lying bastard. They were going to kill me sometime, whatever I said. "Steven we need your decision. Yes or no?"

I was on the back foot. He'd played the patriot card. Say no and you get an automatic 100 points: termination. As if to clinch the deal, on cue, stage left, in walked the Rt Hon J… B…; a face I recognized from the TV. He addressed me directly: "Malik is the point of the lever. The fulcrum is the Middle East; peace is the prize. Enough pressure on our end of the lever, and life will change for millions of ordinary people. You can deliver Malik. I hope I don't need to say any more."

His charisma made the 'arse-speak' sound truly wonderful. I leapt to my feet and shook his hand like a star-struck autograph hunter. I thought the grey six were going to break into applause as he left.

“Steven, now you’ve heard it from the top, what do you say?”

“Yes of course. But if Taylor screws up again, I’ll slot the bastard.”

“Comment ignored. We’ll pretend we didn’t hear that last bit. Well done! Anyway you won’t regret it. It will always stand you in good stead. Now, you go off and get a full English breakfast. You’ll like that. And later there’ll be an intense briefing on the plane.”

Disrespectfully, I sat as they filed out and sunk my hands in my pockets just in case anyone, misguidedly, tried to wish me luck. The chatty one stuck his head back round the door: “I’ve borrowed Corporal Weller’s fake tan cream. She always looks like an orange in the middle of winter – help you blend in. Let me have it back when you’ve finished with it.”

“No expense spared, eh? Nothing like an orange head to blend in with Syrian street fighters.”

“I’m sorry, you would not believe the expense we go to Steven.”

His smile disappeared with my sarcasm. Joe’s killing was being swept away for the ‘greater good’ and my life would be treated the same. He was just trying to do his job, so if peace talks worked, my cynicism would be redundant. I hated them and they were on my side. I hated all sides. It wasn’t right or wrong anymore, it was us against them, them, them and them: multi-sided wars. New alliances splitting old friends, until expediency said otherwise.

‘Stockholm Syndrome’ = sympathy for captors. ‘Croydon Syndrome’ = sympathy for the enemy. What could I call hatred of all sides?... got it: ‘Snake Syndrome.’

Chapter 52

STRAPPED just behind the flight deck in the C130, was an aluminium crate the size of a photo booth. Inside were two seats facing two monitors with a bank of buttons, surrounded by instructions in American speak, stuck on with duct tape: 'Do not use Code J on Screen One'; 'Do not use Coffee in this booth'; 'Do not use Donuts'; and in huge 'fuck off' lettering: 'DO NOT UNPLUG ANYTHING.' Shame it wasn't a Greek flight crew – it would have been turned into a coffee bar with free donuts and battery chargers plugged into every orifice.

The amount of equipment begged, borrowed or stolen from U.S. stores was becoming embarrassing. The trouble was, it was good kit. With the booth door closed, noise was down to a low buzz, but nothing could keep out the smell of warm electronics and aviation fuel .

Briefing officer: "Listen in." There was only me. Who else was he talking to?

"Mission: To escort Malik to Latakia, Syria." He repeated it. Wing Co Bean was past his 'sell-by-date' and losing the edge. He started to ramble: "We were sustaining too many para insertion fatalities from HALO (High Altitude Low Opening) and HAHO (High Altitude High Opening), so now we've developed LANO (Low Altitude No Opening)." He was pleased with his little joke.

I had developed a very unhealthy contempt for all Ruperts. There were good ones but the trouble was, brown snouts got promotion.

He twaddled on: "Uffa Fox developed the idea in World War 2 to rescue ditched aircrew-airborne lifeboats – saved quite a few." Good old Uffa. I didn't like the way this was going. Maybe LANO wasn't a joke.

Sgt 'Gibbo' had said put 'Sir' on the end of a sentence and you can say anything to an officer: "Could you please get on with the relevant fucking detail, Sir." Briefings: the clue is in the first part, 'brief'. I was pissing in the wind. He'd learnt his script and he was going to stick to it.

"We modified Uffa's idea and developed a sealed paper-mache canoe – looks like a coffin. No live trials yet. You're the first."

He certainly chose his words carefully to build up confidence. So I was going to be chucked out of a C130, doing 120mph, in a sealed paper coffin, into a war zone where the RNLI would cut off my orange head if I didn't drown: SNAFU (Situation Normal All Fucked Up)… good and proper. Life certainly wasn't getting any better.

"Sign here, just in case there's an inquiry."

I signed Mickey Mouse. He didn't check. I was rapidly thinking of turning the photo booth into a porta-loo.

"Good. I'll show you the boat."

It looked like a standard sea kayak with a sealed perspex cockpit hatch; webbing harness netted the hull. "Get in, try it. You do nothing on launch. Usual red on, green on. You get pushed out; static line does the rest; count to ten. If you reach ten, you're still alive. She'll impact bows on and hopefully right herself. You open the hatch; press the release clip. The parachute will sink away. Equipment: paddles, fresh water, cash in dollars, seven Mars bars, one Thermos… I hope you don't take sugar. No life jacket, no weapons. That way you might live a little longer if you get caught. Oh, I nearly forgot the mobile phone. Memorize this number. You can call in air strikes. I hear you're good at that. International press badge, might help, but all sides are targeting them, so don't count on it. Cover: you are a freelance photo journalist whose lost his camera and colleagues."

I couldn't help adding: "And his mind?"

He gave me a quaint look: "Yes indeed. So what do you think of Uffa Fox now?"

"He certainly gets a big Greek thumbs up from me."

"Good. Weather: wind light, northerly, fair, partly cloudy sky, sea slight. There's no back up, but Akrotiri is only 70K."

What was I supposed to do – walk it?

"They've got new Russian radar, so we go in very low, 250ft. Parachute should deploy. No reserve, of course."

“Of course.”

“Method: paddle east for 7K, stop 100 metres from beach, sink canoe. It’s biodegradable in 48 hours, as indeed you are. It’s our new eco-green policy.”

Another brilliant one-liner. I tried a laser stare to fry the jokes.

“When I get ashore, how do I find Malik?”

“Easy, there is only one garage on the cornice. No lights, but a 24-hour queue of cars. The owner wants his cash in Cyprus so he will take you to Malik. Questions?”

“Are Qaeda talking to U.K. – U.S. now?”

“No, that’s why you’re going.” He was lying.

“How do I know you’re not going to kill Malik, and I’m being set up as a target marker?”

“Because we would send someone else, not you.” He was lying again.

“How many U.K. – U.S. has he killed?”

“That intelligence is beyond your pay grade.”

“Some?”

“Yes, some.”

* * *

Nevada:

“Who are they sending this time Costa?”

“79 again Sir.”

“Gee, ain’t that guy got no family? If he screws up, we’ll drone the lot. Should have done it last time.”

“Yes Sir.”

Chapter 53

HE WAS RIGHT. It was like being in a coffin. Sgt Watts load master, the exact opposite to Wing Co Bean: confident, calm body language, professional. I felt like a Formula One driver with the chief mechanic giving last-minute instructions. The back ramp went down, my new mate Sgt Watts shouted in my ear a clear briefing: "Get to land. Do it. Get back to base. Sir."

I'd never been called 'Sir' before. He secured the hatch. I was about to be the fastest canoeist in the world. His hand was flat on the perspex, fingers counting down – Red on – five – four – three – two – one – Green on – GO!

The canoe rattled down the ramp into the slipstream – roaring props overhead – noise vibration – tail disappearing – static line jerk – parachute deployed – blackness – impact – sea over hatch… silence, a feeling of peace. I was home.

Check for leaks, open hatch, ditch it… survival elation immediate. Beautiful stars. My mate the Plough: "Hello Plough, good to see you." First thought: how much did it cost to get me here? I sealed the waist band and assembled the paddles as the Herc faded to nothing. They'd be in Akrotiri having a fry-up in thirty minutes.

First job: cup of tea and a Mars bar. Strange place for a tea break, bobbing peacefully under the stars miles from land, but I didn't want to be anywhere else.

Quick release buckle: twist, thump, parachute and webbing gone – deep six. I was now deniable, apart from my accent, brain, uncircumcised dick and orange head.

* * *

I settled into a good rhythm, dipping the paddles smoothly; course due east 7k, calm sea, wind light, Plough on left shoulder. I felt great. Full of energy and an over-inflated sense of my own importance. Rest every 20 minutes, a brew and Mars, muscles warm.

Car headlights just asking to be hammered. People in denial, shopping, chatting until it was too late. The shore always looks closer than it really is; muffled light surf, last Mars bar; double check air support number and chuck. Heat generated by paddling disappeared as the canoe sank. I side-stroked in, jeans and trainers slowing me down . Feet touched sand. I bellied in on the small waves to suss out any cover: a small fishing pier was handy. More tracers skywards from a pissed-off sentry. Phase one, insertion, tick.

* * *

The Press badge could be a life saver or a bullet magnet. Near the queue of cars for petrol were several burnt out wrecks; windows smashed, wheels gone, ideal to rest up. Traffic wardens didn't seem a problem so I got my head down in the nearest and immediately attracted a flashing torch: four armed militiamen. It was time to join the Press Corp. (Did other operators jobs go tits up at first base, or just mine?)

"Why are you in this wrecked car?"

"I'm waiting for petrol." The translation caused a burst of laughter, always a good sign. Quickly I added: "I have lost my friends. I'm an Irish journalist."

"Why are you wet?"

"I fell in the sea – drunk"

More laughter, but it didn't stop them taking my mobile and cash. Phase two was taking a hammering. I eased out, keeping my smile showing. I was not a captive so I wouldn't act like one; shaking hands with them all to emphasise the point. Journalists were in the area so the cover had credibility. With the torch full in my face, they weren't sure what to do next, so I filled the social gap to stop them putting a bullet in my head: "Have you seen my friends – journalists?"

There was a discussion, the coin spun: "We will take you to the hospital. There are two journalists there. Tell your newspaper we are not terrorists."

The garage owner would have to wait. I had no choice.

* * *

From outside it sounded like a choir from hell: screaming tenors with a bass line of agonized groans. It wasn't a hospital anymore, just a roofless abattoir, carpeted with jellied blood and shaded by fly-ridden netting, air infused with sour tasting, metallic smells.

A pair of blue flak jackets, labelled PRESS, topped by blank faces, lay propped against a wall. I grabbed the nearest, shook him until his eyes opened and whispered: "I'm Steve your friend or I'm dead. What's your name?" His stare acknowledged pain and not much else but he did manage to pull my sleeve to his bloody colleague. "I'm David. He needs water and a doctor." (Correction, he didn't need either. He was dead.) 'Nil by mouth' had been written on his forehead, like a sick joke.

Everything was dust covered, except the swarms of violet flies gorging the crimson blood. The militia guards had lost interest since my 'reunion' and wandered off smoking. A pile of arms and legs, rotting in the heat, stacked in a corner waiting to be reclaimed. This was not a Camp Bastion with good survival rates, here was a certainty of a festering death nursed by wailing relatives with appealing eyes and pleading mouths: "Doctor, please doctor." I could have helped but didn't.

The militia men were outside: "I need water for my friend."

The leader looked blank: "Why is your friend more important than my father?"

I went back and decided not to tell David his friend was dead. He probably knew but was in denial: "I will get you and your mate out, but first, do you know an Al Qaeda commander called Malik?"

"No. Al Qaeda are in the northern sector. Get water."

Two mortar thumps nearby racked up my adrenalin: "I'll be back soon to get you out." Unnecessarily I added: "Wait here." My feet skidded on blood.

War zones are like factories, strangers are allocated real or imagined identities depending on facial characteristics, clothing and what's being carried. I found an old car tyre to add to the

Press badge: I was now a journalist with a puncture. What could go wrong?

I jogged unchallenged past disparate groups of fighters. Time to ask: "Malik?" Nothing but suspicious stares – keep moving. Don't wait for questions.

Again: "Malik?" A hand pointed vaguely towards intensive fighting.

I shouted: "Malik!"

His head turned from a group hunched over a map, face out of context, then recognition. He gave orders and walked over: "I said I would kill you if you came to my land. This is my land."

"It's not your land yet. You need help; I can help. In 24 hours the road to Latakia will be closed and you will be surrounded and killed."

"If we fight and die that is God's wish."

"No, fight and live. I can get air strikes for the whole 20-mile wide coastal strip."

"What do you want in return?"

"U.K.-U.S. want to talk to you in Latakia."

"Why should I trust you?"

"If I call in an airstrike now, will you come with me? Trust me or die."

"You said that to me in Greece and my son was saved. I will trust you if the airstrike kills our enemy. What is the tyre for?"

"It is a gift."

"Thank you, then this is a gift for you."

He passed an AK, spare mag taped on, bayonet unfolded.

"They will attack soon. We will attack first. If your airstrike can destroy their heavy weapons, we will win, you will live, and we will go to Latakia."

The challenge was simple and direct.

"I need a mobile phone." He pulled out three and passed one over. "As soon as I make the call their mortars will zero in on us. We will have to retreat. We wait three minutes, then attack. O.K.?"

Now would not be a good time for a low battery or number engaged.

"Malik, do you have smoke grenades?"

“No.” I stuffed rags in the tyre, lit them and dialled.

* * *

Nevada:

“X ray over.”

“This is 79. My position black smoke northern sector, engage all targets east 150 metres. Confirm. Over.”

“X ray – Roger. I confirm all targets. 150 metres east black smoke. Over.”

“79 – Roger, Out.”

* * *

“Malik, run back.”

He gave more orders and dozens of jihadists swarmed back with us. We’d just hit the deck when the mobile I’d chucked was bracketed by Russian HE (high explosives). Another three minutes and American rockets slammed into their heavy vehicles and jellied the contents.

“Malik. We go to Latakia now.”

“Not yet. Follow me.”

Orders to charge are the same in any language. We were off. Fuck it.

“Allahu Akbar!”

I needed a bullet catcher so tucked in behind the biggest bloke I could find. No flanking, no covering fire, just a bunched up, mad, head on assault, firing from the hip… Not in the manual, but it was working. One enemy with aimed fire would have dropped the lot of us. We were halfway across open ground, all screaming with adrenalin, charging to kill… this was fun. The big guy in front fell, splatting blood on my face. I got behind another one. He went down. I didn’t care now. I screamed: “Bayonets, Allahu Akbar.”

We were amongst them thrashing death, shit and corruption – stop – bayonet wounded – six kneeling shot in the head. Their last sight: a mad press badge with bayonet. “Malik get your men back now.” More orders as we raced back, collecting weapons from the dead… “Malik, Latakia now.”

* * *

Nevada:

“Good shooting Costa. Did 79 make it?”

“Can’t say Sir, too much smoke. I think so. I hope so.”

* * *

The Press gang were still there: one still alive, the other still dead.

“Did you get water Steve?”

“Yes David.”

I hadn’t, so Malik gave him his bottle. Uselessly he poured some into his colleague’s mouth. “We go now David.”

“I can’t leave him here. I have to take him home.”

I hefted the dead journo on to my shoulders and set off to find garage man, blood and gunk running down my back.

The Toyota pick-up was ready. Malik sat in the passenger seat. David and I sat in the open back with his dead mate. At the first check point, heading north, Malik waved. The guards fired dozens of rounds in the air in salute. I replied with a full 30 mag. Who cared where they landed? I regretted it seconds later: survival elation had over ridden professionalism. (‘Twat – keep switched on. You may have needed that.’)

The two journos rolled together. David’s arm had fallen over his mate’s chest, their faces close. One smooth, relaxed at peace and dead. The other alive, mentally tortured. It was difficult to see who was better off.

Once or twice David spewed up to confirm he was the live one and prompting a rant: “Never again, never. What do I tell his mother?” I let him go on for a few minutes about murder, water, green fields, before kicking him in the guts hard enough to lay him out. Would their newspaper print that image to illustrate their bravery in the pursuit of truth so others could judge the madness of war? If they’d been in uniform, both would have medals, consequently all sides hated them. My euphoria –

charging and killing people – enemy today, tomorrow a friend – made me ashamed. I hadn't been brave, I was just having fun. Great motives camouflaged mans' sickness… the thrill of war: to look serious and important, to show false modesty, to get admiring hero worship… crap, crap, crap.

Bollocks to war – 'What Is It Good For? Absolutely Nothing. Fuck All.'

Unarmed journos were the real heroes, not strutting, Kalashnikov-posing twats.

By standing and hanging on to the roof bar the desiccating wind eased my anger. I tried saying it was just the after effects of action, that getting Malik to talks would stop the suffering. Both were partly true. It was the other parts of my head that worried me. I'd been fighting with terrorists, killing people. I'd enjoyed being so close to death and surviving. I looked at the dead journo. He'd lost – I'd won. I was better than him. I hadn't been acting. I was worse than Taylor. He just gave orders. Obeying evil orders excused nothing. It said you are sick.

(Eric: 'Sickness can be cured. It's people who don't know they're sick – that's the real problem. Walk on Steve. You'll get there.')

Random check points waved us through. I waved the AK above my head in pathetic machismo. If I saw my photo in a newspaper, what would I think? Brave, good looking hero? No, I'd think what a twat, an evil twat… an evil twat causing suffering.

War distorts values: everything we do is right; everything the enemy does is wrong. Wearing pretty uniforms and badges afterwards to sanitise the butchery. Our atrocities excused by their atrocities, like a child's argument. Demonise the enemy with their real or imagined atrocities: Germans were evil in 1940, now they are good guys. Mick was once spouting off about evil 'rag heads'. Broadening his rant to everyone not 'White Anglo Saxon Protestants'. (WASP's.)

'Easy Mick. What about our mate Tola – a brilliant Fijian?'

'He's different. He's a good bloke.'

We agreed racism was not only evil but illogical. Everyone was colour blind when Tola was patching them up or when

Chelsea's new forward scored, so why when an atrocity occurred, everyone went racist?

(Mick had the solution: earthquakes! 'Have you noticed in a natural disaster everyone helps out?' 'You're right Mick, let's start a few earthquakes and stop war crimes.' I saw his point: a common enemy to fight. 'Yea, why not?')

We arrived in Latakia as more NATO jets flew over, and since we hadn't been vaporized I assumed the new 'no fly zone' was in operation. Plan A was still Plan A. My job ended at the ferry but, and it was a big but – Rule 7: 'Things go wrong when you relax at the end.'

David had eventually acknowledged his mate was dead. We bought a plywood coffin in a carpenter's workshop, wrapped him in plastic bin bags from the supermarket and screwed the lid down. The chippy was proud of his work and lined up the screw heads. We declined another coat of varnish.

Malik went off to find the go-betweens, fixers and diplomats; essential for the smooth progress of talks about talks. We didn't shake hands, didn't say goodbye – just a look, which said… I didn't know what it said. I'd done my bit, so David and I went to get ferry times, leaving the coffin in the shade of the yard.

All around the Eastern Med, ferries are used like landing craft. Ramp goes down, cars, motorbikes, overloaded lorries, foot passengers crowd off, jostling a new crowd trying to get on. We collected the coffin, covered it in a blanket to dissuade interest and carried it to the stern. David sat on it while I went for coffee and a piss.

Paperwork was nil until we reached Cyprus, where we were waved through with suspicious efficiency while the rest of the passengers – refugees, smugglers, terrorists, NGO's, had more hassle.

A mini bus was waiting. David, garage man, dead journo and me relaxed at last. RAF Akrotiri held my ticket home. We were waved through the gates and followed the ring road to a hanger. Half a dozen blokes in civvies stood in a group nearby: too big, too weather-beaten, too balanced. One came over and shook my hand: "Well done. Flight leaves in 30 minutes."

A C130 was warming up 100 metres away, fanning the scent of hot aviation fuel into the hanger. David was sitting on the coffin – rocking slowly. The organiser came over again: "That's your plane. No in-flight movie. We'll load the coffin. Give David four of these when you get on board."

As we climbed the ramp, the load-master handed out ear defenders, a bag of grub and a big smile: same Sgt Watts, same plane, the same ramp I'd been pushed out of only days before. He mimed canoe paddling and slapped my back. There was a good chance I'd get another grub bag. When we were buckled in, I gave David the four pills, waited till they knocked him out and stole his Mars bar.

Blue Med below; Turkish mountains to the north. A cloudless perfect day. Suddenly I realized our course would take us over the Cyclades and Argolic Gulf. No problem. I'd sleep, or maybe clouds would obliterate my paradise. Like a child I stuck my hands over my eyes and like a child I had to sneak a look. Rhodes was easy to spot, then Naxos. I searched intently, then there she was, Hydra, riding at anchor, basking five miles off the mainland. The shape, the bays, everything still there. The harbour easy to identify. A ferry, just leaving, showing a V-wake. The pain physical – face pressed hard against the perspex, using every second as the view faded.

The island was a woman who everyone had shagged and no one possessed.

I sat down, stuffing grub into my face for distraction. From up here, nothing moved, down there it was alive with people, boats, tavernas. Manoli's was just there. I could steal a parachute and land in minutes.

The feeling of being looked after, not in control after all the decisions – just like a package – instilled a soporific mood. The spooks face opposite seemed too self- satisfied. The freezer bag by his feet full of duty free. I closed my eyes. The aircraft's buzz soothing the remains of a job I considered well done. Malik negotiating in Latakia, with communications established to sideline extremists. Labels – 'Taliban', 'Al Qaeda' – elevated to faces. The path to compromise established; pragmatic discussion; peace started and I'd played a part: me, me, me. I was chuffed to bits. I was going to give myself a holiday treat. Somewhere like Australia, somewhere like Perth. Angie couldn't be that hard to find. I was smiling at the day dreams: 'Stevie! Come in, meet mum and dad. I'll leave my husband. I still love you! I'll go anywhere with you!'… Pathetic.

So what niggled? Garage man's easy access to the base? Lack of surprise at the coffin? The unobtrusive heavy gang? I recognized them – not individually, but the way they looked and moved: too confident in their own skins.

The niggle wouldn't go, no matter how hard I tried. The coffin was lashed with webbing to the side of the plane. I went over and stared. The Syrian carpenter had been professional. All the screws had lined up, now they didn't. Obviously someone had checked the journo's status. That wasn't good enough for me. I went back to my best mate Sgt Watts, for a screwdriver: 'Yea right. If you think I'm going to give a lunatic, who voluntarily gets pushed out of my plane in a paper canoe, a screwdriver, think again.' That's what he should have said, instead, he followed me. 'Freezer bag' spook was asleep with still the same smug look. Spook 2 had gone to the flight-deck looking for shiny things to steal . (Spooks love shiny gizmos and the flight deck must have seemed like Christmas.) David was horizontal in another world or wherever the pills had sent him.

Military casualties are always screened for unexploded ordinance hidden in body cavities. I put on my best professional face while 'loady' undid the coffin lid. A black plastic body bag marked: 'Remains. Body. Human.U.S.A.' – fair enough – I undid the zip – alarm bells were going off in my head. When not enough of a casualty was left to make a respectable weight, sand bags were added, O.K., but David's mate was all sand bags. Ducks were waddling into line. I shrugged to the confused 'loady', and gave a thumbs up, to indicate no live ammunition or whatever. The lid was screwed back down.

I swore to myself, my hands clenched, my brain started churning wild scenarios. What if dead journo was left in Syria? What if Malik was tortured and killed in Latakia then substituted for dead journo's body to smuggle into Cyprus?

What if Taylor had wanted to torture and kill Malik all along and I was just a deluded courier? Any job satisfaction was rapidly disappearing. I was sweating from mental angst. Had it been a set up? (Mick's voice – 'Haven't you learnt fuck all yet? You can't believe a single word they say. I hope you've got some insurance handy.')

I was generating more 'Ifs' than Kipling.

Spook 1 was still asleep, mouth open, freezer bag beside him full of duty free. Who was he trying to kid? If he woke, I'd say I was looking for a beer. Zip slid open – ice cubes – suspicion cleared. I raked around – now something soft – a leg of lamb – good, sorted… a leg of lamb with hair and eyes – a head: Malik! My chest thumped, pumping sweat, involuntary shaking, deceiving treachery forcing a silent scream. Betrayed. Malik had trusted me.

I staggered back to my seat. 'Loady' was still sorting out his tool kit. I tried to close my eyes. They wouldn't close. Shock needing distraction: I counted, breathed deep and tried to hang on to sanity. My eyes wouldn't leave the bag as I moved my head – gyroscopically staying locked on. Spook 1 still slept. Malik's son would seek revenge and then his son. Generations of war to come because someone wouldn't take risks. The bastards – the stupid bastards.

Chapter 54

RAF BRIZE NORTON: "Anything to declare?"

He must be having a laugh. My thoughts were like sea ice grinding together: 'Yes I certainly have! One coffin full of Syrian sand – supposed to be a dead reporter and one freezer bag containing the head of a Jihadist called Malik. The former tried to report the madness of war, the latter tried to negotiate to stop war.'

('There is a corner of a foreign waste tip that is forever England… If you can lose your head, when all about you are keeping theirs and blaming it on you…')

'Oh Yea, I nearly forgot the other journalist, David. He's alive but he left his mind back in the shite hole, so he has nothing to declare and never will have. Is there any duty to pay on these items?'

I prayed David wouldn't open his mate's coffin, or become suspicious of the weight or let his mum have one last look. Let his memory lie in a peaceful English graveyard. His body can stay in a Syrian rubbish tip.

Spooks 3 and 4 hustled me into a bland, windowless room for debriefing. Violence was now a serious option – fuck 'em all. Then, surprise, surprise, in slid Taylor, the body snatcher, carrying a self-important folder, and a wide smile which said: 'I know something you don't.' I'd never seen him look so happy. What a happy little Snake he was? Evil vindicated, thoughts of promotion dribbled down his chin as he arranged himself behind the desk – fingers tapping, longing to justify his poisonous policy. I wasn't going to roll over and die: "Where's Malik?"

U.S. crime DVDs hadn't been wasted on him: "He's been taken care of Steve. We spoke to him. Your job is finished. You can now retire with your 3 R's (Reputation, Resources, Relationships) intact, or you can ask more silly questions and leave with nothing. Don't cause us any problems and we won't cause you any."

"Where's Malik? You tortured and killed him didn't you?"

His smile dispersed into a weary frown as he shook his head: "He is with us. His DNA has been confirmed. Why do you care so much about him? We don't want to start worrying about your 'Croydon Syndrome' again Steven."

"Bollocks to your meaningless crap. I have no sympathy for his cause."

A memory of charging across open ground screaming Allahu Akbar a few days ago came back. "I know you've killed him. Why? He was going to negotiate. Why didn't you tell me?"

"Would you have taken him to Latakia?"

"No."

"Well, there you are then. We were never going to let him die of old age."

It stung. Malik trusted me: "What happened to the peace talks? God help you if you ever get a conscience. You'd have to blow your brains out. If you'd talked to him, anything was possible. Stop playing your stupid games. Sign an agreement and stick to it. It's too easy."

"You don't know the big picture Steve."

"Crap. I guarantee you don't. What are you going to do with his head?"

A smidgen of surprise that I knew, then callous words: "Cryogenic library, head bank: OBL, Walt and now Malik... useful for future research, bringing the dead back, proof of history."

He was mad. Nightmare scenarios spun casually, civilized codes trashed, Frankenstein rules: "I've told you Steve, and if you tell anyone else, we can top you with a clear conscience."

It made him feel good sharing and knowing I was not a believable source. He was really saying: 'I'm so powerful, I know stuff you wouldn't believe but I'll tell you, just to see the look on your face.' Actions called insane by an outsider. I hated him and we were on the same side.

He tilted his chair balancing on the two back legs in the superior way of a manager at a board meeting: "I know what you're thinking Steve." He didn't. What I was really thinking was: 'You're an evil bastard and I hope you die soon and if I could pull the trigger, I would.'

I stared into his face and leant on the table as if to say something. It was easy to give it a nudge to unbalance him. Panic and fear registered. Arms windmilled as he went arse over tit. His head hit the wall – lovely. It was worth the gut punch from the spook.

Surprisingly, they didn't let me stop at duty free. Taylor hadn't been joking. I had nothing but jeans, sweat shirt and desert boots – all ingrained with Syrian dust and a journalist's blood.

The transition from intense ops to U.K. normality never failed to shock me. I was standing beside a busy road counting cars; one pulled over – a friendly female RAF corporal with a bright orange complexion. "Get in, I can drop you at the A40 junction if that's any good."

"Corporal Weller?"

"Yes, how did you know?"

"Just a guess."

It was only a couple of miles: "Thanks for the lift."

"Wait. This is yours. Inside is £2000 and a passport."

It didn't make up a fraction of the betrayal I felt.

* * *

Nevada:

"79 clean now Sir?"

"Yep. Malik's head on ice – End Op – I fancy a cold beer."

"79 off surveillance Sir?"

"Hell no. He never will be. The more targets we keep, the more our budget from Uncle Sam. Job security and a well paid future, that's for us to look after Costa."

Chapter 55

I WAITED. Bollocks to the lot of them. I decided to go where 'there is no enemy but winter and rough weather': the Costal Path.

Vague chat was what I needed, so I did the unfashionable thing and hitch-hiked north. The driver who stopped certainly wanted to chat; trouble was it wasn't vague. I was given the most detailed and graphic accounts of medical operations, failed marriages, fraudulent bosses, affairs and random ambitions: climb Mount Everest, swim with sharks – things to do before death – most of which sounded to me like things to do to cause death.

Eleftheria had given me good listening and confessional training. I adopted the role compassionately as steely eyes watered, tattooed hands white-knuckled steering wheels and family financial disasters were released. I was the perfect stranger, never to be seen again. Silences were not threatening. They were opportunities to chew over more confessions. I realized that the thousands of cars on the motorways were all boxes of happiness, love, hatred, sadness and all of the other 83 human conditions.

One exception to the pattern was a computer salesman whose ambition to be a pilot encouraged a snippet of my own on the subject. I decided to miss out the story about canoeing from a C130; instead I mentioned my granddad Pilot Officer Hamilton and his co-pilot Flight Sergeant Woods, who'd flown Mosquitoes during the war. It was finally my turn to link half-remembered family anecdotes into a potted biography.

Inevitably I got to the 'after the war' bit. The salesman sustained my flow like a professional interviewer. My memory built: "They found themselves alive and unwanted, so they turned the garden shed into a research centre. Ideas from insulated kettles to electric-powered rotating frames for drying clothes came and went in clouds of pipe tobacco, laughter, fun and austerity. However, the secret to a profitable business sat on the desk in front of them: a typewriter with sticking keys. They upgraded it with aircraft aluminium and fine tolerances. The Hamilton-Woods Mk 1 was born – light, sleek, efficient. Granddad used to say it would fly if it had wings.

"Mk 2 included a patented key movement that was silent, wouldn't lock up and would respond to a feather touch. Thousands of London typists could now grow long finger nails. That clinched its popularity. Mk 3 was smaller, labelled 'portable', and had electromagnetic keys. Granddad said he could modify it to make toast.

"Success lasted till 1953, when tiredness and a wet road killed Sgt Woods. The business kept going, but the fun had gone. Mk 4 incorporated speech recording, but silicone chips made it out-of-date before it could go into production, so granddad went bust.

"Before he died, he carefully explained that the binary system (0 – 1s) was not the only way to transmit messages. Each letter could be allotted sound, colour or time, then transmitted using micro spacings. Even though I was struggling with maths and girls at school, his clear explanation stayed in my memory."

The salesman responded with increased interest: "Cyber security applications, faster transmissions: patent it and you could make a fortune."

Taylor would have another place to hide his grubby little secrets. All he'd need would be a bucket of wisdom and he might be useful.

The salesman pulled in for petrol as an 'artic' flying the Scottish flag was pulling out. Pushing my luck I opened the passenger door: "Heading for Glasgow?"

"Rangers or Celtic?"

"Chelsea."

"Get in. I like a good argument. If we spent money like Chelsea, we'd be in Europe too."

Conversation petered out, apart from regular cursing at 'granny' drivers. So by the time he dropped me off, I'd joined in the cursing fun.

Chapter 56

THE BUS to Fort William from Glasgow was so warm, dry and safe, I didn't want to get off. But a squeal of brakes as a cyclist had a near miss, sent my head banging. I had to walk it off in fresh air. I'd nothing to lose.

* * *

Nevada:

"79 on the Coastal Path again Sir."

"Good. He can run as fast as he likes now. Is laser-audio available on Predator?"

"Yes Sir."

* * *

Scotland has a right to roam policy, except on MOD land and in living rooms. First steps difficult – one in front of the other – one hundred metres achieved, stop – one hour, walk, stop – two hours, walk, stop – food. Unhealthy external warmth: enervating. Natural, internally-generated warmth: invigorating. Whatever the weather, just turn it on.

The time factor became unimportant. The fractiled coast made distance immeasurable. It could be 10 or 20k from A to B, depending on how many inlets, rocks, bays and peninsulas you wanted to follow. Surfaced roads were easier, shoreline hugging mentally more stimulating, distance travelled irrelevant. A pebble, a rock pool or a piece of drift wood could occupy an hour. No future, no past – constant change. The paradox of life we try to understand. My perception of days grew longer, just like when you're a kid. Obsessions for finding food and shelter receded into, 'something would turn up'. Searching for reassurance and safety changed to the animal immediacy of 'when needed', 'just in time.'

* * *

Just when I'd got it all worked out along came Ardna Vaig. It was not possible to follow the shore line because of barbed wire and big red fuck off signs: 'MOD Danger, Unexploded Ordinance.' Someone had crudely added: 'We don't prosecute the dead.' I replied: "You have a nice day too." At first I was minded to ignore it. The established path cut the sheep-worn green desert from a wooded wildlife haven. Nature's barbed wire of brambles made access difficult, but badger runs let me through if I pushed on all fours. I was in. Nature hadn't only reclaimed her rights, she'd flourished with exuberant growth. It was a paradise of oak, beech, ash, with under-stories of rowan, apple, hawthorn... clearings, glades, tracks sheltering butterflies, insects, birds – most of which shouldn't be this far north. The geography and the Gulf Stream had conspired with the sun to form a warm micro climate. All protected by unexploded military waste.

More rusting signs, losing meaning: 'Beware Mines in... No... past this point.' Wildlife couldn't read. I'd found the land based equivalent of Klondike Spoil Ground. Forgotten, forbidden, unmanaged, unregulated; sanctuaries returning naturally to nature. The secret of all secrets – nature didn't need man. Before and After writ large.

The MOD signs unintentionally implied: 'Fuck Off Man. Leave Me Alone signed God.' Nature didn't want charity, uni research, environmental funds or green protectors. It just wanted... 'TO BE LEFT ALONE.'

I stood still in the wonderful glade, surrounded by nature's beauty: "God I'm sorry."

(Far away, a voice – 'I'm sorry too.')

Each turning, each track, gave new vistas onto a world rioting with health. Huge mushrooms of glistening, emerald green moss, twisted oak branches zig zaging into Kodachrome blue skies – colours courtesy Disney 1955.

Blackbirds chirped surprise, not fear. Generations of them had never seen man. An old ash tree gave a useful leaning post. A deer highway led to a view of the whole peninsula. It was a land only our genes remembered. It stunned me just as the view from Manoli's had when I first saw it. High ground rose gently to the west then fell away steeply in sea-bird clotted vertigo. A kilometre wide plain ended in a harbourless shore where even a seal couldn't land. But what changed the usual west coast view were the stands of deciduous trees, from ancient monarchs to saplings, upright and symmetrical, not wind pruned; force 10 could rattle overhead and stir only a few top leaves; random ancient trunks gently going back to soil, feeding insects, feeding birds: nature's cycle.

Scanning further, a rocky outcrop took the shape of a Kirk, tracks radiating. I picked one and cautiously headed off, reasoning that if deer hadn't detonated mines I wouldn't either. Dead ground hid the outcrop until I was upon it: a row of two-storey houses, not crofts, with the proud Kirk dominating. Most of the roofs had collapsed, the nearest had slates over half, ivy and buddleia crowded windows and doors. The garden gate drew me closer. A fox came out, stopped, looked and meandered off. Human habitation made me wary – slowly I moved in. A rusting kitchen range; birds' nests; debris swept by winter lay around in piles; windows, doors, floor boards gone.

One wall was covered in military graffiti, showing the usual obsessions with swastikas, flying genitalia, and the ubiquitous 17th Dragoon Guards with Camel and Drums badge. It had attracted the motto: 'Are Shit.' Equally obscene criticism was directed at a certain Sgt Gough – awarded the .V.D and Scar back in 1944.

Over the fireplace, female spread legs with creative perspective and the caption: 'I'd rather be in that than the Fleet Air Arm.'

And one I hadn't seen before, looked recent: 'Silex B no good in your tea.'

A series of lines crossed out, 'Days to do are but few', and warming to his literary skills, 'Fed up, Fucked up and Far from home.' All passed down through overlapping generations of squaddies. Graffiti now reproduced in Afghan sangers.

I made my own nest by the range and crashed out for a couple of hours. A shadow at the door woke me. Fox had come home. She padded in, sniffed and settled in the opposite corner: "I know it's your home. I hope you don't mind if I kip here tonight?"

I took it as a compliment that I was accepted by the wildlife, just like another creature. The graffiti didn't bother them but it offended me. This had once been someone's home. As I dozed, I gave them a name: Mr and Mrs McTavish. It was good they couldn't see it now. Ordered to leave, destruction as sure as if it had been bombed. It must have been a fantastic place to live: Mr McTavish fishing, farming, keeping bees. Mrs McTavish, cooking, gardening, weaving – sustainable, clean, low impact, happy – like Greece. They would have had kids and pets, a Kirk for weddings and funerals. All natural – until war broke the cycle. My dreams were full of ghosts: Mrs McTavish would be bustling making tea and porridge. Where were they now? Where were their kids?

I woke alone. Foxy had gone rabbiting. The poisonous past couldn't smother the atmosphere of peace and safety. Most of the treads on the stairs had disappeared but I made it to an upper window. The sea's horizon showed between giant caledonian pines; tracks lured for exploration like childhood adventures.

I tidied up, left my pack in Mrs McT's B&B, and strolled off into the secret world of Treasure Island. Feral blackcurrants, rhubarb, cabbage, gooseberries and the rest, could only be so fruitful and healthy with help from the sea's warmth and a constant supply of fresh water. The garden perennials, which kept nettles and brambles at bay, had found niches to flourish and propagate. Once, hard back-breaking work had provided food. Now nature produced abundance without a spade to tame or constrain. The huge variety plants were in balance.

The north coast looked as if a small harbour had once given shelter, but storms had shattered man's intentions. A constant refracting swell made the calmest sea destructive.

I kept reminding myself animal tracks were my safety. The comparative weight of a red deer's hoof must be more than a human foot. Detonating a land mine was impossible… I hoped. By keeping a rough bearing on the Kirk, I could track a circular route back to the village.

A clump of flowers, ideal for Mrs McTavish – less than three paces from the path. I moved, ignoring a sudden coldness… a metallic scrape as my right foot primed a mine. Instant recrimination – shaking – now I'd pay with death.

"Stupid, stupid, shit. My own fault, basic mistake, so simple. Bollocks."

A blackbird came to watch. I shouted: "Don't sit there mate, you'll get it too. Fuck it." Warnings had flashed. I had ignored them: "I told you so."

Imagination went into hyper drive: it must be antipersonnel, WW2, detonated when foot pressure lifted. Corrosion had given the tell-tale scrape. I stared at my stupid death.

Reaction started. Sweat soaked my face, armpits, crutch. I shivered with fear and cold. So this was it. Not a bayonet charge on enemy lines; not fighting sharks; not gutted by bullets or shot by a jealous farmer; not assassinated on contract; not old age; not a London bus… no, no, no – just self-inflicted stupidity, picking flowers.

"Fuck, Fuck, Fuck."

The last casualty of WW2. O.K. I'll get it over with… But what if it's designed just to take my legs off, draw rescuers in. Only there are no rescuers, no casevac, no field surgery.

I shouted at the blackbird again: "Bugger off or you'll be tripe and offal dangling from the branches too." He didn't move. A robin landed closer, pecking for worm. My last words – "Goodbye robin" – What else?

How many have been killed in the world today – now I would be one of them. What a club to join – it was my turn. What shall I do?

Never give up. Instinct: run… not a good idea.

Breathe: Yea, slow deep breaths.

Think: perhaps I'd imagined the sound. I scraped around my foot until I confirmed the worst: metal.

Action: nothing. So that was it.

How long can I stand in one position? The blackbird eyed me. I clapped my hands to scare him off: what a considerate dead bastard I was. I had to make a will. Twat – it'll get blown to pieces with you. No one to see my death. What shall I do? Easy, pray. In seconds I'll find out which religion was right or if it was all bullshit.

O.K. try it. Pray to God – do it: "God, help me. What shall I do?"

A voice: 'Walk on.'

* * *

Nevada:

"What's 79 doing Costa?"

"Looks like yoga or he could be looking at something on the ground, Sir."

"Goddam Brits. I bet he's seen a frog. Remember when they called off an airstrike because cranes were nesting?"

"Yes Sir. 79 called off in Afghan because of goats and no weapons."

"Correction Costa. There were weapons; he just couldn't see them. If we waited for weaponisation on every target, where would we be?"

"Somewhere else Sir?"

"That's right Costa – somewhere else."

* * *

'Walk on.'

"I can't walk on. I'll get killed if I'm lucky; if I'm not, my legs and balls will be shredded and I'll die slowly. I want it quick."

I bent over and put by head between my knees. Much better – my brains would get blown up my arse. The pure insanity of the pose made me laugh hysterically. I could still laugh even though my muscles were burning.

(A voice: 'Walk on. Have faith. When you have no choice, walk on. It's your decision. You are a free man. Remember the sharks who were dolphins?')

My body braced for the impact of vaporised oblivion. Then a calmness came. I don't know from where... I'd decided. Head up, to walk on...

I stepped one pace, two, three. I was back on the path. I collapsed and puked my guts up. The flowers nodded. I was alive.

Now what? Never go back. But I had to find out. Prodding and crawling on my belly until I reached my footprint – metal casing – scrape away leaf litter – black explosive smell – rusting metal – leave it now – I kept scratching – indentations – lettering – FRA – I knew it! – Fragmentation – B – Fragmentation Blast? – I was right – now get out of it – I scraped again – BENT... FRAG... BENT – got it – FRAYBENTOS CORNED BEEF – Dickhead!

(Mick's voice choking with laughter: 'Tosser. As a mine clearance dude you'd make a fucking good gardener.')

Hysterical convulsions racked my guts. I'd stood still for three hours, sweated piss, froze with fear, ranted, raved, blubbed, screamed, converted to every known religion, including Voodooism and Satanism... Now I would dance: I stamped my feet; jumped up and down like a loonie on the tin, killing my fear and fighting my cramp.

I picked the flowers and headed back to Mrs McTavish.

* * *

Nevada:

"What's new Costa?"

"79 dancing again Sir."

"Do you know how much this operation costs to run? Drones, manpower, buildings, pensions, all to watch a guy dance?"

"A lot of dollars."

"That's right Costa. A lot of dollars."

Behind them stood an English officer. They'd nicknamed him 'Colonel Snake'. He pointed at the screen.

"Your drone is armed, right?"

"I cannot confirm its lethality status Colonel."

"But you could eliminate a target if you had to?"

"Yes, but not without Gold permission."

"I give you permission – eliminate 79 now."

"Sorry, can't do that. It has to be Gold approval."

"Never heard of it. I'll take responsibility. Eliminate target."

"Sorry Colonel. We need Gold and you're not it."

'Colonel Snake' was losing his cool: "79 is a terrorist implicated in a London bombing; he's wrecked U.K.-U.S. operations; his associates include Malik; he fought with Al Qaeda in Syria; he's smuggled weapons, drugs and bombs. Now we have him in the open, on line, perfect, no collateral – kill him."

"Sorry Sir. No authorisation, no vaporization."

Colonel Snake fumed. He looked at the monitor. The cross hairs were still on 79. He tried to guess which button for a kill. Costa flicked to wide angle, losing the aim spot. The Snake stamped out and got the first military flight heading for Scotland.

Chapter 57

I PLACED the flowers on the window ledge and crashed out. Dreams included renovating the house, the village and the Kirk. Cleaning up the whole peninsula of poison. It would take time and a lot of dosh but what a place to live. And good people would move in and live happy lives and kids go to school – foxy would have to move out – but apart from that everything would be perfect. It would be so perfect, more houses would be built; an estate; overcrowding and overloading the land. Animals and birds frightened away; trees cut down. Pollution and crime would destroy the paradise. I woke and decided the peninsula was better as it was.

I scraped the swastikas off the wall, but left the rest, adding enigmatically: ‘No snakes, only corned beef’ and ‘Thank you Mr and Mrs McTavish for a wonderful holiday’… It was the only trace of my visit.

* * *

The Costal Path was still there. I crested the first rise and made a conscious choice not to look back – no ghosts of the past, no phantoms of the future – except one: a grey Lexus slunk in the corner of a distant car park, trying to look anonymous; number plates different; same poisonous driver.

The Snake raised its head as I walked towards it; the same girlie pistol. It looked as threatening as a tube of smarties. After having escaped a killer tin of corned beef, I was ready for anything.

“Get in Steve. Stay in the passenger seat this time and don’t touch anything. You have been making too many of your own decisions. You are paid to obey orders. You are now a liability to national security, not an asset. Your priorities do not line up with ours. We cannot trust you to do the right thing anymore.”

Fuck! I suddenly realized it wasn't a job offer – he wanted to kill me. Obviously he hadn't done the full assassin's course or I'd be dead. He wasn't totally committed. It was time to turn vague guesses into hard facts.

"Colonel, you have lost your way. 'Listen this is important.' You don't know what is right or wrong any more. You have killed more of our people than terrorists for reasons you define as 'the greater good'. You have lost track of morality or any ethical code, let alone U.K. law. The blood on your hands cannot be justified. Your excuse was, collateral damage would gain future advantage over the terrorists. You were wrong. It did the opposite. The crimes you sanctioned were hideous travesties of what our country stands for."

I'd said what I wanted. He rested the pistol on his knee and stared out at the waves. The threat had gone. His conscience had finally reacted. It was hard to believe he'd folded. I could have taken the pistol and shot him as gently as a dentist.

Talking quietly, he tried to explain: "We were supposed to be the good guys. Our morals and standards should have come with us into the job. That didn't happen. Idealism went out the window in the real world. Old hands soon initiated us: 'Forget what you've been taught. This is the way we do it.' Process didn't matter; outcomes did. Even our language changed to make it acceptable to lie, cheat, steal and kill."

He paused, letting the silence order his thoughts, his apology: "We traded one of our junior agents for a high value terrorist. Neither died quietly." I'd heard similar stuff before. "Another time we captured a drug baron. They took hostage one of our diplomats and sent his thumb to encourage a trade. We don't trade, so posted the drug baron's thumb back to them. We received another body part the following week; until after many bloody parcels, we realized they had sent us three thumbs in total. It was an eye for an eye literally. However, we were civilized – we used anaesthetic. The gruesome exchange only ended when a postal strike caused a stink.

"Ruthlessness was rewarded with promotion, so I became more ruthless. It was a way to be superior over people like you. Then 9-11 changed everything and we came out of the closet. Our methods were sanctioned in U.K. and U.S. The rules were no rules. Whatever works, do it. Suspicions were reclassified as 'facts'; terminations tripled per month; budgets also tripled; we had to justify the expenditure. Results were manufactured; fake information gleaned from newspapers; whole operations were based on incomplete, inaccurate evidence and distortions: spinning always spinning. Innocent deaths rewarded with promotion, because he or she had the guts to take 'a difficult decision'. The ability to smile when disaster struck, kept many in post. A sane person would have shot himself – some did.

"I tried to persuade U.S. to kill you, Steve. They wouldn't, so I came to do the job. Now I've changed my mind. As a whistleblower, I wouldn't last an hour. You can last longer. I always knew I wouldn't make old bones. The weight of guilt is too much for anything except SIT. (Self Inflicted Termination.)"

"You mean suicide?"

"Yes Steve. A year ago an egotistical nut-case spouted off: 'It takes a real soldier to kill innocent woman and children.' That was it – we'd lost it in one sentence. We'd accepted some collateral damage, but to hear a perverted statement like that from the top, shocked me.

"The first rule of war is that evil can only be beaten by a greater evil. Their atrocity spawns our bigger atrocity. The Geneva convention exists only on paper. Every country needs its butchers – SS by any other name. The kudos of being part of an elite, pressures egos to stay: it means glory."

"Yea I know what fucking kudos means. Just keep talking."

"What was I saying?"

"You said evil psychos kill innocent people for 'the greater good', but then they lose their way and kill anyone for the kudos of being in the gang."

"Yes I did, but you must understand why. There have been three world wars since 1914-18. The Second World War, then the Third we define as including Korea, Vietnam, the Cold War and all connected surrogate conflicts. The Fourth started with the collapse of the Soviet Union, which removed macro controls on religious, political and financial extremists. However, full on heavy metal destruction didn't start till after 9-11. Afghanistan and Iraq degraded into typical asymmetrical warfare. Farmers with old mortar rounds (IEDs), came up against multi-billion dollar arms industries. There was no contest – the farmers won. What happened next was also predictable. The power vacuum was filled by the evil triumvirate: extreme jihadists, cyber warfare and drugs terrorism. All without borders. Where there is Medicin Sans Frontiers, there is also La Guerre Sans Frontiers. Unfortunately the latter is state sponsored.

"The common factor that feeds all three is money: banks look after it for anyone when the amount is large enough. Then they not only become too big to fail, but also too big to reveal their evil financial sources.

"Offshore accounts in Cayman contain trillions of criminal dollars, yet the island totals less than 100 square miles and is U.K. territory. Even with these vast sums it is still only a branch office. Headquarters is Switzerland where laundered money is legitimized and invested in the London stock exchange and property market. The U.K. economy is now financed by evil: the people we are fighting.

"The situation got out of control after the Second World War when the allies refused to raid Swiss banks. Nazi money from the Holocaust remained to be invested in sympathetic corporations and countries. Russian, Italian and Balkan mafias followed the same route, so did Columbian and Mexican drug cartels, African dictators, insurance scammers, slush funds. And the most dangerous of all – legitimate U.K., U.S. and E.U. pension funds. Swiss banks had become untouchable. Their top staff had an easy choice: a million dollars or a bullet in the head. Occasionally, a banker would be found dead (Blackfriars Bridge), not because he refused, but simply as a message, a warning to others. It's no exaggeration to say criminal funds could pay off all countries' debts, double global GDP, end world starvation, save the earth from polluted hell and make weapons of mass destruction obsolete."

He gave no smile; no indication of hyperbole. He was genuine and sincere: "Your containers Steve were a small part of a big picture. A strategy designed by my boss."

"Who is your boss?"

"You met him before you went on the Syrian job."
"The politician JB?"
"Yes. They're not all self-centred bastards."
"What's the big strategy?"
"One: Invest in cyber war assets to close mega accounts hidden by national borders.
"Two: The enemies' nuclear, biological and chemical weapons switched to self-destruct using Silex. We don't need Trident. Silex has made it obsolete. The Russians and ISIS want us to keep it because it puts half our defence budget on the bottom of the Atlantic – unusable.
"Three: UN peacekeepers given muscle."
"So what sort of magic kit is Silex?"
"Silex B Crystal. It enables intrusive, destructive reprogramming of any programmable system. U.K., U.S. and France can now hack anything: banks, phones, aircraft, nuclear weapons, traffic lights in Beijing, heart monitors in Buenos Aires et al. We do not need Trident. First strikes, pre-emptive strikes would be impossible. It's the equivalent of the World War Two Enigma machine times ten. Good, eh?"
"What is Silex B?"
"A crystal found in Tibet. Lamas made small Buddha's about the size of pineapples from it. The Chinese destroyed all they could find in 1960, but a few remained in mountain monasteries. Its potential was only realised a few years ago by a student on a physics retro course. The course was to reassess inventions from the 20th century, to see if modern technology, materials and computer capacity could make old inventions relevant in today's world. The student worked on an old-fashioned crystal set. Do you know what that is?"
"Yea, my granddad made one for me. It's a radio using tiny vibrations from crystals to demodulate radio signals."
"Good. Alternative therapies and the skulls found in Mexico, have all given crystals an aura of power. Anyway, the student, unconfined by scientific dogma or stifling grants, used her blue-sky mind and melded the crystal with a modern laptop. Luckily, one of our talent scouts who slink around unis, recruited her before anyone else. O.K., so now the hunt was on for the best

crystal to expand its performance. Not all crystal is the same. Our research teams went into overdrive and pinpointed a Tibetan monastery which had two Buddhas made from Silex and persuaded a French Buddhist to get them. He was the only one we could find who fitted the role. His motive was not patriotism or money but peace. He saw fulfilment of the Buddhist sutras."

My head went cold. My right heel bounced on the floor uncontrollably. I could see the little smiling Buddha on Eleftheria's bulkhead.

"Was the Frenchman's name Eric?"

"Yes, your friend Eric. And your stupid actions in the Aegean caused his death. You killed Eric and sank his boat. Now you know how it feels to do my job."

"I won't take that crap. You gave the orders. I didn't."

"And what would you have done, Steve? It was the middle of the night, miles from land, a boat manoeuvring over our container ambush. Who else could it be but terrorists? Would you have pulled the trigger?"

I wouldn't answer. It was checkmate. He offered me the pistol so I could kill myself. I shook my head, eyes averted. He'd won the argument. A sane man could not kill innocent people and accept the consequences.

"So Steve, now you understand. It's 'Tailor' not 'Taylor'. The verb is to 'Tailorise' and part of my job is to estimate collateral damage: Dresden was 'Tailorised'. It is a consequence of every war. Even terrorists use it as an excuse. A recent IRA apology explained: 'We wouldn't be where we are today without the bombers.' Blatantly meaning we shredded innocents for political gain."

Why couldn't the politicians have worked it out and bypassed all the pain and suffering? I gritted my teeth: "So where does Silex B fit in?"

"It's a tool to make politicians talk."

"I'm sensing a 'but' coming."

"Yes you're right. So far it is classed as ultra secret, which means it is useless unless its existence is declassified. Potential enemies won't know its power, so won't be deterred. As a weapon it will be effective, but as a means to peace it has to be publicised, and no politician so far has the balls to do that. Nuclear weapons were only effective because the threat of mutually assured destruction prevented their use. Everyone knew of their power. QED."

"So how do you know about it if it's so 'Ultra'secret?"

"Eric snowboarded out of Tibet with two Crystal Buddhas in his pack. It was my operation. I ran it. He refused everything we offered him because he saw the beauty of the ancient Buddhist ideals creating peace in a techno-saturated world."

"So why don't you just leak the secret?"

"I am Steve. Can't you hear what I'm saying? Of course it's a capital offence to leak Ultra. If someone tried to kill me, I'd fight back, but I'm prepared to kill myself. It's like the iron spikes at the base of a suicide cliff. No one jumped because they didn't want to get hurt." His sanity was being tested.

"Are both Crystal Buddhas stashed away in a secret vault?" (I knew the answer.)

"One is. The other disappeared."

My right heel started pumping again. Eric had made no effort to hide it. It had sat benignly against the bulkhead on Eleftheria. I'd patted it, even talked to it. Eric had bowed to it and I was the only one in the world who knew where it was.

I'd been concentrating too hard for too long, so took three deep breaths to feed my aching mind, fighting to keep it afloat in all the shit and corruption.

"You killed Eric, Leila, Malik and god knows who else, and you would have killed me…"

"One mustn't be squeamish Steve. When I first started, I wasn't even told why targets had to be assassinated. Now we are: innocents get killed."

"Like Leila?"

"She wasn't innocent, but we did use her – and you – to extend the chain. It was my duty…"

I was close to losing it before I had all the answers: "Duty! Fucking duty! Who said it was your duty? O.K. I'll tell you what your duty is: your rank is Colonel?"

"Yes."

"O.K. Colonel Taylor."

"No, I told you 'Tailor' is my MOD job title – you know: 'Tinker, Tailor…' My name is Drew."

"O.K. Colonel Drew – duty calls."

Silence, just waves pulsing on the nearby shingle beach. He offered me the pistol again – and again I refused it. I spoke very slowly: "This is important… This is important… This is important… Use the pistol."

"Yes, but don't burn the car Steve. It would be a waste; wipe your prints."

"Did the heroin you allowed to reach U.K. have any effect?"

"It kept prices down on the streets. Before 2001 the Taliban were destroying the crop. If we'd allowed them to keep doing it, crime would have rocketed, prisons would have blown and prices would have tripled – you work it out."

"Please tell me I'm wrong. You mean U.K. troops were dying to keep the heroin supply going?"

"It's not as simple as that. We had to feed the devil."

"That is the most evil justification I've ever heard. You're mad, insane … it stands everything we were fighting for on its head."

"Welcome to the real world Steve. Leila's bomb was the atrocity which pushed the 'Ultimate Personal Surveillance Bill' through parliament, and doubled our budget. Hence my new Lexus, which is why I don't want it damaged again."

"Bollocks to your Lexus. You have been brainwashed."

"But do you understand now, Steve?"

"Shut the fuck up – 'this is important' – just do it."

I was witness. I had to live.

"Pass me the 'Cashmere' from the back seat please."

What was a 'Cashmere', a silencer, a knife? It was a green jumper to prop behind his head so his beloved Lexus would be easier to clean.

"There's a Tesco bag in the boot. I need something to sit on."

"Fuck the plastic bag. Get on and do it."

"Alright. I need privacy – get out."

As the door clicked behind me, a metallic tapping sounded on the window. Fuck he'd changed his mind. I'd have to kill him myself.

“Steve, remember, Silex B will get you into their accounts. Work back and use their money to destroy them.”

“I got that twenty minutes ago. Now do it.”

I slammed the door hard. One and two and three and ‘CRACK.’ Hazed smoke filled the car. Fucking amateur: oil in the barrel.

Snake dead. That was another hundred points. They’d have to kill me twice now. As I went back to the Path, I wondered if there was a Mrs Snake coiled at home, waiting.

* * *

Nevada:

“Can you read the plates Costa?”

“Yes sir. U.K. assigned military.”

“Who’s walking away?”

“79 sir.”

“Pass it to liaison. Have you noticed how computers don’t get tired, or forget or have morals? Have you noticed that Costa? Have you?”

“Yes sir, I have.”

“Tracker locked on target 79. Armed. Gold approval for vaporisation?”

“Yes Sir. Is there no other way?”

“No. Stand by Costa for kill.”

* * *

(Eric’s voice: ‘Did you have to kill him Steve?’

‘I didn’t. He killed himself.’

‘But you didn’t stop him?’

‘No.’

‘What was your motive?’

‘To stop him killing more innocent people.’

‘Then it was a necessary evil?’

‘Yes it was.’

‘I am dead, so who is talking to you?’

‘My subconscious memory of you.’

‘Exactly. So I live with all your other voices, in ideas for you to pass on. My koan for you: If two people walk away from each other on the Path, they will eventually meet.’)

“Thank you Eric. I like that.”

And so it is. Walk on.

* * *

Obituary, from *Reptiles Weekly.*

Colonel Vincent Drew. MOD assigned ‘Tailor’. Affectionately nicknamed Snake Shit.

Annally challenged from an early age, nevertheless gained a place at Cambridge, where he is remembered for his stage performance of Walter Mitty. Critics said ‘a natural.’

Saw active service in Whitehall for nine years, despite suffering eye strain and debilitating baldness.

Found dead in a remote Scottish car park. Police say the circumstances were not suspicious, no one else is being sought. However, comparisons will inevitably be made with Dr Kelly’s death since Colonel Drew was negotiating for peace in the Middle East. And even in that dangerous environment, he was convinced a breakthrough was imminent…(!)

The Secretary for Defence said he was another casualty in the ongoing war against terrorism – no enquiry would be held. He added that the peace process was in a different place because of him and his ilk: ‘We will remember.’

A close colleague, known only as Steve, gave us a quote, which unfortunately we cannot use. Suffice to say a wire brush should never be used in any colonoscopy procedures.

No flowers. Donations only to Spitting Cobra Conservation Trust, c/o Sir Arthur Shagnasty, Fuck-up Hall, Burton on Shite.

* * *

Snake dead – Job done – Walk on – ‘Tomorrow do your worst, for I have lived today.’ – A sea-weed smell across grass swelling fields.

Question: What is two foot wide and four thousand miles long, or longer if you want?

Answer: – The Costal Path – A wonderful circular, endless pilgrimage, fractiled to infinity. Walk on.

* * *

Ahead four men – one hundred metres – nothing unusual. Another four to the right with a dog, fuck, unusual. Here we go. They didn't waste much time. I was almost flattered they'd sent eight to kill me.

One detached from the front group and walked towards me. I recognized him: "Bob! Come back for more mackerel?"

"They were good Steve. It was good crack, but we're here to do a job."

Options: Unlikely he'd get a stoppage or snag before I got to him. He was fit; killing wouldn't be easy; plus he had back up; bound to be a sniper. I could jump the cliff: survival remote. Inland: too open. No orange smoke for cover, so it was eight and a dog against one unarmed dickhead – never give up. O.K., spin bergen catch first bullet… then… I thought. What a bloody state to get into, working out how to kill your own mates.

"Need to go mob handed to do a simple hit Bob?"

His back-up fanned out.

"Cool it Steve, we're on your side. There's a vacancy now for a 'Tailor'. You've got the job if you want it."

I let his words hang quietly as he chatted on: "You remember the blokes from the barbeque? Dasher, Digger, Lofty, Ginge, Buster, Tinker. Jill Two is our new medic and of course Ben the dog." They waved and Ben wagged his tail.

My brain was still recalibrating. This was not what I expected. Bob continued: "The job is difficult. If it was easy, we wouldn't be here. U.K. has a shed load of enemies; killing them all is not an option; we want new ideas. Pay grade sergeant, plus generous expenses. Your file says you are risk averse to long-term relationships, so that fits in well with us. If you accept, I recommend you treat Jill Two with the greatest respect or she may get a bit casual when she's trying to sew your bollocks back on.

"Another thing, we had to clarify one piece of intelligence, that you are a 'lover of animals'. Unfortunately when transcribed in the office, it came out as: 'Enjoyed having sex with animals.' Worryingly, they cleared your security status with a note saying: 'We have an open recruitment policy. Everyone needs a hobby.'

"Do you want the job?"

"O.K. Bob, cut the crap, I'll do it. Get a brew on. I'll have tea – I know what your coffee's made from."

At last I had back-up; U.K. loyalty reinstated. I knew what I was fighting for and I knew where the Silex Buddha rested. Four aces in one hand… Walk on.

* * *

Nevada:

"Have they eliminated 79 Costa?"

"No sir. They're shaking hands."

"Why do Brits have to make it so goddam complicated? We have to assume terminalisation has cancellation tag. Confirm with Gold if 79 now friendly."

"Yes Sir. Gold now confirmed, 79 friendly."

"I need a beer Costa, with ice."

Chapter 59

WHOEVER SAID: 'Love doesn't last but the pain does', got it the wrong way round.

*   *   *

Perth, Western Australia:

"Mum quick. Your pommie team's on the telly."

From the kitchen Angie could hear the chants: "Chelsea, Chelsea, Chelsea!"

She walked through drying her hands, resting them on her husband's shoulders – searching the crowd for a face… memories were not being unfaithful.

"Mum, why do you support Chelsea?"

"I'll tell you one day Stevie. Let's all go sailing after the match and I'll teach you how to tie a bowline."

Jeff grinned and kissed her hand: "Sure thing Angie."

Stevie rolled his eyes heavenwards in mock disgust.

"C'mon Stevie, give your mum a kiss and I'll get the pizza."

"Mum, call me Steve. Stevie's a baby's name."

"O.K. Ste…eeeve."

London, same time:

When it's cold, grey and raining I'll remember.

Windscreen wipers metronomed, red tail lights blurring heavy city traffic. Stamford Bridge (Chelsea's ground) next turn, bland music on the radio – then Santana breaks through – volume full, bass thumping – drumming the steering wheel. I carried a bottle of coconut sun oil in the glove compartment. Slapped a dollop on the dash board and there they all were. Immediately a memory video: Angie, Sophie, Mick, Maria, Manoli, Kim, Eric – lovely Molly – God I loved them all. Where are they now? I lowered my window – not cold rain but warm sea spray – dolphins gliding alongside – surfing the wet road…

When I'm old, raddled with worm, rabid with pain, incontinent, impotent, retching my last breaths, exhausted on a tide line, killers quietly approaching – I'll remember and make it new. It was one season, less than a year, but it was a gauge for the rest of my life. A spirit of place – an escape into blue and white.

Taste the music; hear the sun; touch the laughter; talk to dolphins in the language we've forgotten. A pebble, an olive stone, a lock of blonde hair, a sun bleached menu from Manoli's where I first tasted ouzo. All hidden away in a baccy tin pleading for freedom, begging for sunlight and a soft pine breeze. They yearn to escape into blue and white… One day.

* * *

The complete Costal Path officially does not exist; perhaps just as well, since bureaucracy has a habit of screwing things up. Anyway, those who need to know will find out from their mates. No qualifications needed, no restrictions, just the ability to love this Island. It's worth fighting for.

'And remember – clockwise'. Also a big thanks to MO Brian.

'Seriously, thank you, Sir.'

Chapter 60

SOUTH COAST ENGLAND. MFV 'Just Dawn'. Mick's note:

Dickhead left this story, said it needed to see some light. A few bits have been changed to satisfy MOD pen-pushers.

The last I heard, he was somewhere off the East African coast. He's a good bloke to have on our side, though I wouldn't tell him that. If I'd shot that kid in Afghan, I'd have regretted it all my life. Steve called stop, he was right.

He said: 'Destroy your enemy by making him your friend.'

I said: 'Bollocks.'

He said: 'Got a better idea?'

I said: 'No.'

He said: 'Well then, shit or bust. See you in six months.'

I said: 'Hope you make it.'

We almost shook hands, but Sophie and the kids were slobbering all over 'Uncle Stevie.'

I wish he'd been at Harry's last New Year's Eve when Maria and Manoli came over. Manoli helped behind the bar. Greek style – gin full tumblers with a tonic and lemon top. Harry did his nut, until he realized how much money he was making.

Before Dickhead left I gave him a couple of Jimmi Hendrix C.Ds, so he could keep up his air guitar practice… Malaka!

Chapter 61

EASTERN MED: Way out deep – a Dolphin leapt, sighted a schooner, chased to play. More followed – a pod, a school. More still – a fleet, hundreds, old guiding young, flying, surfing white crests on blue. All on the same ancient course. The music of genetic memory – all streaming south, past Monemvasia, past Capes Maleas and Matapan, past the restings of Jupiter, Hermes, Gloucester – past the homes of Gods – then further, scything, sea alive, as fast as the hot Meltemi: the perpetual rhythm of immortal beauty, life's meaning. And sailing with them a young couple at the wheel of the most beautiful schooner in the world – Eleftheria. (No translation required.)

* * *

Mombasa Harbour, East Africa:

"Are you still writing Steve?"

"Yea, nearly finished."

"Come to bed now."

"Yea O.K."

"Love you."

"Love you too." (Got it right at last.)

Walk on.

THE END

Lightning Source UK Ltd.
Milton Keynes UK
UKHW01f1912210618
324610UK00001B/70/P